EXECUTIVE COMMAND

GARY GROSSMAN

DIVERSION
BOOKS

Also by Gary Grossman

The Executive Series
Executive Actions
Executive Treason
Executive Force (August 2018)

Old Earth
Red Hotel
Superman: Serial to Cereal
Saturday Morning TV

Diversion Books
A Division of Diversion Publishing Corp.
443 Park Avenue South, Suite 1004
New York, NY 10016
www.diversionbooks.com

For more information, email info@diversionbooks.com

Second Diversion Books edition July 2018.
Paperback ISBN: 978-1-63576-470-3
eBook ISBN: 978-1-938120-08-4

LSIDB/1807

To Chet Huntley and David Brinkley, Walter Cronkite, Edward R. Murrow, Dave Garroway, Hugh Downs, Frank McGee, Ernie Tetrault, George Reading, Tom Ellis, Arch McDonald, and all the great anchors, journalists and commentators who helped shape my political awareness through their national and local broadcasts.

To all those who sit in their chairs, remember the age-old quotation, attributed to many writers, including Mark Twain,

"A lie can travel halfway around the world while the truth is pulling its boots on."

PROLOGUE

In sixth century BC, during the siege of Krissa, Solon of Athens contaminated water with herbs. The Romans used arsenic, a popular and readily available poison. Toward the end of the Civil War, Union General William T. Sherman tainted Confederate drinking supplies during his march to the ocean. The general had developed and perfected his methods during the war on the Seminoles in Florida years earlier. Poisons continued to be dispensed during World War I, and in 1939, the Japanese reportedly poisoned water supplies in Mongolia.

In the 1970s, wells in Bangladesh were contaminated with arsenic. Decades later, Palestinians on the West Bank claimed that Jewish settlers poisoned their only source of drinkable water.

The FBI derailed a plan in the mid 1980s to introduce cyanide into the water supplies of major U.S. cities. Four Moroccans were arrested in 2002 just before lacing water in Rome with powdered potassium ferric cyanide.

In 1996, America's Safe Drinking Water Act identified contaminants and poisons, which, in the hands of terrorists, would pose one of the greatest risks to the infrastructure of American life. Since then, law enforcement has investigated tampering at hundreds of U.S. water sheds, reservoirs, and water supply tanks.

But the worst is yet to come.

PRINCIPAL CHARACTERS

HOUSTON

Abdul Hassan
Carlita Deluca
Miguel Vega
Manuel Estavan

DURHAM, NH

Dr. Satori

THE WHITE HOUSE

Morgan Taylor, President
Scott Roarke, Secret Service Agent
Katie Kessler, Deputy White House Counsel
John "Bernsie" Bernstein, Chief of Staff
GEN Jonas Jackson Johnson, National Security Advisor
Norman Grigoryan, Secretary, Dept Homeland Security
Eve Goldman, Attorney General
Bob Huret, Secretary of State
Louise Swingle, President Taylor's secretary

WASHINGTON, D.C.

Duke Patrick, Speaker of the House
Shaw Aderly, U.S. Senator, Missouri
Nathan Williamson, Chairman, Center for Strategic Studies
Christine Slocum, speechwriter
Jim Vernon, sales executive
Lily Michaelson, sales executive
Leopold Browning, Chief Justice U.S. Supreme Court
Richard Cooper, former Lt., U.S. Army

CIA

Jack Evans, Director National Intelligence (DNI)
Vinnie D'Angelo, CIA agent
Raymond Watts, CIA officer

THE PENTAGON

CPT Penny Walker, Army intelligence

THE FBI

Robert Mulligan, Director, FBI
Curtis Lawson, Assistant Director, FBI
Shannon Davis, agent
Duane "Touch" Parsons, facial recognition expert
Roy Bessolo, agent
Komar Erkin, agent
Nancy Drahushak, agent
Chuck Rantz, agent
Raymond Watts, agent
Greg Ketz, agent

MONTANA

Ricardo Perez
SGT Amos Barnes
Cheryl Gabriel

MASSACHUSETTS

Charlie Messinger, a businessman
Paul Le Strand, a businessman

NEW YORK

Paul Twardy, journalist

MEXICO

Oscar Hernandez, President
Elder Cabrera, Chief of Staff

PARAGUAY

Ibrahim Haddad, a businessman

MINNEAPOLIS

Lawrence Beard, U.S. District Court Judge

RUSSIA

Arkady Gomenko, an analyst
Yuri Ranchenkov, Deputy Director, FSB
Vinnie D'Angelo, CIA agent
Major Sergei Kleinkorn, supervisor
Aleksandr Dubroff, retired Russian Colonel

CENTERS FOR DISEASE CONTROL

Dr. Glen Snowden
Dr. Bonnie Comley

NAVY SEALS AND U.S. COMMAND

Vice Admiral Seymour Gunning
Commander B. D. Coons
Commander Robert Shayne
Anthony Formichelli
Jim Kaplan
Steve Smoller
Joe Hilton
Walter Canby
Rob Perlman
GEN Jim Drivas, Special Operations Command
CPT Susan Mitnick

PART I

CHAPTER 1

HOUSTON, TEXAS
GEORGE BUSH INTERCONTINENTAL AIRPORT
JANUARY 3

He tried not to look nervous.

"Step forward."

At first, the man didn't hear the order. The thick, bulletproof glass of the U.S. Customs and Border Protection officer's booth muffled the sound.

"Step forward," the agent at the Houston terminal repeated.

The man wanted to be invisible. Mistake. His instructions were to blend in, act casually, and make small talk. He was five-eight, clean shaven. He kept his brown hair medium length; normal. Except for a small scar under his chin, there was nothing memorable about his look. Nothing distinctive.

"Step forward!"

He tensed. Not good. He should have smiled politely and done as he was told. However, the man was not used to being told what to do by a woman. He hesitated again and was slow to hand over his passport.

The agent didn't know how much harder the president had just made her job. Generally, work came down to evaluate, stamp, and pass. Sometimes it took longer, but it was usually the same thing every hour of every day. Evaluate, stamp, and pass. In twelve years, she'd probably only flagged twenty people, principally because they were belligerent to her and not a real threat. It was different today. Houston was beta testing a new system that was sure to be on a fast track everywhere. But right now it was slow, and Agent Carlita Deluca was already feeling pissed off.

The man finally passed his papers under the glass in the booth. With the Argentine passport finally in hand, she studied the picture; then the man before her. The *evaluate* part. She made quick assessments. Recent scabs on his face. *Cuts from shaving?* Sloppy knot on his tie. *Not a professional.* She rose up from her chair and examined his rolling suitcase. *Brand new.* Then Deluca looked at the passport more closely. *Armenian name, but citizen of Argentina.* She checked whether he had traveled in the Middle East. No stamps.

"State your business in the United States."

The man cleared his throat. A bad signal, but he didn't know it.

"Job interview."

She listened to the accent. Carlita Deluca had become pretty good at detecting certain regionalisms. Not Armenian. *German?* She needed more.

"Where?"

"University. I'm a professor." He put his hand out impatiently, expecting his passport, which Deluca didn't return.

"Of what?"

The man shifted his weight from one foot to another. "Philosophy. Comparative religions."

"Have you taught here before?"

"No."

"And where is your interview?"

"New York."

Deluca nodded, scanned the passport through her computer and waited while the photo traveled as data bits across the Internet. *The accent? Definitely not German. Not European at all. More....*

A video camera also captured the man's image at the booth. The new image and picture on the passport were instantly cross-referenced against millions of other photos through FRT or FERET—Facial

Recognition Technology. Some of the process was standard post 9/11; some as recent as the president's last sentence.

"What school?"

"Universidad Nacional De Cordoba," he answered, almost too quickly.

"No, where is your job interview?"

"Oh, New York University."

Middle Eastern? She couldn't quite peg it yet. So, Deluca continued to study the man. It also gave the computer—which she understood very little about—time to talk to whatever it talked to. It was definitely sluggish, and the line behind the man was growing longer. She stamped the passport and wondered whether the computer was even working. It was.

• • •

A 2004 report to Congress concluded that America's intelligence and law enforcement agencies missed, ignored, or failed to identify key conspirators responsible for the September 11, 2001, terrorist attacks. The public agreed. People who should have been flagged as dangerous or, at the very least, undesirable, entered the United States undetected. Once here, they engaged in highly suspect activity that went unchecked.

It's not that the system didn't work. There was no effective system. That changed with the establishment of Homeland Security Presidential Directive 6. In Beltway speak—HSPD-6. The White House directive, issued September 16, 2003, consolidated interagency information sharing. The avowed goal—to put the right intelligence into the hands of the right people; securely and in a timely manner.

At the center of HSPD-6 is TSC—the Terrorist Screening Center. The department has been charged with identifying, screening, and tracking known or suspected terrorists and their supporters. Feeding TSC is the FTTTF, the Foreign Terrorist Tracking Task Force, and TTIC, the Terrorism Threat Integration Center, all administered by the FBI.

In addition to establishing the TSC, HSPD-6 effectively rerouted watch lists and terrorist identification programs through another service called TIPOFF.

This is precisely where the photograph of the man at the airport was being examined electronically against hundreds of thousands of other pictures.

TIPOFF began in 1987 with little more than a shoe box full of three-by-five-inch index cards. Now it ran through a complex computer network; one of the most secretive in the world. Every nanosecond, search engines mine data from CIA deep cover reports, to Customs photo scans, right down to Google, Yahoo, and Bing images. Until recently, the subjects in the TIPOFF database were primarily non-U.S. persons. Out of necessity, that changed. Today, the program cross-references records of American citizens and even legal permanent residents who are "of interest." It feeds that information to the U.S. Customs Service, now administered by the Department of Homeland Security.

• • •

The man's "biometrics"—the physical characteristics including facial geometry—were being interpreted at the speed of light by the TIPOFF computers. The nation's interlocked FRT programs rejected more than 99.999999 percent of the matches. That took less time than the next step. The program kicked the photograph back into the database for further analysis when it registered positive against some fourteen other pictures.

"Can you tell me where I can find Southwest Airlines?" the man asked as politely as possible. He was beginning to feel this was taking too much time.

"After baggage claim, go outside. There's a tram."

"Thank you." The man shifted his weight again and forced a smile, hoping this would speed things up.

Egyptian. Deluca decided. But the computer's identity program still hadn't given her any reason to hold the man. She reluctantly returned his passport.

"Proceed to your right and straight through the doors."

The man smiled again and then let out a breath.

A sigh of relief? Deluca could hold him, however travelers behind him were growing impatient after their long international flights. *But still.*

"One more question." The fifty-nine-year-old mother of four was clearly stalling. Agent Deluca wanted to give the computer another moment. That's when a short pinging sound indicated an incoming message onscreen. She checked the monitor. One word appeared under the picture captured by the new Customs surveillance program.

DETAIN

When she looked up, a couple and their child were now standing at her window. The subject had taken his passport and left.

"Where the hell?"

Deluca rushed out of the booth, down the hallway, and through the doors where she had directed the man. She reached for her walkie talkie, but she'd left it at her post. On the other side of the doors she faced the concourse lined with luggage turntables. *Which flight?* She remembered. Aeromexico out of Mexico City.

Another customs agent read the urgency on her face as she passed him.

"What is it?"

"Got a detain. White male. Well, white-ish. Medium build, brown sports jacket. Short brown hair."

Carlita Deluca had just described dozens of men within fifty yards. The second customs agent did what Deluca hadn't done. He radioed upstairs. But it was already redundant. Homeland Security computers had signaled an alert. Simultaneously, the conveyer belt froze. The outer doors locked. No one was going to get through.

Five agents converged in the baggage area; all with printouts of the subject's photograph. Deluca pushed past some arriving passengers to get to the arrivals board. She read it aloud until she came to Aeromexico 4325/Mexico City. Baggage Claim 7. "Yes!" Deluca turned and looked down the line.

From twenty feet she spotted the man who was walking near the conveyor belt. She signaled the agent closest to radio the location. Seconds later, agents appeared from everywhere. People automatically made room for the uniformed officers whose 40-calibre Glock 23s were out.

The Egyptian sensed the mood change in the concourse. Three of the largest men he'd ever seen were now running across the expanse on an intercept course. Behind them, he saw the cursed female agent who was pointing him out. She had a gun. So did the others. He couldn't place the weapons. That wasn't his expertise. He panicked.

Abdul Hassan started to run. There was no time for *how* or *why.* All he could do now was escape. *The exit.*

Hassan ignored the shouts to "Stop!" He pivoted right and bounced off an elderly couple. The man nearly fell down. A pregnant woman next to him was not so lucky. She hit the ground hard. This brought screams from another family and the crowd began to scatter. People tripped over one another. The route to the doors clogged. He darted to the left and suddenly found himself running at full force toward the customs agent from the kiosk. He jammed his head into her gut, instantly bringing Deluca down. The Egyptian grabbed her gun.

"Drop it!" shouted another agent.

He answered the order with a wild shot. Twenty feet away, a father of two fell to his knees. His last thought before his head cracked on the cement floor was for the safety of his twin boys.

People screamed and dropped low. Only five remained upright. Hassan and four of Houston's most experienced U.S. Customs and Border agents. Their guns rang out from nearly 360 degrees to the target, each finding its mark—a difficult-to-make head shot, two bullets to the lungs, front and back, and two more in the heart. Any of the agents could have taken credit for the kill.

CHAPTER 2

WASHINGTON, D.C.
THE WHITE HOUSE PRESS ROOM
THE SAME TIME

"Why, Mr. President?" shouted a dozen reporters in one voice. Each hoped to be the loudest. Morgan Taylor knew this would come. Even his chief of staff warned against making the announcement. But it was time.

The president of the United States looked around the room. It didn't matter who he went to. The question would be the same.

"Okay, Mark." He pointed to Mark Montgomery, Washington bureau chief for *Time.* He'd tell Montgomery. The rest of the world would hear it.

"Why, Mr. President?"

Why? was the most important follow-up question any reporter could ask. *Why?* was exactly what he expected. *Why?* hadn't been asked enough in recent years. And it was hardly ever answered honestly.

In that single moment, Morgan Taylor cautioned himself. *Be clear. Be precise.* With seventy-five reporters in the room his answer could be reported seventy-five different ways. *Be very clear.* That wouldn't be a problem. Taylor suffered from clarity. It was his trademark, particularly in his second term as president.

Now *Why?* would take him where he needed to go. He would tell the nation why every traveler passing through U.S. Customs, whether at an airport or a border crossing, whether American or foreign national, would be photographed. And that photograph would be checked against the largest bank of interlinked computers in the history of the Internet.

"Why," Taylor began. "Today we face the greatest challenge of our lives. The enemies of freedom and liberty are out to destroy us." He stared at the faces in the room and shook his head. *Shit. Too political. Sounds like another stupid campaign stump speech*, he quickly told himself. The president ran his hand through his hair, still trimmed to military regulation length. "No," he continued, "Let me give it to you straighter. They want to see us dead."

Everyone in the room sat mesmerized by the man in the black pinstriped Brooks Brothers suit. He was fifty-four, the average age for a president these days. But nothing about his character was average. Taylor was a former fighter pilot. He had experienced war firsthand; as recently as the previous fall in the jungles of Indonesia. He could fly an F/A-18 off a carrier or bring *Air Force One* in for a crash landing in the Pacific. Morgan Taylor was a force of nature; a man who wasn't used to the word "no." He drilled that point into his cabinet and staff. World leaders also knew he meant what he said. That was ultimately more important than how the reporters reported his answer. Still, he wanted to be unquestionably precise. No more *Whys*.

He had stature well above his 5'11"—not just because of the electorate, but because he commanded. Morgan Taylor really commanded. It earned him respect and made him hated. He represented American ideals more than any American political party. And though he was a Republican, as a rule he was neither left, right, nor center. In this, his last term, he viewed the country and the world from a white house, not tainted or painted with a red or blue political brush.

Taylor was an Annapolis graduate, earning top honors in his class. As a Navy pilot, he was praised for his skill. The fact that he was brought down by enemy fire in Iraq during the war which drove Saddam out of Kuwait only elevated respect for him.

After his discharge, Commander Morgan Taylor, USN (Ret.) signed a lucrative contract with Boeing, the parent company of McDonnell Douglas, which manufactured his high-performance jets. In time, he used his military contacts to score an appointment as a strategist at the State Department. A few years later, he made a run for the Senate from Washington State, where he was elected as a moderate Republican from a progressive state. Two terms later, he took his place in history as President of the United States.

Now, he brought all of his experience, all of his jobs, and all of his sensibilities to bear. He evaluated problems with the perspective of a highly skilled pilot who had delivered death from twenty thousand feet and considered life from the position of a downed flier who had crawled through the desert sand hoping to see his wife and family again. He publicly embraced science and personally maintained his faith. He was a hopeful man and a realistic leader. If anything, as commander in chief he didn't mince words. Not in the cabinet room or during a press conference.

"I'll give it to you again, Mr. Montgomery. They want to see us dead. You. Me. Your wife and children. Your sister, your brother, and everyone you know. That's what they want. So from this day forward, we're going to start thinking the unthinkable. That is the way we'll stay alive in today's world."

CIA HEADQUARTERS
LANGLEY, VIRGINIA

Jack Evans cracked the seal on the file. He'd waited months for the report. It was finally here and as complete as it was going to get—for now.

Evans, the director of national intelligence, oversaw the entire intelligence network that included the NSA – the National Security Agency, the CIA, the DIA—the Defense Intelligence Agency—and elements of the FBI. America's chief spy, a former top cop, and head of civil service investigations from New York state, opened to the first page.

DNI ONLY

The report was commissioned by, and intended solely for, Jack Evans. Depending upon its contents, he'd be sharing it one office up.

THE WHITE HOUSE
PRESS ROOM

"Now I'll save you the trouble of asking the next obvious question," Taylor volunteered. "*What* is the unthinkable?"

There were rumblings of *yes* in the room. The former Navy vet bore down on the young turk *Time*reporter who got frequent airtime on *Meet the Press*. "Everything is unthinkable. Everything that turns civilians into armed combatants, cities into the front lines, cars into explosive devices. The enemy is not working off the playbook we teach our military at West Point, Annapolis, or Colorado Springs. They're not equipping uniformed officers to take ground and lead troops. They're arming women and children to blow themselves up. They don't see defeat in death. They see victory. But a suicide bomber is just one means. We've also seen them turn hijacked airplanes into missiles. Thinking the unthinkable means we consider where we are most vulnerable, and we defend against attack. We cannot allow ourselves to be blindsided, either by natural disasters or holy wars."

Taylor almost wished he could have called back his last comment, an attack on a previous Republican administration and a worldwide religion. But it was time to tell the truth. He had already enumerated and acted on his policy to go after terrorist strongholds and arms caches *anywhere* in the world. Now he needed to prepare Americans for the same at home. *No more platitudes*, he told himself.

"Sir Ian Hamilton, in his Gallipoli Diary in 1920, said, 'The impossible can only be overborne by the unprecedented.' 9/11 was unprecedented. A bomb on a London subway was unprecedented. What else do we need to add to that list? Because each time, under the headline, are names of people. And whether it is one, ten, hundreds, or thousands, we share the blame for not recognizing the unprecedented. But we will not be blamed for ignoring the unthinkable.

"Now I'm going to tell you how we're going to do it."

DURHAM, NEW HAMPSHIRE

The second-year doctor looked up from the chart and saw the teenage girl doubled over. She had no color in her face.

"Hello, I'm Dr. Renu Sitori," she said through an Indian accent. "What do we have here? Appendicitis?"

The nurse at the rural New Hampshire clinic in downtown Durham, NH, who had already seen her said no. "But severe abdominal pain, like the man who came in yesterday. One-hundred-three fever."

The girl barely opened her eyes.

"I have a few questions for you. Then we'll get you taken care of. Can you speak?"

She barely nodded and clutched her stomach.

"This won't take long, but I have to know. Did you eat anything unusual?"

"No," she whispered.

"Did you take a fall?"

Another labored *no*.

"Did you touch anything unusual around your parents' farm? Especially any dead animals?" She was trying to rule out birds.

"No."

"Is anyone else in your family sick?"

She blinked once and tried to nod *yes*. It was becoming too uncomfortable for her.

Dr. Satori turned to the nurse who shrugged her shoulders.

"Who brought her in?"

"Her father. He's in the waiting room."

"Stay with her." Satori tore out of the examination room and found the forty-year-old farmer pacing the floor, ignoring the president's speech on the TV. The young doctor introduced herself, and then asked him the same questions.

"Dunno," he kept answering. "Dunno."

"And what about anyone else? How are your other family members? Your daughter indicated that someone else was sick."

"My wife. She's in bed."

"With what?"

"Dunno."

"Like your daughter?"

"Kinda. Maybe."

The doctor considered food poisoning. However, the nurse had already pointed out that the girl's symptoms were similar to another patient's. This was going to take more time. She told the farmer to wait for a few minutes.

Satori went to the nurses' station down the hall and pulled the chart for the patient she saw the day before. The diagnosis was relatively the same. Abdominal pains, high fever, developing nausea. "Where's this?" the resident pointed to the address. The nurse didn't know. Nor did the senior nurse on duty. "Come on, you all live here, it's a small town. Where is Foss Farm Road?"

An aide called out. "Past Oyster River Reservoir on Mill Road."

"And Lee Lane?" That's where the girl lived.

"Lee's west of town. On the 155."

Dr. Satori walked back to the waiting room to speak to the girl's father. He was still pacing.

"Is she all right?"

Satori ignored him. "Does your wife have a high fever, Mr. Huggins?"

"Well, a little."

"Bring her in." It wasn't a polite request.

As the father turned to leave he grabbed his side and stumbled over a metal folding chair. Satori caught him before he hit the wall. "Get a gurney!"

Satori helped Huggins to a chair and saw that his eyes were suddenly cloudy and vacant as if he were going into shock.

CIA HEADQUARTERS
THE SAME TIME

The first few paragraphs simply rehashed the history. A shooting in Moscow that wasn't really a shooting.

There were eyewitnesses. People saw the chase. An elderly man was hunted down at the Gum Department Store blocks away from Red Square. But officially there was no police action, just a cover story. Something about a training exercise with an undercover officer disguised as an old man; a drill to determine whether citizens might note a terrorist, possibly a Chechnyan, in their midst.

Considering how quickly the "crime scene" was contained, it seemed plausible.

Tourists bought the story. Muscovites knew not to question it.

Days after the "training exercise," a *New York Times* reporter was shot to death in the Bronx. On its own, it could have been written off as a simple robbery. But this particular reporter had been at Gum; a witness to the shooting and a recipient of some remarkable information. Jack Evans knew some of it. As director of national intelligence, he was anxious to learn more.

Evans read what five grand could buy in Russia today. The cash went to a thirsty, horny Moscow police officer; the first to arrive at the Gum shooting. He was happy to take the money. After all, the cop was talking about a man who didn't exist. The FSB, the new KGB, had made certain of that.

The Moscow cop explained that when he got to the famous Gum mall complex, a trapezoidal Neoclassical structure built in the time of the tsars, he did exactly as he was told by the FSB agent in charge.

Leave. But doing so, he overheard another agent mention the name of the old man who had been shot.

"Dubroff. Aleksandr Dubroff."

He remembered it and told the CIA officer. It really didn't matter to him. There was no police report to back it up.

Jack Evans continued to read. Once CIA analysts had a name to work with, they began to find a great deal.

> Dubroff, Aleksandr. Former Politburo member. Former Colonel, KGB. Former Chief Intelligence Officer of Red Banner training program (see footnote on Andropov Institute). Widower.

There were additional biographical hits, then a qualitative note.

> Based on the following information, Aleksandr Dubroff could be considered one of the KGB's true Cold War henchmen.

Evans continued. Next came excerpts from online blogs, posted by an assortment of Dubroff's associates, underlings, and a few who survived his wrath. They were all writing or rewriting their version of Soviet spy history; most without a publisher; most unsubstantiated beyond their own accounts.

Jack Evans believed all of it. Dubroff had sensitive information for the West; information even the new Russia didn't want out.

The DNI finished reading. Good, but not good enough. Before he went to the president he needed more verifiable data. Not just a tip from a cop on the take. Not just Google searches or even Interpol's assessment. He needed more from the inside. He had just the man who could find it.

THE WHITE HOUSE PRESS ROOM

"I've called on the secretary of Homeland Security, Norman Grigoryan, to tighten the screws; to identify weaknesses in our infrastructure, from airports to power grids to transportation hubs. We will divert resources to strengthen these possible hard targets. Do not expect life to get easier as we do this. We will be faced with more surveillance cameras, admittedly an assault on some of our traditional rights. And we will require tighter entrance and exit policies. Count on being asked to prove who you are and what your business is. It won't be popular, but it is necessary. We will improve our ability to process data quicker and determine who belongs and who doesn't. It's not what I want. It's what it's come to. Do you belong on the airplane? Do you belong on the bridge? Are you allowed in the building?

"We will think the unthinkable. Why? Because three fishermen walked onto the grounds of Kennedy Airport undetected and were not stopped until they came to a security building. They were not terrorists. But they could have been.

"A pickup truck stopped along Interstate 405 adjacent to the San Onofre Nuclear Power Plant between San Diego and Los Angeles. The door opened. A man pulled a long cylindrical object out of the flatbed. It was a section of three-inch pipe that had become dislodged. Not a MANPAD, a shoulder-fired missile. But it could have been.

"A plane crossed above the fall foliage of Delaware and bore down on the White House. F-15s were launched to chase him away or eliminate him. They had less than a minute to decide to commit. The private pilot realized his mistake and broke away. He was not on a suicide run. But he could have been.

"We must learn from those scenarios and think the unthinkable; consider how and where an airplane, a shoe bomb, a MANPAD, or a truckload of fertilizer can be deadlier than an advancing army. Thinking the unthinkable is not even letting a twelve-year-old girl pass through the gates at the Super Bowl with her backpack or an unobserved boat moor off a runway at JFK, Boston's Logan, San Francisco or any other airport near a body of water.

"We must think the unthinkable. Sadly, there is no more important rule. Not anymore."

CIUDAD DEL ESTE, PARAGUAY

Travel posters don't tell the story. Ciudad del Este, a city of a quarter million, is an unimaginable haven for drug runners, money launderers, and criminals of all stripes—killers and bankers alike.

The notorious Paraguayan city is a long way from the civilized world. It sits at the apex of the triple border region of Paraguay, Brazil, and Argentina. Those who are drawn to Ciudad del Este usually aren't there to buy postcards to send home. Many visitors who cross over the Paraná River via The Bridge of Friendship from Foz do Iguaçu, Brazil don't want anyone to know they're there. They traffic in weapons, illegal immigration, and terror.

Ciudad del Este is an ungovernable center for transnational crime and most recently home to a man named Ibrahim Haddad, a successful art dealer who earned his fortune in imports-exports. To the few people he socialized with at his compound, he was retired. That was not true. He had a job; actually more of a passion than a vocation. Ibrahim Haddad was still trying hard to bring down the American presidency.

What better place to set up camp than where criminals run things? Ciudad del Este was the closest thing to Baghdad in the Western hemisphere. The description is not so far from the truth. Over the past decade, the Muslim presence has rapidly grown. At the last imprecise census, nearly a fifth of the population was Arab. Many of them Hamas, Hezbollah, and Al Qaeda members.

Ciudad del Este attracted Arab rebels because its uncontrollable environment helps sustain criminal activity, or worse, outright terror.

It works like this: Many Arab businessmen export large sums to purchase goods for import. Since much of the export business of Ciudad del Este operates underground, the people who trade can easily siphon money and supplies to terrorist organizations.

Of course, proving this has been difficult. Still, authorities have little doubt. Paraguayan police estimate that 70 percent of the six hundred thousand vehicles on the road are stolen from Argentina, Brazil, and Uruguay. Brazilian law enforcement claims that Paraguay's thieves trade cars for drugs. Those drugs end up in the United States and Europe.

Virtually everything is for sale. Cigarettes, TVs, computers, soybeans, marijuana, cocaine, and guns. Early in the last decade, a Paraguayan national in Miami was arrested for allegedly selling some three hundred passports, various shipping documents, and visas. Among the sales—sixteen passports to terrorist suspects from Lebanon, Egypt, and Syria.

Ibrahim Haddad lived in Miami at the time. He was Syrian born.

CNN described the border as a terrorist paradise. A *New Yorker* article said it is "the center of Middle Eastern terrorism in South America." Even the Paraguayan daily *Ultima Hora* wrote of the lawlessness of Ciudad del Este. It was wild and open with unprotected airspace; the perfect place to hide in plain sight.

Even the head of USASOUTHCOM, the nation's Southern Command for all military operations in Central and South America, argued that the Tri-border is refuge for "the narco-terrorist, the Islamic radical fundraiser and recruiter, the illicit trafficker, the kidnapper, and the gang member."

A few years earlier, the governments of Paraguay, Brazil, and Argentina attempted to stem the rising crime. They established a "tripartite command of the Tri-border;" a joint criminal database interfaced with the banks. But with so much money laundering at risk, and the banks hardly interested in seeing their accounts dwindle, the Tri-border cooperative quickly fell apart.

Ibrahim Haddad is one of the reasons for its failure. Long ago he bought off key people who, through the course of time, rose in the ranks of the banking community.

For years, Haddad worked out of Miami's luxurious Fisher Island. Then he moved to Chicago. All the while, most of his financial transactions went unchecked through the banks, his banks, at Ciudad del Este.

Now, Haddad was untouchable in an untouchable city. He was protected by white collar workers on the take, local militia who drank and fucked away most of their payoffs, and a band of paramilitary thugs who protected him day and night in his fortified country-club mansion.

Rarely did Haddad venture into the city's souk with its twenty thousand tin-roofed shops, makeshift stalls, and slipshod mini-malls jammed into fifteen blocks. His *sacolerios*, his couriers, did the work for him. They brought back food to his seemingly impregnable fifteen-thousand-square-foot fortress and guests he deigned to meet.

• • •

Haddad had aged in the last year.

After fleeing twice from the United States, time was catching up to him. He was no longer a young man, and a sixth sense told him that he was not well. His last breathless escape from American authorities took a physical toll. His run through a field ten miles from Chicago's O'Hare airport triggered severe asthma attacks. This led to serious bronchitis and habitual coughing that had only recently begun to subside. He knew he'd never be able to exert himself to that extent again. And he'd probably never go back to the United States.

But he didn't have to. He could exact the damage he wanted from his new home. The Internet continued to afford him the means to securely manipulate his riches, execute his plan, and track the panic that would ensue.

So far there was no news. That was all right. But soon.

The sixty-four-year-old businessman handled his final plans in the manner he had handled everything over the last four decades—with meticulous planning. His mastery of English, French, German, Russian, and Arabic gave him the ability to trade in a variety of commodities globally: art, stocks, motion pictures, terrorism, and now natural resources.

His appearance changed over the years. Sometimes from age, sometimes by his own hand. He could hide a great deal with the length and color of his hair, a new beard, and an accent. But the man could never mask the coldness in his eyes and the hatred in his voice.

He was Ibrahim Haddad. He was Luis Gonzales. He was a dozen other people over the course of his life. Upon arriving in Paraguay, he decided to take his family name again. The name his wife accepted. The name his daughter shared. It was his way to honor the memory of his beloved and their daughter, killed by an Israeli missile attack. When his work was finished—which would be soon—the Americans very well might find him. But revenge would be served. Then, he could join Allah and his family, having fulfilled his mission—his personal *jihad*.

For more than thirty years, he had patiently pumped millions into a plan to plant a sleeper in the White House. His ultimate goal was to undermine the United States' relationship with Israel, discredit and undermine the administration, turn American support from the Jews, and forever change the political structure of the Middle East.

He had come so close to succeeding. Now, sensing that he no longer had the benefit of time, Haddad launched a quicker, more strategic plan. Israel would crumble once the Great Satan collapsed under its own political weight. Americans would experience the horrors of Rwanda and Bosnia firsthand. He alone would be the architect of the destruction.

This time, he prayed. *This time, my sweet wife and daughter. This time.*

THE WHITE HOUSE PRESS ROOM

"Mr. President! Mr. President!" shouted the reporters.

Morgan Taylor pointed to Ed Baron of AP. "Eddie."

"Mr. President," the wire service editor began, "What you're suggesting…"

"What I'm saying," Taylor correcting him, "is going to be policy of the United States."

The reporter rephrased his point. "Mr. President, this policy could have serious Constitutional implication. I suspect, curtailing freedom of assembly for one. Do you have a sense of what kind of pill you're asking the American people to swallow? I can foresee both the left and right claiming bloody murder."

"Bloody murder. A very appropriate description. Bloody murder is precisely what I'm trying to prevent, Eddie. Do you think our museums and hospitals would be safe? Your D.C. apartment? Shopping centers in cities across the country? I'm sure you consider most security a joke. At a concert? A stadium? Everyone talks about it, but little else except for show. The price of a ticket must include the cost for true vigilance.

"We are not going to go the way of the dinosaur. When the meteor struck was their last conscious thought—if they had one—where the hell did that come from? We have the means to see where the danger is coming from. And I'm going to do something about it.

"Constitutional implications? Yes, there will be." Taylor allowed himself a quick smile. "Learned minds will certainly have their work cut out for themselves."

THE WHITE HOUSE

Katie Kessler was one of those learned minds. She had history weighing heavily on her as she rolled another Constitutional boulder up Capitol Hill. The work was indescribably difficult, but Kessler was living her dream as deputy White House counsel; catapulted to Washington virtually overnight.

Katie Kessler had been a quiet and successful junior attorney in a Boston firm on a slow track to the middle. But after a chance meeting, she was propelled into a world she never could have imagined. She found herself in the inner chambers of government, meeting the country's most powerful people. Nothing short of a miracle for a woman not yet twenty-nine.

So was the fact that she was alive.

During the past year, Kessler had to persuade the chief justice of the Supreme Court not to swear in a president-elect and that a sleeper spy plot went all the way to the White House. She also had to convince President Morgan Taylor why the presidential succession laws were a disaster in the making.

This was all due to the man she met, fell in love with, and now dared to think about a future together. The only thing that made that hard was that he was a special agent for the Secret Service, with duties he could never fully reveal to her.

Kessler worked the computer keys as she watched the president on TV. She was deep into the constitutional law archives, researching the dangerous ground the president was charting. *Six months*, she expected. Six months before a related case might reach the Supreme Court. *Max. Maybe sooner.*

Kessler was five-six, alluring, and fit. Depending upon her mood, she wore her curly hair down or put it up in a bun. By day, she favored black suits, colorful silk blouses, and pearl necklaces. At night, it was back to jeans or a loose-fitting jogging suit, unless she and her boyfriend were out for drinks and appetizers. However, as the White House's newest and brightest counsel, there weren't too many nights out. She spent hour after hour in law books reviewing precedent and case history with two pressing assignments: the president's avowed doctrine which stretched borders like giant rubber bands and a proposed radical change in the rules of succession. Her proposal.

Katie heard the president's press conference in the background. Her days were getting longer. That meant less time to see the man she loved.

THE WHITE HOUSE
A BASEMENT OFFICE
THE SAME TIME

Scott Roarke was not watching the TV, though it was also on. He was absorbed in an online *Atlanta Journal-Constitution* newspaper report. Through his reading, Roarke tapped his fingers to the rhythm of the *William Tell Overture.* He did this unconsciously; a Lone Ranger himself with the gun to prove it.

Roarke actually wasn't working alone. He reported to a man he usually just called "boss." Others called him Mr. President. He got away with the informality strictly because of their past, which was off the record books. That's because Roarke often went on missions as a lieutenant in the army's secret Defense Intelligence Agency that *never happened.* One occurred well inside the lines of Saddam Hussein's fierce Republican Guard just when Morgan Taylor dropped out of the sky.

Taylor was zeroing in on a suspected biological weapons plant with one Rockeye bomb left in his stores. As he was coming around to his target, a trio of SAMs locked on from a portable launch facility. Taylor was fast, but not fast enough this day in low-level combat. He evaded two of the missiles, but not the third.

The Navy commander ejected from his $24-million machine fearing he'd never see home again. But he landed close to Roarke's dugout, which meant that his mission was scrubbed and now he had to get both himself out and this Navy flier who was pretty useless on the ground.

That pilot however was always grateful. When he became president, he brought Roarke into the Secret Service to man a department designated PD16 for Presidential Directorate 1600; an homage to the president's local address.

And now Roarke had a job in the basement. Not any old basement. A very secure, high-tech and extremely wired staging area where Roarke launched to different parts of the world. Few people beyond the Director of National Intelligence, National Security Advisor, FBI Chief, and a few key members of Congress actually knew who Roarke was and how he served the president. There were those in Washington who had their suspicions.

Scott Roarke topped off at six feet, just an inch or so taller than the president. He had a swimmer's physique, or someone skilled in the martial arts, which he surely was. Unlike others in the Secret Service, he wasn't a suit-and-tie guy. He didn't wear a lapel pin or talk into his sleeve. He dressed casually, wore sneakers, and preferred a Blackberry.

He kept his thick brown hair longer than required. Regulation would have looked incongruous. But there was very little regulation or structure to Scott Roarke's life. He was unique in the ranks of the Secret Service; Morgan Taylor's go-to man. He earned $114,300 per year but had access to so much more, whether it was in Yen, Euros, or Rubles.

Roarke was loyal and principled. When necessary, he was also calculating and lethal. But he could be warm, witty, and flirtatious. Those were the real traits that drew Katie Kessler to him in Boston less than a year earlier. Those were the characteristics that she loved. Those qualities made him a whole person. But without her, he wasn't complete.

Roarke was engrossed in the *Journal-Constitution* account. It was a murder story, unrelated to the protection of the president, but something caught his attention. He'd been searching the Internet a great deal recently, most of the time aimlessly. However, he trusted his hunches and he continued to look for connections that no one else might recognize.

The wall opposite his desk and the one around the side were full of clippings. He'd written question marks on some. Others were marked with a big red X. Most were murder victims; some were obits of prominent citizens who died of natural causes. *Or seemingly natural,* Roarke quietly considered. So far, none appeared related.

He keyed on a list of names a friend at the bureau had researched. They covered the gamut of high school and college teachers, career army officers, retired servicemen, and a host of other everyday people. There were hundreds of names. Some were obviously going to be meaningless; many had died. He was particularly interested in hearing what those people could tell him. He was certain even the dead could find a way to speak up.

Fortunately, Roarke had friends in high places. A good deal of the heavy lifting was done for him by the FBI. As a result, he received extracts from files, full biographies, and obituaries. He could call upon the bureau to conduct field interviews whenever and wherever necessary. And why? It all came down to a gut feeling.

Now another obit. Roarke read it closely. A CEO of a software company outside of Atlanta. Graduate of an arts school in Cincinnati. *Right age. Possible.* He'd have to check.

The agent sent the file to his HP Color Laser printer. It quickly spit out a hard copy. Roarke highlighted key words: *Victim. Hit-and-run. Veteran. Chairman of the Board. 42.* In Roarke's mind, nothing distinguished this particular sad death from the scores of others he found. But it was going to go on his wall.

Only three people knew what he had been doing in his secluded office since September—the president; Shannon Davis, his close buddy at the FBI; and his girlfriend, Katie Kessler.

Katie noticed mood changes. So far he had nothing to show for his time. What started as intuition was becoming an obsession; a long, slow, unfulfilled obsession.

Now he had 221 clippings and the belief that there was a thread through some of them. *But what?*He went back to the computer and once again was unaware of the song he was tapping out.

THE WHITE HOUSE PRESS ROOM

"We've struck in Indonesia, the Philippines, in Mexico, Venezuela, and Saudi Arabia. We have done so with the permission of those governments," Morgan Taylor continued without the benefit of notes. "We have destroyed weapons caches and training camps without committing troops. But there's no victory to celebrate. And I don't stand before you to claim one. I can't, because like it or not, the enemy is here."

"Next question?" So far no one had touched the other hot button—Taylor's plan to overhaul the laws that govern the line of succession. Maybe now. He pointed to a legendary *Wall Street Journal*reporter midway in the first row. "Yes, Bill."

"Mr. President, you must realize what civil liberties activists, as well as Democrats, will say about this."

"Yes," Taylor said. *No question yet*, he thought. *It'll come.*

"Sir," the reporter continued, "Do you intend to sell this up the Hill in the name of National Security?"

The president took a deep breath. "Mr. Barlow, within the last two years we have learned a great deal about the lengths to which seemingly ordinary citizens will go to destroy our republic. Their means always surprise us. Did any of us recognize the enemies among us? Would we now?" Taylor paused. The response, unstated, was nonetheless in the minds of everyone in the White House press room.

"So what will I do?"

The reporter put his pencil on his pad ready to write.

"I will keep expanding the sphere of influence of the Pentagon's Counterintelligence Field Activity, CIFA, which was created under President George W. Bush during his first term in office. At that time, CIFA was transformed from an office that coordinated Pentagon security efforts around military facilities, protecting them from attack, to an agency which can investigate crimes within the United States, such as terrorist sabotage, treason, and, of utmost interest to the *Journal*, economic espionage."

The reporter was now fully engaged. But as he listened, he wrote down the year *2003* and double underlined it. It was his reminder to check the date. He recalled that a Department of Defense directive from 2003 prevented CIFA from engaging in the kind of law enforcement activities the president now proposed.

"In my estimation, we did not go far enough at that time. It has left holes in our intelligence gathering efforts. So, in answer to your question, yes. I will be sending legislation to Capitol Hill this week that, in this age of terrorism, gives intelligence and law enforcement authorities more equal footing on already tenuous ground."

Hands shot up in the air, but Taylor was not finished.

"I will save you the trouble of asking your follow-up," the president noted. He grasped the podium with both hands and leaned forward. "What will this mean? Stepped-up domestic-based missions by Marine Corp Intelligence with bureau cooperation and Jack Evans' oversight. Without the mumbo jumbo—they'll investigate people who are believed to be threatening or planning to threaten the physical security of Defense Department installations, operations, visitors, and most importantly employees.

"Greater analysis of threat assessments across the country. The Pentagon likes to call it 'data harvesting.'"

There was a chuckle in the room. Despite the news that personal freedoms could very well be devalued, most of the reporters admired the moderate Republican president. They admired his candor. They were about to hear more.

"There will be no torture. But we will not stop at 'polite' questioning."

"Mr. President," the reporters shouted.

"What I mean is that investigations will be conducted under the letter of the law, but bail will not be a safety net for the uncooperative. Now for some bad news for the conspiracy theorists among you," the president added. "The government of the United States is not out to invade the privacy of law-abiding citizens or disrespect your life, lifestyle, or religion. There will be no wholesale arrests, no coercive practices. I will not allow it, Congress will not abide by it, the Supreme Court will not uphold it. The purpose is to make our domestic facilities safer while we continue to target terrorist strongholds outside of America. The purpose is to protect America.

"And to that point, let me add that I will not tolerate actions taken by vigilante or political groups that do not respect the rights of others. I will go as far as legally possible to discover and disrupt terrorist or would-be terrorist plots.

"There will be debate, which I have no doubt, you as members of the press will find rich in copy. There will be disagreement, which I implore you to report in a balanced manner for your readers and viewers. This isn't the time to fan partisan political fires. It's time to figure out what we can do within the letter of the law."

This triggered disturbed looks and mumbling. The president had to talk over it.

"I know you're concerned. And for some of you, it is about personal freedoms. Well, I'll ask everyone—do your news organizations tell you that you can't investigate a lead? Do your news networks say you can't question sources? Do you think that life would be better if you simply waited to report what happened?" Taylor surveyed the room. There was no argument even from the journalists who would skewer him later on the TV talk shows appearances, their commentaries, and political blogs. But for now, they were silent.

"Let me do my job. I guarantee you'll have plenty to report."

Taylor didn't say a word about another story that would break soon if a phone call in his office didn't go well.

"Thank you." The press conference was over.

CHAPTER 3

GEORGE BUSH INTERCONTINENTAL AIRPORT
A FEW MINUTES LATER

The ten-year-old Buick circled the airport perimeter waiting for the arriving passenger. The driver had a specific description and a password. But on his first and second pass, no one flagged his car. The third trip around took longer. A pair of police cars cut in front, sirens blaring. Traffic began to build up. By the time he got back to the Aeromexico terminal he ground to a halt. Passengers were streaming out. Police secured the entrances preventing anyone from entering. An officer tried to direct cars away to make room for more police and an ambulance. His rubber-necking told him nothing. "Fuckin' shit," he swore. He maneuvered to the left lane to make it around once more.

Thirty minutes later he was creeping by the terminal again. This time he managed to ask a cop what happened.

"Keep moving."

The driver hated police. But he needed to ask. "What's going on?"

"None of your fucking business," the officer shouted to the young Hispanic. "Now move!"

The white officer was wrong. It was Miguel Vega's business.

Vega was twenty-one and he had a great deal of responsibility today, and for the next few days. He'd been ordered to pick up a very special visitor. Now he was scared. If he couldn't make his pickup he'd have to come back empty. That could prove to be very dangerous. There would be consequences. There always were for members of 13-30, a new and deadly spin-off of one of America's growing internal threats—the MS-13 or Mara Salvatrucha. Better known as the Maras.

Originally, MS-13 was a street gang with its roots near MacArthur Park, west of downtown Los Angeles. After two frustrating decades, L.A. police attempted to break up the gang. They instituted a deportation policy and sent thousands of immigrants with criminal records to Central America. But the deportations backfired. The first deportees returned from Central America almost to the man. Now the Maras had organized cells in Washington, D.C., Boston, Baltimore, Houston, and many other U.S. cities.

Even the Department of Homeland Security's Immigration and Customs Enforcement Agency acknowledged that deportation essentially amounted to taxpayer-financed visits with family and friends before their inevitable return north. The result—a never-ending string of gang members shuttling between the United States and Central America.

The common joke for Maras facing deportation in one city is, "See you in L.A." They were guaranteed to be back in the United States in weeks.

Estimates are that Mara Salvatrucha members number fifty thousand or more. They're involved in hard-core immigrant trade, extortion, and racketeering. Thirteen-30 was rumored to be involved in even worse crimes. Little was known about it. Neither the FBI nor the ATF had successfully infiltrated the tight organization. Members were recruited at thirteen. At age thirty there were initiation rites that considerably thinned the herd. Those who "graduated" were set for *life*. There was, however, no definition how long that meant.

Now Miguel Vega didn't know if he'd make twenty-two. "Fuck!" he exclaimed as he drove around again. A few minutes later he parked, but he failed to retrieve his "package."

MOSCOW, RUSSIA
THE SAME TIME

Arkady Gomenko chose one of the doors at B2. There were many in the complex of lounges, restaurants, and pool halls. He liked B2 because the building had character. In days gone by, it had formerly housed departments of the old Soviet ministry. Now, it was a bar. And the stories people told were different than the confessions heard under torture in its many rooms years earlier.

Arkady sat on a stool. He removed his unstylish black frame glasses, rubbed his tired eyes, and studied his reflection in the mirror behind the liquor. He was less interested in seeing how he looked. *Who else is here?*

It was quiet for the next two hours, which made the forty-four-year-old functionary perfectly happy. He shared some small talk with the bartender, a few words with a blonde half his age—that went nowhere, and listened to one lost soul who believed Khrushchev should have stood his ground in Cuba. The whole world would be different and every Russian would be rich like the Americans, the man argued. Arkady thought he was full of shit, but the conversation helped him waste the evening away.

One more check of the mirror. He didn't like what he saw. Too much flabby skin under his chin, receding hairline, and gray coming in. *No scoring tonight*, he realized. Arkady settled up, put down an adequate tip and waved good-bye to the bartender. "*Dosvidonya*."

"Dosvidonya," came the reply. The bartender waved automatically, happy for a tip. At least Arkady left one. So many other beleaguered middle-aged government workers on their fixed incomes didn't.

THE OVAL OFFICE
LATER

Three of America's most powerful men were gathered for the meeting.

Jack Evans, the director of national intelligence, was seated on one side of a brown leather couch. Next to him, General Jonas Jackson Johnson, the president's recently named national security advisor. In the chair opposite them, Norman Grigoryan, secretary of the Department of Homeland Security. He was absorbed in a file.

The president settled into a seat he recently brought out of storage. He decided to update the Oval Office. Update to him meant that the colonial furnishings of the last administration went back to the White House collection in favor of some familiar and historic Navy-issue relics. His pride and joy was sitting in the captain's chair, which had belonged to Admiral Isaac Hull when he commanded *The USS Constitution* during the War of 1812.

"Thank you for coming," he said rising from his coveted seat. "We're going to start without Mulligan." Robert Mulligan was the director of the Federal Bureau of Investigation and a close friend of the president's. "He'll join us when he can."

Taylor looked at his secretary of Homeland Security. "All set, Norman?"

Grigoryan was the last to read the report. "Mr. President, this is...."

"Hold onto that thought for awhile Norman. First, a little background that's not in Jack's file."

Grigoryan closed the folder and put it on his lap.

"I asked Jack to do a little paperwork to maybe ease a serious case of K-PAN."

Evans laughed. He knew the term. Grigoryan and General Johnson didn't.

"K-PANs," Taylor explained, "are simply the things that Keep the President Awake Nights."

There were light smiles.

"And that describes most nights."

The men agreed.

"Jack generated the report. Mulligan added to it. Now, maybe I won't be alone at 2 a.m."

More laughter.

"Now, let me tell you what it's all about."

CAPITOL HILL

"This is just great!" Duke Patrick shouted to the crowd of aides who had assembled in his office to watch CNN. "The best that reality TV has to offer."

Just then, the Speaker of the House's leggy new political aide walked by his office. She caught everyone's attention; something she was quite capable of doing anywhere on the planet. "Mr. Speaker, do you need me?"

"Come in, come in, Christine. Watch what political suicide looks like on national television. Taylor's just put a big fat target on himself and asked us all to end his misery."

Christine Slocum stood to Patrick's left, brushing slightly against him. He shifted back in his chair and eyed her exquisite body, which he was determined to experience. *Soon,* he hoped.

For years, Patrick had been a loose cannon; speaking before thinking and not framing those thoughts particularly well. But he could be molded. Slocum knew it and used it. That's why she was there. For the man, currently second in line of succession because the nation was without a vice president, Duke Patrick was definitely someone who needed to improve his game and up his public persona if he was going to make it to the White House. Christine Slocum was now close enough to counsel Patrick; to coach him on what to say and when, and who to say it to, whether it was Ed Schultz or Rachel Maddow on the left or Bill O'Reilly to the right. And with every well-positioned sound bite, Patrick gained ground.

Duke Patrick would have to consider how to respond to Taylor. Or more accurately, Slocum would, though he would still think it was his idea. He was good. She was better.

CHAPTER 4

NORTH SHORE BOSTON

Charlie Messinger stepped off his G-4 at the Beverly, Massachusetts, Airport. His flight from Chicago was made all the more easy since he didn't have to go through Logan. But that hadn't been a problem for years; not since his government contract. Messinger developed key software used in the intelligence community's newest generation of Echelon—the telephone and Internet probe that listened for and identified words that might be used by terrorists, anarchists, or spies.

Messinger was not a computer expert himself. He was a man with connections, family money, and the ability to capitalize on opportunity. He retired from the military with honors and Pentagon contacts. He then set up a business, and struggled only as long as it took to build one of the leading Route 128 software companies. Within three years, Globix ComPrime, went from nothing to a firm valued at more than $3.5 billion. He commuted anywhere in the world from Beverly Airport, which was minutes away from his exquisite home on the ocean, along Route 127.

Obviously, Messinger could have had chauffeurs, but he preferred driving himself. He kept his Bentley in the garage for the sixteen-mile commute to his office and drove a pale blue Thunderbird back and forth from the airport.

Today, he wasn't going right home. He scheduled a luncheon meeting not too far away in Rockport. A French software manufacturer was interested in a new program Globix was developing. Messinger intentionally leaked news of it to trade magazines. On the open market, it could increase the company's price per share. The Frenchman represented a buyer he hadn't cracked yet. And though the former army colonel did not trust the French government, he believed in the Euros they traded.

The visiting Frenchman flew in the night before, and Messinger proposed a favorite North Shore haunt. The plan was to meet M. Paul Le Strand at The Greenery, a small restaurant with one of the best views of Rockport's famed Motif #1 on Bearskin Neck.

Messinger arrived thirty-five minutes after landing. He might have made it quicker, but a late afternoon storm slowed traffic along state highway Route 128. He easily found a parking place on Main Street.

With time to spare, he took a stroll along Bearskin Neck, which could be shoulder-to-shoulder crowded in the summer months, but in January only attracted diehards and locals.

Messinger enjoyed the quaintness of Rockport, though he didn't get there often enough. As a kid he used to bring dates to the rocks at the far end of the jetty, share a lobster, and watch the ocean slam against the breakwater. There'd be no eating outside today. Light rain was still falling. The air was raw, and, most importantly, Roy's, the great lobster joint along Bearskin Neck, was closed for the season.

Still, a few people were out, determined to get a snapshot of Motif #1, a simple red shack that jutted into the harbor and was purportedly one of the most photographed and painted buildings in America. It certainly was one of Messinger's beloved sites.

Motif #1 stood out against the sky in any weather. It was originally constructed in 1884. It survived the harsh New England winters until the massive blizzard of 1978. Donations from tourists, friends, and residents paid for its complete restoration. But no cameras were out today. At least one visitor was happy about that.

Messinger pulled his collar up and wished he had grabbed an umbrella from the car. The rain was getting heavier again and the wind off the ocean had picked up. Messinger doubled his pace along Bearskin Neck. Suddenly, someone brushed by him from the side. Messinger didn't take much notice, but an instant later he thought he felt a prick on the back of his left thigh; nothing bad, more like a mosquito bite. He turned, first in one direction, then another. By now all he saw were people scurrying in different directions under their open umbrellas.

Messinger continued down Bearskin Neck. He felt a momentary wave of light-headedness which soon passed. He was much more aware of the rain than anything else.

Soon, he had rounded the corner onto Main Street, making a left and the last fifty yards to The Greenery along Dock Square. He had called ahead for reservations and was happy that his table was ready. He left the seat with the view for his guest, so he could easily see Motif #1.

Five minutes later Le Strand arrived.

"Mr. Messinger?"

Messinger stood and offered his hand. His left leg buckled a bit under him, but he quickly balanced himself. "Monsieur Le Strand. So good to meet you."

"Please, you'll do me the honor of making it simply Paul," the Frenchman said politely.

"Paul it is. But only if you call me Charlie."

"Charlie." They laughed and shook hands again.

Le Strand was a younger man. He sported a goatee and wore a thin, black leather tie, a black shirt, and black leather sports coat. Quite rich. Quite fashionable. Quite French. And a dangerous looking businessman.

"I have been looking forward to our meeting for some time."

"Oh? I had no idea. I've only recently learned of your interest," Messinger replied.

The waitress interrupted the conversation to take their drink order. "Oh, I should warn you Paul, Rockport is dry."

"There's no alcohol here?"

"No," the young waitress replied. "Not even wine."

"What a shame. Water then. Sparkling, please."

For the next ten minutes the conversation covered a variety of topics from the exchange rate of Euros to America's footing in France, and vice versa. It was a natural segue to their business. But as the first course arrived, Rockport crab cakes with horseradish tartar sauce, Charlie Messinger began to perspire. He wiped his forehead with his napkin.

"It's unusually warm in here," he observed.

"A bit." Le Strand smiled. He poured his companion another glass of water from the bottle.

"Thank you." Messinger took a quenching sip. "Better," he said.

But he wasn't. And he wouldn't be. Le Strand knew it. He had seen to it. He had bumped into Messinger on Bearskin Neck. And there, the tip of his umbrella made perfect contact. In a fraction of a second, Le Strand shot an injection of ricin into Messinger. It was a classic maneuver right out of the Cold War. A Bulgarian Interior Minister had reportedly done the same to Bulgarian émigré writer and dissident Georgi Markov some thirty years ago.

Messinger experienced the same immediate stinging Markov had. But he had not yet noticed that there was a small spot of blood on his pants. Nor did he see a pimple-like red swelling on his thigh. But the fever had already begun.

Le Strand had carefully crafted the umbrella, using old KGB specifications easily available on the Internet. He drilled two 0.34 millimeter holes into a tiny pellet, the size of a pin head, and filled the projectile with the biotoxin. The pellet, coated with a thin layer of wax, would dissolve on contact with warm skin, allowing the poison to seep into Messsinger's bloodstream. The poison, much more lethal than cobra venom, was now working its way through Messinger's body.

The only difference between Strand's work and that of the Bulgarian assassin years earlier, is that Strand doubled the lethal dose. Instead of shock setting in the next day, Messinger would feel it in hours. Instead of suffering for days, he would be dead before he made it home. Doctors would most likely rule his death a result of septicemia, a form of blood poisoning, perhaps the result of kidney failure. Or the coroner might never look beyond the car crash Messinger would likely experience as he lost control of his Thunderbird.

Messinger hardly touched his main course, steamed mussels in a garlic white wine cream sauce. Le Strand politely recommended that he return home. "We can wait until tomorrow, Charlie." But actually, the Frenchman's business was concluded.

"I'm really sorry," Messinger said, slurring his words. "I don't know what came over me."

No apologies by Charlie Messinger would save him now. Le Strand was only doing what Colonel Charles V. Messinger had done to him years earlier. Pronouncing his death sentence.

Le Strand considered giving Messinger something to think about as the fever, pain, and delirium shut his system down; some way for him to realize why this was the day he was going to die. But he decided not to. Instead, Le Strand accompanied the retired army colonel to his car. He wanted to make sure Messinger, becoming groggier with each step, would get on the road. As a final irony, he raised the death-delivering umbrella overhead to keep them dry.

"Get home as fast as you can," Le Strand said coldly. "You're not well."

Messinger pulled into traffic. Le Strand's parting words swirled in his mind. *You're not well. You're not well.* Messinger took the winding coast route, fighting to keep his focus. He was a few miles away when he realized that Le Strand hadn't said that at all. It came to him the instant he took a sharp curve too fast and was airborne over the cliffs that abutted the Atlantic. It wasn't, "*You're not well.*" Le Strand had said, "*See you in hell.*"

CHAPTER 5

GULFTON, TEXAS

Miguel Vega feared he would pay for his failure with his life.

He didn't know what happened at the airport. It wasn't his fault his "package" wasn't there. Police were everywhere by the time he managed to park and reach the terminal. They sealed off the airport. The only thing he actually learned was over the radio coming back.

An all-news station, which he normally never listened to, reported a shooting at George Bush Intercontinental. They were "looking into it." They should have talked to Vega.

But it's not my fault, he thought over and over. That wouldn't be good enough for Manuel Estavan.

13-30 had been contracted to deliver the "package" to some Godforsaken, freezing place called Massachusetts. That was the deal. That was Vega's responsibility.

Estavan always made examples of fuckups. He'd seen it before. His cousin, the one who recruited him, wore an ear-to-chin scar for a mistake he made two years ago—coming back a grand short on a drug transaction. Another member of 13-30 was less fortunate. He and his girlfriend died together with one bullet as they were locked together fucking. This was retribution for the gang member's skipping a drive-by shooting in favor of a Jamie Foxx movie.

Surely Estavan would do something brutal to Vega. Better he accept punishment than try to run.

THE OVAL OFFICE

"Let's get a bead on Russia," barked General Jonas Jackson Johnson, the president's national security advisor. Johnson preferred things plain and simple, like the way members of the inner circle addressed him. He was usually "J3" for the three Js in his name.

It was a topic everyone could weigh in on, but no one person had all the answers. Not Homeland Security Secretary Norman Grigoryan. Not DNI Jack Evans or Chief of Staff John "Bernsie" Bernstein. Most of all, the president didn't like what was going on there. Everyone knew it. The trouble went back to when Vladimir Putin started this march toward a return of Soviet-like control.

Putin had centralized control of the judiciary, the regional governors, the media, and the major oil companies. He used corrupt courts to seize the highly valued energy conglomerate Yukos. Its former chief ended up in a Far East prison camp joining others Putin systematically put away.

Through this period, Russia rolled back pluralism and limited contact between the East and West. But he didn't return Russia to Soviet rule. It was more like Soviet-light. But now President Josef Gudinsky made Putin's work look like child's play. Gudinsky's grab for total control over Russian life was another quickly developing K-PAN.

"Jack, am I correct to say that his FSB is looking every bit as bad as Stalin's KGB?"

"It's getting there," the director of national intelligence paused, not certain if the president wanted him to pick up the story. When Taylor almost imperceptively tipped his head, he got his cue to continue. The country's number one spy sat straight up. "Gudinsky is becoming more insulated and paranoid. His squads are eliminating Muslim dissidents. You can image where that will lead. At the same time, his paranoia about the West is turning Russia into a closed society again. He believes that everybody working in Foreign Service within Russia, whether it's business or human rights, medicine or education, is merely a tool of western intelligence. And our sources close to him suggest that he thinks we're behind plans to organize a popular uprising in Russia."

"There's no truth in that," Morgan Taylor said.

"But he believes it," Evans replied. "And he's right about one thing."

"Pray tell?" Grigoryan asked.

"We do have people inside. And another going in."

"Who?" Grigoryan asked.

"No names," Evans stated. "But rest assured that my asset will come back with valued intelligence."

Evans began to outline the operation. He was cut off by the president's phone. Taylor motioned for him to continue. However, by the fourth ring it was obvious the call from the president's secretary wasn't going to go away.

On the seventh ring, Morgan Taylor finally walked to his desk. "Hold that thought, Jack." The president pressed the speaker button. "Yes, Louise."

"I'm sorry to disturb you, Mr. President. I have Director Mulligan for you. He's quite insistent. He said it couldn't wait."

"Put him through." Taylor picked up the phone. The rest of the conversation would at least be semiprivate. Not everything could be viewed as public, even in present company.

"Hello, Bob."

This was the only thing the group heard. And nothing on his face gave any indication what they'd soon learn.

"Customs officers shot and killed a suspect attempting to enter the country through Houston."

Two minutes later, the president recapped the conversation. He was stone cold. "FRT flagged a subject at George Bush Intercontinental Airport. He was on a federal watch list. They took him down while he attempted to escape."

"Took him down?" Norman Grigoryan asked.

"Shot him." The head of Homeland Security was about to ask the next question. The president saved him the effort. "He's dead."

"They had to kill him?" Grigoryan was furious. "Do they think they're in the fucking Wild West?"

"He seized an agent's gun and shot a man in the crowd."

"Any idea who it was?" Grigoryan pressed.

"An alias, most likely on his passport. Working on bonafides now," the president said grimly. "*Where* he was going and *what* he was up to…no, not yet."

The two advisors to the president couldn't hide their worry.

"The bureau is checking hotel reservations across the country and his travel itinerary."

After a long silence, Taylor took his seat in the Halsey chair across from his advisors. They picked up the conversation where they left off, but Taylor had only one thought right now. *Another Goddamned K-PAN.*

GULFTON, TEXAS

"I'll make this easy for you all to understand," the Salvadorian gang leader shouted. "You lose something of mine, I take something of yours."

Miguel Vega tried one more time to explain what happened; what he heard on the news.

"I don't listen to the fucking radio," Estavan shouted back. "I listen to the sound of money. And because of you, I don't hear enough." Without another word he picked up a leather sheath on the table between the two men and drew his Gil Hibben III Combat Machete.

The loss was tangible for 13-30. And so it would be for Miguel Vega.

For each sleeper smuggled into the United States, the gang could take in ten-to-thirty-five thousand dollars. Upon successful delivery to remote locations across state lines, there'd be a bonus. Easy money.

Expecting no problems, and with the advances already wired, Estavan had shelled out cash for a late-model used car. Now he figured he'd have to refund the full down-payment or apply it against the next "package" to come through…if there were another. Either way, he was not happy. Proof was the fact that he called all forty gang members together.

"Hand on the table!"

Thank God. Only my hand. "Which?" Vega cried in thanks.

"Whatever one you don't need to jerk off."

Miguel Vega began to cry. He suddenly looked more innocent than he had in years. He placed his left hand on the wooden table.

"Flatter!"

Vega never wanted to join this cruel branch of MS-13. He had plans of leaving the horrors of the Houston ghetto. His natural ability at the computer keyboard was going to be his ticket out. But no longer. He had his cousin to thank.

"Look at me, asshole! Eyes forward."

Vega complied.

"Do you have anything to say?"

Why even try. Vega had seen how Estavan dispensed justice. It would only make Estavan angrier. "No."

The MS-13-30 gang members quietly realized it could have been one of them facing Estavan's 15.5-inch blade. It was merely good luck that spared them this time.

Estavan raised his machete, the principal weapon of the Maras. He swept it across the young man's face. One cut. A mark for life, but not anywhere near the true punishment for the crime. In a lightning-swift move the blade came down on the tip of three fingers. Only his thumb and pinky were sparred. The gang leader smiled at his work and with a nod. A lieutenant tossed Vega a towel.

"Now go and lick your wounds!" he ordered. "The rest of you remember the price for failing."

"Everyone out! Now!" Estavan's lessons worked. Everyone obeyed him. He'd never read Machiavelli, but he was an apt student of the sixteenth-century writer. Without knowing history, he ruled his own limited territory much like Lenin or Mao; two men he'd also never heard of. But for dictators it was always the same. It was all about fear. Estavan led, not through cunning or intellect, but because he instilled more fear than anyone else. His own spies insured that there were no secrets he didn't hear. And his bloody machete? Once again it put fire in his men's bellies to do unmitigated harm to others.

As Vega rushed out of the front door of the run-down apartment building in the center of gang territory, he couldn't possibly have known that he actually owed his life to the man who lay dead on the airport floor.

CHAPTER 6

THE WHITE HOUSE
LATER

"J3, I want you here for my little talk with Hernandez," the president said.

Talk wasn't the right word. But General Jonas Jackson Johnson understood the nuance. Talk was warning. Morgan Taylor was advancing the field of play on the basis of the Melbourne Accord.

"2030 sharp," Taylor said using military time. In one hour he was going to give Mexico's president Oscar Hernandez one chance to respond. One chance only. No negotiations. No rhetoric. No grandstanding. If he didn't agree to the terms of the "chat," there would be a response with extreme prejudice and incontrovertible meaning.

Morgan Taylor would have to notify the Speaker of the House, the president pro tem of the Senate, and members of the Armed Services Committee. He would also brief his cabinet based on the latest damning report prepared by Homeland Security and the FBI on drug snuggling into the United States and gangland-style kidnappings and killings working their way north. *The president of Mexico be damned if he didn't comply*, thought Morgan Taylor.

WASHINGTON, D.C.
THE HOTEL GEORGE STEAM ROOM

Duke Patrick sat in the steam room with two other key players from the Hill. He was closest to the senior senator from Missouri, Shaw Aderly, and the chairman of the conservative Washington think tank, The Center for Strategic Studies, Nathan Williamson. While they often disagreed with one another, a fundamental political belief united them now. They wanted Taylor out. Patrick more than any of them.

"The whole succession debate is very confusing to the American public. It gets traction, and then quiets down. Eventually we will see a new amendment reflecting much, if not all, of the noise that's out there," Aderly said. At sixty-six, he was the most senior and most politically powerful of the group. He represented the strongest faction of closet megalomaniacs. Aderly came from the president's party and wisely kept his anti-Taylor criticism to a select few. Time would come when he wouldn't. For now, naked in heat with Patrick and Williamson, he could lay bare his opinions. "Perhaps sooner than later. But we use the debate to our favor."

"You have to look at it this way, Duke," Nathan Williamson said. "Unless there's some divine intervention on your behalf before the likely ratification of a new succession amendment to the constitution, you're going to have to get the presidency the old fashioned way."

Duke Patrick had already resigned himself to that fact. The cable news channels debated the issue. It became a unique topic in the world of division and derision that usually clearly delineated Fox News from MSNBC or Current TV. There was no conservative or progressive stand; no real Republican vs. Democratic position. Of course, some Democrats saw real merit in maintaining the status quo considering the Speaker of the House's party affiliation. But in any Congressional election, meaning every two years, leadership could, and often did, flip.

So some Fox talkers argued in favor of the proposal. Others did not. The same thing occurred across the spectrum on CNN, political blogs, and in editorials. As a result, loyal followers of the normally ideologically separated channels had to come to their own decisions; a surprising phenomenon in the recent marketplace of biased political ideals.

And according to the popular political discourse, the country was generally buying into Morgan Taylor's new plan for presidential succession—a proposal developed by Katie Kessler. The plan garnered her two astounding job offers. One as a court clerk for the esteemed Chief Justice of the Supreme Court, Leopold Browning; the other as a deputy White House counsel. Not surprisingly, Kessler chose the White House. Her decision wasn't based on Scott Roarke also working there. It was the excitement that she felt about the address and the commitment she had for the job.

A draft of the amendment was already working its way through Congress where political wars were going to be fought over more than just language. The fundamental concept would take one of the country's most powerful men out of the Number Three position in the order of succession; something that Duke Patrick, Speaker of the House, didn't like at all. And he liked Morgan Taylor even less.

Taylor embraced Katie Kessler's plan for establishing the office of president and vice-president-in-waiting. These positions would be held by presidential appointees and would serve only upon the death of both the president and his vice president. They would live outside the District and be afforded Secret Security protection and daily White House briefings. Taylor presented the idea to the public before the holidays. His aides were still selling it up, but the country seemed to be behind it.

The plan sought to guarantee the stability and sanctity of the executive branch should Washington be the target of a catastrophic attack that eliminated the heads of state, the Speaker of the House, the president pro tem of the Senate, and the cabinet. This was one of Taylor's "unthinkables" that he'd acted on. But from Patrick's point of view, and his power base, it bumped the speaker—it bumped him—way down the line.

"So when do I get into the debate?" Patrick asked. It was apparent the decision was less his. It belonged to the people with him in the sauna.

"Formally, after Taylor's State of the Union. But you start tickling the tiger now. A few calls to the White House. *The Daily Show* likes you. You go there. We find the right news talkers to go on. You mention the concerns, never personal, of course. All for the benefit of the country. Then you'll hit it hard.

"It will look personal, like I'm an opportunist just out for my own hide."

"No, it won't," Williamson said in an even tone.

"How?"

"You're going to offer to step down as Speaker of the House,"

"What?" Patrick was completely flabbergasted.

"You *offer*. It will diffuse any concern that this is self-serving. You won't have to."

"And if you're wrong and I do?"

"That's easy to answer," Williamson said. He looked over at Aderly.

The powerful Washington senator smiled. It was the convincing, photo-perfect smile that helped him win elections. "You become a more viable, more honorable candidate come primary season in two years. You make a lot of money in speaking engagements, and then the nation elects you president of the United States."

Patrick wasn't so sure.

"Don't look so worried, Duke," the lobbyist added. "This will be very scripted, starting with a speech at the Jefferson Memorial. You'll be, well, very Jeffersonian.

"Scripted? I write my own speeches," Patrick blustered.

"Not any more."

"But…"

Williamson was in total control. "Don't worry. We've got someone to write it for you."

"I always…"

"Everything must be carefully choreographed," Aderly explained. The election is still three years out. We'll take care of you."

"Who?"

"Someone already in your office. A woman named Slocum."

"Christine?" Patrick felt an immediate stirring at the thought of the attractive legislative aide. He tried to casually cover himself with his towel, but not before his problem was apparent.

"You're not the first to notice her," Aderly laughed.

Duke Patrick was clearly the most powerful man in the House of Representatives, but right now he felt like a pawn, played by two great masters. They were naked in the sauna, conspiring like old Roman senators. But once in the White House, he would remind them who was in charge.

"We'll time everything. We'll whisper in ears, plant op eds that raise your visibility, and get you all the airtime you'll need," Williamson said. "The blogs and the radio talkers will all be behind you. And TV. Then there will be real noise. Hell, maybe we'll even have you switch your party affiliation. Now that'll make news."

"Put a bead in that," the Democrat Aderly said.

Patrick pursed his lips and nodded. On some levels it was like the old days. Party bosses made the decisions and played puppet master. Mayors, governors, congressmen, and even presidents. However, Congressman Duke Patrick's run for the White House would be crafted by a committee of two scoundrels. They'd market and elect a winner. It was all detailed in a confidential white paper prepared by Williamson's Center for Strategic Studies, a think tank that Patrick knew very little about. And yes, switching parties was an active scenario.

"Now, let's review some talking points you can go with right away," Aderly said in his booming voice. "This will be great."

CHAPTER 7

THE OVAL OFFICE

The day was going to end as it began. With hard, harsh words.

"Good evening, President Hernandez. I'm sorry that this call is coming so late. I appreciate your time now."

"No hours shall ever get in the way of our friendship," the former importer, now president of Mexico, lied.

The CIA reported that Oscar Hernandez's imports were not always legal. Taylor had been fully briefed before their first meeting a year ago. Hernandez had made multimillions in contraband—drugs and weapons. Much of his profit was earned at the expense of U.S. citizens—many of whom were now dead from overdoses or gangland assassinations.

"Thank you for that. Mr. President, you're on a speaker phone and General Johnson is with me."

J3 offered only a curt hello. He'd hadn't perfected pleasantries yet.

"I'm honored to be on with both of you," Mexico's president noted. "My chief of staff, Elder Cabrera, has joined me."

Cabrera said hello. But before they lost more time with small talk, Taylor went on point.

"Mr. President, I will start with geography we are both familiar with." There would be no interruption for five minutes.

"We share a two-thousand-mile border that is porous. By conservative estimates, a quarter of a million illegal aliens, many of them Mexican nationals, enter the United States from other-than-official border crossings. Mind you, that two-hundred-and-fifty-thousand estimate is conservative, even though illegal immigration has slowed. A more accurate account suggests a half million to a million. You know how border states like Texas and Arizona feel. It's not pretty."

"We wish it were otherwise, Mr. President.

"Agreed," Taylor said instantly shutting down a response. "Two years after 9/11, the U.S. Border Patrol apprehended"—for this he consulted his notes—"39,215 illegals and OTMs." Other-than-Mexicans required no explanation. "The next year, the number increased to 65,814. Three years later, twice that number. Now it's doubled again.

"Our records show that while many crossing the border are admittedly hard working men and women seeking to make an honest living for their families, many are not. More than 20 percent of illegals entering last year had criminal records. Twenty percent, Mr. President.

"They come through Mexico, though their countries of origin vary. Honduras, Brazil, Paraguay, El Salvador." Morgan Taylor paused so his next point—the object of the call—would truly sink in. "They come from other countries as well. Iraq, Iran, Saudi Arabia, Afghanistan, and Pakistan.

"Mr. President, the problem is twofold. By not controlling your side of the border between our two great nations, you have created a terrorist freeway—a Highway One to the United States. Highway One with hundreds, if not thousands of off ramps.

"We detain. You don't control. We disarm. You allow re-arming. We move to close the entrance points. You even publish and distribute guides for those who seek to enter. We deport. You turn them around and point them back north.

"Specifics, must be on your mind, Mr. President. So, I will give them to you. A Juarez television station, on more than one occasion, reported that suspected terrorists have paid taxi drivers to take them across the border. Their destination—Sante Fe, New Mexico. But if that is unsubstantiated, then the crossing of Mahmoud Youssef Kourani was not. He was smuggled into the United States in 2001, caught and pleaded guilty to providing material support to Hezbollah. Kourani was not a hard-working itinerant Mexican. Kourani was an Iraqi national; a man on the FBI's terrorist watch list; an Al Qaeda operative. He had been in Mexico. In Sabinas Hidalgo, just southwest of San Antonio. I believe your wife came from there, Mr. President." Taylor had done his homework. "She still has family in town. Think about whether your nieces and nephews are safe?

"In the time since we arrested Kourani, we have learned a great deal, Mr. President. There are more active Al Qaeda cells in Mexico. The Department of Homeland Security gave this information to your intelligence officers eighteen months ago. You've made no arrests, Mr. President. Not one. Not in a year and a half.

"Here is what is happening. Arab nationals with known terrorist Al Qaeda connections set up shop in your country. They change their Islamic surnames to Hispanic sounding names, obtain false identification, learn to speak Spanish, and then pass themselves off as determined immigrants. They are not migrant workers simply trying to better their lives." Sarcasm slipped in. Taylor delivered it quite deliberately. "Oh, and they come here, too, on Aeromexico flights under false passports, claiming to be college professors looking for jobs. We have a dead one in a Houston morgue right now."

Taylor heard muffled chatter on the phone as President Hernandez and Secretary Cabrera conferred. Up until now there had been nothing new to Taylor's rant. But this new information was dramatic.

"Mr. President, may I…."

"I'm not finished yet. Believe me, you'll want to hear me out."

Taylor and General Johnson noted a frustration on the other end of the phone.

"At least three gangs are known to be assisting these sleeper spies," Taylor continued. "And yes, they are sleeper spies, Mr. President. I assure you they have not come to Texas to take in the Superman ride at Six Flags." More sarcasm. "They have thrived in El Salvador, Paraguay, and Brazil, but they also flourish in the Mexican state of Chiapas, along your border with Guatemala. It seems you have a problem to the south as well as the north.

"There, the Maras run their smuggling operations, which includes people, drugs, and weapons." Taylor wanted to bring Hernandez personally into the conversation, but he resisted. "They travel north on a cargo train, which departs every week out of Tapachula." More homework now. "Your father's hometown, Mr. President.

"Now to my most important point. Both our nations signed a "Declaration of Security in the Americas" at a Special Conference on Security of the Organization of the American States. That was in 2003 before either of us took office. But our predecessors considered it an important agreement. As I'm sure you recall, it recognized that the hemisphere faces more than traditional threats. We are confronted with global terror, which requires a multidimensional response."

"Mr. President!" Hernandez tried to cut in.

"That response?" Morgan Taylor continued; his voice more resolute. "You and I both know the answer. I recently helped forge a new security doctrine in Southeast Asia. You have seen the results. We strike at terrorist strongholds, weapons supplies, and training camps, just as President Obama did in taking down bin Laden. But even we have been lax when dealing with the Republic of Mexico."

Morgan Taylor drew a long breath. "President Hernandez, that is about to change."

• • •

Five minutes. That's the time it took to dress down the leader of Mexico. The country was currently one of America's greatest problems and certainly its closest.

"Mr. President," Hernandez managed, "you can accept that there is more than one hundred twenty-five years of standing good will at risk. So grant me the privilege of a rebuttal. You do a disservice to our great nations if you do not." The fifty-eight-year-old ex-smuggler was known as an expert debater. Morgan Taylor expected a counter argument. He was going to get it.

"Your assessments are not correct. You assert that the Maras are cooperating with Al Qaeda. Not in my country. Contrary to your police reports and intelligence provided by your historically flawed CIA analyses, they are not a centralized organization. They do not have the kind of infrastructure that would support a relationship with an outside organization, let alone a nonindigenous one.

"Moreover, the Maras do not have an anti-American agenda. They are, without a doubt, criminals. But they are committing no political crimes. They are not terrorists."

An intelligence report on Taylor's desk told him that historically Hernandez had solid ties to the Maras. The Mexican president's protestations meant nothing.

"Come now, my friend," Hernandez continued. "The Maras are disorganized and terrible with details. They'd make the worst partner for Al Qaeda, which is highly security conscious.

"As I acknowledged, the Maras are criminals. Perhaps deadly criminals, but they are not enemies of the State. Not ours or yours. Should you attempt any breach of our border to strike at these gangs, you will undoubtedly cause the death of hundreds, if not thousands, of my countrymen. Women and children included. The elderly and the pregnant. It will *not* solve your problems, Mr. President. It will increase them. You will succeed only in creating a new enemy. Examine your recent history to see that I'm correct."

The Mexican president paused, but not to allow Morgan Taylor a chance to re-enter the conversation. He used the moment to add a sharper tone to deliver and read Cabrera's notes.

"There are no terrorist training camps, Mr. President. Your hard targets are elsewhere. Not the Republic of Mexico. You cannot seriously consider Mexico farmland or our bustling cities home to terrorist bases. I repeat, Mr. President, the United States has no targets in the Republic of Mexico.

"We do, however, have a border crisis. For that, you are right. And who's to say that OTMs, the name you so readily apply—and an offense all its own—are not a problem. But I suggest you look to the north. Canada has more accessible routes to the United States. It shares two borders with you. Alaska and the mainland. And those borders receive less scrutiny than ours. It seems your immigration authorities prefer the warm weather.

"Fly your drones elsewhere, Mr. President. Mexico is not your enemy unless you make it so."

• • •

Now it was Morgan Taylor's turn again. Hernandez would not have the last word.

"You must be familiar with the name Adnan G. El Shukrijumah, Mr. President," Taylor blasted. He repeated the name. "Adnan G. El Shukrijumah."

Taylor picked up a file and read a summary.

"Known Al Qaeda. Suspected in the planning of 9/11. Positive ID in Honduras, July, 2004, meeting with the leaders of Mara Salvatrucha. Shukrijumah had reportedly sought entry routes into the United States through Mexico. From Matamoros to Brownsville, Texas."

Morgan Taylor lifted his eyes from the report. "This Al Qaeda operative, who you maintain would have no reason to do business with the Maras, tried to acquire radioactive substances to manufacture a dirty bomb. A bomb they intended to transport through your nation to mine. A nuclear bomb, Mr. President."

Taylor's voice was now far sterner than Hernandez's. "Our bilateral agreements state that we share security responsibilities along our border. If it is not bilaterally maintained, then it will be unilaterally enforced. We *will* act. The Maras will be targeted and removed with extreme prejudice. We will take the battle to them. That is our course of action. If you have another, I recommend you make it operational within fifteen days. Fifteen days, Mr. President. Not a moment longer."

Taylor ended the call with a request that his best regards be conveyed to the president's wife. The hollow pleasantry was returned and the Mexican president hung up.

"Well, J3?" Morgan Taylor asked.

"We shall see what we shall see," General Johnson replied.

"In two weeks you may very well be implementing this." Taylor held a folder in his lap. It detailed an executive command that would far exceed what Morgan Taylor hinted on the phone.

The National Security Advisor was well acquainted with the plan. He'd written it.

CHAPTER 8

WASHINGTON, D.C.
THE J. EDGAR HOOVER FBI BUILDING

At ten that night, Curtis Lawson stopped in to say goodnight to Director Mulligan. He had his trench coat over his right arm and leather gloves in his left hand. It had been another long, exhausting day. He knocked on the door, well aware that the head of the FBI would be at his desk.

"Yes," came the reply.

"Lawson."

"Come on in, Curtis," the director said to his number three.

Mulligan was at his feet to greet Lawson, one of the senior African American men in the bureau. The chief kept a file on the forty-two-year-old up and comer. It was filled with praise that might eventually work into a recommendation to the president for the head job. Praise that noted his management ability, his award-winning marksman awards, and his achievement as a Rhodes Scholar.

Curtis also had great looks and the body of an NFL quarterback. Quite a contrast to the older, balding director he had been working under for six years.

Bob Mulligan poured a glass of aged Bacardi 8 rum. "Join me in a nightcap, Curt? We've been through the ringer today."

"No thanks, sir. Too wasted and I still have a stop to make on the way home. Gotta pick up some things for my kid."

Lawson definitely appeared tired. The events of the day in Houston sent the entire bureau into a frenzy, and Mulligan had put Lawson in charge from the first alarm. This pleased Lawson for a few reasons. He'd been on the outside of other recent key investigations, solely working off gossip, which he valued. Now, finally, he was on the inside.

"What the hell is open at this hour?" Mulligan was always full of questions; part of his DNA.

"Target."

"Jesus, how old is your boy now?" Mulligan asked pouring himself a brandy. "Eight?"

"James is eleven," Lawson said with pride.

"Christ, where do the years go?"

"When we only see them a half hour a day, seems like they grow up in about a week."

"That's the truth," Mulligan agreed. He was the father of three adult children he rarely saw. "Sure you won't have a quick one?"

"Another time." Lawson offered his hand. "Night, sir. You should go home, too."

"Maybe in an hour or so," the FBI chief said.

"Shame we didn't get to talk to the guy. Would've been a real prize," Lawson noted.

"Missed opportunity." Bob Mulligan patted Lawson on the back. "But you know Touch Parsons is doing his magic. We'll see what turns up. Now get!"

Lawson put on his trench coat preparing himself for the January air. As he did so, he offered a word of encouragement. "You know, Mr. Director, we'll get more on him."

"You better hope so, Curtis. This one's yours. And he fucking better talk to you from the grave."

• • •

Curtis Lawson was permitted a driver for late-night duty, but he preferred to be on his own. He relished the thinking time to and from the J. Edgar Hoover FBI Headquarters just blocks from the White House. He always had a great deal to think about.

Lawson lived in College Park, Maryland, with his wife of sixteen years and his son. He usually made the commute in under forty-five minutes. Tonight he'd take longer with his stop at Target

He arrived with nine minutes to spare before the 11 p.m. closing time. His shopping would only take a few minutes. Lawson walked swiftly past the bank of cash registers, the cards and crafts, the clothes and toys, CDs and DVDs, and finally into the electronics department. Without comparison pricing, he picked up what he was looking for and went directly to the check out in under four minutes.

His purchase was $29.95. He paid cash and left. Soon, he'd be home, but not before Curtis Lawson did two more things that night. First he made a quick call with his new pay-as-you-go mobile phone which included ten minutes of preloaded airtime. When he was finished he trashed the cell.

SCOTT ROARKE'S APARTMENT
THAT NIGHT

Roarke slid into bed next to Katie. It was late and he had no intention of waking her. Roarke just wanted to feel her warmth. They could create great heat together. But there was far too much on his mind tonight.

He snuggled up to her back, perfectly spooning with the beautiful brunette, the love of his life.

She stirred and automatically reached around with her right hand and found him. Roarke gently kissed the back of her neck, but failed to respond to her touch.

Katie then rolled onto her back. "Rough day?" she whispered.

"Pretty well sucked."

"Anything you can talk about?" She snuggled up under his arm, resting her head against him. Katie expressly used the word *can*, which was quite different from *want to*.

"No," he sighed pulling her closer.

"Same old, same old?" she asked referring to his frustrating investigation.

"That and more."

"What did you think of the president's speech?" Katie was working so hard at the conversation she was really waking up.

"Hardly caught it."

"Well, you'll be hearing about it for a long time." Katie Kessler's new job at the White House was probably going to become hell because of it, too.

"CNN was already blasting it as 'The Ex-Patriot Act'."

After a minute of silence, Katie raised herself up on her arm. The softness of her breast lay against Roarke's muscular chest. It felt good to both of them.

"Anything you want to share?"

Roarke did. But without assurance that her one-bedroom, second-floor apartment at Seventeenth NW and Willard, not far from Dupont Circle, was clear of listening devices, he wouldn't. Also, there was the law. He wasn't allowed to share details of his job with anyone, including Katie. He'd violated U.S. secrecy code in the past, revealing details of his work to her. The president could have fired him, but didn't. If Congress had learned about the conversation, he would have been arrested, tried, and convicted.

"Anything?" she asked again.

"How much I love you."

"You better," she murmured. "I moved to this political hornet's nest to be near you. I've never done that for anyone." With her free hand, Katie reached under the covers for him again—hoping.

"I do. And I'm sorry. It's just work. I've been kind of absorbed."

Overwhelmed would have been Katie's frustrated word.

THE WHITE HOUSE
THE SAME TIME

"Coming up next," the local TV anchor read, "The president's declaration on pre-emptive strikes. Will Capitol Hill be the first battlefront? Speaker of the House Duke Patrick fights back. And ahead, taking stock of the soft drink wars. Who's bubbling up to the top this week? And in sports tonight, you've got to see what led up to this shot!" The video went from the thirty-three-year-old anchor to a clip of a miraculous half-court basket at the buzzer by the Washington Wizards.

"Well?" the president asked from his side of the bed.

"Well, what?" Eleanor Taylor was reading and had successfully ignored the tease and most of the late news. But it didn't mean she didn't know what he was really asking.

To the public, the first lady was a quiet, nonpolitical player. But in her fourteen years in Washington, she had been active in a number of key charities, particularly those that dealt with the arts.

In executive sessions, and the privacy of their bedroom, she often complained about the people right down the street—the narrow-minded representatives, the high-paid lobbyists, and the ever sanctimonious commentators. Eleanor Taylor was appalled that the United States offered itself up as the leader of the free world, yet not one president—including her husband— considered it important enough to have a cabinet level post for cultural affairs. She wanted her husband to announce the creation of that position.

"You know, the speech."

"You left something out."

"Today wasn't the day."

"Today was the day. You missed an opportunity."

"It wasn't the right time. Soon."

She'd heard that before. "Right." She returned to her book.

"I promise. But what did you think?"

The first lady looked at him through thirty-five years of marriage and caring. "You deserved better play."

Taylor agreed. The news recapped the president's speech after stories about an emergency airplane landing in Cancun, lipsticks that kill, the shooting in Houston, and an eighteen-month-old baby who can correctly point to most states on a map.

"I don't think I quite captured the hearts and minds in the newsroom."

"Make that baby your pick for vice president and you'll lead the news." Eleanor was hardly joking. She hated how vacuous local TV news had become. And these days, national coverage of significant issues was no better.

"What's it going to take for people to pay attention? Another catastrophe?" the president rhetorically asked. He pointed to the TV. There was a commercial for the latest Hollywood action movie based on yet another Marvel comic hero. It was filled with explosions and a great deal of CGI animation. He muted the set. "Nothing has meaning anymore."

"Your neocon friends and the extreme right don't help either," she said for the bedroom only.

"They're not my friends."

"Well, they're not your enemies either, and if you want my opinion…"

"I guess I asked."

"Just keep on message. Over and over. Tell them what you're going to do. Do it. Just like you did coming out of Australia."

Eleanor Taylor was referring to the doctrine the president forged months earlier among Southeast Asia and Pacific rim nations that authorized the coalition to seek and destroy terrorist weapons supplies, money sources, and training camps.

After the commercial break the president fumbled with the remote, "I need help," he admitted.

"Press the button on the left."

"No, at work."

"Well, that's easy, darling. You need a good vice president."

"You're right about that." The nation was still without a number two. Taylor was close to making a decision. But until he did, Duke Patrick was next in line.

Morgan Taylor took the audio off mute in time to hear the depressing news that a couple of soft drink companies were doing better than he was.

WASHINGTON, D.C.
FOUR HOURS LATER

Roarke bolted out of bed, roused from his dream as if hit by lightning.

Katie Kessler felt the bed shake. "What? What is it?"

"It's okay."

It wasn't. He'd been having nightmares recently. All the same. Assassins with different faces laughing at him. But the more he looked into their eyes, the more obvious it was to him that they were the same man. A real man. A killer named Richard Cooper who had served bravely in Iraq as a U.S. Army officer, only to die—but not for long.

"I've got to walk around," he said. Roarke got out of bed, pulling the covers down below her waist. Ordinarily, her body would be a warm, inviting, and very open invitation for him to return. Not tonight. He paced, fully naked, in front of her. The streetlight cast equal streams of light through the slates on her blinds. Katie's eyes went right to him. "Come back to bed."

She reached under the sheet and touched the wetness he was causing. *Is he going to take advantage of it or not?*

"I'm lost," he admitted. "I'm totally lost."

"You're lost because you're trying to do this all by yourself. How many people are there gainfully employed in law enforcement in this country? But Scott Roarke, my Scott Roarke, thinks he has to be the nation's top cop?"

"Davis is helping."

"Okay, there are two of you. But I bet Shannon's sleeping okay and probably getting a little more action than you have recently." She tugged at the sheets with her toes, exposing the rest of her beautiful body.

"So come here and let's even the score." Roarke half listened. He sat next to her on the bed. She rested her head in his lap and automatically reached over to him. He filled her hand.

"Cooper thinks he's dead to us. That's our only advantage."

"What makes you think he's even out there taking orders for new hits? He could be long gone on vacation in Greece, counting his money and drinking Ouzo." Her fingers played him like a piano. "Speaking of ooze…"

"Hon, I can't." Roarke stood up.

"Then get some more fucking help and stop trying to fix the world by yourself." Katie pulled up the sheets and rolled over.

"I know him. I could have been him."

"You were never like him," she said.

"We were both in Iraq. Both under fire, both…"

"And you're not a killer." *Not the same kind,* she thought.

"But if I had survived a bombing like that, who knows."

"I do. You're not him. You're not."

Roarke returned to bed. He rolled Katie over and kissed her gently. It was a passionate, thankful kiss that they both felt. It was what he needed the most. He rested his head on her breasts and held her tightly.

As they found that restful state just before sleep, Katie whispered into her lover's ear. "Get some help, Scott. Promise me. Please, get some help."

She felt him nod. She hoped he meant it.

CHAPTER 9

MINNEAPOLIS, MINNESOTA
JANUARY 4

Before Lawrence Beard donned his court robe in the morning, he was like millions of others. Just another guy in line for a cup of coffee.

Beard held a District Court seat, and was recently mentioned in the *Minneapolis Star* as a promising candidate for a Supreme Court nomination. That might be two years out depending on who retired, but the *Star* was right. Beard was definitely on the White House's short list.

The fifty-five-year-old, former Minneapolis DA was everybody's perfect compromise. His beliefs ran straight down the center. He'd managed to avoid politically and polarizing issues. He was viewed as a centrist and a strict Constitutionalist, which curried favor with members of both parties. His rulings were widely quoted. So were his rants from the bench. No one wanted to be the object of his stinging lectures, especially the ones he delivered to convicted murderers and incompetent lawyers.

His name had been brought up to every president since Bush. Morgan Taylor was the man most likely to elevate him. But today, Lawrence Beard was simply an anonymous customer ready for the line to move.

His morning ritual also included checking out the newspaper's front page and inside opinion pieces. The lead story above the fold reported the president's press conference. A sidebar explored the legal ramifications, which Beard immediately scanned.

"Sure is something," a stranger said over his shoulder.

Beard glanced back. Behind him—a man in a jump suit a good three or four inches taller than his five-eight. He had to look up.

"Taylor," the man continued as if he were talking to an old friend. He tapped the newspaper. "Think people will put up with this?"

Beard's rules of conduct extended outside the courtroom. He wouldn't comment, even casually. Not here. Not anywhere. Just a raise of an eyebrow, then he turned back as the line moved forward.

"Makes you wonder what's going on in America," the man persisted.

Beard took his place at the counter, ready to order. "Morning," the clerk said. "What can I get you?"

"Large black coffee and a cinnamon scone."

"That'll be three-eighty-five." Beard put down a ten.

Now the tall man was by his side with his order. "Make mine the same," he said. "Guess we're two of a kind." He also laid a five dollar bill on the counter and tapped the fingers of his left hand while he waited for change. The noise and the action drew Beard's eyes downward.

It was the ring that caught his eye. A white gold band with interlocking snakes and deep red ruby eyes.

Beard suddenly stiffened. He'd seen it before on one man in Iraq; a man who was now dead. His entire body tensed and then he felt a sensation on his thigh like a bug bite. Justice Lawrence Beard left the cash register not waiting for his change.

"Sir?" the cashier said trying to get his attention.

But Beard didn't hear him. He was someplace else. He joined the customers waiting for their morning coffees to come up. Beard folded his newspaper under his arm and kept his eyes straight ahead. A minute later, he was out the door, never to look back and never to return. The stranger with the army ring who had stood behind him; the stranger who had arrived from a late night flight from Boston, had already seen to that.

MONTANA
INTERSTATE 15 NORTH

The best Ricardo Perez could get was coffee from a Union 76 station. He drank it slowly, not knowing where he'd find the next gas station. But close to every three hours he made a pit stop to use the bathroom and buy another cup. He needed it to stay awake. He was well into his second day on the road. Except for some quick naps at a rest station, he had to push through. Those were the orders.

These were strange roads and Perez definitely felt out of place. It wasn't so much that *a* Ricardo Perez couldn't drive the interstate. It was that *this* Ricardo Perez had no real explanation why he was there.

So far it had been uneventful. The used Lincoln with tinted windows blended in, and Perez kept to the speed limit exactly as ordered. He was chauffeuring an important passenger who needed to remain safe. He retrieved the "package," as the man was called, at the Houston airport. For more than thirty-four hours, Perez had two jobs: transport the "package" north to some state called Montana and avoid getting stopped.

He thought about what he'd tell police if he was pulled over. "We're on our way to Butte to look at real estate." *Would that sound right? Not if the car was searched.* He'd been trying to think of a good reason for a day and a half. No one thought of that when he took off. His only instructions were to keep moving, stay on schedule, drop off the "package"—his lone passenger—then leave.

The whole thing would have been easier if the man had talked to him. He didn't. Worse, he wouldn't allow Perez to play the radio. When he tried, the passenger hit the driver's seat from behind; his signal to turn it off.

Miraculously, Perez had made it to age twenty-three. The gang member accomplished the feat by doing what he was told. Always. Drug deals, rape, and murder. They'd all come his way, and so far without any threat of arrest. Perez's accomplishments fell under the category of unsolved gang crimes that worked their way from the front page of newspapers, quickly to the second section, and then into oblivion.

Ricardo Antonio Perez was originally from El Salvador. He came across the Arizona border with his older brother. They were teenagers then. Ricardo was ready to escape the memories of home.

Now eight years into life in America, he was a full-fledged gangster. He carried a handgun and a knife. He always had a knife. Most recently, he used it against an elderly couple in a parking lot. They had just seen a dinner theater production of *Man of La Mancha*. They had less than $100 in their pockets.

He turned the money over to his only family now—the leaders of Houston's MS-13 splinter gang. But he was punished for picking such a worthless target. He wore the scar on his forehead as a reminder of his fuck up.

Ricardo Perez vowed to improve. The responsibility he now had was proof that he'd become a valued member of the organization.

"We'll be there in another three hours," he told his passenger, without expectation any longer that he'd be answered. "I drop you off, and you pay the remaining amount due." Still no comment.

They passed a sign for an upcoming truck stop. "Sure you don't want a cup of coffee? We've got another stop ahead?"

The man looked out the window. He didn't drink coffee or alcohol. Besides, he needed some more sleep so he would be ready for the work ahead.

In the rearview mirror, Perez saw the man fold his jacket and put it between the door and his seat. Then he rested his head against the makeshift pillow and closed his eyes again.

For an instant, Perez thought of pulling over, shooting the asshole, and taking his money right now. Five thousand dollars. It was right there in a briefcase. Estavan had told him, "Make sure you count it!" There would be hell to pay back home if he screwed up. *Fuck it,* he thought. He could suffer through another three hours of silence.

MINNEAPOLIS, MINNESOTA

"Your Honor, are you feeling okay?" the court clerk volunteered during a morning recess. The judged appeared out of sorts today.

"I'm fine, Melissa," Judge Beard said.

"Are you sure?"

"Yes, thank you."

At one point during morning testimony, Beard looked like he had completely tuned out. He had to ask the witness to repeat an answer. He carefully phrased the request so the defense would not have cause to file an appeal. Still, the prosecutor noted the lapse, as did Beard's clerk.

"Do you want to call a recess, sir?" she leaned in to whisper.

"No, I'll be fine." With that, Beard tried to put his bench face back on, but all that came to mind was the ring and the man at Starbucks who was wearing it. Without realizing it, he wrote down a word on his pad. The last letters of the name *Cooper* trailed off just as Judge Lawrence Beard's hand relaxed and he slumped into his chair never to hear another word of testimony.

CHAPTER 10

MOSCOW

Arkady Gomenko left work at precisely 1830—6:30 p.m. Since he was, as he liked to say, between marriages, he had no need to go right home. He rarely did. He loved watching sports on TV, meeting friends at bars, and trying to talk his way into some middle-aged woman's bed.

In truth, Gomenko was more successful watching TV and talking sports. So, this was his routine, three or four nights a week. Pretty boring for a forty-four-year-old civil servant who might still have a little potential left.

He wasn't bad looking. The kind of person who never stood out. Though he talked about the personalities of the people at his work, he never discussed his occupation or politics. Arkady Gomenko was the typical Russian of the new regime—which was pretty much a copy of a Soviet citizen-comrade from the old regime.

Arkady Gomenko appeared to live his life this way—from work to bars, from bars to home, from home to work. It was this way ever since wife number two ran through his savings and left with a true capitalist, an Austrian stock broker. Now, six years later, Arkady did his job efficiently, but no better. Most importantly, he never raised concern from his supervisors.

It was noted by those who occasionally tailed him over the years that he had his familiar haunts and there was nothing dangerous or subversive in his pattern. He seemed to have fewer than a dozen bars, cafes, and restaurants on his list, and he visited them quite spontaneously, with no predictable frequency.

To his boss, Yuri Ranchenkov, the new deputy director general of internal intelligence of the Federal'naya Sluzhba Bezopasnosti, better known in abbreviated form as the FSB, Gomenko was a reliable enough, semi-unnecessary official who would either die at his desk of old age or retire into oblivion. The perfect functionary. There was probably no need to tail him anymore. Of all people, Gomenko was harmless. Still, there were rules.

Arkady Gomenko must have known he had been spied on by his

boss. He'd processed reports on others who declared loyalty to the state but were still tailed off hours. In two cases, people disappeared. Like in the old days.

Today, Gomenko turned right from his office at Lubyanka Square and walked down Myasnitskaya Street to a small sports bar. He spent a few hours there. No one scored that night. Not even the Russian soccer team on TV in a repeat of a World Cup match.

At 2212, he went home alone, none richer for the experience.

WASHINGTON, D.C.

"Penny, it's your long lost."

The army intelligence officer recognized the voice over the phone. "For never more," she corrected him. CPT Penny Walker and Scott Roarke had had a torrid, but short-lived, affair three years ago. Somehow they managed to maintain the heat of their relationship in their conversations without giving into the sex any more. "But if you ever say so long to your sweetie, you know who to call."

"I thought you and Touch Parsons were an item?" Roarke asked. Parsons was the FBI's leading IT expert, having helped Roarke twice in the past year. His real name was Duane, but the agency dubbed him "Touch" because of his special abilities with complex computer programs, particularly manipulating and interpreting facial recognition photos.

"Well, yes, Mister Matchmaker. I had a momentary lapse. Your voice can send me to such warm places."

It was all quite innocent; merely the cost of engaging Walker's expertise.

"What can I do for you this time?"

"I need help." Roarke had not told her what he'd been working on recently.

"Go ahead, baby. Fill me in." It was an intentional double entendre.

"I'm up to my ass in alligators and I can't figure my way out of the swamp."

"What is it?"

"I can't say."

'But you need my help."

"Yes," he replied.

"On business you can't tell me about."

"That's about right."

"You are the most frustrating man I've ever had the pleasure to take to bed," Walker admitted.

"The pleasure's all mine."

"That's debatable. So what *can* you give me?"

"Some army records. Nothing out of the ordinary."

"You're such a liar."

"Really. Basic research," Roarke said, explaining nothing.

"Okay then. Now if you remember, honey, army records go back about two hundred fifty years. So care to narrow it down a little?"

"I'm going to give you a bunch of names. See what you come up with. If you start connecting the dots, then you'll make me a happy man."

"I doubt that," she laughed. "No more hints?"

"Nope. I'll e-mail you names. You do your thing. You're the best at it."

"I know," Penny Walker said.

Scott Roarke quickly e-mailed a Word doc. Walker would soon discover everyone on the list was dead. He hoped she'd find a lot more. He was acting on a hunch and on Katie's insistence to get help.

CHESTER TOWNSHIP, OHIO
LATE AFTERNOON

Gloria Cooper wasn't thinking about anything as she walked down her long driveway to bring up the weekly *Chesterland News*. It had been years since she'd read much of it, but her husband Bill still liked to follow local sports. It was a throwback to when their son Richard played high school football. A few cars rolled along the suburban street lined with contemporary homes, none more magnificent than the Coopers'. But that didn't matter to her. Little did anymore.

About twenty yards off, on the opposite side of a street, a black SUV slowed and came to a stop. Its warm exhaust hit the cold air and sent a cloud billowing upward. As she walked to the end of the driveway she casually looked at the vehicle. The woman wondered why it was there. Someone seemed to be looking at her, but she couldn't tell who.

Gloria bent over to pick up her paper. When she looked up, she was startled by the sound of a car horn. The SUV had pulled out into traffic and nearly sideswiped a passing car. Her first impression was to call out *idiot!* But as the SUV sped off, she held the thought: *The man at the wheel!*

For a moment, a fleeting moment, the sixty-seven-year-old woman's heart seemed to stop. *He looks like…*

The driver felt a piercing stare in his peripheral vision. He floored the SUV.

Bill Cooper wouldn't want to hear what his wife thought; what she wanted to think. So she wouldn't even share it. Yet, the man in the car looked so much like their son—their long dead son.

• • •

It was a mistake. Possibly his first one in years. He wished he had never returned to Chester Township. *Why?* he asked himself. It was stupid and dangerous. He never intended to be seen. After all, he had died twice. Once in Iraq, years ago; and more recently in Washington. *Stupid! Never again.*

Richard Cooper drove away with the image of his mother's surprised face staring at him. As soon as he reached Interstate 71, he floored the accelerator wanting to add miles between his past and where he was going.

Richard Cooper is dead, he affirmed. *And the people responsible for killing him will all die, too.*

Years earlier, the army officer known as *Cooper* had been leader of a squad ordered to take a building in Baghdad and rescue a family. Cooper viewed the tip as highly suspicious. It came from an unreliable source that disappeared when army intelligence tried to question him.

Cooper complained. "It's a fucking setup." His appraisal was curtly dismissed. Cooper tried again. He could clearly see the danger. Why couldn't they? Again his request was denied. The order came back, "Take the damned objective!"

But the building was too quiet. He was certain no one was inside. Cooper radioed command. A captain, a major, a lieutenant colonel, a colonel, then a brigadier general. He was ignored. He skipped over them and went to a two-star. The general didn't take his call. He stopped short of going higher under threat of court martial. Against his better judgment, and those of his fellow soldiers, he obeyed the order.

Cooper and seven other squad members went into the building. He was right. It was a trap. A bomb exploded. Four floors pancaked on top of his fellow soldiers. Everyone but Cooper was killed. Somehow a retaining wall protected him. Although dazed, he made his way through the rubble. At first, revenge was not on his mind. Surviving was.

A family found him stumbling through an alley. Realizing that a lone American soldier would be the prime target for snipers, they took him into their home. They had their own motives. They were Shiite insurgents and they wanted information on American weaknesses and soft targets.

The army never found Cooper's body. They assumed it had been incinerated in the blast.

Cooper's captors didn't need to torture him. He willingly cooperated, not because they turned him, but because the army ignored him.

And if he had any doubts about his decision, they evaporated when his immediate command changed the story. They released a statement that the squad was attacked in the course of a rescue attempt. They put up a heroic defense, but died when a suicide bomber stormed into the building.

The lies killed the man who had been Richard Cooper, not the bombs.

The former lieutenant remained in Baghdad, helping the rebels. Weeks later his new associates introduced him to a man who could help him. His name, Ibrahim Haddad. Like Cooper, he was a man on a mission. He saw great potential in the American soldier, especially when he learned that Cooper was an extraordinary athlete and an accomplished actor in his high school.

"You shall become an instrument of revenge, my young friend," the Syrian explained. "Yours and mine."

Haddad told Cooper how important a role he would play in bringing down the Americans. The ex-soldier cared more about his personal vendetta. But soon the millions Haddad transferred to Cooper's new Swiss accounts made him put his own cause on hold. Until now.

Haddad had taught Cooper how to change his look, manner, and identity; how to move through crowds yet never be seen; how to become the world's stealthiest assassin. It worked time and time again, right through his most recent passing. That's when he faked his own death at the hands of the man who most wanted to see him dead—Secret Service agent Scott Roarke.

Now America's Secret Service, the FBI, and even Haddad thought Cooper was gone. The dental records of the deceased would not prove anything, for a man who survived a bomb blast at ground zero could have a whole new set of teeth.

As he drove out of Chester Township, Ohio, he vowed *never* to make another mistake. He had more money than he could ever spend, the ability to travel anywhere in the world, and the knowledge of how to kill more successfully and effectively than any assassin since the Jackal.

The image of his mother's face was nearly gone now. He'd provided for his parents' welfare. They had their memories. That was better than knowing who he was today and where he was going.

Richard Cooper didn't exist. But as any number of other people, he had more work to do and all the time in the world.

INTERSTATE 15
A TRUCKSTOP NORTH OF HELENA, MONTANA

Ricardo Perez exited the highway thinking only of getting his cursed passenger out of his life. As he angled toward the far end of the parking lot, he hit his brights twice. A signal. Two hundred feet away a car answered with three flashes. The flashing lights identified the cars to one another. Perez drove to the waiting vehicle, made a wide turn, and backed into the space next to the green Toyota Camry.

"Stay in the car." These were the first words from the man Perez had driven 1,138 miles.

It was obvious his passenger was not an American.

Another man, about the same age as his forty-something passenger, stepped onto the pavement. Perez's "package" did the same. They hugged and kissed one another; left cheek, then right. Next they returned to the green car where they talked for ten minutes.

Perez grew impatient. He wanted his money and he wanted to leave. The whole thing was making him nervous. Just as he was about to get out to try and hustle the men along, his passenger returned.

He reached into the backseat and fiddled with something. Perez presumed he was getting the money ready. "Here." He passed an attaché case forward with pretyped directions. "This is where you'll go now. Follow the instructions on the paper. Then you will be through."

Perez checked the case. The money was there in hundreds. He counted it out twice, which took more time. $5,000. Then he looked at the directions. "It's all there, but I wasn't told about any other stop," he complained. "This isn't part of the deal."

"You are mistaken. It is right here on the paper. You have one hour."

"Am I picking up someone else?"

"There will be someone there. Another driver for you to meet. Now go. Do not be late. One hour. Exactly."

The man left Perez's Lincoln and rejoined the other in the Toyota. Perez watched. He was pissed off. He punched the steering wheel. "Jesus Christ! This wasn't the fucking deal!" He needed rest more than anything else. He wanted to drive a few miles and find a safe motel. Instead, he slammed his foot on the gas pedal and tore out of the parking lot. He nearly hit a guard rail as he merged back onto Interstate 15. *One hour?* He figured he'd get there early. If no one was there, he'd leave. *Fuck them! Fuck every one of them.*

The directions called for him to take an exit east off I-15 exactly twenty-two miles out, make a right on a two-lane road, and keep going at twenty-five miles an hour for exactly eighteen miles. *Simple and stupid.*

He followed the instructions with the radio finally blaring loudly. He hated every station he found, but at least there was music. He turned off the Interstate at the precise point and drove down the county road. Eventually the pavement ended, but the road continued. Perez picked up his cell phone and thumb-dialed a number. The call went nowhere. He checked the display. No bars. *Damn it!* Perez speeded up. According to his odometer he was less than a mile away and a few minutes early. There was a rise ahead. *Got to be just over the hill*, he thought.

Ricardo Perez began the descent and immediately slowed. He saw smoke rising from the road ahead. "What the fuck!"

He crept forward barely above five miles an hour. A car, or what was left of it, was smoldering. It looked as if it had stood at ground zero for a high-explosive attack.

Perez stopped short. He checked his watch. He was a minute early. Did the person he was supposed to meet have an accident? "Shit!" He was going to be in serious trouble when he got back home.

The young gangbanger took his gun out of the glove compartment and cautiously stepped out of his car.

"Anyone there?" he yelled. It was a useless call into the cold air. No one could have possibly survived such an explosion and fire.

An accident? There were no skid marks. Perez walked around to the front of the car. The driver hadn't hit anything. *The driver?* Perez looked in the wreckage. The skeletal corpse of a man was burned beyond recognition. The stench made him pull away.

It was too much for him. Perez broke into a full run back to his car. He had to get away. This was no accident. Then…

Ricardo Perez couldn't intellectualize the blinding flash. It was too sudden; too unexpected. It simply happened. It was followed by a blast of raw energy and skin-searing heat. Perez was at his top speed, but the force of the explosion hurtled him a dozen yards back into the lifeless dirt of the Montana high desert.

CHAPTER 11

WASHINGTON, D.C.

Christine Slocum hadn't wasted a moment to invest herself in her new job. She was an excellent writer with a full command of history and a talent for working "closely" with others. Her credentials were impeccable: a Smith College graduate with honors, work at Associated Press and MSNBC, and a short stint with Congressman Teddy Lodge. Rumor had it that she'd served Lodge in more ways than one. After meeting the young beauty, Duke Patrick hoped he'd be as fortunate. But right now, it was all about work.

"This asinine succession proposal of Taylor's. I want to know how we can defeat it," Patrick barked from his desk.

Christine crossed behind him to read over his shoulder. She leaned close enough to him that he could smell the understated but inviting scent of her Calvin Klein Euphoria floral fragrance, an inviting combination of orchid, lotus, violet, and amber. She pointed at a line in the proposed amendment, rose up and offered her first commentary.

"It won't be the first time it's changed," she said displaying her knowledge."It started with Article II, Section 1, of the Constitution, then the Presidential Succession Act of 1792, The First Presidential Succession Act of 1886, the Presidential Succession Act of 1947, and more recently the Twenty-fifth Amendment."

"Christ!" he said turning into her full body. "How do you know all this stuff?"

"I eat history up," she explained. "Always have. A real history junkie."

"Aderly was right about you."

"Senator Aderly?"

"Yes."

"But I've never met him."

"Apparently your reputation precedes you," Patrick said, taking in her extraordinary figure.

She recognized the look and the intent. "Then I hope I live up to your expectations," she added, turning quickly and circling his desk.

"So, unlike the present law, the succession line went from the president to the vice president, then onto the secretary of state, followed by the secretary of the treasury, the secretary of war, and the rest of the cabinet."

"I really had no idea." That was obvious.

• • •

A similar, but more dignified conversation was underway in Attorney General Eve Goldman's office as Katie Kessler discussed the milestones with Eve Goldman. Both women were dressed in linen pants suits, part of the Beltway uniform. Goldman's was from a Nordstrom in Bethesda, Maryland, where she lived. Katie picked up a similar outfit at Nordstrom Rack on Wisconsin Avenue in Washington at a considerable savings.

"After President Truman succeeded Franklin Roosevelt, he decided to change the first line of succession from cabinet to Congress," Kessler noted.

"Right," the forty-nine-year-old AG added, demonstrating her understanding. "Truman didn't even name a vice president until he ran for re-election in 1948."

"And without a vice president serving under him, George Marshall, his secretary of state, would have become his immediate successor if he died."

"Didn't Truman think that in a democracy, the position of president is elective, and therefore it should fall to someone who had stood the test of the electorate? Hence the Speaker of the House, the leading officer of Congress?"

"Yes," responded Kessler, "but the speaker is not a nationally elected representative, and is only elevated to national prominence by gaining the support and vote of the majority of the members of the House.

"Interestingly, the 1792 statute named the president *pro tempore* of the Senate as the first officer in the line of succession, not the Speaker of the House. But without a vice president, the power in the White House could switch to the opposition party."

"Like now."

"Exactly. And if that person is not, shall we say, presidential material, the country has a bigger problem. That was Truman's perspective on the president pro tem at the time, a vindictive and powerful seventy-eight-year-old, good old Tennessean named Kenneth McKellar. On the other hand, Speaker of the House Sam Rayburn was a good friend of Truman's."

"Good enough to have been drinking with him when he got word about Roosevelt's death," Goldman noted. "But we've had extended periods since 1947 when the president's party is not the majority party in either the House or the Senate, or both. So wouldn't it be more advantageous to have a cabinet member appointed by a president to continue his policies than a legislative officer with a divergent political agenda?"

"Then this is all about me," Patrick said, following the explanation from Christine Slocum in his office.

"Politically, at this moment, yes, but put yourself in the president's shoes."

"That's my plan."

She laughed.

"I'm serious," he said. His demeanor switched to underscore the point. "Stick with me and this time you will make it to the White House."

"I believe you could," Slocum said.

"More than could. Will."

"I stand corrected, Mr. Speaker. Will." Slocum refocused. "Let me explain some more."

"Okay."

"President Grover Cleveland's vice president died in office in 1886. Congress was out of session, and according to the 1792 act, there were no statutory successors if, in turn, Cleveland died or he couldn't discharge his duties. So Congress reconvened and pulled together The First Presidential Succession Act, which set the line of succession after the vice president with the secretary of state, then the rest of the cabinet department heads, in order of their department's establishment. Approved, the 1886 Act required the successor to convene Congress, if it wasn't already in session, to determine whether or not to call for a special presidential election."

"Kinda foreign notion. I don't like it."

"Neither did Congress, including the whole definition of who's an *officer*. For example, would even the Speaker of the House be considered an *officer* in Constitutional terms?"

"Yes? No," he settled on. "Hell, I'm elected, so…"

"Yes, but an *elected officer* of Congress," Kessler said, reviewing the same argument. "The Constitution, Article II, Section 1, Clause 6, states that Congress may, by law, specify what *Officer*—capital *O*—shall act as president if both the president and vice president are unavailable. That's the foundation of all the laws that followed. But does the Constitution view elected *officials* as *Officers*?"

"That's a question for the Supreme Court," Goldman offered with authority.

"Correct. But how would they rule? Cabinet members as officers? They're *officers* appointed by the president, ratified by the Senate."

"James Madison maintained officers are those appointed rather than elected."

"Correct again, but it got sidestepped with the ratification of the Twenty-fifth Amendment. In the strictest sense, it focuses on how the president is succeeded in office, under the terms of the 1947 Act. But there's a big old hole that's there to fall into."

"Take me through the worst case scenario as it now stands," Goldman asserted.

"Worst case? There's a terrorist attack. The president dies. The vice president, Speaker, and Senate pro tem are also killed. The secretary of state resigns his office in order to be sworn in."

"But imagine that the Senate moves at light speed to elect a new president pro tem. The appointment will bump out the secretary of state."

"So he's now in," Duke Patrick chimed in.

"Or *she*," Slocum said with a seductive smile. "But it's not over. Minutes later, the House names a new Speaker."

"*She* or he," Katie noted to the Attorney General, "would bump the Senate president behind the Speaker. The Senate is in disarray and the former secretary of state is out of a job."

"Craziness," Goldman commented.

"But possible."

Eve Goldman was impressed with Kessler's command of the subject. She'd heard much of it before, amidst the chaos before Teddy Lodge was about to take office. Now it all meant so much more.

"Since September 11, 2001, we've lived under the specter of this reality. Terrorism, treason, and other unimaginable plots point to the flaws in the existing structure of succession. One bomb, one missile, or God knows what could throw the country into utter chaos. This is not fiction. It just hasn't happened yet. We need to have clarity for once and for all over the definition of *Officer* and eliminate any scenario that leads or contributes to Congressional chaos. That's why I thought that a system that allows for a president and vice president-in-waiting, of the president's choice, provides for political stability until the next election."

"It's bullshit," the Speaker exclaimed. "Pure unadulterated bullshit. And Taylor's doing this only because we're in opposite parties."

"Maybe so," Slocum said only partially agreeing. "But similar ideas have been talked about for some time on both sides of the aisle. From Representatives Brad Sherman to Senators Cornyn and Lott."

"Well I'm not them. And I'm not going to vote myself out of a job if something happens to Taylor before a vice president is confirmed."

"Fortunately, it's not Patrick's decision," Goldman declared. "It's the state's job to ratify an amendment."

"And that's where we need to be heard," Kessler added.

"With a lot of explaining."

Kessler nodded her agreement.

"It'll take allies across the country. Governors and members of Congress. Talk show hosts and community leaders. That's Bernsie's area. And prep. And that, my dear young colleague, will be your domain. Things like this don't happen overnight, but you'll be spending a lot of time at your desk worrying about it. More work, less boyfriend. Sure you're ready?"

"I am," Katie said, really selling her confidence.

"What's her plan?" Patrick asked, now standing and looking out his window at the Washington Mall which stretched out for blocks from the Capitol.

"To get the states in line with the idea. If passed, the president will nominate a candidate as the immediate successor after the vice president. This could be a well-respected or beloved former president or vice president, or someone else with national visibility. Probably a safe choice, but a member of the administration's party. The nominee would be subject to Senate confirmation. If approved, this person would receive regular intelligence reports and protection from the Secret Service."

"Utter bullshit putting someone up who hasn't been elected," Patrick complained again.

"You could say the same for the members of the cabinet who are already in the line of succession," Slocum responded.

"Yes, but…"

"Positioned correctly, it won't be such an impossible plan to sell in."

"And this Kessler woman is the prime proponent of this?" the Speaker asked.

"As far as we've heard."

"Where the hell did she come from, and who made her God?"

"Word on the streets is she's hooked up with a boyfriend in the Secret Service." Her innate competitive sense took over. "But that can change."

CHAPTER 12

JEFFERSON CITY, MONTANA
LATER

They'd been on the road for a little under two hours.

"Shhh," the driver of the Toyota said. "There might be something on the radio. He set the car radio to scan until it landed on a news station out of Missoula, KLYQ. Maybe the news would have a report.

"No loose ends." Those were the orders. Five thousand American dollars were wasted in the two executions. But the man in Paraguay considered it a small price to pay considering the secrecy it bought.

Eventually the news came on after the weather and American sports scores, which meant nothing to the pair of foreigners. Not understanding the difference between national and local news, they caught the network broadcast at the top of the hour.

> "From Houston, comes this update. The FBI is investigating the identity of the arriving passenger shot by U.S. Customs and Border Protection agents yesterday at George Bush Intercontinental Airport. Authorities said that the man resisted arrest and killed one passenger with a gun he seized from a federal officer before other armed customs agents opened fire."

"Do you think he was with us?" asked one of the passengers.

"No. Probably just a deranged American zealot," the driver replied. "The country is full of them."

The two passengers in the back nodded in agreement. They were, after all, not familiar with America beyond the violent movies and uncivilized reality TV shows they'd seen. They'd spent their lives in their books and their laboratories. One was a chemist, the other a biologist.

The men waited for news more relevant to them; word of the explosion. But there was nothing. The final story was about a man named Duke Patrick who had the title *Speaker of the House*, whatever that was. It seemed to them that he was making some worthless speech.

When the news finished, someone called Savage came on and started yelling. The driver turned the radio off.

OREGON, MISSOURI
HOLT COUNTY HEALTH DEPARTMENT CLINIC

Dr. Noam Adam was confused. In the span of just two days the Indonesian immigrant had treated three patients with the same symptoms; some seemingly flu related, some not. The headache and weakness were consistent with a flu diagnosis. But the ringing in the ears bothered him and the intermittent waves of nausea confused him. The disorientation his patients experienced was unexplainable.

Avian flu? He asked himself. *Another strain of H1N1?* He really didn't know and he certainly didn't want to be an alarmist, not in rural Oregon. Adam would run more tests on his own time. After all, three sick farmers in a week didn't add up to a pandemic.

So far, the basic blood tests proved inconclusive. The white blood cell count on the first to get sick had decreased, but not exceptionally. He would have to watch the others. They each had temperatures that peaked a little over 101.5—nothing out of the ordinary. He excused the red spots on the second patient's skin as fever related. Again, nothing out of normal range.

Everything pointed to the flu. It was January. Quite normal. Adam simply needed to check Holt County Health's vaccine supplies and maybe order more. There was no need to panic.

THE PENTAGON

CPT Walker read the detail she'd collected from researching the names Roarke provided. They all had one thing in common: they died in the last month. Yet, with the exception of one possible fatal heart attack victim, whose death near Rockport, Massachusetts, she just found on the Web, nothing jumped out at her. The only reason she gave Charlie Messinger more than cursory examination was that he died close to where Walker and Roarke spent a wonderfully wild weekend. Later, she'd chalk up the random connection as a "God Wink;" a reference to a series of books she enjoyed reading about how people should pay attention to powerful coincidences. This was definitely one.

Walker typed the name *Messinger, Charles (Charlie)*, into her computer. Hundreds of references came up. *Too many.* She was about to hit delete when her mind went back to the small B&B a stone's throw from Bearskin Neck. *Okay, Mr. Messinger. Who the hell are you?*

She stuck with the search for a good two hours. Walker had to refocus a few times because she kept getting lost in her memories. At one point she cursed Roarke. But she knew he was happy now. Besides, Roarke had played matchmaker and set her up with Touch Parsons over at the FBI. *You get ten more minutes, Messinger. Talk to me.*

He did.

Charles V. Messinger, Colonel, U.S. Army, ret.

"Hello," she said. "What do we have here?" She decided to see. Walker logged onto a secure Pentagon site which she opened with her personal password.

She sat back and read. Well into the third page of his record was an astounding story. That's when she realized she had experienced a full-fledged "God Wink."

MONTANA HILLS

The cold woke him. Freezing cold. Perez reached for blankets that weren't there; for his girlfriend; for his mother. But there was only the cold and the dirt.

Where am I? The pain cut short his first conscious thought. He forced his eyes open. Even then he didn't instantly remember what had happened. *Driving. A lot of driving. Making the drop. Driving through the hills. Then… The burning car. The explosion!*

He survived. Now he had to live. *How?* He was miles from help and alone in a God-forsaken land. No jacket. No way out.

The young man slowly raised himself up. He stretched. *Sore, but nothing broken.* His clothes were ripped. The back of his shirt all but burned off. The sun was going down, which meant he'd been out for hours; critical hours when he could have been walking back to the highway. Now it would be suicide to leave. He had to survive the night.

The smell of burning rubber and gasoline was still in the air. He turned around to see the rubble barely fifteen yards away. His survival instincts took command. *Gotta stay warm.*

For the next eight hours Ricardo Perez sat by the charred wreckage of his car, throwing anything flammable into the fire.

He drifted in and out of sleep dreaming fitfully about the explosion and finally bolting awake with the realization that he had been double-crossed.

FBI HEADQUARTERS

"What do we have here, people?" Roy Bessolo felt he'd given his highly focused team enough time to produce some theories. They were fast and smart agents. All handpicked by Bessolo himself.

"Got a probable ID," volunteered Nancy Drahushak, one of Bessolo's rising super stars. "Try this on for size. Abdul Hassan. Egyptian born. German educated. It appears this was the first time Abdul Hassan has been in the United States. But it's not the first time this man's been here."

"What do you mean?" asked Komar Erkin, the newest member of Bessolo's A-plus Team.

Drahushak held up one photograph, then another. "Looks like Hassan may have made an appearance or two under some aliases." Drahushak tossed them on the table. They certainly resembled the deceased. The photographs were in the FBI database and they had triggered the Houston DETAIN alert. "Touch Parsons is into them now."

"Touch?" Komar wondered.

"Duane Parsons," explained Bessolo. "We call him 'Touch.' Because that's exactly what he has. A real touch for facial recognition programs. He works closely with us and FTTTF."

The Foreign Terrorist Tracking Task Force shares information with the FBI's National Joint Terrorism Task Force and eighty-four regional joint task forces. Their principal duty—data-mining; creating "electronic footprints" of known and suspected terrorists. Hassan was not one, but his other identities were. That's why his picture produced a positive at the airport.

"I've got more," Drahushak continued. The brunette, the only PhD in Criminology in Bessolo's team, handed out more photographs. Four good *maybes*. Take a look."

The pictures went from hand to hand. Soon, all of Bessolo's crack team had a chance to see them.

"The best ones are from Syria. Oh-eight. Looks like he was at a trade convention. See the banners in the background?" Drahushak was well into researching the event, sponsored by a chemical consortium. "I should have more later today. Now for the *maybe.* This one is from South America."

"Oh?" Bessolo said. Hassan's flight originated in Buenos Aires, with stops in Colombia and Mexico City.

"This could be him, too." She handed over a somewhat blurry picture from a soccer match. "Second row up. He's third from the left."

"How'd we get this? Bessolo asked.

"Sharp field work. A CIA officer I know takes his camera everywhere, especially soccer games. He puts everything in the hopper. Just in case. He says you never know what's going to be important later."

"What did this cost you," asked Aaron Phillips in an all-too-snarky manner.

"Something you'll never get to enjoy from me!"

"Smart ass."

"Well, thank you."

It was the kind of banter that Bessolo liked. He promoted team spirit, which was particularly important during marathon investigations—like this was sure to become.

"The shot's fuzzy," Bessolo said, returning to the job at hand.

"Parsons is working on it. By the time he's through with it, we'll see what his fillings are made of."

Chuck Rantz, Bessolo's fingerprint expert, tapped the photo. "Do we know who he's sitting with?" It appeared that the two men sitting to Hassan's right could be Middle Eastern.

Bessolo liked the question.

"Don't know yet. Gotta wait until Touch is through with his run at it. Then we'll cross-reference," Drahushak explained.

"Who the fuck's playing?" Bessolo asked.

"Who's playing," Drahushak answered. "I don't know." She thought it was a joke.

"Find out. I want to know if Hassan is just out for a good time at a match or whether he's rooting for his own home team."

"Good question." Drahushak made a note to check. She wished she'd thought of that.

"Who's next?"

Komar Erkin raised her hand. "Unconfirmed, and unrelated to the photos, but interesting. BND may have something." BND stood for the *Bundesnachrichtendienst*, the German intelligence service.

Erkin was on tenuous ground for a newbee. President Taylor had made it very clear that during his term, America would not act on unconfirmed intelligence or handpicked information that might be suspect.

"Give it to me," Bessolo barked.

"Hassan may have also gone by the name of Musof al-Mihdhar. They have a nice thick file on an al-Mihdhar. Chuck, check the fingerprints on file. Until we've got real confirmation, I hesitate to go much further."

"Pique my interest, just for argument sake," Bessolo said.

"Well, your guy Parsons should run these pictures, too."

"Yes, yes. And…"

"If they're the same, I'd personally worry a little bit more." Erkin had everyone's attention. "Al-Mihdhar is a Saudi. He holds a doctorate in chemistry and a masters in geology, with some dubious credits in Israel thanks to Hamas. BND had been tracking him around the world. They lost him six months ago."

So he was an Egyptian or a Saudi? A chemist and a biologist?" Bessolo's entire body language stiffened.

"Whichever worked on any given day," Erkin stated.

"Then I want to know if the others at the soccer game were also into geology and chemistry. And what kind of deadly cocktail those two ingredients make." Bessolo left his team with a lot to do.

CHAPTER 13

CIUDAD DEL ESTE, PARAGUAY

So far he'd sent thirty-six men to the United States. Eighteen teams of two. Only one didn't make it. *At least he died in the process*, Ibrahim Haddad thought gratefully.

Haddad had everything that money could buy and none of what

he really wanted. He lived like a recluse in Ciudad del Este. He wanted his wife and child back. That would never be. One day he would join them, welcomed by the Prophet, reunited with his family killed by an Israeli missile. That very fact shaped his life, dictated every action, and ultimately led him to Paraguay.

He first learned about what this country could offer him years ago through a chance acquaintance at a Beirut souk. There they were—Haddad, a well-respected businessman, and the stranger, a professor at Beirut Arab University. Two men unsure of what present to buy for their wives. They met at a counter displaying fine dining linens made of the best Indian cloth. Only one would see a great family dinner served on it.

"Ah, both of us with the same thought," the Beirut professor offered when they found themselves together in line with their presents. "For your wife?"

"Yes," Haddad happily responded. "The Prophet Mohammad bore witness of the goodness of his wife, for she was the first to embrace Islam. We honor the Prophet by honoring our wives."

"That is so true."

"And my wife reminds me of that on a daily basis," Haddad said with a smile. I suspect yours says the same thing?"

The man laughed. "Yes. Exactly her words."

"Then we shall both be rewarded when we return home," Haddad said. His intent was quite clear.

The men continued their lighthearted conversation as they paid for the linens. Outside, the professor invited Haddad to tea. What began as small talk moved into global politics and the teacher's own expertise. Haddad learned that Dr. Akbar El Deeb was one of the leading experts in a commodity that existed in far too short supply in the Arab world.

Haddad found the discussion interesting and well beyond any of his reading. They talked about the problems that faced each of the Arab nations and how they dealt with the need. Then Haddad's questions turned to the rest of the world. "Is the resource as challenged in the West?"

Dr. El Deeb explained the difference. And in explaining it in such detail, Haddad learned as much about America's vulnerabilities.

Everything he said was completely fascinating. The history, the science, and the transglobal political ramifications.

Over the next two hours Haddad learned how little the Americans knew about the magnitude of the potential danger and how important a role a little country like Paraguay could play. The facts were absolutely amazing and worth further research.

The men ended the evening with a sumptuous dinner. Dr. El Deeb returned home near the university with his wife's present. Haddad went the few miles south with his. He could just imagine his wife's reaction. It would be the most magnificent weave she had ever seen. He would tell her, "We shall wait to use it for when we break fast on the last night of Ramadan, my love. And over a wonderful meal that I will prepare for you, we will pledge our love for eternity."

Ibrahim Haddad loved his wife and infant daughter. But he would never see them alive again. They died while he was shopping. They died without his protection. They died without a gun in their hands. A bombing run, retaliation for a Black September attack, sealed their fate.

That night, with his daughter's lifeless body in his arms, Ibrahim Haddad vowed the ultimate revenge. It would take years, a web of international coconspirators, foreign partners, and money.

Haddad plotted to bring down the Zionists. His goal required the complete undermining of support from America. They way to do that was attack the very heart of the political, moral, and constitutional power in the United States.

One plot had failed, but Haddad survived and escaped and immediately began to set things in motion that started the night he met Dr. El Deeb; the night his beautiful wife and daughter were killed.

It had taken years to plan and millions of dollars. He worked with research from old Soviet Union intelligence officers, disenfranchised scientists, Arab fanatics, and even Americans with a cause or a craving for power. It became his life's work. Soon the United States would have to stop worrying about the rest of the world and take care of its own needy citizens. Israel would be alone and fall.

All of this because of a chance encounter with a college professor in Beirut and the primer he got on a most vital natural resource.

CHAPTER 14

GULFTON, TEXAS

Manuel Estavan used 13-30 for his own personal gain. While the people who served him lived just above the poverty line, making money by killing civilians and their countrymen, Estavan had some $870,000 in a high-yield account with Citibank. The deposits from the Syrian came easier than cash on the streets. Typically, 13-30 dealt in drugs, stolen cell phones, prostitution, racketeering, and hard-core extortion. All of it required management and huge risks. On the other hand, the kind of immigrant smuggling he was now into was easy money.

His biggest challenge was competition. There were MS-13 gangs throughout the United States and an ever increasing number of 13-30 branches.

Only a decade earlier the gang had numbered a few thousand. Today, as many as fifty thousand. Manuel Estavan was finding that running a gang was much like running a business. He had to stay ahead of the competition and provide better service.

Now he needed to keep his new client happy. *Refund the deposit on the dead guy before it's demanded.* That's what Estavan decided. Show that he could be trusted no matter what.

Though he lost one "package" at the airport, his young followers had successfully retrieved others. They were not the typically poor El Salvadorian farmers that other 13-30 gangs transported across the Mexican border. These men were well-dressed, professional-looking travelers on their way, he thought,*to conduct some serious shit.*

Al Qaeda? Estavan didn't know. Moreover, he couldn't even spell it or explain why we were at war with terrorists. However, he knew they were involved in something *muy grande.*

So, Manuel Estavan wanted to demonstrate his loyalty and be first in line for more work. Two successful pickups. One already delivered to Maine. Another on the way to Montana. *Two for three. Not the contract,* he thought. *But not my fault, either.* Estavan called a number on his phone; a number he was told not to use unless it was "vitally important."

But this is extremely important, he presumed. *They're going to need help bringing more people in.*As he punched in the international telephone number, Estavan allowed himself to think of the money. Tens of thousands for the handling of each "package," based on degrees of difficulty, and a bonus for sacrificing his drivers. That money came to him separately. Twelve thousand five hundred dollars per. That's where the profit really was.

CIUDAD DEL ESTE, PARAGUAY

The cell phone rang. The number that only ten people had. The one that he never wanted to answer. He was amazed the batteries were even charged. Yet, he could hear the ring tone coming from a bureau drawer beside his bed.

Ibrahim Haddad wondered who was calling and why? There was only one way to find out, but picking up had its own risks. *The Americans can listen.* That fact had been publicly established with the 2005 *New York Times* investigative article on the Bush administration's controversial eavesdropping on telephone calls. For that reason, he sat up in bed, but didn't move. The ringing stopped. *Good. Wrong number.*

Less than a minute later the phone rang again. Haddad tried to ignore it. On the fifth attempt, he grabbed the Samsung phone off his dresser. On the seventh set of rings, he finally answered it…carefully.

"*Hola.*"

"*Hola, Solon,*" the caller replied.

"*Esta es Manuel.*"

Haddad didn't say anything.

"I know you said not to call you unless there was a serious problem. There is. U.S. Customs pigs killed one of your…"

Haddad threw the phone on the bedroom floor. The battery popped out and the device broke. His display of anger alone didn't quell his fury. He flung the bedroom bureau from the wall onto the phone. "Imbecile!" he screamed. It was followed with more.

One of his body guards instantly ran into the bedroom suite.

Haddad waved him away. *Just like that stupid maniac in Libya!* he told himself. He was remembering the late night calls more than a year ago from Abahar Gharazzi, the son of the Libyan dictator. Those calls very well contributed to the discovery of his plan to put his own man in the White House. *Now another incompetent.*

He calculated the time they were on the phone. Ten, maybe twelve seconds. Possibly not long enough for the Americans to establish a trace. Then he replayed the conversation in his mind. Were there any words that the NSA's Echelon computers would pick up on even in Spanish? *There was a problem? Return the money?* Hardly. *U.S. Customs? Houston?* That began to worry him more. *Killed your…* That phrase could positively connect him.

Haddad wished that he could contact the one man who could take care of the gangbanger. But as he surmised from the cable news, his number one assassin had been cut down in Washington by the FBI. He'd have to put the job in someone else's hands. A lesser assassin. But it had to be done. *Manuel en Houston*, Manuel Estavan, had violated his express order and put his life's work in jeopardy. For that he would die. Any number of people in Ciudad del Este could do it. However, the job wasn't a priority right now. Other things were more urgent.

CHAPTER 15

THE WHITE HOUSE

"How's the market?" President Taylor asked his chief of staff. He wanted to judge what the Wall Street barometer had to say about the political climate.

"Surprisingly good," reported John Bernstein. "The Dow and NASDAQ are both up again. Some profit taking at Boeing after the 777 sales to the Chinese. Tech is soft."

"Ford?"

Bernsie nodded his balding head. "Up more. GM, too."

John Bernstein had been a friend, associate, and confidant since

Taylor served in the Senate. He was ten years older than Morgan Taylor and much the political curmudgeon that most people could only take for short periods. But Bernstein was shrewd, knowledgeable, and daring. He ran the White House and had a direct line to corporate leaders across America. That made him an influential fund-raiser and a good pulse taker. The joke around Washington was that John Bernstein never slept. Just when people thought they were returning phone calls too late into the night to reach Bernsie, he would pick up. He was, in fact, the man Morgan Taylor relied on the most, even though they rarely agreed on anything. That was part of the attraction. He would willingly engage the president on policy and philosophy. Their differences made Taylor think twice about every critical governmental decision and three times on political ones.

Bernstein's personal life was another matter. He was twice divorced, overweight by forty-five pounds, and ordinarily wearing fairly rumpled suits. His appearance, however, was part of his personal deception.

"But something feels wacky to me. There's a lot of activity at Nestlé. Coke is going through the roof. PepsiCo, too. Apparently, the new distribution deals they were making in South America are beginning to pay off. Don't know if it's the cola wars or what, but why now?"

"The Latin market is huge."

"I guess," Bernsie said, not really willing to leave anything to a guess.

"Okay," Taylor continued. "The fact that the stocks didn't take a nose dive after the press conference was encouraging. Let's keep a sharp eye on those sector leaders, though," Taylor added.

"If there's the hint of a blowback, I want to hear immediately."

Bernsie agreed.

The president was ready to move on to other topics. He opened a new water bottle. He didn't really have a favorite label. They were all the same to him. Furthermore, the White House chef didn't play favorites. The shelves were stocked with Dasani, owned by Coca Cola, Arrowhead and Calistoga from Nestlé, and Pepsi's Aquafina, which were all experiencing a run up in the stock market thanks to some insider trading.

CHAPTER 16

GAYLORD, MICHIGAN
JANUARY 5

"One-oh-three point two. We're going to work on getting that down, Mr. Mooney." Dr. Sheila Gluckman noted the temperature in the patient's chart.

"Well, give me what you need to give me," replied the sixty-three-year-old farmer. "Then I gotta get going." He started to stand up.

"Ah, not quite yet, Mr. Mooney. We need to check a few more things.

"Just the flu. Give me the prescription and..."

"Take your shirt off, please." The hospital's senior physician in internal medicine was quite insistent.

Mooney was not in the habit of going to doctors, let alone disrobing in front of a woman physician. He unbuttoned his red flannel shirt slowly, but left his shirt on.

Gluckman gave a reassuring smile. "All the way off." She handled the man's modesty well. "It's easier to listen to your breathing."

"I can breathe fine."

"Good. Then it will only take a few moments."

Mooney continued to unbutton and slipped his arms out the sleeves.

"The undershirt, too."

It was almost comical until Gluckman saw the red blotches on the man's chest. He winced as soon as the doctor's stethoscope came in contact with his skin.

"Sorry," she offered. "Now, breathe in and exhale quickly."

Mooney did as asked. He had a hard time and coughed.

"Again. Big breath, then push it out."

She didn't like what she heard or saw. She returned to her desk and wrote more in the farmer's chart.

"You got a prescription for me?"

"We're going to try some things, Mr. Mooney. But I'm checking you in for more observation."

"What do you mean?"

"You can't leave."

"I can't."

"You really have to stay." She explained why.

MONTANA
INTERSTATE 15

Reality began to set in with Ricardo Perez. He was an illegal from El Salvador with no business in Montana. It might as well be the moon.

His clothes were charred. He had no way to get back to civilization except on foot. If he made it back, he'd need help. And money? The five thousand was gone, and he had only a few hundred crumpled bills in his pocket. Most of all, he didn't have a reasonable story that would keep him out of trouble.

Ricardo Perez was weak, hungry, and lost. His own people had double-crossed him; sold him out. The hatred that burned through his veins had kept Ricardo Perez alive through his cold sleepless night.

He was supposed to die. He realized the bomb was intended to kill him. Like the driver of the other car, he was some sort of loose end.

If he ever made it to the main road and found help, he certainly couldn't go to the police. Not with his poor English and gang tattoos. Not as an MS-13-30 member with a record. No doubt he'd be arrested and held for the death of the driver who got killed.

Mas opciones. Perez couldn't return to Houston; not easily. Probably not ever. Manuel Estavan, his gang leader, sold him out. *And for what? Hundreds? No,* he reasoned. He was worth more dead. *Thousands.*

Why? he wondered.

Perez gathered up everything that might keep him warm. A yard of fabric left from a smoldering blanket, even maps and papers that had been scattered from one explosion or the other. He stuffed them under his clothes and then wrapped everything else around him the best he could and hobbled back toward the road at first light.

Ricardo Perez had to find transportation, shelter, and food or he wouldn't survive another night. As he walked, every step made him stronger rather than weaker. Every yard filled him with greater revenge.

He would make it. He just wished he had his gun. That was lost in the explosion.

•••

The ride from Interstate 15 where Perez was supposed to die was twenty-two minutes. His walk back to the off-ramp, over the hills and against the wind, took five hours. The El Salvadorian was smart to have started early in the morning.

He reached the Interstate a little after 11:00 a.m. Now he needed a ride. *But to where?* Wherever he could find food and a warm place to sleep.

As he stood along the side of the road, with his thumb out, he remembered the first time he hitched into Santiago de Mara, El Salvador. That was merely ten years ago. Perez was a playful child looking to catch a fast ride into town to visit his uncle's *groceria*. He thought of the handful of candies that would come his way along with the vegetables and chicken his mother sought.

That day an old beat-up Dodge truck stopped for him. It had been dark green before rust took over. Now it was basically down to the metal with replacement doors and bumpers lashed on. It spewed a cloud of deadly exhaust. But the driver wouldn't die of lung cancer. "Need a lift?"

The young Ricardo knew he shouldn't have gotten into the truck. From the moment the pickup pulled over and he had a good, hard look at the driver, he was scared. The 260-pound man behind the wheel reeked of a horrible combination of beer, sweat, and piss. The boy tensed, but there was no time for second thoughts. The driver locked the door and flashed a terrible, toothless, telling grin as he drove.

"Come here," the fat man said, unbuckling his pants. The boy slid far right, into the smallest space, as far from the man as possible. Not small enough.

The driver grabbed the back of Perez's head. Ricardo struggled, but the man was far too strong, too insistent, too drunk, too horny. Once the man had the boy where he wanted, he slowed the truck and then came to a stop farther down the dirt road.

Convinced he wouldn't live through the next few minutes unless he did something, Perez suffered indignity for only a moment—enough for the man to lean back and close his eyes.

That's when Ricardo Perez left his childhood behind forever. He pulled a switchblade from his right pants pocket—a present from his older brother.

He ended the crime in a most brutal, unforgiving manner. The slice from his switchblade was so quick, so surgical, that the man first thought he was feeling the delicious sensation of the boy's mouth. But when Perez squirmed out of the vice-like hold, the rapist realized the warmth was blood pouring from his own crotch.

He looked up with utter dismay. His cock was in the boy's hand.

Perez threw it at him and opened the passenger door. He scrambled out of the truck, fearing that the man would be on him in an instant.

Panicked screams reverberated from the truck. But Ricardo did not look back. He ran as fast as he could. Seconds later, he heard the pickup start again and steer over the gravel. The screams, mixed with an unholy litany of curses, came closer. The truck gained on him. Perez prayed as he scrambled up a hill. Yet, the faster he climbed, the faster he lost his footing in the dry dirt. He slipped and had to hold on to a rock in order not to slide under the truck.

The boy stood up, but he had nowhere to go. The truck was inches away. The boy looked into the most hate-filled eyes he'd ever seen. But they came no further. The truck began to slip on the loose soil, rolled backwards, picked up speed, and crashed into a tree.

The sharp whiplash broke the man's neck. Ricardo Perez sat frozen for fifteen minutes. His life was changed forever. The last thing he did before leaving was to spit on the driver through the open window of the truck. The coyotes, bugs, and buzzards would do the rest.

Perez resumed his walk, far more grown-up than when he started. His knife was gone, but he felt he could kill anyone now.

That's what he thought of as he crossed onto the Montana highway. The first dozen vehicles passed him by. An 18-wheeler signaled and pulled over. When the driver examined Perez, he saw that the haggard youth was covered with blood. He gunned the gas, and swerved back on the road.

A cold half hour later, another long-haul driver slowed to a stop. Perez cautiously walked toward the truck. When he was at the door, he looked in. The driver rolled down the window. He was fifty, maybe older. Perez really couldn't judge.

"Well, you comin' or not?" the man offered through a bad smile.

Perez tried to size him up. He'd done some hard living, but the man was soft-spoken.

"Up to you?" the man said.

Perez made a quick decision. He nodded. It looked safe, but nothing was safe.

"Okay," Perez replied in his best English. He opened the door and climbed up. The semi was back in the speed lane seconds later.

Perez said nothing, but he studied the driver. He had a close-cropped beard, some sort of cowboy hat, and a checkered shirt and jeans under a long leather coat. His belly spread over his belt just like the man ten years ago.

"Looks like you've been to hell and back," the driver noted.

Perez nodded.

"None of my business. Right?"

No response.

"That's okay. You're a little out of your element. Just tell me where you're going."

The young man didn't really know. He shrugged his shoulders.

"Well, Helena's up the line."

When it was obvious that the young Hispanic didn't know what he was talking about, the driver explained more. "Helena. Helena, Montana. A city. It ain't big, and they haven't seen a lot of people who look like you, but you'll be able to get a good night's sleep and some new clothes."

After a moment's thought, Perez spoke up. "Okay."

The driver sized up his passenger more. "Don't suppose you'd like a bite to eat?" He motioned to a cooler behind them. "Help yourself."

Perez didn't need a second invitation. He was hungrier than memory allowed. And thirsty. The driver also offered him a bottle of water, which he took without complaint. After that, the one-sided conversation got even quieter.

Sixty minutes later, the driver pulled his truck up to a gas station. He opened his door and started out, then leaned back in. "There's a bus station down the street. Just before the next light. You might want to know it's near a police station, though." He said it like a warning.

The man turned to pump gas and tipped his hat to his passenger. Perez opened his door and looked up and down the street. Then he walked around to the back where the driver was and said two words he hadn't said to anyone in a decade.

"Thank you."

MOSCOW

Tonight, he'd start at Cult at 5 Ulitsa Yauzskaya. This was Gomenko's favorite watering hole. The bar was housed in the basement of a liquor store; full of noise and the intoxicating mixture of the cheap vodka and heavy smoke from the imported Lucky Strikes. He opened the red door and stepped in.

The bartender welcomed him. "Arkady! Come in!"

Unlike many of the other establishments, where the help changed with the seasons, Cult had its regulars on both sides of the bar. Gomenko decided on a stool dead midway along the bar opposite the largest assortment of vodka bottles in all Moscow.

The bartender, an ex-Russian paratrooper named Igor Solchev, often set up dates for Gomenko. Never hookers. But they also weren't sexy young secretaries looking to get laid. It was more likely they were divorced, mid-to-late forties, horny, and hoping. All Arkady's speed. He didn't want a relationship. He wanted a good fuck. Anything more than that would get in the way. When he had enough money saved, maybe then he would try to settle down again. At least another year or two of pushing papers for Yuri Ranchenkov by day and bar hopping at night.

Solchev gave Arkady a high sign from his side of the bar. "Good to see you, Arkady."

"And you, my friend."

"The usual?" Forty-proof Dovgan on the rocks.

"Please."

Solchev poured the drink and leaned forward. "To your left. At the end," he whispered. "The brunette. She's been here for almost an hour. I mentioned I had a friend."

"Oh?" Arkady asked.

Arkady raised his eyebrow. He liked what he saw. "Thank you." He slapped a few bills down and slowly walked along the bar.

Solchev smiled. Cash tips made living in today's Russia so much easier. Gomenko was very good to him.

The not-so casual repositioning was noted by a sports fan at a table behind him. He never had eye contact with the man, but he saw everything in the mirror. The conversation with the bartender, the more than ample tip slapped down before the bill came. The nods and smiles. And now the conversation being struck between the Gucci saleswoman and the FSB researcher. He knew what she did. He'd overheard her talking to the bartender. And he certainly knew what Gomenko did. That's why he was there.

THE WHITE HOUSE

"How do you rate this report of Bessolo's?" President Taylor asked.

"Scary," FBI chief Robert Mulligan said. General Johnson, Jack Evans, Norman Grigoryan, and John Bernstein listened. "Thanks to FERET, we've got a number of very clear photographs that link up to a couple of identities for this character. Abdul Hassan for one. Aka Musof al-Mihdhar is another. Forget the name on his passport. It was forged for the trip. But the first name, his real name, matches up with a Syrian geologist."

"A geologist runs from customs agents?" the president asked.

"There's more," Mulligan continued. "Look at this picture. It's enlarged from the original. See the three men we've circled?" The FBI chief handed it to the president. It would eventually work its way around to everyone.

"Spectators at a soccer game at Westfalenstadion Stadium in Dortmund, Germany. But not just any fans. Abdul Hassan is on the left. Next to him, we have a positive hit on a Saudi biologist and a possible ID on the third. Another chemist out of Hamburg. These guys are all scientists. What's most disturbing, customs posts in Miami and Atlanta recorded their entry into the United States ten days ago. But with no reason to stop them then, they all cleared without a problem."

"So, we've got an invasion of geeks," piped in John Bernstein, the president's resident contrarian. "I mean, three middle-aged eggheads. Come on."

Bernstein pretty well described himself. The group laughed except for Taylor and General Johnson. The national security advisor brought the room back to reality with a sharp reminder. "One of those eggheads killed a father at the airport. That means everyone we can connect him with has to be considered dangerous and deadly, too."

"And Bernsie, three is all we know about," Mulligan argued. "There very well could be more. Trust me, Abdul Hassan was not in the United States for an interview at Columbia as he told the customs agent or a rock hound convention. But he was sure as shit here for a job. Something's in the works."

"Then what are they planning?" Bernsie asked.

Now Jack Evans spoke up. "In my estimation, he…they…are beyond the planning stage, Mr. President. The planning is over. They're operational. They're here because they've identified their target. We have to determine what that target is."

"And since they could be anywhere…" Bernsie complained, "Where do we look?"

"Where it would make sense for a geologist to be."

"The ground," offered Norman Grigoryan, Homeland Security secretary. "Or under it."

"Point well taken," Evans answered. "We must ask what they asked themselves. Is the target worth the time, the expense, and the risk."

"But?" Bernsie didn't get his sentence out.

"Later," the president whispered.

"There are principally six factors that a terrorist has to consider before selecting a final target," Grigoryan explained. "Criticality, accessibility, recognizability, vulnerability, effect on national interests or the public welfare, and recoverability. You can remember that all by the acronym CARVER."

"Carver?" Bernsie had never heard the term before.

"It was coined by Bill McCrory, former U.S. Army, counterintelligence, and U.S. Secret Service," Grigoryan explained. I can explain them one by one if you'd like."

"Jack, you want to take it?" Grigoryan said, turning the floor over to Director Evans.

"Criticality. By hitting the target, will it achieve the terrorists' objective? Assuming that it's to interrupt normal life, is it worth the trouble? Accessibility. Can the terrorist reach the target? Recognizability. Is the target recognizable once they have access to it? And conversely, is it something we may not recognize as a target? Or would we not recognize it from the air even if we're directly overhead? Vulnerability. Is it vulnerable or too well protected? Effect on the country. What will the impact be? The political, economic, or even psych effects if the attack is successful. And finally, recoverability. This is the ultimate unknown. How long will it take for us to recover to an acceptable degree and at what cost? Taking 9/11 into account, it could be decades."

Evans was finished. The room was stone cold. Even the president had never heard as clear a description of what a sophisticated terrorist must consider. It was chilling commentary.

"Well then," Taylor said, "Since they didn't come to the U.S. to be on *American Idol*, tell me what they are here for. They're trained and they have special knowledge. Gentlemen, what's their target?"

"Well, Mr. President, considering the fact that we have one dead geologist, I think we can safely narrow down the potential targets to a few hundred fault lines, a couple thousand dams and levees, and a volcano or two," National Security Advisor General Jonas Jackson Johnson said more seriously than it sounded.

"Jesus!" Chief of Staff Bernstein muttered under his breath.

"Jesus is right," the president solemnly added. "Take me through it, J3."

"I'm not sure I can do any better than Jack. But I will add that the goal of a terrorist attack is to deny the use of an asset, be it civilian, government, or military," the general said. He and the head of Homeland Security had weekly meetings about the dangers, covering everything from shopping centers, amusement parks, state capitols, and nuclear power plants. "But the goal might not be the destruction of a strategic asset, it could be to create civil havoc. Should a strategic asset go down? Well all the better in the terrorist's mind."

"Jack, Bob, Norman, and I are working with some forty security agencies to define and refine the possible target."

"Or targets," said FBI Chief Mulligan.

"Quite correct. Or targets, Mr. Director," J3 agreed. "Anyone's guess. Keep in mind attacks don't have to achieve one hundred percent success to be effective. A threat, once made public, can produce its own devastating results. Primarily fear. And fear can lead to a disastrous drop in the stock market, unemployment, spiking oil prices, or even greedy sector profit taking."

For a moment, the president flashed on his previous conversation with Bernsie about the stock market. Then it was gone.

"Something concrete, gentlemen," Taylor said. "We have hundreds of earthquake fault lines, for example. Can these people set off explosions that would trigger, say, a major earthquake in Los Angeles or here? You know how the one in 2011 was so unsettling up and down the East Coast."

"Unlikely. That would require strategically placed nuclear devices and sophisticated drilling. The risk-reward is too high. Too great a chance that they'd be discovered. I think that's more of a plot out of science fiction. And if they have nuclear bombs, I think they'd go for a hard target."

"Like Hoover Dam?" Bernsie asked.

Now General Johnson jumped back in. "Yes. We saw what Katrina did to New Orleans. Imagine simultaneous attacks up and down the Mississippi, Iowa, and along other rivers with levees, locks, and dams."

"We should look at every major city that sits down river of a dam," Bernsie stated.

"We do," said Norman Grigoryan. "Every day. And not just because of this alert. In the twentieth century, levees failed more than 140 times. They're an aging system. Ones built and inspected by the

Army Corps of Engineers may be more reliable than those locally constructed and maintained. But they're all on our scope.

"For example, in Northern California there's the Sacramento-San Joaquin Delta. It's not all that different than New Orleans," Grigoryan explained. "Levee breaks there could seriously affect the water supply for twenty-two million Californians. Right where those rivers meet and dump into San Francisco Bay. I'm sure you won't remember, but in 1997, one hundred thousand people were evacuated when fifty California levees broke. Twenty-four thousand homes were destroyed. Eight people were killed."

"So it's a likely target." Bernsie pointedly said.

"Only if it's one of many. Not on its own. More likely, The Tennessee Valley Authority. TVA alone controls thirty-two major dams. More that are smaller. The good news is that the larger dams, one hundred fifty feet plus, can likely hold unless hit by a small nuclear device. They are also the best protected in the country. The small ones are where the real danger resides. Soon we'll see winter snowmelts, and according to the computer models, we can expect heavier than normal rains in the Midwest this spring. The levees should be considered a prime target. The downstream death toll would be very high."

"And its impact on the greater society?" Taylor asked rhetorically. They all knew the answer. Devastating.

"What other likely targets?" Bernsie wondered.

"Sewage treatment plants," continued National Security Advisor General Johnson.

The men reacted predictably to the thought of massive sewage spills.

"No joke. If sabotaged, sewage could seep into groundwater aquifers and pollute fresh water supplies for a *long* time." He stretched out the word for maximum impact.

"Seems like it's a lot of work," Mulligan offered. "Wouldn't be my choice of a target."

J3 nodded affirmatively.

"Airports and shipping ports?" asked Bernsie.

"Viable targets, but I wouldn't send geologists, biologists, or chemists to take out those targets.

"Then what about power lines? The big ones?"

"Same, Bernsie. We need to stick with strategic targets that are in our terrorists' wheelhouse. If customs and border had taken down a munitions expert, then this conversation would be a whole helluva lot different. These people are here to deny us the use of something we need. I believe the end game is much greater than the attacks themselves."

"And what is that?" Morgan Taylor stood up and looked out the window overlooking the Rose Garden.

"Over the last eighteen months, the presidency itself has been assailed. First through the election process, second through the media. I think the target hasn't changed," General Johnson charged.

Taylor bowed his head. "It's all about faith in the government. Destroy that faith and you destroy*everything* America stands for and what we represent to the rest of the world."

"Exactly, Mr. President." J3 now addressed him more as the Commander-in-Chief. "I believe they want to create the kind of havoc that will make a typical natural disaster look like a walk in the park…a crisis on such a grand scale that FEMA, the National Guard, and local authorities together couldn't begin to contain. If that happens, the gangs and the private militias take over. God help us if that day comes."

The thought stung everyone.

The meeting broke up. Everyone had an assignment. As the room cleared, Morgan Taylor tapped General Johnson on the shoulder. "Stay for a few more minutes, will you?"

"Sure, Mr. President." He knew not to ask why.

Bernstein politely ushered the FBI director, the director of National Intelligence, and the secretary of Homeland Security out, then returned to the Oval Office. He took a seat next to the president. The couch remained open for J3. He didn't wait for an invitation to sit. Morgan Taylor had something on his mind.

"General."

"Yes, Mr. President?"

"I have a proposition for you."

THE RAYBURN BUILDING
CONGRESSMAN DUKE PATRICK'S OFFICE

Christine Slocum was surfing the net, looking for breaking stories that the Speaker could comment on. Since she was Duke Patrick's new principal speechwriter, she helped create media opportunities for him in print, on air, and via social media.

Slocum, a drop-dead beauty with long straight blonde locks usually tucked up in a conservative bun, was careful when and where she let her hair down. She did it with the last Democratic presidential candidate in the privacy of his hotel rooms. A little over a year ago, she wrote for Congressman Teddy Lodge and slept with him. She was very, very good at both.

She was a true political predator. Sexy, powerful, tremendously capable, cold, ruthless, and wild in bed. She had no aspirations to emerge from behind-the-scenes, but she was groomed to rise to the top. Groomed by a man she never met, but who made all the right doors swing open for her and provided enough money to retire for life at thirty. The problem, unknown to her, was that most people who came in contact with this man never lived to fulfill their dreams. Only his.

After an hour, she checked her e-mail. There were notices about committee hearings, opinions on bills, editorials and op eds from a dozen newspapers, a few press inquiries, and a heads-up about an eBay sale she might be interested in.

After she worked her way through the work correspondence she opened the eBay listing. Slocum collected Beatles memorabilia. Apparently there was something special coming online she might want. On the surface, the alert was for low numbered tickets from the Beatles Shea Stadium concert. But it actually gave her more specific information which pleased her a great deal.

THE WHITE HOUSE
ROARKE'S BASEMENT OFFICE

Roarke reached for the phone. Penny Walker's number at the Pentagon came up on the caller ID.

"Whatcha get?" he asked.

"No hello, just what did I get?"

"I'm impatient."

"Impatient was one thing you never were," she giggled. "But you did give me up too fast."

"My bad. But enough of memory lane. What road are you going down today?" Roarke leaned forward ready to take notes

"Remember Rockport, Massachusetts?"

"Memory lane again."

"You're lucky I remember it, sweetheart, because that's the only reason I pinged on Charles Messinger."

"Who?"

"One of your dead guys," she explained. "Car accident driving home from a business luncheon in Rockport."

"So?"

"So a healthy guy just drives into the Atlantic?"

"It happens," Roarke said.

"Yeah. Sure it does. And who cares, except his wife. But you should care, Mr. Roarke. You should care because Charles V. Messinger was a colonel in the U.S. Army. One of the people who served under him was a lieutenant." She paused to make sure Roarke followed her. "A certain Lieutenant Richard Cooper."

"Oh, my God!" Roarke exclaimed. His nagging feeling returned. "How did you say Messinger died?"

"He drove into the drink. Possible heart failure."

"Ten to one it wasn't."

"We're going to have to prove that."

"Can you send…" Roarke didn't have to complete the sentence.

"I already called in an army medical team to examine the body. He's not scheduled for burial for another two days."

"What about this business meeting. Who was it with?"

"You're right on the ball, Sherlock. I'm checking that out.

According to his office, there was a French businessman on his calendar. A Monsieur Peter Le Strand."

"Who I bet doesn't exist," Roarke concluded.

"So far."

"Penny, I love you."

"No you don't. If you loved me, you'd still be fucking me. You sure can't live without me, though."

Roarke had to agree.

"There's more," Walker said.

"I can't even imagine," Roarke answered.

"Messinger was about middle in the chain of command in Iraq the day that Cooper was ordered to take the building. Wanna hear about what happened to some of the others?"

Roarke wrote everything down. She told him about LT Don Nicholson, who died in a small airplane crash; Major Gerald Fox, dead rappelling off a cliff. Walker went through the untimely demise of two sergeants, one named Riverton, another Sandeman. And a judge in Minneapolis yesterday. Also U.S. Army retired.

"He was in court when he collapsed. I talked to the clerk myself. She said he was trying to write something down. He got as far as three letters. She has no idea what they refer to. Want to know what they were?"

"Yes?" Roarke begged.

"Three little letters. A *C*, an *O*, and another *O*. Then the judge lost consciousness."

"Oh Jesus." Roarke couldn't believe it. "Cooper really is alive."

"And the Honorable Lawrence Beard of the U.S. District Court in Minneapolis is dead as a result. All vets related to Cooper's case. Now you want to hear the really interesting part?" she added to pique his interest.

"The rest wasn't?"

"Not as much as this. They generally died in the order of their rank. He's been working his way right up the ladder."

"Holy shit!"

"That was exactly my reaction, but I put it more delicately."

"Who's left?"

"Well, sweetheart, that's what I'm working on."

"You better hurry."

CHAPTER 17

WASHINGTON, D.C.
WASHINGTON SPORTS CLUB
JANUARY 6

Ten more. Nine. Eight. Scott Roarke was counting off the crunches left. He started with four hundred.

It was hard keeping up with the demanding Special Forces workout. Harder every year—twelve since he'd been out. But recent experience told him all he needed to know. *Gotta stay in shape.*Remaining physically fit was absolutely necessary.

As he slowed down to the final few sit-ups, Roarke noticed a woman; a beautiful woman in a form-fitting red leotard. She was working out directly opposite him on an elliptical machine. In an oddly sexual moment, she let out a relieved gasp at the end of her drill. It came at the same moment as Roarke's.

Roarke hadn't seen the blonde before. He was sure he would have noticed, even though he wasn't looking.

The Secret Service agent made instant assumptions, as he always did. He assigned a name to the dynamic body. *Scarlett.* For the actress Scarlett Johansson. He often used easy-to-remember Hollywood names. Then again, he'd certainly have no trouble recognizing and remembering her anytime.

Scarlet smiled at him, noting that they'd shared some pain…or pleasure. He returned the greeting and that was that.

Roarke went to the weights. When he finished, she was gone. Not that he was interested in her, but he was half surprised she left so quickly.

Minutes later, in the shower, the image of the woman in the leotard came to mind. *No.* He willed away the thought. Roarke was truly, madly, and deeply in love with Katie. As far as he was concerned, there'd never be another.

Outside, the January cold slapped Roarke hard and another face formed before him. He hoped that today he'd get even closer to the person who really filled most of his conscious thinking— Richard Cooper.

Roarke was oblivious to a pair of eyes that followed him from across the street. The blonde. Christine Slocum, was watching him. She'd made first contact, as ordered.

AN HOUR LATER

"Got another for you." Penny Walker stayed the night at her Pentagon office. She was glad she did. Another name on her list came up dead. Major Gene Wesley, veteran of Iraq. Right place. Right time. Right assignment.

"I think you'll want to check this out yourself," she said on the phone. "It's recent. Watch for my e-mail and be ready to travel."

CHAPTER 18

MOSCOW

Gomenko struck out at Cult the night before. Apparently references to American jazz chased away his potential conquest. Tonight, he was at Yuri's, a smaller establishment closer to his apartment. He was only half watching a soccer game on the TV monitor when a tired patron took the bar stool next to him.

"Hello," he said. "What's on?"

"Another old game."

The man watched for a half minute until he recognized it. "Ah, the match against Germany. We win."

"We always win in the reruns."

Once again, the state was trying to control the media as best it could. It included pushing patriotic gymnastics and soccer wins like in the old days. Most of it came off silly.

"Ready for a refill?" the stranger asked.

Gomenko got his first look at the man. He was eight, maybe ten years younger, but unshaven and not particularly well dressed. For a moment he wondered if the look was deceiving. After all, these days everyone and everything was worth questioning. Even the women he picked up.

"Maybe in a bit." He decided to lose himself in the game and leave the newcomer to his own drink, which ended up being a glass of deep, red burgundy.

The man examined the color of the wine, took in the aroma, swirled the drink, and sipped.

Gomenko couldn't ignore the ritual. He had to ask. "Good?"

"Just awful. But it's going to make a cheap vodka taste so much better by comparison."

Arkady laughed. His bar companion was all right.

After an hour of small talk, which included yelling at the German team unnecessarily since the outcome had been decided years earlier, the conversation turned to the women at the bar. The women who had been ignoring them all night.

"You'd think we're invisible to them. Not even the time of day."

Arkady had the same general feeling. But midway through the comment, he lifted his head out of his drink and stared into the mirror. The man had his vodka at his lips, nodding agreement to his own pronouncement. "Not even the time of day," he repeated.

Arkady didn't take his eyes off the reflection of the man. He replayed the aside. *Invisible to them.* Then the next sentence. *Not even the time of day."* The words were precise. There was no mistaking them. They required a reply.

Arkady whispered the words he memorized years ago. He said them automatically and without any emotion. "And in ten years, they'll be whores wishing they had a man at home as good as us."

Then he waited, nervously. What would the stranger say next? The Russian felt his leg shaking. He willed it to stop.

The man raised his drink. "A toast," he proposed to the women, who in fact looked very attractive and were simply out for a good time together. "Here's to the ones who get away and don't even know it."

Gomenko had one more reply. Direct and unmistakable. "Fuck them."

It was a conversation that could have played out between any two men and meant nothing. But between Arkady and CIA agent Vinnie D'Angelo it meant a great deal.

Light talk turned from women to weather, to the old soccer game on TV, and eventually to Moscow's worsening traffic. All safe topics. Through the conversation, Gomenko never learned the name of the stranger or his identity.

Russian? He spoke like a Russian, but he was not a Muscovite. Perhaps he came from farther North.

The man was on his third drink, Arkady on his fourth, when the years of waiting came to an end. To everyone else, they looked like two drunken friends, talking nose to nose. But the stranger suddenly cut to business and sounded completely sober.

"Tell me about the man who ran Red Banner."

Five years of discrete payments. First, ten thousand U.S. Then twenty, twenty-five, and thirty. And last year another $35,000 in discreet accounts. All for waiting. Now he would have to work for the money. This required another stiff vodka. He signaled the bartender for a double.

Arkady gasped. *Why would he ask about the long-gone KGB facility? The secret Soviet city where Russian spies were trained to pass as American and infiltrate U.S. institutions, corporations, and even government. A realistic version of hometown U.S.A. in the middle of the U.S.S.R.* Even today, it was better not to talk about Red Banner.

Vinnie D'Angelo, one of the CIA's most valued agents, squeezed Gomenko's arm. It was not a friendly gesture. He was letting the Russian know that this was non-negotiable business.

"We need to know about a former chief intelligence officer at KGB. Aleksandr Dubroff."

We? We had to be the CIA, Gomenko's paymaster. He shivered. The money was real. So were the risks, which suddenly became greater. *And Dubroff?* He knew that name. Dubroff was a legend. So were his means. However, there was no record of his accomplishments. At least as far as Gomenko knew.

"It will be very hard."

D'Angelo squeezed harder and smiled broadly. "You want to live to enjoy your savings?"

"Yes." Arkady answered. "I will try."

The CIA agent made his point. He lightened his grip. "Dubroff was trying to get information to us when he was intercepted and killed at the Gum Department Store in August. I need to know what he had. Why he was talking to an American reporter. I want to know who he trained. The names of his protégés. In particular, a Syrian named Haddad. Can you remember that?"

In spite of the liquor, Arkady's head completely cleared. He committed all of the questions to memory and answered, "Yes."

"Good." D'Angelo raised his glass in a mock toast.

A loud cheer from the TV broke their chain of thought. The Russian team scored the winning goal against the Germans…again. D'Angelo used it as a cue to slap Gomenko's back and clink his glass. From then until the end of the evening, there was no more talk about the Cold War–era colonel who plotted to infiltrate America with KGB spies.

At 2350, just shy of midnight, Gomenko offered to pay the tab. He lost the argument after loud complaints from his companion.

D'Angelo stayed for another twenty minutes, trying to make passes at the women down the bar. But it was just for show. Vinnie D'Angelo had been faithful to his wife throughout their fourteen years of marriage, even though she had no idea what he really did for a living.

CHAPTER 19

MAYVILLE, NORTH DAKOTA
THE BLUE NOTE DINER
JANUARY 7

"What'll it be?"

"What's good?" Roarke asked.

"Depends what you like," the waitress answered.

Roarke had planted himself at the counter. The food off the

grill smelled good and he was hungry. He'd traveled all day from Washington. Reagan to Chicago, Chicago to Fargo. A thirty-minute drive from Fargo to the small town of Mayville. Hunger brought him to The Blue Note Diner, more famous for a juke box filled with songs containing the word *blue* than the food. *Blue Moon, Memphis Blues, Blue Velvet, Blueberry Hill.* Hence, the blue note. It was a 60s diner. Not because the owner was marketing nostalgia. He just hadn't updated it from when he took it over from his father.

"What's the blue plate special?" The printed price on the menu was crossed out. It was now six dollars higher.

"Turkey, peas, corn."

"Anything fresh?"

The waitress laughed. "Freshly cooked."

She was thirty, thirty-five, maybe forty. She would look the same at forty-five, and she'd be doing the same job at fifty. She wore a wedding ring and she looked happy. *A simple life,* he thought. *Uncomplicated. Safe.* He reflected on his own life. High stakes. People in shadows. Enemies of the state. These were the things that were going through his mind since he met Katie. Maybe finding a place like The Blue Note to eat instead of The White House commissary. Putting his gun away. Having a job he could talk about with others.

Scott Roarke wasn't solely evaluating his life. He was considering *their* future. Because over the last year, it all changed. Everything. Katie completed him. Her softness compared to his toughness. Her smoothness to his edge. Katie's sensuality to his masculinity. Her regard for the law to his lawlessness.

For their relationship to grow, let alone survive, he truly contemplated leaving the service. He thought about finding that simple life. Then, like most times he went there, he snapped back.

"Cup of coffee?"

"I'm sorry?" he said.

"Would you like a cup of coffee?"

"Sure, black. And a glass of water."

"K. But I gotta charge you extra for both."

Extra? "Whatever." Roarke leaned over and looked at the songs on the juke box. He loaded a dollar's worth of quarters and started with

Blue on Blue by Bobby Vinton. Dolly, the waitress, was back with his coffee and a bottle of water. It looked out of place in The Blue Note.

Roarke removed a small notebook from his vest pocket, careful not to open the flap too far to reveal his Sig Sauer, 9mm pistol. He studied the notes he'd made before he left Washington. CPT Penny Walker's findings. They told the story of an army officer who served in Iraq. His rank of lieutenant colonel put him in a chain of command; a now deadly chain of command. He heard that a young lieutenant in the field was complaining about taking his men into harm's way. LTC Gene Wesley could have ordered the squad to stand down. He could have saved the lives of 1LT Richard Cooper's squad. He ignored the request.

Now, Wesley was dead, too. According to the report, he was a very successful rancher. His horse threw him. He cracked his head open on a rock. *Plausible,* considered Roarke. But much more likely, Wesley was murdered by the assassin he was tracking.

Roarke hoped he would learn more tomorrow. It was too late tonight. Traveling ate up his whole day. Tomorrow, Wesley's son promised to drive him out to where he found his father. He also said he'd show him some personal letters his father sent from his last year in service.

The Secret Service agent also had an appointment with the coroner. His close friend at the FBI, Shannon Davis, gave him some very specific questions to ask.

HUTCHINSON, KANSAS
THE SAME TIME

Dr. Sam Brown now had three unrelated patients suffering from the same symptoms. He didn't know what he was looking at, much less, what he was looking for. *Appendicitis? No. Flu? E.Coli?* Unknown to him, he was going down the same checklists that Dr. Satori, Dr. Gluckman, and Dr. Adam tried at different hospitals in different cities. The same checklists that a dozen other small-town doctors were scratching their heads over in nine other communities, too. But

Brown had unique experience that put him above the others. He had spent a year working in Atlanta at the CDC, the Centers for Disease Control and Prevention. He still had friends there, and he thought a little advice couldn't hurt. One of them was a doctor he studied under at Boston University Medical School.

A RANCH OUTSIDE GREAT FALLS, MONTANA
THAT NIGHT

The target, like the others, had been selected by Haddad's team of scientists based on accessibility, active and passive security, and impact on the community. Big or small, all were strategic. For the two colleagues who met on Interstate 15, one a geologist and the other a biologist, this was a small target. A single ranch well. They had four others of equal size tonight. An easy night. Each would take about forty-five minutes. Tomorrow they would hit the larger, conventional water treatment facility, which produced an average of 12,327,876 gallons of safe drinking water per day for some 58,000 people who lived in Great Falls.

One of the foreigners, the biologist turned bioterrorist, considered it ironic that the city took its name from the series of five waterfalls. Water would create such havoc for its citizenry in the coming days, weeks, and, if all went well, months.

But first things first—the well that provided water to the sixteen-thousand-acre Colin Baker ranch. It was the perfect size for what they had in mind. Direct distribution to an influential family whose death would be noticed.

Haddad's research was accurate. The site was vulnerable. The ranch was serviced by submerged pumps which collected water from underground aquifers. With a confined volume of raw water, the agent of choice was a biological toxin, costing less than $10,000 and requiring little more than a home brewing kit, protein cultures, and personal protection. Money was no object, training was simple. The only real risk they faced was stupidity in handling the trillions of bacteria. That was not going to happen.

And so, they parked the Toyota they now drove midway down the road leading to the ranch. Google satellite photos showed them exactly where to go. The snowfall, which had begun two hours ago, would cover their tracks by morning. Though they were from warmer climates, Haddad had his men train in the Alps. They learned to drive in unfamiliar weather and work in freezing temperatures. Lights were out in the Baker house, and the property, which had never seen a robbery in thirty-five years of operation, had no active alarm. If all went according to plan, the seven members of the Baker family and the eleven employees who would be back by daybreak would not live long enough to regret the lack of security.

Given lax infrastructure protection, most of the targets were virtually open for business.

The terrorists, using new pseudonyms, found the well casing, and in minutes introduced *Vibrio cholerae*. It would hit the digestive track and lead to nasty watery diarrhea, rapid dehydration, a state of collapse. Maybe not death, but a good scare.

This was a precision bioterrorism attack. North, south, east, west of Great Falls, Montana. The Baker Ranch on Millegan Road, a second spread off McIver, the third along Eden Road, the fourth adjacent to Bootlegger Trail. Then a satisfying prime rib dinner at Clark & Lewie's, a play on the area's founding history by Lewis and Clark. The next day they'd hit the city's plant, right at the critical downstream point in the distribution system. All was ready, from fake IDs to the *Turlaremia,* which is stable in water and chlorine-resistant. After that, they were on to their next destination.

As the two experts worked through the night, Haddad's other teams were at their newest targets: Nashua, New Hampshire; Trenton, NJ; Lake Worth, Florida; Big Bear, California; Tucson, Arizona; and Verona, Wisconsin, also known as "Hometown USA." They served *Shigellosis, Anthrax, Botulinum,Cryptosporidium, Saxitoxin* and other equally lethal cocktails, all shipped to staging points across the country by overnight delivery, long-haul truckers, and MS-13 couriers.

MAYVILLE, NORTH DAKOTA

Roarke was not one to ignore warnings. Even ones hastily written in soap on a motel bathroom mirror. "The water's awful." *Okay, I won't drink it,* he said to himself. Roarke was happy he'd grabbed his unfinished bottled water from the restaurant across the street. The four ounces left would cover him for the rest of the night.

After finishing in the bathroom, Roarke sat on the double bed in his spartan room. He spread out the contents of a folder and committed the next day's schedule to memory.

0800 Coroner
0900 Chief of Police
1030 Meet Family
1230 Depart for airport
1400 Flight

Roarke checked his watch and did the quick math. Given the time difference, Katie was still at work; maybe for another two hours. The promised good night call would come later. Now his choices were exercise or rest. He opted for rest.

The Secret Service agent stretched out and tried to get comfortable on the lumpy mattress. His head sank deep into an old feather pillow. Roarke stared straight up at the cottage cheese ceiling, which drastically needed a fresh paint job. The ridges in the speckles reminded him of flying high over the snowcapped Alps, only upside down. His eyes passed over Austria, Switzerland, and on to Northern Italy. He'd been there before, on government duty. Now he thought about vacationing there with Katie. Perhaps a honeymoon.

He surprised himself. They hadn't talked about marriage. She'd only recently moved to Washington. They weren't even living together full time. Now he was thinking of a honeymoon. *Where'd that come from?* He knew fully well. He loved Katie. This was the one woman he would marry.

Roarke smiled to himself as he continued to look at the ceiling. But suddenly the relief of the ridges formed an image in his mind. A familiar face emerged. A killer's eyes bore down. He closed his eyes and willed the vision away. For a minute or so, there was only the sound of light traffic outside and he started drifting off to sleep. But then another notion came to mind. *Cooper could have been right here. Staring at the same ceiling.*

On one hand his thinking was purely anxiety-driven. But increasingly, Scott Roarke felt that he and Cooper shared a great deal in common. Most of it revolved around death.

Were you here? Roarke had a sinking feeling he had been. He decided to get up and find out.

• • •

Lou Panini. The name was the giveaway. Everybody knew someone with a name that just fit their line of work: Harvey Strum, the guitar teacher. Dr. Eitches, the allergist. Well, according to the ledger, Lou Panini was an executive with Subway. The front desk clerk remembered him and explained to Roarke that he'd been in town to meet with people interested in opening a local franchise of the national sandwich company.

Roarke thought that Cooper was either getting sloppy or he was having fun. Deadly fun. *Panini.* He had to laugh.

The Secret Service agent was certain that a check with Subway would prove there was no Lou Panini on salary. A late call to the FBI set that in motion.

According to the ledger, Panini stayed one night, paid with cash, and left his room spotless. In fact, the maid told the front desk she thought the bed was never undone. He apparently slept on the covers and didn't use a towel. *Definitely Cooper's m-o.* He didn't want to leave DNA traces on the sheets or in the bathroom. *Chances are he even wore a hairnet.*

"Can you describe him?"

"Maybe."

"His height and weight?"

The clerk looked at Roarke.

"Kinda like you."

"Exactly like me?"

"Nope."

"How was he different?"

"Darker hair. A bit taller."

"That's all?"

"He limped."

"A lot?"

"A little."

"Like a war injury?" *A trick. A diversion of Cooper's.*

"Maybe. Or sports. Now that I think about it, it wasn't that bad."

"How'd he sound?"

"Different."

This was painful. "How different?" Roarke asked, trying to remain polite.

"Southern."

"Any recollections of what he said?" he asked the motel clerk, a young man who had obviously found his life's work.

"Nope," he said through a pronounced Dakota accent. "But he was nice to everyone."

"Did you get any confirmation that the name and address he gave you were accurate?"

"Nope."

"Did you see him when he checked out?"

"Nope."

"Any chance you still have the bills he paid with?"

"Nope."

Roarke wondered if this was the future of America? People who saw nothing, who questioned nothing, who grunted monosyllabic answers.

"Is there anything else you remember about him?"

"Nope."

Roarke bet his reputation that the six-foot-one black-haired salesman was Richard Cooper. Take away the fake Southern accent, a bogus limp, and a big salesman grin, and in Roarke's mind, Cooper had come to Mayville and accomplished his personal mission.

Of course, there wouldn't be any evidence. Certainly nothing physical. There was only a coroner's report which cited a fall from a horse and a massive concussion. Roarke was convinced that neither gravity nor poor horsemanship had anything to do with it.

JANUARY 8

"An autopsy?"

"Afraid it's too late," the coroner explained the next morning. "Mr. Wesley was cremated."

"Cremated? He wasn't going to be buried for another two days."

"You're right about that, Mr. Roarke. Buried yes, in two days. But cremated first."

"Shit!" Roarke exclaimed. The bureau had fucked up. He had fucked up.

The rest of Roarke's questions didn't matter. The same was true at his next meeting. The Mayville chief of police had nothing. Roarke hoped for more with the victim's wife.

"Any history of dizziness or heart problems, Mrs. Wesley?"

"No, sir. My husband was in perfect health."

"And how was he on horseback?" A silly question.

"He was the best rider in the county."

Roarke left the Wesley house and decided to reconstruct the rancher's last day on Earth. Breakfast at The Blue Note. A haircut down the street at Ligerri's. Then, Wesley went home and rode his horse into the hills. Between the haircut and going home somebody might have seen something. Roarke found more people to question in town.

"Did anyone see a black-haired man with a limp?" he asked around town. "A stranger? Someone you haven't seen since?"

A realtor did. Panini asked him to show him an empty storefront down the street from the bank. But after a few minutes he said it didn't meet company specs. "That was it. Ten minutes at the most."

Roarke worked that into a recreation of Cooper's day. That was at 10 a.m. Ninety minutes before he killed Major Gene Wesley, U.S. Army retired.

"And he had no interest in seeing any other property? That was it?"

"Yes, that was it. He went to The Blue Note. Don't know a thing after that."

Back at the diner, Roarke asked the inevitable follow-up. Dolly remembered Panini coming in. He trusted her memory. Not many out of towners stopped by. "Then the guy left. He got in his car and headed out of town."

Roarke opted for a cup of coffee before leaving. He was surprised it was twenty cents more today than yesterday. He attributed it to the rising gas prices and the cost of doing business. He was wrong.

CHAPTER 20

HELENA, MONTANA

Ricardo Perez awoke after a nine-hour sleep. He showered for a full half hour and then looked outside his Motel 6 room. The city was blanketed with snow. A ten-inch snowfall had blanketed everything. He thanked God it hadn't snowed a night earlier, otherwise he would not have survived the road to hell and back.

The first thing he did was buy a pair of jeans, a shirt, and a heavy parka at a local Goodwill, one of the only stores open in the storm. Then he ran through his *opciones* again. There weren't many.

Going to the police was out of the question. They'd hold him. A report would lead to an investigation; an investigation to his arrest. *No police.*

Home? He could hitch a ride or steal a car. But he was a dead man if he returned without a plan. The gang member trudged through the snow trying to think of something. He never felt so isolated; so confused; and so fucking cold.

Revenge kept him alive the night in the mountains. But that wouldn't save him in the short run. First he needed a plan.

Perez continued his walk. Fortunately, it was quiet. He didn't draw any attention. Still, he knew he needed to be more than an El Salvadorian gangster in the middle of Santa's Village.

He walked past a storefront on East Lyndale Avenue. A dramatic poster caught his eye. He never would have looked twice at it before. *Now?* It depicted a young man wearing the same kind of *don't fuck with me* attitude that Perez lived by. They were about the same age. He, too, belonged to a large group, an extended hierarchical organization. Perez wondered how much they really had in common.*Don't fuck with me*, was a good start.

Perez looked beyond the poster. There was a light on inside and he could make out two men. The gangster hesitated. He was more nervous than he had been since that day he was on the way to his uncle's for candy. That awful day.

He sucked in a breath. The cold air filled his lungs. *No going back now,* he thought. But there was also no going forward without serious help.

Ricardo Perez made the most important choice of his life. He turned the door knob and entered.

THE WHITE HOUSE
THE SAME TIME

"Mr. President, I'm still thinking. I've got one hundred reasons for saying no."

"You only need one to make it yes. I want you," Morgan Taylor told General Johnson. "Look, J3, there has never been a better time than now. I'm not into trying to make history, just run things more efficiently and not fuck up the world. But this is the right thing to do. And you're the best man for the job."

"I'm a soldier, not a politician. I can design, evaluate, and task a mission. I'll tell you straight to your face whether you're making a good decision or your head is up your ass. I'm you're man for that. You're paying me to be your national security advisor. And honestly, you couldn't have picked anyone with more experience. For vice president? Keep looking, Mr. President. The country wouldn't elect me."

Morgan Taylor smiled. He expected the push back from General Jonas Jackson Johnson. What surprised him was that they were having a conversation about it. J3 could have just come in and said, "No fucking way. Now for today's agenda." He hadn't. So the general was open to it.

"The country doesn't have to elect you, Jonas. I'm appointing you. Who's going to object on the Hill? It would be foolish for Patrick to try. This is a slam dunk. And, you'd still head up National Security. It's a perfect way to streamline and save some salary." The last comment was sure to help in the confirmation hearings.

"And you think the country is going to be happy with a standing general as veep?"

"You'll need to hang up that uniform, at least for now. Think of it as a way to pick up another retirement package. And who knows, you just might like the feel of a good suit. It fit Washington well. Grant and Ike, too."

"They were presidents."

"I guess I am getting ahead of myself," Taylor said. The comment had double meaning.

"You son of a bitch," J3 exclaimed. "You're trying to put me in place to run in three years. Did you crack your head that badly when you got shot down in Iraq?"

"And you'd be happy to see Duke Patrick sitting in that seat?" Taylor swung around and pointed to his chair which was tucked under his desk. "Of course you'd make a great candidate. A distinguished military career, a proven leader, head of National Security, vice president. Damned straight!"

"I'm not a politician," the general said again.

"Good. The nation doesn't need another politician. Look around. No one's complaining about any shortage. There are thousands of them. There's only one of you. You're the man I want in the job."

CIUDAD DEL ESTE, PARAGUAY

There's an age-old myth. The Arabic language has no word for *compromise*. There is victory. There is defeat. War and Peace. All extremes. But the West has argued that there is nothing in the middle. And because of it, it's widely believed that Muslims will not negotiate. In fact, that's not true, though it makes for good copy. The word compromise exists. Over the millennia, compromise has brought families together to form tribes, and tribes together to create nations.

However, compromise was no longer in Ibrahim Haddad's vocabulary. *Compromise? There is no compromise.* He would never know happiness again. His wife and daughter were long gone. Enemy missiles had done their work. Now there was only the satisfaction of seeing his vision come true.

For more than thirty years, he plotted to exact revenge. He wanted Israel to suffer as a result of the withdrawal of U.S. support. But his plans failed. Now he was running out of time. Personal time. His coughing worsened. His inhaler helped less and less. He required oxygen more frequently. Doctors told him he had emphysema. It would get worse.

So this would be his last strike. He would honor his family in the deaths of Americans. The great Satan would be on its knees, struggling with its own economic and social collapse, and then the Arab armies could do what it wanted with Israel. *Yes, I will live to see it.*

THE PENTAGON

"So what do you want me to do?" the army recruiter asked MSG Tom Quinn over the phone. "This guy could tear out of here if he thinks we're stalling him."

"Give me thirty minutes," Quinn said. "Feed him, play cards with him. I'm sure you can keep him busy for a while."

The master sergeant hung up the phone in his second floor Pentagon office and whispered to himself, "That was the weirdest call I've ever had." The enlisted man looked out of his Pentagon office window on to the parking lot wondering what to do. "Just plain weird."

On first blush he thought it was a crank call. The story was just plain wacky. Still, as part of the DOD intelligence team, Quinn went by the book. Check out the source.

Quinn quickly confirmed that the phone number and the name of the caller were legitimate army. Next, he reviewed the recruiting officer's full file from the database. *Nothing out of sorts.*

He now wondered just who to report this to. Local Montana police? Army Intelligence? *Who?* Just then his answer walked by his cubicle.

"Captain, sir." Quinn stood up. "Do you have a sec?"

"Sure, Tom," CPT Penny Walker replied. She was holding a folder with more information for Roarke.

"What's up?"

"I took a call from a recruiting officer a few minutes ago. A Montana storefront that doesn't get much traffic on a snowy day. But in comes a guy, a young Latino with a wild ass story."

The blonde army captain was curious, partly because she always liked a good story, but mostly because it was her job to be curious. "And?"

"And he said someone had tried to kill him the day before."

"Who?"

"He wouldn't go that far."

"Does he want to go to the local police?" Penny asked.

"No. The guy said he couldn't."

Can't or won't, she wondered. "Okay, start again. He walks into an army recruiting office and..."

"And there's more. He felt he wasn't just walking into an army recruiter, he saw it as walking into an official U.S. government office, not to enlist but to talk directly to Uncle Sam."

"Make this easier for me, sergeant."

"He asked for asylum."

"Holy shit."

"He's probably an illegal. Maybe even a gang member. A real fish out of water in Montana."

"What does he want?" Walker asked pointedly.

"Protection."

"Why the fuck does this guy need protection?"

Quinn checked his notes. "He claimed he was transporting a 'package,' as he called it."

"A 'package'?"

"A man. He drove someone all the way from Texas to Montana. He figures it was some suit who just entered the country and needed to go somewhere without being noticed. Not Hispanic. And not a young guy. Someone older, well dressed. Maybe Middle Eastern. After he dropped him off, he was given instructions to drive somewhere in the boonies and meet up with another car."

Walker's mind raced to an alert that came across her desk while she was on Roarke's case.

"Where did you say he picked this guy up?"

"Texas."

"Where in Texas? What city?"

He looked at his computer notes. "Houston. Probably a bureau matter, not for us…except…"

"Except what?" Penny asked.

"He said that when he reached the other car it was burning. He got out and saw that the driver was dead. That's when his own car blew up."

Walker came around to Quinn's computer screen. "Give me that number, sergeant," she said urgently. "And print out your notes. All of them. Word for word."

MSG Tom Quinn took in a relieved breath. "Yes, sir." Now it was someone else's problem.

MINUTES LATER

"Johnson." It was J3's one-word hello on the phone, sure to fluster any would-be flunkies, congressional aides, or as he liked to say, media weenies, from trying to get anything past him.

"General, this is Walker, CPT Penny Walker, DOD intel."

"I know who you are."

He was clipped and intentionally impolite. Penny Walker expected as much. She'd met the general at Pentagon functions and knew his manner well.

"I assume you're calling for a reason," he continued.

"Yes, sir. That's why I skipped command."

"I'd say you did. What is it?"

"Something very interesting. I think it may be related to the Houston shooting."

General Jonas Jackson Johnson suddenly showed interest. "Go on."

"Sir, a young Latino gang member, or presumed gang member,

walked into a Helena, Montana, army recruiting office. He wasn't there to sign up. He wanted protection."

"Protection. Why?"

"Try asylum. I'll give you my theory in a moment. But this was after he finished transporting a man, he presumed to be Middle Eastern, from George Bush Intercontinental to a truck stop in the middle of Montana. He was paid $5,000 in cash for the delivery, then sent alone down a remote country road an hour away. The next thing—kaboom."

"Kaboom?"

"The damned car blew up. Fortunately, the driver was out."

J3 was writing it all down. He'd already flagged key words. *Middle Eastern, cash, and explosion.* Together they were lethal. He could see where this was going.

"He's only alive today because he saw another car he was supposed to meet up with—or what was left of it—burning on the road. Lucky he got out of his when he did. That's when it exploded. The driver of the first vehicle was not so lucky."

"A MANPAD or missile?"

"He doesn't think so. More likely a bomb on a timer that was set when he dropped off his passenger."

"Have you talked to him?" asked General Johnson.

"No, a sergeant down the hall took the call fifteen minutes ago. The recruiter is keeping the subject busy in Helena. But the guy's panicky. He doesn't know if he can trust anyone."

"You said a gang member."

"Yes, sir. By the sound of it MS-13 or a splinter group."

"Dangerous sons of bitches. Here and south of the border."

"That's what I understand, sir."

Penny sensed the wheels turning. "You think that recruiter can buy a little more time and keep this guy occupied? Some java, travel folders. Someone like you to keep him busy?"

She chuckled. "I'll talk to them. I'm sure they can come up with ways."

"Good." Another pause from the president's national security advisor. "Captain, how quickly can you meet me?"

"Upstairs?" She was referring to General Johnson's Pentagon office. "In five-to-ten depending on the elevator traffic, sir."

"No. The White House."

CHAPTER 21

WASHINGTON, D.C.

Jim Vernon's taxi pulled up to the Marriott Metro Washington on H Street, NW. The chain-link fence manufacturer was getting in two hours late to the hotel. The weather out of the Midwest delayed the afternoon flights for hours. Because of another stop he made, he missed the opening session of his convention and the chance to meet with potential clients. But that didn't bother the salesman who looked to be in his mid thirties. He was very good; very, very good at what he did, and there was really no need for him to attend.

Vernon was single, eligible, and desirable. He got laid a lot. At last year's convention, he slept with three different women, all married, and all who dreamed about a second night they never got. Nor did they get their phone calls answered. Still, each of the women returned, hoping to satisfy their year-long fantasies.

Before Vernon was halfway through the lobby, he had committed every face in sight to memory. There were four conventioneers hanging outside The Metro Grille to the left. A couple and their two children stood talking with the concierge to the right. Straight ahead, a pair of bellhops waited for work. Past them at check in was a woman who shifted her weight from one leg to the other.

Vernon carted his black Samsonite suitcase forward and quietly fell in line behind her. She wore an expensive black leather jacket set off by two dangling pearl earrings. A set he had given her twelve months ago. Her red hair fell just below her shoulders, standing out against the black of her jacket and complementing the color of her powder-blue blouse. His eyes drifted down. She wore a short black pencil skirt which emphasized strong, sexy legs. Her Pradas gave her an extra inch and a half, which placed her neck right at Vernon's lip level.

The salesman inhaled. He recognized the perfume. *Pleasures by Estee Lauder. Very nice*, he thought. He leaned forward and whispered in the woman's ear. "Bar or minibar?" He pressed up against her ass. She felt him and without turning around, smiled. He gently kissed the back of her neck, taking in more of the perfume.

The forty-six-year-old saleswoman leaned her head to the right, inviting more. This was sexier than her fantasies. The desk clerk handed her the room portfolio. Though distracted, she examined it. "Room 314," she said just loud enough for Vernon to hear. "And may I have an extra key?" she asked the desk clerk.

"Certainly, Mrs. Michaelson." The clerk fulfilled the request. "Have a nice stay."

"Oh, I will," she replied. "She pushed up against Vernon, felt his hard cock and slipped her card key in his hand. "As a matter of fact, I'm looking forward to jumping right into bed."

The clerk, oblivious to the exchange, just smiled and looked to the next guest. "May I help you, sir."

Vernon stepped forward and indicated that he'd be paying in cash.

"I'll still need a credit card on record."

"No problem." He had one just for the occasion; only this occasion, bought at CVS and loaded with cash.

Minutes later, Jim Vernon checked into his room. That was all he did there. He quickly walked down the two flights of stairs and inserted the electronic key card into Mrs. Michaelson's door. She was already in bed and so very ready.

Her hair was enough to turn him on. He loved redheads. True redheads. Lily Michaelson was the real deal. She pleased him a great deal the year before. Depending on how hungry she was, he might not need to look any further to the other women on his list.

BLOCKS AWAY

Roarke and Katie lay in bed. He held her, but nothing more. He was exhausted from his trip. A weather delay in Chicago cost him a connection, which meant a later flight into Reagan.

There was something else that kept him from making love with Katie. An inner voice distracted him with a *"come find me"* attitude.

Katie played with the hair on his chest and talked softly and lovingly to him. It took a few minutes before she realized he wasn't paying attention.

"Scott, are you with me?"

"Yes, baby," he finally answered.

"I need to talk to you."

"Sure."

"I mean a real talk."

Roarke shook the other voice out of his head. "Yes." It wasn't very sincere.

"Is this what our life is going to be like?"

"What do you mean?"

"This. I don't feel you with me. You're here and not here at the same time. You didn't even know I was talking to you."

It was all true. "I'm sorry."

"You have only one thing on your mind. There's no room in there for me, is there?"

He half expected the question. "Of course there is." Roarke swallowed the words.

"You know what you're really great at?" she asked.

"What?"

"You're a really great lover and you're really great at your job. But you're a terrible liar."

Katie Kessler was right. Even though he loved her…even though they planned for a future together, there was almost no room for her right now. This man—Cooper, who had threatened her life as well as Roarke's, was more present than she was.

"I want you back."

"I'm here, sweetheart."

"Really back. Heart and soul."

Roarke sighed heavily. He looked over to her and nodded. "I love you."

"I know that." Katie rolled up under his arm and nestled her head on his chest. "I love you more. But I'm afraid of losing you, and…"

"You won't."

"And I'm afraid you'll lose me if we don't get back what we have," she said sadly. "It's so hard to be this much in love and be so afraid of having it disappear in an instant. It's too hard for me."

Roarke understood. He understood completely. It's not that he was in a serious line of work. That part was true. But, he made it more dangerous. He put himself on the line for the president of the United States. In doing so, he put Katie's life in jeopardy.

He was convinced Cooper was alive. And as long as he was, Katie's fears would be inescapable.

The image of Richard Cooper returned to Roarke's head. He was laughing.

Katie's mind was working on something, too.

• • •

Lily Michaelson swore her throat tickled when she came. It was the second time, the second way. Jim Vernon was an aggressive, hungry lover. Now it would be her turn. Over and over again. It was better than she remembered. More exciting than anything she had at home. It would end again in the morning, or if she was luckier, in a few days.

Vernon slipped his cock out of her and rolled on his back. She reached down and felt him; felt their shared wetness, then reached for her own. She would start, then he would take over—she hoped —just as he had last year.

Right now it didn't matter that she really knew nothing about her lover; that he failed to call her all year long; that he never even mentioned the company he worked for. She was lost in exquisite pleasure. And quite frankly, Lily Michaelson, wife, mother of two from Buffalo, New York, and PTA president probably wouldn't have given up the moment even if he whispered in her ear that he was a cold-blooded murderer.

CHAPTER 22

WASHINGTON, D.C.
JANUARY 9

Roarke peddled his exercise bike with full resistance. It was a conscious way to deal with his feelings. Maybe Katie's move to Washington had been a mistake. Everything was overwhelming—her White House appointment, the danger he brought to her life, the physical intensity of their relationship.

Roarke desperately wanted her, but now he needed to concentrate on work and shake the cobwebs from his mind.

Penny Walker was a huge help. He'd get more out of his friend Shannon Davis at the FBI, too. He just needed to beat Cooper to a kill. Roarke was convinced it was going to happen.

As he toweled down, Roarke looked through the *Washington Post*. A story in the metro section caught his eye. An interesting story. Particularly the line at the end.

> Jason Trumbolt will be interred Thursday at Arlington National Cemetery during a private service. In lieu of flowers, friends are encouraged to make donations to The Iraqi War Veterans Fund for the Disabled.

He reread the account from the top. A lobbyist for Northrop had dropped dead on the Metro. He was a decorated Iraqi Freedom war vet, since retired, and a senior consultant for one of the leading aerospace contractors.

The obit noted that Colonel Jason Trumbolt served in Iraq. It was enough for him to stop peddling and call Walker at the Pentagon.

"Penny, it's Roarke. Have you seen the…"

"Paper? Yes. Trumbolt?"

"Yes. Was he?"

"Yes he was. High up on the command. I've already put in a request for an autopsy. No fast cremation this time," she said, referring to Roarke's report from Montana.

"Shit. Right here in D.C.!" Roarke exclaimed. "Yesterday! Blocks away." Roarke was close. "Pen, I have to know who's left. Who he still has to get to?"

"I'm trying. But I hit a wall. Some of it's classified. You know anyone who can help me cut through the bullshit?"

Of course Roarke did. His boss, the president of the United States. But Captain Walker also knew the president now. General Johnson had seen to that. It was a separate matter and, as far as she knew, it didn't involve Roarke.

Roarke finished the conversation and jumped off his bike. He nearly ran down a woman in blue tights.

"Excuse me!" he offered in apology.

The woman smiled. "No problem."

It barely took Roarke a second to remember her. The blonde from a week before. He figured she was in her late twenties, like Katie, but different. There was a calculating edge to her; disguised but there. It made him instantly uncomfortable.

They stood facing one another. Roarke apologized again.

"It's totally okay," she said. "I like meeting great looking guys at 40 miles per hour."

He laughed. "I'll slow down next time."

"Not on my account."

As he walked away he thought about her comment. It seemed completely seductive and absolutely intended.

WASHINGTON, D.C.
LATER

Curtis Lawson took a long lunch. Instead of ordering a sandwich from the FBI commissary and taking it at his desk, or going to one of the nearby restaurants, he opted for a scallops-and-clam chowder at McCormick & Schmick's at Ninth and F Street. It wasn't because of a craving. During a meeting with the director, he was texted with a come-on for a new mortgage rate of 2.055 percent.

"Absurd!" he said. Lawson deleted it, complaining to Robert Mulligan that the damned cell phone solicitations, even on unlisted numbers, were getting worse. "I'm about ready to throw the damned thing out the window."

The FBI Chief agreed. Since spam filters blocked almost all of the garbage coming through the e-mail server, many spammers switched to text messaging. The FBI was even investigating sales personnel at phone stores who were selling newly activated numbers on the side to third parties.

But it wasn't spam. It was a message definitely intended for Lawson, the assistant director, and no one else. It was his cue to take a lunch.

Lawson got there at 2:05. He aimed for a particular barstool, but a man was sitting there, talking with a fellow worker over lunch. Lawson had seen them before on the Hill. They were young legislative aides, a year or two out of George Washington Law School. Not wanting to be noticed, he simply faded back a little, ordered an iced tea, and pretended to read the newspaper he'd brought along.

Twenty long minutes later they left, and Lawson saddled up to the seat even before the bar was clear. If the drop had been made, it would be under the counter; easy to extract. Lawson placed the newspaper on his lap. That gave him the opportunity to feel for the note. It was, taped up. After his lunch arrived, he placed a napkin on his lap, over the newspaper, and recovered the folded piece of paper with a simple tug. He neatly slid it between the pages of the day's *Washington Post.* Lawson was back at the office by 2:05. There he read the nine-word note. If it fell into anyone's hands it might look like a Super Bowl tip. But decoded it really belonged on the front page.

CHAPTER 23

THE WHITE HOUSE

"Mr. President, not many people penetrate my armor. Fact of the matter is that I really don't let people even near. My whole life I've listened to command and authority. And no doubt, I've given my fair share of orders to those under me. I've tried my damned best to make decisions based on intel and instinct. Now, out of nowhere, you have me reaching for something I'm just not used to doing."

General Jonas Jackson Johnson was one of America's most decorated soldiers. As a wartime general he could dispassionately deal, live with, and compartmentalize the most weighty go/no-go decisions responsibly and dispassionately. And as the president's national security advisor, he was privy to unspeakable truths about real-world dangers.

But four days ago Morgan Taylor asked him the most profound question of his life. It required an honest, emotional response, for it rose above rank. It touched his heart; a place a warrior avoided.

"You have it within you, J3," the president replied. Believe me, you use the same strength of character you have always relied on. The difference is, you sleep a lot less at night and you have to listen to the voices of everyone who has carried the weight of the nation on their shoulders from the beginning of the republic. At least that's how I see it."

"You ask a lot from me."

"No doubt about that." There was only seriousness in President Taylor's reply. "All that you are will come to bear. You will learn and you will grow. And should it become necessary, you will lead. General Johnson, how about making some history with me?"

Through the conversation the president and the general had been sitting across from each another. Morgan Taylor was at his desk. J3 in a chair facing him. Suddenly, General Johnson realized that his reply required him to come to attention. He stood, straightened his uniform, and looked deeply into the eyes of the president of the United States.

Sensing the importance of the moment, Morgan Taylor also stood.

"Mr. President, your offer demands more from me than I have ever delivered. Patience I have never had for bureaucracy. The ability to let things roll off me, which is not my nature. The requirement that I listen to multiple points of view rather than act on my own experience. And the need to be damned nice in polite company. Hell, I might even need to learn how to dance."

"You can be sure of that," Taylor laughed.

"You're asking the wrong man to do all these things."

"I'm asking the man most qualified."

"Well, you finally got that right, Mr. President. That's why I'm ready to be your vice president."

Morgan Taylor flashed the biggest smile he'd had in a long, long time. "Jonas," the president said, using the general's first name for probably the very first time, "You're out of uniform. Go buy a new suit and get ready to face Congress."

THE FBI
THE SAME TIME

In the world of *holy shit*, this was *holy shit*.

FBI agent Shannon Davis stopped short when he scanned the critical daily report assembled for him based on key search words. Some extracts were aimed at his ongoing investigations; others were requested by Scott Roarke. In this case it served both their needs.

Prior to Davis receiving the report, the agency search engine scoured more than 3,000 local newspapers, 3,500,000-plus blogs, 8,300 law enforcement agencies, as well as state and regional crime databases. In this particular case, it filtered 2,434,212 people with the same last name, 1,154 in the target state, 152 in the county of interest, 22 in the local municipality, and 2 on the street in question.

In general, the name in question was Cooper. Specifically, Bill and Gloria Cooper. Today there was an exact hit on Gloria Cooper in the right state, on the right street, and the right city—Chester Township, Ohio.

It would have been an innocuous notation to anyone but Shannon Davis and his friend in the Secret Service, Scott Roarke. But it was anything but innocuous.

Shannon was on the phone within seconds after reading the 911 report vacuumed up by the powerful agency computers.

"Pick up, pick up, pick up," he said as Scott Roarke's cell phone rang. On the fourth ring Roarke answered.

"Hello, Shannon," Roarke answered, seeing the caller ID. Roarke was walking to the White House after his morning workout at the YMCA gym at Seventeenth and Rhode Island. "What's up?"

"Got something for you."

"What is it?"

"Probably not for the phone. Let's just say the mother of a soldier presumed to be killed in Iraq popped up in a small police report today in…"

With that, Roarke made a quick about-face on K Street and headed to the FBI headquarters. "I'll be there in fifteen. Dig up anything else you can. Whatever it is, it's relevant!" Roarke hung up. His sudden change of direction was noted by only one person. A woman. Christine Slocum who walked quite casually, but intently, a half block behind.

Shannon Davis's FBI office at 935 Pennsylvania Avenue could have been anybody's. Barely 250 square feet. White walls. Three filing cabinets. A view of The Corporation for Public Broadcasting Building across the street. However, Shannon Davis didn't need much more than his computer and his intellectual curiosity. In the hands of a talent investigator, these tools were often more powerful than the bureau's standard-issue Glocks.

"Pretty interesting, Scott."

"For damned sure," Roarke replied. He read the simple Chester Township police report again."

> Distress call; F. Gloria Cooper, age 67. Possible stalker sighted outside residence. No direct contact. Black Lincoln Navigator. No ID on license plate. WM. Estimated late '30s. No positive ID. Woman reports individual resembled family's deceased son; killed in Iraq. Officers sent to scene. No report of suspect. No further action taken.

Davis referred to his notes for the rest of his briefing.

"We'll have a transcript of her 911 call. It's bizarre. She didn't want her husband involved. She was distraught, as if she'd seen the dead. This could prove he's not." The FBI agent turned to Roarke. "Would he be that stupid to go back and see his mother?"

"Not his mother, but his roots," Roarke answered. "Richard Cooper was trying to connect with his roots. Seeing his mother was an accident. A mistake he's not likely to make again. You can be sure he's put on six hundred miles on since then."

"Six hundred? To where?" Davis asked.

"Right here. Cooper is back in Washington. He's been busy. Check the obit page in today's paper."

THE MANSION ON O STREET
THAT EVENING

"I want to know how to see trouble coming," Katie said.

The comment caught Roarke off guard. At first he thought it was the *mojito* speaking, not his beautiful girlfriend.

"You what?" Roarke asked.

"I want to be more prepared."

"Why?"

"Oh because someone…*many someones*…have tried to kill you, just two, three, oh, four times by last count. I was stalked as a result of being with you and I didn't have a clue how to notice things."

Katie and Roarke were having dinner in one of the most unusual hotel restaurants in Dupont Circle, let alone the entire district. The Mansion on O Street had more than one hundred rooms and dozens of secret doors leading into bedrooms and down winding hallways. The establishment was actually four 1890's brownstones linked together. Its eclectic clientele came from all walks of life: authors, musicians, politicos, corporate executives, K Street lobbyists, and club members and their guests. The management never disclosed the identity of the hotel clientele. Even more unique, the mansion is filled with floor-to-ceiling art and memorabilia. Every glass, plate, salt and pepper shaker, painting, and trinket is for sale. The only things not tagged for purchase: the priceless collection of electric guitars autographed by legendary rockers.

Given the surroundings, Roarke figured this was a perfect location for lesson number one.

"Okay, I get it."

"Then take me out to a shooting range. Get me a gun. Teach me…"

"Slow down. To jump out of the way of an oncoming bus you have to see it first. Let's work on those skills."

"What skills?"

"Making you more observant. More aware."

Roarke took in the room again. They had been seated in the middle of the restaurant on the one night of the week that it was actually open to the public. It was not the best position, but it gave him a view of the most open area. In front of Katie, three rows of tables and a standing bar for wine and cocktails. At dinnertime, the restaurant was alive. It was the perfect place to be seen or get lost in the crowd.

"All right Ms. Kessler, school's open," Roarke offered. He leaned in a bit. "Don't actually look anywhere, but take mental pictures of everything you can. Use word associations. Note manner, attitude, clothing…if people are paying attention to one another or not. Count steps to the entrance, find escape routes, question why people are together and who doesn't belong. And keep talking the whole time."

Katie automatically turned her head slightly.

"No, no, no. No real peeking. It all has to be while you're engaged in normal conversation. You talk, you gesture, you take it all in."

"Well, Scott," she began marching her fingers to his hands and up his arms. "Let's talk about something else. Like after we're through with dinner."

"Okay," Roarke said, thinking the lesson was suddenly over.

"I want to take you back to my apartment," she said coyly.

"Oh?"

"Then I'm going to undress you very, very slowly." Her fingers marched up farther and her foot, now freed from her shoe, caressed his leg. She moved across the table, closed her eyes, and kissed him on the lips.

Roarke automatically closed his eyes. When he opened, Katie inched back. That's when he saw her glance ever so slightly from side to side as if to see if her kiss drew what would be natural observations.

"Oh, you're good," he whispered, impressed with her technique.

"Shhh," she said, "I'm talking." Her foot went back to work under the table. "First I'll unbutton your shirt, though one day I just want to rip it open. You put your arms down and it'll drop to the floor. Then I'll unbuckle you. No problem there. I can do it in the dark. But we're going to leave the lights on…for both of us."

Katie worked her toes up higher. Scott was definitely into the conversation.

"Your pants will fall down. Then your underwear, unless, of course, they get stuck along the way. If so, trust me, I'll help. It might require bending down. And while I'm there, if my hands aren't busy, I'll take your socks off. One by one. You know my rule."

"Can't be naked with socks on."

"Good boy."

"And then," he managed to say.

"And then?" She suddenly pulled back laughing. "And then I get your cell phone out of your pants pocket and throw the damned thing out the window so it doesn't interrupt us while I fuck your brains out!"

Roarke laughed, too.

"I'm serious," Katie said.

"How about I mute it before you get to the belt buckle?"

"Promise?"

"I promise."

"Okay," she replied, flipping her hair, which gave Katie a chance to check out more of the room. Then, with a smile, Katie Kessler was back to business. "Wanna know what I saw?"

"Go."

Katie began describing people in the room with astounding detail. "Over your right shoulder is a couple on their first date. Awkward conversation; no touching. I'd say he's a year or two out of law school, probably working on the Hill, not for a law firm."

"Why?"

"If he were at a firm, at his age and level, he'd be there until midnight. So he has the look of a lawyer, but he's definitely not with a firm. She's a legislative assistant he picked up. No more than twenty-three and very Midwest."

"Assess the threat."

"No threat."

"Go on."

"Another table over are three guys, mid-twenties. They keep splitting their attention between the game on the monitors and watching the waitress's ass, the one with the short black hair. And when we came in you checked out her ass as well, Mr. Roarke. Looking for concealed weapons?"

"Always." That part was very true. "Back to the guys. Are you sure they're not doing that as a cover, trading off keeping an eye on us?"

"They're definitely more interested in her ass than you."

Roarke laughed again. She was getting good at this, but he asked, "Even the one with the blue shirt, tan jacket, and stripped tie? Medium sideburns, hair over his collar."

"What's he do?"

"Young writer. Probably a blogger for one of the progressive sites."

Roarke perfectly described a man behind him.

"How did you do that?" Katie asked incredulously.

"When we came in and you were checking out whether or not the waitress's ass was catching my attention, I was actually evaluating a lot more."

"Really," she said, feeling even better about her sweetheart.

"Really. Now go on."

Katie did, describing the lesbian couple three tables away and the busboy with a limp.

"Does his limp change at all?"

"I didn't notice."

"Notice. It's all important. Sorry, but I have to be hard on you."

"I like when you're hard on me," she said in a very seductive whisper.

"Katie," Roarke reprimanded. "Stay in school. What about behind you?"

"Oh, two corporate lawyers. A senior, mid-sixties in a three-piece suit. Corporate, rich, talking to a younger member of the firm who's trying to impress his boss."

"How'd you see them?"

"A few of my moves and catching reflections in the tilted mirror at the bar and the chandelier above."

"How successful would you view the conversation."

This was a harder question; judging intent. She had to think.

"Not very."

"Why?"

"The older guy," she starts laughing, "was also more interested in the waitress's ass."

Roarke had a clear view that Katie lacked, but she was right. "Very good." He was impressed, and thought again how important this was to her. Their relationship did put her in jeopardy. That very thought was the one thing that prevented him from fully committing to her.

"And the guy standing at the bar is interesting," she said, getting back to her descriptions. "He's trying to hide a good body in a loose-fitting suit. He's had a drink since we've been talking that he hasn't touched, and he's keeping to himself. Maybe waiting for someone. He glances at someone, then another, never paying much attention to anyone."

"How old is he?" Roarke's tone changed; his eyes narrowed.

"Thirty-five, maybe forty. Hard to say. Probably somewhere in between."

"Right-handed or left?"

"Right, the side where the drink is."

"Where's his left arm?"

She reached across the table again and kissed Roarke. It gave her a better angle to see. Pulling back she said, "Close to his body. Tight."

Roarke spoke quietly. "Katie, I'm going to shift my body like I'm about to turn around. I won't. But you tell me what he does."

Katie sensed the lesson was over. This was practical now.

Roarke put his left hand on his chair and adjusted slightly, appearing as if he was trying to get more comfortable. Not happy, he did this again, then looked around and signaled the busboy with the limp and showed him his empty water glass. A very innocent move.

"And?" Roarke asked, settling down.

"As soon as you adjusted he looked away. Like you were connected."

Roarke said with stone-cold directness, "Maybe we are."

Roarke turned around and looked back, not disguising any move now.

The man was gone.

CHAPTER 24

THAT NIGHT

"Next, let's go to the Mountain-Time line. Hello, you're on *Coast to Coast.*"

The host of *Coast to Coast AM,* America's top-rated all-night radio show was into his third hour for the night. It was time for "Open Phones America," the unscreened call-in portion of the show. This usually followed a one- to two-hour interview that featured the latest sightings from a leading UFO authority, the author of a new book on remote viewing or out-of-body experiences, researchers into the paranormal, historians reviewing ancient prophesies, and more than a fair share of conspiracy theories considered by many absolute gospel.

"Hello," the caller said through a cough. "Something's going on here."

"What's going on?"

"People are getting sick and they're dyin'," the male caller said.

The host could already tell this was going to be a good conversation. There was already intrigue.

"Who's dying and where are you calling from?"

"Up the road from Boulder. Three neighbors, perfectly healthy people a week ago, went into the hospital. Two of 'em are already dead." The man coughed again. It was a throaty, ugly sound over the radio. "They're killing us off."

"Wait, who's killing who?"

"They're killing us. My neighbors. My friends. Me. My wife went in this afternoon. Nobody knows what's happening."

The conversation went on for another five minutes. It was followed by a listener from outside Ogunquit, Maine, with a strangely similar story; then another from rural Mississippi. The accounts were sprinkled with references to big government, aliens, and terrorists.

This was *Coast to Coast AM* at its best; intriguing, mystifying, and on the edge. But tonight there was truth. Truck drivers, insomniacs, and the curious heard about the impact that a group of men, driven to different parts of the country by members of MS-13, were having.

HELENA, MONTANA
THE SAME TIME

Ricardo Perez tuned the radio in his motel room. There were no Spanish language stations, no gangsta rap, nothing but talk shows with a lot of static. He settled on a talk radio show just because the drone of the conversation would lull him to sleep. People were calling in about what-not; things he didn't understand, from parts of the United States he had never heard of.

Actually, Perez was feeling pretty good. The army had treated him well. He certainly didn't feel like a prisoner. True to their word, the soldiers had not called the police. They alternated taking him out to dinner, going to movies, and walking the snowy streets of Helena. They explained it would be too dangerous for him to contact anyone, especially since he was presumed dead. So Ricardo Perez, grateful to be alive, was happy to live off the government in protective custody.

He fell asleep listening to some show called *Coast to Coast AM* and conversation he really didn't understand.

WASHINGTON, D.C.
JANUARY 10

The White House press secretary sent an e-mail blast to the networks. The president would have an important announcement at 8:00 p.m. ET. It was clearly a surprise, coming only days before his scheduled State of the Union address.

In years gone by, the broadcast networks would have cleared their schedules. Now, coverage fell on Fox News, MSNBC, and CNN and talk-radio consensus-builders. News producers and fact excusers requested information on the nature and substance of the president's appearance.

The only heads up they got was the indication the statement would have a profound effect on the executive branch. Speculation went from a major policy decision to the deteriorating relationship with Mexico. It was enough to fuel conversation for the next six hours and deliver a huge audience to the president.

• • •

"Good evening." The president stood at a podium with the long hall of the East Wing behind him.

Morgan Taylor wore a classic black suit, set off by a red tie and the requisite American flag lapel pin.

Scott Roarke had settled into the couch with Katie at Katie's apartment to watch their boss's speech. He heard Taylor's "Good evening," then his cell phone rang.

"Come on," he complained under his breath. But the caller ID indicated this was one to take.

"Penny," he whispered to Katie as he walked across the room.

"Okay. If the president was about to announce World War III, you'd probably know."

Roarke laughed. He got up, and on the fourth ring, before the call went to voice mail, he answered.

"No time for the speech?"

"Speech?"

"Oh, just the president of the United States." Roarke kept his voice down so Katie could still hear the TV."

"Oh that."

"I guess you're a tried-and-true Democrat."

"You would have found out if you'd stuck around long enough to go into the voting booth with me, sweetheart. Now you'll never know," Penny Walker teased. "But I've got some more that I think you're going to want to know."

• • •

The TV was on in room 421 at the Marriott Metro where Jim Vernon was otherwise engaged in the pleasures provided by the conventioneer from Buffalo, New York. Lily Michaelson rose above him. He was deep inside. Neither of them was paying attention to the TV. They certainly weren't going to stop now to turn it off.

A few words came through the sighs and moans. Nothing that would make the housewife having an affair stop or the assassin having a good fuck care. At least not yet.

"We live in unpredictable times," the president stated. "In the past few months, we have experienced an exciting, but polarizing, election, the horrifying events that unfolded prior to president-elect Lodge's inauguration, the unscripted succession, and then another which has me speaking to you today and serving as the nation's president.

"In fact, the uniqueness of my term is that I believe you truly have a president of the United States, not the president of a single political party."

On any other day, this comment would have surely resulted in endless talk-show debate. Today it would get buried because Taylor was about to make more news.

"This means that first, foremost, and completely, my decisions will be based on what is best for the entire country. And this is what leads me to my time before you tonight."

Speaker of the House Duke Patrick watched CNN in his office. Christine Slocum stood to his right, taking notes to fashion a few inevitable quotes for his post-speech interviews. Ever since she came in the picture, his image improved. She cautioned him to count to three before responding on camera. He could nod, smile, and appear to think. It allowed him to look like he was patient, understanding, and thoughtful. In fact, it was a device which gave him time to consider how to reshape the question into something he was prepared to answer. Three seconds brought Duke Patrick more prestige and began to erase his reputation as a hothead. If he was to become president—for either party—he had to be, for lack of a better term, more *presidential*. He had his job. She had hers.

"I have made serious proposals regarding the succession process that I've asked Congress to support, states to consider prior to ratification, the justices of the Supreme Court to weigh in on, and you—the American people—to view as an utmost necessity. This would revise the law of the land, through an amendment to the Constitution, to provide for a new rule of succession for the benefit of the country, should we face an enormous, unspeakable crisis in the Executive Branch."

"Bullshit!" yelled Duke Patrick, while Christine Slocum crafted a quotable response in an even, reasonable tone that could be quoted and heralded as statesmanlike.

"Seriously, Penny. The boss is on the air and I don't know why. What do you have?" Roarke asked, trying to keep an ear tuned to the TV.

"I put together the rest of the missing link in the chain of command."

Roarke's silence communicated to her that his attention was split between the call and the president's speech."

"Look, if this is a bad time…"

"No, sorry. The chain of command," he said indicating he'd followed part of the conversation.

"Yes, I found who was at the end of the line. Who made the final decision in Iraq. Or more accurately, the senior officer who did not overrule the field appraisal. There's only one left."

Roarke was completely engaged. Knowing this name could help him set a trap for Richard Cooper and allow him to end his obsessive search and leave this awful business behind. It was the key to opening the door to the rest of his life with Katie Kessler.

"But the road to a constitutional amendment will not be overnight. And the business of the United States currently has a process with an unfilled seat. Between the president and the Speaker of the House, in the direct line of succession, should be the vice president. The nation does not have one now."

Jim Vernon felt the energy build up inside of him. Each deeper and more powerful thrust brought him closer to release. Lily Michaelson tightened around him. She was holding on for him, only moments away from letting her muscles relax. The tingling was reaching right up to her throat again. She blocked out the sound of the TV but moved to the rhythm of the president's speech, finding speed as the president built to his climax.

"Get to the point!" Duke Patrick demanded.

"I can't hold it," screamed Lily.

"You're not going to believe this," said CPT Penny Walker. "I had to dig pretty damned deep, and if you ever breathe a word it was me…"

"I won't," Roarke said excitedly. "Dammit, who?"

"And so, I present to you tonight a man I will place before the

Senate for confirmation; a man with a most distinguished record to the country, to this White House, and to the nation…"

Duke Patrick leaned forward. Whoever it would be would separate him from direct succession to the nation's highest office.

The president looked directly through the camera lens to the thirty-seven million people watching. "My choice as vice president of the United States is…"

Penny Walker said the name over the phone exactly as the president did. Scott Roarke watched the TV as Taylor's lips moved in sync with Penny's voice.

"General Jonas Jackson Johnson."

"Damn him!" Duke Patrick blurted out.

"Yes!" screamed assassin Richard Cooper as he began to explode inside Lily Michaelson. He heard the president utter the name of his next target and the sheer excitement led him to the most powerful orgasm he had ever experienced. The woman, he forgot who it was, collapsed over him as he continued to flow into her.

PART II

CHAPTER 25

MINUTES LATER

Katie tried to read the expression on Roarke's face as he walked back to the couch. *Surprise? Concern? No,* she thought. It took a few more seconds for her to recognize what he was feeling. *Worry.*

Roarke sat down, nestled her head on his shoulder and returned to the TV coverage. He wrapped his right arm around her. Neither said a word until the president concluded. Katie Kessler knew there were things he couldn't talk about, things he shouldn't talk about, and things he had to talk about.

This was the price of loving Scott. Katie wasn't sure if he'd share the conversation he had with the army intelligence officer. If he wanted to, it would come. She wouldn't push.

"Katie," he began after taking a deep, soulful breath.

This was something he *had* to talk about. "Yes," she responded still snuggled in his arm.

"It's all gotten more complicated."

Now it was her turn to take as deep a breath as his.

"Cooper is alive and I know who he will go after next," he said in the most measured tone she'd ever heard from him.

Katie pulled back to be able to look into his eyes. "Who?"

Roarke took in her loving look and gazed back at the news. His attention sharpened and she naturally followed his line of sight to the

40-inch HD screen. There, she saw footage and understood exactly why she read the worry in her lover's expression.

• • •

Five minutes later Roarke stood in the corner of Katie's apartment typing out a simple text message.

Priority Apple. Bring Zeus Home tonight. Repeat Apple.

Seconds after he hit send, he received a reply.

kk

It was that easy for Roarke to alert the president that General Johnson had to be brought Home immediately. *Home*, the only word with a capital letter, meant the White House.

That night, Katie and Roarke tenderly folded into one another. She felt that their lovemaking eased some of his stress. But it was going to take real strategic planning and his 9mm Sig Sauer to end this. That was the realization that kept Katie awake while Roarke slept in her arms.

• • •

"Next caller, Midwest line. You're on *Coast to Coast AM.*"

"Hi. This is Willard in Gaylord, Michigan, and you had someone on the other night saying how they're killing people where he lives. Well, the same thing is going on here. My wife is in the hospital now and I'm really worried and I want to know what's going on."

The host didn't immediately recall the conversation.

"What do you mean?"

"My wife. She's not the first in our area. I can't get any straight answer from the doctors. But we all live in the same area and now my wife is in here, like she's been poisoned."

"Poisoned?"

The word quenched the thirst of listeners throughout the United States who found sustenance in conspiratorial theories. It was the first time it was mentioned in the media, but not the first time it was talked about in a lab.

• • •

Bonnie Comley was listening to the broadcast while she was driving home from the Centers for Disease Control and Prevention in Atlanta. She'd considered using the same word herself a few hours earlier to describe the report of multiple deaths from similar causes in different parts of the country. But she felt it would have been premature. Now it was late-night radio.

She pulled over at a well-lit Atlanta gas station and wrote down the name of the town the caller had said: Gaylord, Michigan. She remained there for the next forty-five minutes as *Coast to Coast AM* fielded similar calls from Oregon, Missouri; Hillsdale, New York; Bakersfield, California; and Jefferson City, Montana.

Comley got home a half hour later but didn't go to sleep. A phone call she'd received the other day nagged at her; a call from Sam Brown, a former student, now a practicing physician. She spent the night on the Internet with her radio tuned to a broadcast that was sounding less and less like a conspiracy.

AURORA, NEBRASKA
THE SAME TIME

Two men were also working the late shift on municipal property. They were in a small Nebraska town, but they weren't on the city payroll. Rather, they were paid handsomely by Ibrahim Haddad.

The pair of chemists followed procedure with great care. They had to. They were handling a deadly toxin.

The water system in Aurora is supplied by five wells, each with an average depth of just more than two hundred feet. They feed an iconic tower, which promotes the town's name for miles. The tower's capacity is three hundred thousand gallons, delivering via gravity fifty-five- to fifty-seven-degree water 24/7.

The area's water table hadn't significantly changed in recent years. As a result, the quality of the product remained high and the need for water treatment, low. This made it a perfect target for Haddad's men.

With an average daily demand of 911,117 gallons, the plan was to introduce precise amounts of toxins into the output over three consecutive nights.

The typical morning rituals of Aurora's citizenry—brushing their teeth, having their morning coffee, or drinking a few glasses of water would produce the desired effect.

CHAPTER 26

YMCA OF METROPOLITAN WASHINGTON
JANUARY 11
0620 HRS

Roarke attacked the elliptical machine with a vengeance. Back strengthening. Weights. Sit-ups. He focused on an image of Cooper, which masked the pain of his regimen. He stopped just short of his stomach muscles feeling like they would tear apart. Only then did he see the blonde working out directly across from him.

She was on a machine he'd never attempted, probably because it was more for dancers than law enforcement officers. It had one obvious purpose: stretch the legs and groin muscles to create perfect splits. There were, however, other benefits as well.

If there were another purpose, however, Christine Slocum was certainly using it correctly. The machine made for a most inviting sexual invitation that was impossible to ignore. Her rhythmic, throaty breathing only heightened the image. And then, with one last deep breath and her eyes shut, she stopped and released her legs, as if collapsing from an intensely fulfilling orgasm.

Seconds later, she opened her eyes very pleased that Roarke had been watching. "Hello there," she said to him. "Hope I wasn't too noisy?"

"Not for me," he answered.

"This used to be easier. I guess I need more practice."

"Are you a dancer?"

"When I was growing up. Right through college. Not anymore." Slocum slowly stood up. Her jet black leotard clung tightly to her body and contrasted her fair skin. Beads of perspiration dropped from her forehead making her perfectly beautiful face glisten. She wrapped a towel around her neck and walked closer.

"If I don't get in early, it feels like I'm cheating," she said.

Cheating. It didn't seem like an accidental word to Roarke. None of this encounter did.

"What do you do?" Roarke asked.

"Oh, I work on the Hill. An assistant. I'm on the bottom, which is okay. And you?"

Another veiled sexual reference. That would make two.

"Oh, like everyone else around here, I'm a civil servant. Not much to talk about."

She studied his physique. "I bet you're very good at what you do." Sensing she might have gone too far, she softened. "I mean, you really throw yourself into your workout. It looked like you were someplace else; someplace serious."

"I just push myself as far as I can. No big deal."

"Well, we both work in government and we both workout. A few things in common." She offered her hand, which he politely accepted. "That's enough for an introduction. I'm Christine Slocum."

"Nice to meet you, Christine Slocum."

"And you are?" She still held his hand.

Here was a woman who could be best described by most men as "hot." For the record, Roarke added another adjective. *Calculating.*

"Sorry, yes," he answered. "I'm Scott Roarke."

Now having his name, which she fully well knew already, she let go.

"And what exactly do you do as a civil servant, Mr. Roarke?"

"Scott." He was sorry he said that.

"Okay, Scott," she replied appreciatively. In conversational terms, she felt she made it to first base.

"Recently, a lot of clipping and filing."

She laughed. "Me, too. I'm working for my second congressman. And it seems everything comes down to clipping, filing, collating, and stapling, even with computers everywhere. This town is going to drown in paperwork."

"You've got that right," he offered lightly.

"Eventually I'd like to run for Congress myself. To be perfectly honest," which she wasn't, "that's the real reason I try to stay in shape. It's a helluva routine and not everyone comes in healthy or leaves healthy."

Christine Slocum, the very last speechwriter for Congressman, then-President-elect Teddy Lodge, had summed up Lodge's sudden exit from government and life.

"And why do you really hit the gym with such abandon, Scott?"

"When work doesn't work out, my workout does."

"Like now? Like today?"

"Yup. Some tough days." He had said enough. Maybe too much.

Then came the awkward silence. Where was this going to go? Since Slocum set it up, she decided to take control.

"So, Scott. Nice to officially meet you."

"Likewise." Another thing he shouldn't have said.

• • •

Ten minutes later, Roarke was out of the shower and toweling off. The general quiet and solitude of the men's dressing room at this hour was interrupted by a commotion building at the entrance. Roarke heard a few *whoas* and whistles and turned to the excitement. To his complete surprise there was a woman in their midst. But not just any woman. Christine Slocum. She was made up and dressed to kill in a tight pencil skirt, white blouse, and heels.

The blonde breezed past the ten men in various stages of undress—primarily young lobbyists and Congressional aides. She took no notice of anyone except for the one man she came to see. And she saw all of him.

Without any embarrassment she said, "Give me your hand."

Shocked by her presence as much as her bravado, Roarke extended his right hand. She turned it palm up and wrote a series of numbers with a red Sharpie she had readied. “My phone number.”

Looking down she whispered, “Try not to rub it off before you call me. I’d love to see you again.”

With that final suggestive remark she left to the same *whoas* and whistles she heard on the way in.

Scott Roarke added another descriptive adjective to the list. *Fearless.*

MARRIOTT METRO HOTEL
THE SAME TIME

Richard Cooper looked out his window onto Fourteenth Street, NW. He, or the man he pretended to be, had just gotten laid again by Lily Michaelson. After showering, she left for the airport and her real life in Buffalo, New York. There, she would dream about next year’s tryst. It would sustain her, though Cooper had no similar fantasies. His mind was elsewhere, planning an assassination that would bring him completion that sex with Mrs. Michaelson would never provide.

Cooper had conceived an operational strategy after reading an online *Washington Post* article a week earlier. According to the story, the Johnsons were going to host a charity reception for the Walter Reed National Military Medical Center at their home. That reception would be tonight. CEOs, philanthropists, and members of Congress were due to attend. The evening would move from cocktails and *hors d’oeuvres* to speeches, and then on Cooper’s schedule, the general’s death. He reasoned that no one would want dessert after that.

He already figured out how to infiltrate the party, even if the Secret Service or Johnson’s army buddies were running defensive patterns. Ex-filtrating might be more challenging, but the Google map of the property, now up on his iPad, provided a clear escape route.

With General Johnson dead, Cooper could disappear forever. Thanks to his earnings from Ibrahim Haddad, he had the means to live anywhere under any identity he created. Richard Cooper was long gone, twice killed. Maybe he would reinvent himself as a novelist. He always felt he could write political thrillers. And with more actual experience than anyone in his stock and trade, he thought he might be able to make the bestseller list.

CHAPTER 27

0715 HRS

Roarke ducked his head down to shield the stinging January wind. It made talking on the phone almost impossible.

"What?" Penny Walker asked. "Hard to hear you."

Roarke stopped and turned his back to the wind making it easier to talk and listen.

"Why don't you just call me when you get where you're going,"

"Can't wait."

"Let me guess. You need a secretary again."

"Sort of," Roarke said above the wind. "Jesus, it's cold."

"What this time?"

"Hit the computer keys. I need some background."

"Okay, shoot."

Roarke switched the phone to his left hand, opened the palm of his right and read the sequence of ten numbers Christine Slocum had so provocatively written down.

"A phone number," Walker noted.

"Right, Sherlock. A cell," Roarke replied.

"I have a thought. Why don't you just dial it, sweetheart?"

"Not until you can tell me more about the person on the other end."

"Male, female?"

"Female. That's all you get."

"Uh oh, trouble in paradise?"

"Just trying to figure out that if this woman means trouble, what kind is it going to be."

"Got it. Be back to you soon as possible. Working on some other things, too."

Roarke braced himself against the wind for another six blocks. He calculated his pace. He'd be at the White House within ten.

THE WHITE HOUSE

"Good morning, Louise." Roarke greeted Louise Swingle, President Taylor's dedicated secretary and his eyes, ears, and virtual keeper. She'd been by Taylor's side since he was in the Senate and could read his moods better than her own husband's. Basically, the fifty-four-year-old mother governed the private life of the man who governed the nation. Swingle also took a personal interest in Scott Roarke and was pleased he had a remarkable woman by his side.

"Good morning, Scott. I'll let him know you're here."

Roarke removed his parka and slung it over his right forearm. As Louise Swingle punched a button on the phone she noticed the writing on his palm.

"And what's that?" she said, recognizing it as a number.

Before he could respond the president was on the intercom.

"Yes, Louise?"

"Mr. Roarke is ready, Mr. President."

"Send him right in."

"Yes, sir."

Roarke smiled and started to walk. Louise, still curious, pointed to Roarke's right palm. "And that?" she asked again.

"I've got a stalker," he replied.

"Oh? Get rid of her," Louise Swingle remarked. She wasn't kidding.

Roarke waved good-bye with his left hand.

• • •

Roarke strode into the Oval Room. The president was standing, sipping coffee in an official White House mug. Next to him was his national security advisor, now Taylor's appointee for vice president, pending Senate confirmation.

"Good morning, boss," Roarke offered. It was a highly informal greeting, but considering their history, the president allowed Roarke to get away with it. "Morning, General."

"Mr. Roarke, good to see you. The president tells me I'm a prisoner here because of you. Care to elaborate?"

Morgan Taylor motioned for both men to sit around the coffee table at the center of the seating area. Taylor took a high-backed, hand-carved oak chair that had been Thomas Jefferson's. He chose to sit in it whenever he felt the conversation would take on historical proportions. Roarke's text the previous night certainly suggested that.

"Okay, Scott," the president said. "To J3's point, what's going on?"

"In the most basic terms, a highly skilled assassin has been working his way through the country, targeting a variety of men in various occupations."

"Targeting?" General Johnson questioned.

"Killing," Roarke continued.

"To what end?" J3 demanded.

Roarke looked at President Taylor, who encouraged him to go on.

"As retribution, sir. You'll know him from his involvement with Lodge and the Inauguration Day shootings. At first he was presumed dead. He survived. And he's on a new mission; a personal mission. He's been working his way up the chain of command he served under in Iraq, eliminating one subject after another.

"He's taken out salesmen, ranchers, teachers, realtors, judges—all ex-GIs who overruled his field decision in Iraq. I believe you are aware of the case, General."

Jonas Jackson Johnson remained stone silent.

"His appeal was denied…by everyone. Before storming a building, which he considered a trap, a suicide mission, he appealed to command. Acting under orders, he led his men into the building. They all died. Or at least it was assumed they all died. All but one did. The mission commander, then a dedicated army lieutenant, survived. Now he is a killer. He has remained one step ahead of me for more than a year. But for the first time I know where former U.S. Army 1LT Richard Cooper will strike next."

The general unconsciously began nodding.

"Based on what we've pieced together, only one man in this scenario remains alive. You, General Johnson. You."

CHAPTER 28

MOSCOW
THE SAME TIME

Arkady Gomenko discovered that the best way to uncover state secrets was to do it out in the open. For this he needed just a couple items: official Kremlin stationary and a copy of a signature that would open doors. He had both. Gomenko counted on a cumbersome bureaucracy that spun in circles through dynamic inaction and bureaucrats who would pass work off rather than be troubled by it. Two more things that worked in his favor.

After giving into the American spy's request, Arkady Gomenko brought what he needed to his apartment. He wrote a draft of a memorandum, crossing out a few words, inserting others. Once he was satisfied, he typed it on his Sony laptop in Cambria, a font known to be used by the one government official whose name he was forging—Petrov Androsky. Androsky's name would make the correspondence stand out for its authority and as a waste of time. Androsky was the prime minister's brother-in-law, useless as a high commissioner of internal affairs and a pain in the ass to his family. He was notorious for requesting reports he never read, launching studies that were never needed, and wasting everyone else's time.

Yes, reasoned Gomenko. *Androsky would order this report.*

It was actually a very brief document issued on official stationary with Androsky's scrawled, but completely identifiable, signature. In the fake document, Androsky demanded a detailed synopsis with key names and dates on the old, retired Red Banner project, also known as the Andropov Institute. No reason was given. No reason was needed. The prime minister's brother-in-law wanted it. The report would become someone's bad luck in the FSB's research department. Considering the memo was directed to Yuri Ranchenkov, the overworked and constantly annoyed deputy director general of internal intelligence of the Federal'naya Sluzhba Bezopasnosti, it would end up in the hands of the ever-beleaguered Arkady Gomenko. For that he was certain.

Gomenko looked at his finished work; a masterful piece of espionage if he said so himself. It would go in Ranchenkov's inbox tomorrow.

THE WHITE HOUSE

General," Roarke continued, "this man never misses. Therefore, it's our responsibility to take away his opportunity. But, he is also a master of disguises and dialects.

"J3's getting round-the-clock Secret Service protection," President Taylor offered.

"Like the protection Teddy Lodge had?"

"That was different," Taylor argued.

"Really? Cooper is capable of penetrating *any* security. You're a marked target. And we can control where you'll be. Here."

The general looked at Taylor flashing an expression that Roarke couldn't miss.

"What?" Roarke asked. "What?" he repeated.

"It's not as easy as that," the president said. "The general is hosting a reception at his house."

"When?"

"Tonight."

"Good lord! Cancel it."

"No," Johnson proclaimed.

"With all due respect, General, that's just plain nuts."

"It's in my home. Everyone is vetted and that's it."

"Have you explained how things run around here, boss? We take assassination threats seriously."

"Scott, you're not going to have any more luck talking any sense into this horse's ass than I've had."

"Horse's ass or not, General, you are putting others at risk."

"Acknowledged, Mr. Roarke. But I've been in battle before and never run."

"This is neither a battle nor a retreat, General Johnson. There is a skilled assassin out to kill you. He is greater than the Jackal, and you are already in his crosshairs."

"Then I'll be the bait in a trap that the bureau will spring."

"General, maybe you haven't fished or trapped for a while. Sometimes the bait is already dead."

CHAPTER 29

ATLANTA
THE CENTERS FOR DISEASE CONTROL
BUILDING 21

Dr. Bonnie Comley was at her desk in Building 21 on the sprawling Atlanta campus of the Centers for Disease Control and Prevention. She worked in the new, sweeping seventeen-story secure facility, one of the tallest on the Roybal Campus. Many of its 472 laboratory and lab support personnel were either known, or suspected to be working on, the CDC's research on parasitic diseases, foodborne diseases, and AIDS research. Some were true investigators as much as scientists; frontline detectives in the expanding realm of CW/BW, the abbreviation for Chemical Warfare and Biological Warfare. Comley was one of them.

Her professional home, architecturally dynamic, was a fortress. Building 21 was a brilliantly designed curved structure encased in blast-resistant, heavy architectural precast panels, reinforced glass, stone veneer, and metal. The construction included horizontal and vertical sunshades made from perforated metal and glass, which enhanced the natural light in the work spaces and provided for a more energy-efficient operation.

But it wasn't the exterior that made Building 21 unique. It was the interior.

Within Building 21's twenty thousand square feet were top secret impenetrable labs. Impenetrable so outsiders couldn't get in and bio organisms and chemicals within couldn't escape.

Dr. Comley worked behind three secure doors, sometimes not leaving for days. "Threats," she told young colleagues, "don't take time off."

The Centers for Disease Control and Prevention was formed October 27, 1997. It was preceded by The Office of National Defense, the Office of Malaria Control in War Areas, and The Communicable Disease Center, among other iterations.

The CDC has been charged with protecting the public's health and safety by providing information, conducting research, and working to prevent the dissemination of infectious diseases, food and waterborne pathogens, and other microbial and chemical infections.

The agency was originally established in Atlanta because malaria, its earliest target, was endemic to the Southern United States. For years, more than half of the agency's personnel focused on mosquito abatement and habitat control with the goal of eradicating the disease.

In 1946, a budget of roughly $1 million covered the 369 employees. Only seven were medical officers.

Today, it's a very different organization, shaped by the times and the dangers. The annual budget is now well north of $7 billion and pays for the CDC's 15,000-plus employees in 170 different occupations in multiple locations.

A great deal of its work is public in nature. But much of it exists in Level 4 Containment Labs, or BSL-4 for Biosafety Level 4.

The facilities, referred to as "Hot Labs," belong to a subset of four distinct safety levels which deal with a scope of micro-organism designations starting at P1. The worst of the lot, P4, are highly dangerous bacterial and viral pathogens that require extreme containment.

Comley was actively screening five search windows on her computer. They were opened to online portals from regional newspapers. Each one of them backed up what she heard on the radio.

She rolled her chair backwards to a file cabinet and reached for an old Rand McNally map she stuck away years ago. Low tech and perfect for what the forty-eight-year-old scientist needed to do now.

Comley taped the map on a wall to the left of her desk, crafted flags with yellow stick-it paper and pushpins, and stuck the flags into locations that matched up to her research.

Staring at her work she deeply feared she was only scratching the surface. While the reports varied, there had to be a common variable. She ruled out contagion. *Too random.* But there had to be an independent factor that entered into normal life situations. *What was it?* she wondered.

Needing to give herself a break and seeing that her Black and Decker coffee maker was empty, Dr. Comley removed the old filter, replaced it with a new one, put in another eight scoops of Starbucks Espresso Roast, rinsed and filled the pot, and then watched the simple extraction process begin. Basic chemistry. Two heterogeneous composites coming together to form a mixture with immediate sensory impact. In that moment, as the heated water passed through the ground beans and the first dark blend dripped down, releasing a wonderful aroma, Comley was hit with a powerful, terrifying thought.

THE WHITE HOUSE

Scott Roarke had given General Johnson a great deal to think about. But Jonas Jackson Johnson wouldn't budge. Not for the president and certainly not for Roarke.

"Before your head spins right off, we need you on another matter, Scott," Morgan Taylor said.

"Boss, all things considered, I've got to get things rolling with the service and the bureau. We've got less than eight hours before the general's reception, and at least I can be there and…"

"Scott, hold on. There's something else," the president said.

"Oh?"

"J3, your turn."

General Johnson began slowly. "We're keeping someone under

wraps in Montana that you need to debrief. The president thinks your background is the key to the subject opening up."

"Me? Not the FBI. We're mixing up a whole bunch of priorities here, guys."

"Scott, listen," Taylor implored.

"A gang member checked himself, quite smartly I'd say, into an army recruiting office to avoid the police."

"So?"

"He asked for asylum."

"And this is more important than keeping you alive, General?"

"First of all, I plan on staying alive. Second, maybe yes.

"Scott, this situation requires special attention. We haven't wanted to turn him over to the bureau…"

"Or Evans and the CIA," added the president.

"And why is that?"

"It may be tied to the death at the Houston airport. And that moves it up the game board, immediately passing *Go*."

"Don't get me wrong, but this is one fucked day and I don't get it."

"We may have a terrorist threat, Scott," Taylor stated. "Believe me, Mulligan and Evans will get a piece of this, but we need a debriefing first. You're the perfect person to do it."

"Me?"

"He's you, Scott. Nearly twenty years ago," the president explained. "Which is why I want you to talk with him. Find out what and why and everything in between. We'll have a plane waiting for you at Andrews. 1930 hrs sharp. You tell us what's going on. We've got a sinking feeling it's not good, and it's in our own backyard."

"But tonight?" Roarke asked again.

"Tonight," J3 stated. "I can take care of myself in my own home."

Roarke had a very different opinion.

THE OVAL OFFICE
MINUTES LATER

With Roarke excused, General Johnson complained to the president.

"If a national security issue exists, a member of my staff should be on that plane to Montana, Mr. President."

"My man will get what we need. He'll connect. They've got something in common." Taylor explained why.

Roarke had come out of a gang in Los Angeles. It certainly didn't have the reputation of MS-13 or any other branch of Mara Salvatrucha. His life of crime was short-lived and inauspicious—a convenience store theft, almost too insignificant to qualify as a gang initiation, but a crime nonetheless. He was nabbed by a Los Angeles policeman. The officer let him stew in the backseat of his squad car. On his way to be booked, the officer gave him a choice: jail, a police record, and whatever punishment his father determined appropriate, or study under a martial arts master.

Scared straight, Roarke chose Tae Kwon Do, training with a taekwondo master. It was transformational.

Roarke learned discipline, a culture of physical fitness, and ultimately respect. He had reached a fork in life's road and chose correctly. He dropped out of the gang and graduated with honors. His policeman friend never told Roarke's father what happened, and Roarke, in turn, learned the importance of honor, helping others, and keeping secrets.

It all led to more levels of training, courtesy of the U.S. Army Special Forces, and a seminal rescue assignment in Iraq which brought Commander Morgan Taylor out alive.

"If anyone can reach this guy, it's Roarke," Taylor confidently told General Johnson. "Count on it. This subject has smarts. Hell, he turned himself into an army recruiter. He'll listen to someone who he can relate to. More than that, he'll talk. Then we'll have a real understanding of what we're dealing with."

General Johnson had seen Roarke in action before. The president was right. "Okay, we'll go with your man," the vice presidential-designee said.

"Good. Now let's talk about how we keep you alive tonight."

CHAPTER 30

LATER

Roarke made a swing back to his apartment to pick up a knapsack he always had packed and ready. Always. Two shirts, a sweater, socks and briefs, jeans, and four magazines for his Sig Sauer. Enough to duck in and duck out of almost anywhere for anything.

Outside, a Lincoln Navigator was waiting with a young, talkative Air Force driver. Roarke wasn't in any mood to converse. He kept mulling over what a bad idea this was and how much he was feeling like a yo-yo—emotionally and physically.

En route to JB Andrews, Roarke called Katie.

"The boss has me on another sales trip," he explained.

Sales trip in their couples' language meant she didn't have to worry. *Nothing Rambo.*

Just to make sure, she asked, "With or without your goodies?"

He always had his *goodies.* His 9mm pistol, a knife, and a combination key chain with an assortment of hidden compartments which included twenty inches of wire, picks, and files that could be used for any number of purposes. He called it "spy stuff." That was more than partly true. It came from Jack Evans, director of national intelligence; a gift, ordered by the president.

"Got 'em. Won't need 'em. I'm just visiting."

Katie couldn't ask where. If she was really worried, she might be able to convince Louise Swingle to share something. However, considering Roarke indicated he was going on a *sales trip,* she'd wait it out.

"Oh, hon, thanks for last night."

"Thank you. I needed you," Roarke added, recalling the overwhelming release he felt.

"I know. Trust me. There's more where that came from."

Unconsciously, Roarke looked at his right hand. Christine Slocum's phone number was still on it. There was obviously more someplace else, too.

MCLEAN, VIRGINIA
HUNTING RIDE LANE
THE SAME TIME

The general's three-story home sat on a cul-de-sac in one of Washington's primo upscale communities. The white brick colonial was more house than he ever needed, but his wife had had enough of barracks life, barracks schools, and barracks kitchens. This was where she wanted to stay and retire. But Morgan Taylor had another move in mind. With Senate confirmation, the Johnsons would pack up again and take up official residency in the United States Naval Observatory at Number One Observatory Circle.

General Johnson liked McLean. It meant nothing to him that this was also where many high-ranking government officials, members of Congress, and foreign diplomats resided. It did mean something that the CIA was located nearby, along with some of the country's major defense contractors and consulting groups.

McLean was situated between the George Washington Parkway and the town of Vienna, Virginia. It was named for John Roll McLean, the former publisher and owner of the *Washington Post.* Today, it would be like naming a town for Rupert Murdoch.

Here, in this prestigious Washington suburb, where the median income was well north of $150,000 per year, the Johnsons were hosting their last party for at least three years. Tonight's was the easiest in quite some time. Colette Johnson wasn't preparing a thing, though she loved to take charge of the kitchen the way her husband ran so much of the army. A venerable and approved Washington catering company took over, freeing Mrs. Johnson to mingle; something she would have to get better at as the vice president's wife.

This was the event of the night in Washington; a chance for Washington elite to hobnob with the usually isolated general, overhear a few conversations, and try to sift through what was real.

Servers, all in black except for white gloves, greeted guests at the door with a 2012 Cantine Maschio Prosecco. Right after a coat check, which utilized the den as storage, invitees—all checked in with picture IDs—proceeded through an elegant and open entranceway to a large formal living room decorated with warm floral wallpaper. The wallpaper definitely was not of the general's choosing. Once inside, there was seemingly no end to the appetizers, from delicious canapés and stuffed mushrooms to mini lobster rolls with a hint of truffle oil.

This was the first time most of the guests had seen the house. As a consequence, Collette spent a lot of her time giving tours. Had it been summer, the party would have expanded through the French doors to the backyard that abutted the woods. Beyond the trees, Kirby and Old Dominion Roads.

A few men actually braved the cold in order to smoke the general's full-bodied imported Diplomáticos Cuban cigars and sip his Glen Livet 18-year scotch. That was until the Secret Service found it too hard to split attention and called them in.

The woods made it prime property, a great place for kids to hide and also a natural killing field.

• • •

It happened just as Roarke stopped at the Joint Base Andrews security gate. A guard shined his flashlight into Roarke's eyes, momentarily blinding him. In that instant an indelible image of Richard Cooper burned into his consciousness, and along with it, the realization that he was the only man who might recognize the assassin.

"You're cleared for Hangar 14," the guard said after approving Roarke's ID. "There's a C-37A up ahead, sir." The C-37A is the military designation for the Gulfstream GV business jet. The guard told the Air Force chauffeur to wait for a jeep with a *FOLLOW ME* sign.

Two minutes of waiting gave Roarke two minutes more of worrying. He couldn't get the idea out of his head that the president had made an error in judgment; a potentially fatal error in judgment. That concern was still front of mind when the jeep pulled up and the procession began.

They took an access road past a row of hangars. They stopped twice to give the right of way to departing F-18s and then continued toward the transport. A hundred yards from the C-37A, they gave a wide berth to a helicopter that was fueling. Suddenly Roarke yelled.

"Stop!"

"What?"

"Stop. Right there," he tapped the driver's shoulder and pointed. "In front of that bird."

"Sir, I can't do that. I'm following the jeep."

"Right. And you can stop following the jeep by pulling over."

The driver did not obey. "I have orders, sir."

"Your orders have just changed. Stop the damned car!"

• • •

Security was especially tight. But this wasn't a problem for someone who had every reason to be there.

Luke Sader was an apt bartender who, when in town over the past few years, had occasionally freelanced for the caterer. The firm would have used him more. He was that good, but he traveled a lot and wasn't always available. When he phoned in the other day, the owner gratefully put him on for the general's party. "Perfect timing," he was told, "my regular came down with something."

Sader knew exactly what the go-to bartender was suffering from. A broken nose and a cracked rib following a mugging.

"So sorry to hear that. Happy to help," he said, calling in just at the right time to pick up the gig.

As a trusted freelancer and previously vetted member of the caterer's team, he passed White House clearance without question. Plus, some of the barflies actually remembered him and his expertise with mixed drinks and bottle juggling. One commented that he flipped and tossed the vodka as adeptly as a knife thrower would his knives. *Ironic, almost comical*, he thought.

The bartender, looking to be in his early fifties, had wavy brown hair, contemporary gun metal glasses, and the required black outfit. He kept everything moving; mixing, pouring, and refilling with a smile. His conversations were all filtered through a slight Scottish accent. That made him more appealing, easy to converse with, and obviously not a threat to the Secret Service officers milling around the room.

• • •

"I need a ride," Roarke demanded.

The lieutenant on duty wasn't about to open up a shuttle service without reason.

"And you would be?"

"Roarke, Secret Service. A C-37A was going to ferry me, but I have a sudden change of plans."

"We're going to need approval, sir."

"I'll get it," Roarke replied, hoping he would. He pressed a button on his cell and turned his back on the pilot. Some heated conversation followed which the Air Force pilot tried to follow. A minute later, Roarke handed his phone to the officer.

"It's for you."

"For me? Who is it?"

Roarke didn't explain. He shoved the BlackBerry in his hand.

"Hello," the officer said, clearly annoyed.

"Hello, son. What's your name?" the voice asked with obvious command of the moment.

"Gerstad. Latham Gerstad, LT USAF. And who am I talking to?"

"To *whom*, lieutenant. It's to *whom*."

"Whatever. I'm busy and if this is going to turn into a grammar lesson the conversation is over."

"Not grammar, LT Anderson. Command."

"I take commands from…"

"The commander in chief."

"Look, I don't know who you are, but…"

Roarke used "The P Bomb;" the president live on the phone.

"Morgan Taylor, son."

The name in isolation didn't register to the annoyed pilot.

"And who gave you the authority to…" His voice trailed off, as reality registered.

"The American people," the president stated. "Now, get *my* passenger where he needs to go. What do you have warmed up?"

"An old UH-1N Huey, sir. But I will need confirmation," Gerstad quite appropriately replied.

"I think we'd all court martial you if you didn't. You'll have it from the tower before Mr. Roarke tightens his safety belt."

• • •

"Nothing," Shannon Davis said as he brushed Curtis Lawson. Davis coordinated the security with the Secret Service which broke the house and property up into distinct quadrants. Lawson was Director Mulligan's man, and also there because he was one of the bureau's best shots.

"Same outside." Lawson was still shivering from the cold. "All's quiet. You really think he'll show up?"

"Not ours to question. Just keep alert. Roarke said he could be anybody. Maybe he'll come as Mrs. Johnson." Davis laughed at his own joke, then more seriously added, "He's that good."

"Nobody's that good."

"Don't be so sure. Ever sat next to a transexual?"

"I wouldn't know," Lawson answered.

"My point exactly."

The bartender watched the officers weave around the floor through the cocktail hour as everyone assembled for the general's speech in the living room prior to dinner. Applause greeted General Johnson when he walked to the front of the room. The clapping came from those who knew and appreciated him and those who feared him.

With no one needing another pour, Sader clapped too, thinking to himself that McLean, Virginia's population of 49,250 would drop by one tonight. He, Richard Cooper, would personally see to that.

• • •

"I'm not a speech maker," General Johnson offered. He scanned the room seeing friends and foes, but no one who looked like an assassin. "So, I'll keep this short. And that will keep you all very happy."

Johnson earned his first laugh as a vice presidential nominee, and it was on an unrehearsed ad lib. In fact, Johnson would have been uncomfortable reading off a page or a teleprompter. The distinguished four star was much more comfortable absorbing briefing papers and spitting out orders. But as the vice president-designee there'd be more listening, which right now troubled him far more than being shot.

"You've heard that President Taylor wants me as his vice president.

He is my commander in chief, and if I've learned anything, it's to follow the chain of command."

Richard Cooper had followed the chain of command, as well. Right up to General Johnson. The general's death would end the line. Revenge served on a silver platter at Johnson's own home. *What could be more fitting,* he thought.

"And so, with renewed honor, upon confirmation, I will retire from the army I have served since my youth, and enter a political world with, I dare say, more landmines than I ever encountered on the battlefield."

The crowd laughed again. It was completely true.

"But once a solider always a soldier. My heart and soul has been with the army. But the United States Army is not a thing. It is comprised of honorable, dedicated men and women, many who return to our shores broken; in need of medical care, career counseling, and assistance reintegrating into mainstream life. That is why we gather this evening. To make their transition and lives healthier and fulfilling…to show we are there for them in the long run, when they need, where they need, and how they need. And for thousands it is through the remarkable work at Walter Reed."

Johnson spoke about the medical facility and how strapped it was for resources beyond what federal tax dollars provided. He appealed to the wealthy visitors to dig deep and make significant contributions. He did so by looking at each and every one of them directly in the eyes with the sincerity and determination he sent young soldiers off to battle. General Jonas Jackson Johnson was powerful and inspiring.

"You know," he said, transitioning to another topic, I've done a little bit of reading recently, trying to understand the mindset of men like generals Washington, Grant, and Eisenhower as they prepared for the Executive Branch. Now don't read that as any aspirations beyond vice president. But when those men hung up their uniforms for civvies, they did more than change their clothes. They had to change the way they viewed things. And, in most cases, it wasn't what they'd planned."

Cooper listened and actually understood what the general meant. He, too, had to adapt in the civilian world. He, too, had to understand how to use what he learned, but make it work outside of the structured environment of the military. Two different men, two different courses. In another reality, he'd probably enjoy talking with General Johnson about the challenges and difficulties. However, that was not to be.

"General/President Eisenhower reflected on that very point in 1957. He recalled—and I'll try to get it right—an old army saw which goes, *Plans are worthless, but planning is everything.* What does that mean? Well, as Ike explained, there's a huge distinction, because when you are planning for an emergency or the unknown you must start with one thing—the very definition that it is unexpected, therefore it is not going to happen the way you had planned."

This made Cooper, above all the others at the party, think. He lived and even survived because of detailed planning. That worked so long as he was in control of all the variables—time, place, strategy, and ultimately, the element of surprise. Death when you least expected. But, the general, and Eisenhower before him, was absolutely right. He only considered one side of the equation, not the unexpected. *What if* the tables turned?

"Well, ladies and gentlemen, I didn't plan on becoming Morgan Taylor's nominee for vice president. Not on your life."

Or yours, General, Cooper thought.

"But rest assured I will give the Senate completely honest answers in my testimony up to the issues of national security. I will be guided by the president in those matters. As it should be. Anyway, I'm too damned new at this thing to run at the mouth. I'm going for the three Bs. Be brief. Be good. Be gone."

The crowd laughed. Most had never heard Johnson speak. Those who had, never knew him to be so glib. Jonas Jackson Johnson even amazed his wife.

"And with that, I am gone."

"Forever," Cooper whispered as he returned to making drinks. In a few minutes his relief would take over and he'd really go to work.

"Enjoy yourselves." The guests applauded and the FBI and Secret Service agents who patrolled the party and the grounds looked for just about anybody Richard Cooper might be tonight.

• • •

Roarke was aloft in one of the real old birds the 1st Helicopter Squadron of the 11th Wing flew. This particular UH-1N had flown in the Vietnam era and now provided rotary wing support to VIPs in the NCR, the National Capital Region. Though the temperature outside was barely above twenty degrees, the helo cabin hit a comfortable seventy-two degrees with the turbine spinning and bleeding welcomed warmth Roarke's way.

• • •

The pilot, LT Latham Gerstad, set a course for McLean. It was not as direct as Roarke wanted, but airspace in and around NCR is full of restricted areas, Military Operational Areas (MOAs) and Terminal Control Areas. Even Roarke's Huey had to obey the TAC and FAA procedures or risk being brought down.

The president's call to the secretary of the air force and the secretary's subsequent call to the Andrews tower cleared some of the hurdles, but not all given incoming traffic, fuel issues, and non-negotiable no-fly zones.

The most direct shot was low over the Potomac River, below incoming commercial flights, then barely above the tree and power lines on a southwest heading to McLean.

The flight took an agonizing twenty-two minutes, worthy of ulcers if Roarke wasn't so focused.

As they neared the destination, Gerstad reported, "Two miles out, sir." He was following GPS coordinates to a supermarket parking lot four blocks from the general's house. "Hope we'll have room," he said. "If not, I'll get you as close to the deck as possible. You might have to take a big first step.

It was the kind of comment Roarke didn't need to respond to; just be prepared for.

"Coming up," Gerstad said a minute later. He pointed ahead and to the right.

"We going to make it?

"You'll know as soon as I do." And with that, Gerstad concentrated on the wind, the telephone poles, and the cars below.

"Dicey, but I see a spot that may work."

Gerstad brought the helicopter down five feet from the deck when a Nissan Sentra careened around the parking lot. "Hang on," the pilot warned. His lifted the bird up fast; a maneuver that sent Roarke's stomach squarely into his throat. He fought the nausea and concentrated on the task at hand.

"Okay, let's try this again." Gerstad came around and hovered twelve feet from the ground. He wasn't going to take the same chance a second time."

"This is as close as I dare get. How are your knees?"

"I suppose I'm about to find out," Roarke said.

"Okay, on three," Gerstad said as he hovered over the jump zone. "And good luck. Looks like you've got yourself a real mission,"

"You have no idea," Roarke replied."

Three came very fast and hard.

CHAPTER 31

MCLEAN, VIRGINIA

Once on the ground, it was a matter of expediency. Roarke needed to get to the general's house fast. Problem solved when the driver of a light blue Toyota Prius rolled forward. Roarke approached, ID in hand, and Sig Sauer ready. In a move right out of an old *Lethal Weapon* film, the driver watched his car tear down the street without him. If Roarke wished for a fast sports car, he was not disappointed with the pep of the hybrid.

"Nice speech, General," a waiter said politely after working his way up. He offered Johnson the last glass of champagne on his silver tray. "For the toast. Everyone's gathering."

"Thank you." Johnson replied.

General Jonas Jackson Johnson gave the man a good sizing up, as he did everyone. *Flunky,* he thought, noting that the waiter wasn't even wearing a jacket that fit properly.

"You never failed to inspire. An illuminating career."

The general wondered if he sensed another word left unsaid. *Was it "sir?"* Before he could follow up, the waiter walked away.

"Ladies and gentlemen, if I may please have your attention?" Carl Lyons had gone to West Point with Johnson and, as one of his oldest friends, was the best person in the room to address the crowd.

The downstairs, filled with some of Washington's military, political, and social elite, quickly quieted again. People moved closer to the speaker, but left room around General Johnson so he could be seen. By now everyone had a champagne flute in hand.

Lyons, distinguished and poised, raised his glass. "I've known this old warhorse since we were cadets. Let me tell you, he was as irascible then as he is now."

People laughed.

"For years I thought his vocabulary consisted of *yes*, *no*, and *what don't you understand about the word no*."

More laughter.

"But time has softened him up a bit. I thought I heard a 'maybe' a few minutes ago. I guess he's trying out a new word he'll need on the Hill."

Lyons had perfectly characterized his lifelong friend and brought his toast to the transition point he wanted.

"And so, with utmost respect and admiration, and in honor of a most distinguished military leader, a wartime general, and a man dedicated to peace, I heartily congratulate the next vice president of the United States, the soon-to-be retired General Jonas Jackson Johnson." Lyons brought his glass up higher. "On behalf of a grateful nation, I wish you true happiness, success, and health."

The general pivoted right and left nodding to his guests' calls of "Here! Here!" Jonas Jackson Johnson then brought the drink up to his lips. Champagne, no matter how good, wasn't to his taste. The scotch that was being drained from his liquor cabinet was. But a celebration was a celebration and soon this god-awful evening would be over. So a little champagne…

"Don't!"

It was more than a shout. It was a command. J3 knew commands. He spent his life listening to them and giving them. He respected them and he followed them.

The general evaluated the voice. It was sharp and direct, coming from over his shoulder; from someone running. It was a familiar voice. And now he saw it came from a familiar face—Scott Roarke.

Johnson didn't need any other warning. It suddenly came together. The unsaid, *sir*, the oversized jacket of his server. The comment.

General Johnson looked at the champagne, and dropped the glass.

Roarke's shout coupled with the breaking glass created a virtual vacuum. The only sounds over the sudden silence—running and a back door crashing open.

Roarke took off in the same direction, squeezing through the door before it closed. He saw his quarry ahead, racing into the woods.

"Cooper!"

Richard Cooper didn't stop. Roarke did. He aimed his Sig and fired, but Cooper dodged left at the last moment.

Roarke picked up the chase following Cooper through the thick maples and oaks.

The assassin slowed, looking for cover and exit points. He stopped when he heard the crunching snow behind him.

"Hands behind your head. Kneel and hit the ground. It's over," Roarke stated.

Cooper ignored him.

"Now!"

"I'll grant you one thing, Roarke. You're a persistent son of a bitch."

"Hands up, kneel, and hit the deck."

Roarke heard rustling behind him, then a voice. "It's okay. FBI. I have him."

Roarke kept his eyes on the target and demanded, "Cooper, my last warning."

"I said I have him. Stand down." The order came from the man now beside him, agent Curtis Lawson.

"He's MINE. I'm Secret Service."

"Stand down, mister."

Roarke carefully lowered his Sig. Lawson's Glock was trained on Cooper. The FBI agent then stepped closer to the subject who still hadn't complied with Roarke's order.

Lawson then made what Roarke considered a dumb move. He positioned himself directly in front of Roarke, blocking any shot the

Secret Service agent might have. Roarke adjusted his position, but was hemmed in by the trees. He thought Lawson was trying to cuff Cooper, but he wasn't sure. Then he saw a blur of arms and Lawson doubling over on the ground and the assassin on the run.

"Dammit!" Roarke ran to Lawson.

The FBI agent waved him on. "Get the bastard."

Roarke heard the crunching of snow ahead. He dodged some bushes and cut around trees in pursuit. Suddenly, his leather shoes failed him. Roarke slid down an embankment and hit a rock hard. The time he lost was the time Cooper needed.

• • •

"What the hell were you thinking?" Roarke was pissed. "That was a rookie-ass move," he complained to Lawson who was still trying to get to his feet.

"I'm sorry," the FBI said. "Didn't know you. We've been waiting to see if this guy would show up."

"Right, because of me! And I identified myself as Secret Service."

"I had my orders."

"Were your orders to let a killer get away? Because that's exactly what you did."

Roarke was disgusted. He didn't wait for an answer. He walked past Lawson and then Shannon Davis and the other bureau agents who were now outside. Mulligan was going to hear about this in no uncertain terms. *He let him get away. He let him.*

THE WHITE HOUSE
LATER THAT NIGHT

"Jesus!" Taylor exclaimed over the phone to his director of national intelligence. "How many lives does this guy have?"

"Not lives, Mr. President. Identities. Cooper is an absolute chameleon, a master of disguises with more personalities than I've ever seen," Jack Evans replied. "I wish he worked for us."

"Well since he does not, I recommend you find him once and for all and get rid of everybody he is or ever will be."

CHAPTER 32

ATLANTA, GEORGIA
THE CENTERS FOR DISEASE CONTROL AND PREVENTION
JANUARY 12

"Hello, you're on the air."

Tonight, that's about all the host had to say on *Coast to Coast AM*. The audience took it from there. For four straight hours callers talked about the mysterious illnesses and deaths that were cropping up across the country. It was as hot a topic as anything had been since alleged sightings of El Chupacabras and Big Foot, the end of the world Mayan Calendar predictions, and the secrets behind Area 51, HAARP, and Project Majestic. More importantly, it was current with names, dates, and places. What started as a trickle a few days ago was a flood of calls now. Certainly some could be written off as conspiracy theorists who trudged through knee-deep suspicion of the government. But many of the callers had the ring of truth. Their family members were dying.

Bonnie Comley listened. More than that, she had her staff listen, take notes, and immediately follow up. The conversations led to more pins in her map. A lot more.

CIUDAD DEL ESTE, PARAGUAY

Ibrahim Haddad had his own map, which replicated many of Dr. Comley's locations and then some.

He turned down the Internet radio Web site of this incredibly popular American radio series. *At last,* he proclaimed only to himself.

Now he would achieve his goal because this time he wasn't relying on the cumbersome American political system or the power of the media to shape public opinion. He dug deeper into history and into psychology. This time it was all about fear; ultimate fear that would bring panic to communities, the stock market, and the government itself. The first things were already happening. Soon it would go viral. *Viral.* The term made him laugh. People were now using the word to explain how fast information flowed. *Flowed, another apt description. From town to town. County to county. State to state.* Haddad was quite certain an already armed citizenry would surely place family over ideals and defend home before country. All of this to severely weaken the United States and remove its influence over his hated Israel. All of this to punish a nation's people for the death of his wife and daughter.

Things were proceeding on schedule. He figured no more than ten days, maybe less.

The Great Satan will choke, Haddad said to himself. The fact that he'd also stand to make hundreds of millions of dollars gave him even greater satisfaction. He would not live forever. But his money would continue to finance terror long after.

Haddad turned the Internet radio station back up and looked at the global market on the CNBC Web site. *Another very good day ahead.*

NEW YORK CITY
WALL STREET JOURNAL OFFICES

Paul Twardy reported on stock trends. He was watching Pepsico, Coke, and Nestlé again, to see where they would go with the morning bell. He charted sharp rises four days in a row. The trend would be understandable in the summer. But *January*?

Twardy was raised in upstate New York, studied business at Wharton, and switched to journalism at NYU grad school. No surprise he could make a business story read like a thriller. He'd written for the*Boston Globe,* the *Philadelphia Inquirer,* and *Time,* where a decade earlier he won a Pulitzer for his cover story on pharmaceutical companies that profited from flu epidemics scares. He exposed two schemes in particular. The award was great, but the magazine lost advertising revenue. He was unceremoniously dropped eight months later. He took his award to *Newsweek*, then *USA Today*, and most recently *WSJ*.

This story had the same kind of ring to it. But he wasn't sure why until he heard the last half hour of an off-the-wall radio show on his way into work.

CHAPTER 33

HELENA, MONTANA
0830 HRS

The C-37A came to a perfect, short landing and taxied to the opposite end of the runway, dropping Roarke off at the general aviation terminal. As soon as Roarke was clear of the wings, the plane was refueled in preparation of a quick take off.

A man, bundled up against the cold, met him halfway to a civilian aviation hangar.

"Mr. Roarke?"

"Yes." Roarke's breath formed a dense cloud in front of him.

"I'm SGT Amos Barnes from Helena. Sorry for the cold." He looked at what Roarke was wearing. "I've got a warmer jacket inside for you."

"Thanks Sergeant." Roarke shivered. "Feels like I'm going to need it."

"A bit colder than D.C.?"

"Sergeant, the less you know who I am and where I come from the better. Hope that's okay, but it's the way I operate."

"No problem, sir."

"Now point me to the bathroom and a cup of coffee. I've had a really long day and I'll be happy to hear all about your special guest."

As he said this, Roarke turned his phone on. The moment it found a signal and reset to local time a message alert sounded. Roarke waited to listen until after he was alone and finished washing his hands at the terminal sink. He washed them thoroughly until Christine Slocum's work was completely gone.

The voice message was brief:

> Sweetheart, word is you've been a busy boy. Figure you're en route now, but you're going to want to call me.

CPT Penny Walker left all the encouragement needed. She had him on *You're going to want to call me.*

"Okay partner, whatcha got?" Roarke asked, now in the passenger seat of a Ford F-150.

"No hello? Sorry to wake you?"

"Hello, sorry to wake you."

"Fuck you very much, Mr. Roarke. And a good morning to you, too."

"Sorry," Roarke said. "I'm a little bit scrambled up right now."

"So I heard," Walker replied. "You okay, though?"

"Yes."

"Did you tell Katie what happened?"

"No."

"Word of advice. You better, especially considering this other stuff you're stepping into."

"Meaning?"

"The phone number. The woman. Miss Sex Appeal."

"Ah, what do you have?"

"Well, starting with the basics, if I were still seeing you, I'd be jealous."

"You must have something else than her measurements."

"I do. Christine Slocum. Age twenty-seven. Magna cum laude Smith graduate in International studies. Interned at the U.N., Smith Barney, and a big ass D.C. law firm with too many names to mention. Apparently she's a damned good writer, too. A few articles came up through Google, I bet there's more. Scholarly stuff on the Middle East, American politics, NAFTA. I also found her through some blogs. But all that seemed to stop about eighteen months ago. No bylines since then."

"Where's she from?"

"Still researching that. Nothing yet. But I'll get it."

"You're holding something back, Pen," Roarke said.

"Ah yes. Her current employment."

All Roarke knew was that Slocum worked on the Hill.

"Your dear Ms. Slocum is no slouch. She's a speechwriter for a congressman."

This was getting more interesting already.

"Care to take a guess who she works for?"

"Nope." Roarke didn't need to make anything more public in the truck than he already had.

"You're no fun."

"Nope."

"Christine Slocum is Duke Patrick's speechwriter."

Roarke let the information sink in. Walker thought he dropped off the call.

"Scott, did you get that?"

"Sure did. Anything else?"

"Not yet. Still digging. But look for an e-mail in a while."

Roarke ended the conversation with a quick thanks. He considered the last, most essential information that Walker discovered. *Christine Slocum is Duke Patrick's speechwriter.*

As a Secret Service agent, Roarke served the office of the president. As a human being, Scott Roarke was fiercely loyal to Morgan Taylor. *So why does the Speaker of House's speechwriter, the president's chief critic since Senator Teddy Lodge, make a beeline to me?* It wasn't a coincidence. She was clearly stalking him, ready in every way to take him. *Why?* he wondered.

Roarke went to a solitary place, a quiet mental state where his martial arts master had taught him to look for answers. There, he saw Slocum. But it wasn't the image of her at the gym. It was someplace else; in the wings of a hallway in a far-off memory. Only the sound of the Ford truck crunching on the snow in a parking lot brought him back.

• • •

Roarke knocked gently on the door. It definitely wasn't the knock of a policeman, CIA interrogator, or army intelligence.

"*Hola, Ricardo. Como ésta*?" Roarke's Spanish was passable, not great. But he thought it might be a good place to start.

"Uno momento," Ricardo Perez replied from behind the door.

Roarke motioned for SGT Barnes and a National Guard private standing vigil to step away. He gave a nod indicating he'd be okay. The young guardsman was reluctant to take orders from the civilian. Roarke looked to Barnes who took care of the situation with a whisper in the soldier's ear. Roarke didn't know and didn't care what he said. He just wanted to be alone and out of earshot of everyone

Perez unlatched the chain and turned the lock. The two men stood face to face at about the same height.

Roarke took the lead in Spanish. "*Me llamo Scott Roarke.*" He offered his hand. Perez, unsure, took it. Roarke then asked in English, "May I come in?"

Asking permission was like the gentle knock; an indication of the nonthreatening, nonauthoritarian tone Roarke wanted to establish.

"Sure." Not knowing what else to do, the gang member volunteered his name.

"It's good to meet you, Ricardo. Is English okay?"

Again, it was all about permission.

"Yes."

"May I sit down?"

Perez was not used to *anyone* asking him *anything.* He lived, let alone, survived in a world of demands with no civility and punishment for disobeying.

"Sure."

Roarke took the chair across from the bed.

Perez sat at the head of the bed, the farthest point from Roarke.

Roarke reasoned that if this went well, he'd move closer and ultimately they'd be sitting side by side, eating burgers and fries together on the bed, and sharing war stories about their common past. For now, the distance was fine.

"I work for the president of the United States, Ricardo. I'm not a soldier, though I was one, and I'm not a policeman. I help the president figure things out that can make this country better."

Perez listened.

"I don't need to tell you, you're a lucky man to be alive."

No response.

"If your gang experience was anything similar to mine, you can't go back to any of your family." Roarke intentionally chose *family.* "They'll kill you, Ricardo. They already tried."

"Not everyone. Not my brother." He was opening up.

"No, not your brother. But they'd have to kill both of you. He'd be too much of a threat."

This penetrated.

"It's over, Ricardo. It's over for you, just like it was over for me years ago."

Roarke shared some of his story; enough to strengthen the growing trust.

"Now tell me about you. Start wherever you want. Take your time. Oh, and how about some breakfast? Pancakes, eggs? I'm starving."

CHAPTER 34

MOSCOW
THE SAME TIME

It was easier than Arkady Gomenko had imagined. He had all the right stamps that trafficked the world of officialdom, and slipping the letter into the middle of the stack for the late-arriving Yuri Ranchenkov was no problem. Even in the world of e-mail, so much of the bureaucratic process was still accomplished through memoranda. In this case, it provided more deniability, because the lame nephew of the prime minister probably forgot half of what he ordered. And without an electronic trail, Gomenko's fingerprints (absent from the letter thanks to the gloves he wore) were not on the correspondence in any shape or form.

Now it was a matter of waiting until Ranchenkov came into work, had his morning coffee, wasted an hour or two, went through his e-mail, and then hit the morning snail mail. Gomenko expected he'd get called in any minute after the ritual.

Like clockwork: "Gomenko, get in here," Ranchenkov ordered over the phone.

"Yes, sir," the hapless official answered.

Gomenko walked the long dingy corridor which needed the same paint job that had been forgotten in the Soviet era. He took his time, not looking to be too eager; just the normal functionary who made work last.

"Good morning, Director Ranchenkov," Gomenko said, entering the office.

"What's good about it?"

"Apparently very little from your tone."

Ranchenkov didn't share the reason for his displeasure, but Gomenko smiled inside.

"What are you working on?"

"The Balkan summary you gave me three weeks ago."

"It can wait. I have something else for you," the deputy director general of internal intelligence said.

"But you told me it was urgent." Slogging through a useless report was hardly urgent, but it is what filled his days, months, and years.

"It can wait another week. I have a most important matter; a request from the Kremlin." Ranchenkov read from the memorandum without referencing the named author, Petrov Androsky. "You can go to the archives, research this thoroughly, and prepare the report."

The beauty of the plan Gomenko had invented is that he was acting under orders that would never be questioned, preparing a report that would never be read—at least in Moscow. It would add to his work week and to his retirement income.

Just to tickle the tiger, he asked, "Where do I start, I've never heard of the Andropov Institute. Is it a school?"

"I have no idea." That was true. Ranchenkov had served in the Soviet army for only a short time. He came up through the FSB long after the collapse of Communism. "Some relic, but you're going to dust off the files and become an expert. The Kremlin," he still didn't say who, "requires a full summary. Names, dates, places. Details. I don't want to see you until it's finished. I'll clear you at records."

Gomenko collapsed his body in mock disgust. He let out a sigh for effect and left for his office.

"And it better be finished fast," Ranchenkov yelled to his underling's back.

Spying didn't get much easier, Gomenko thought.

MONTANA MOTEL

Roarke and Perez were on their second Egg McMuffins from the McDonald's on North Montana Avenue. They'd already had an order of pancakes and a large McCafe latte. The food had done as Roarke intended—satisfy his hunger and bring them closer together. He now sat at the corner of the bed and listened intently as the gang member was up to how he survived being raped by a truck driver.

This conversation took the better part of the morning. Roarke was in no rush to get to the heart of the matter. It was far more important to establish a bond with Perez. In time, and with trust, the relevant information would come.

Just before noon, the young Mara transporter began to describe how he picked up a man at the Houston airport.

"He came in on a morning flight. He'd been told my license plate and what I'd be driving. I just needed to keep circling the airport until he saw me. On the third time around, this guy flagged me. I pulled over. He had a password and I had the answer. That was it."

"What was the password?" Roarke asked, wondering if it would add anything.

"Pretty simple. I had to hear it a few times. The guy had some sort of accent. It was 'I'm going to a soccer match. Who's winning the competition?' Of course, I needed to have the right answer."

"Which was?"

"Guatemala."

"That was it?"

"No, if he responded, 'I wish Brazil was still winning,' I was to let him in. If he got it wrong, I was supposed to still pick him up, start driving north, then find a place and kill him."

"He got it right," Roarke noted.

"Yeah, but only to try to kill me later."

Roarke didn't jump to that part of the conversation yet. He wanted to take things all in order.

"Did he speak with you enough to get a sense of where he was from?" Roarke asked. To be more clear he added, "Did he sound like you?"

"No. He wasn't Latin. European maybe. He had a roughness to the way he spoke. Without ups and downs. Just flat."

Roarke gave a few examples of words and sounds. When he came to a sentence in German, Perez stopped him.

"Like that."

"Are you sure? Roarke tried a few sentences with a Spanish, Russian, and Arabic dialect. He wasn't as proficient as his friend, CIA agent Vinnie D'Angelo, but it was good enough.

"No, it was more like that first one. Maybe with a little of the last, too, when he met up with the other guy."

"It was a long ride. Did he talk to you?"

"Only to tell me he needed a bathroom."

"Any cell phone calls?" Roarke might be able to track something down.

"No."

"What about stopping for food or coffee?"

"He had some food with him. I had a lot of coffee. I offered. He wouldn't drink any."

A German Muslim? That was Roarke's assumption, at least based on the limited variables he was getting.

"What about when you dropped him off?"

Perez recounted the event. The other car flashing its lights. The two greeting one another as long lost friends.

"Whoa. Describe that."

"They fucking kissed each other on the cheeks both sides. And talked in that other language."

"Did you catch anything? Anything like *"Assalamu alikum* or *Salam Alaikum?"*

"Yes, that *Assalamu* thing you just said."

Now Perez had a question for Roarke.

"So who the hell were they? And why did he want to kill me?"

Roarke stepped very carefully. "In a second." Roarke thought for a moment. "Ricardo, you must have gotten a good look at the man you drove."

"Yes. I kept staring at him in the rearview mirror. Whenever he noticed, he moved away."

"And what about the other man? The one he met up with in the parking lot?"

"Him, too."

"Well, to answer your question, they, or someone behind this, wanted to kill you because you could identify them. You're alive and I need you to do just that—identify them." Roarke stood up. He had the young man's full attention.

"Ricardo, I can help you. I mean really help you. We can give you a new name. A new life. An education. You can be somebody. Put all this behind you. Everything. There's the army or even college. But it all begins today with what you know."

"I've told you everything."

"Told me, yes. But it's time for some pictures."

"Pictures. I didn't have a camera."

"In a way you did. I'm going to go out and see if the sergeant can find someone in town who can draw well. Maybe we can get a clear picture of the two men based on your descriptions. All you'll need to do is talk them through it. If we get decent drawings I have a friend who can do miracles with them; maybe even figure out who the hell they are. Think you can?"

"I've never done it before."

"You've never escaped from a car bomb before either."

MOSCOW
LATER

Arkady was waved through security in the FSB archives. He was allowed only pads of paper and pencils. No pens, no cell phones, keys, or anything that could hide electronics or cameras of any design. But then again he didn't need them.

One archivist pointed him to another until he was convinced he was getting the old-fashioned Soviet runaround.

"Look, perhaps you did not hear who requested this information. I am here on the highest authority of the FSB. This authority can make sure that you will never see the light beyond the bulbs you sit under. If you think that such things ended when we stopped calling one another comrade, you are mistaken. Take me to where I need to go."

Arkady made sure that his voice carried far down the vast aisles and put fear into anyone within earshot.

"Mr. Gomenko, I am sorry you've encountered such difficulty," said one older man who suddenly entered the area. "My name is Sergei Kleinkorn. I will assist you."

"Thank you."

There was something about Kleinkorn that instilled some trepidation in Gomenko. *His age, his manner. His tone?* He was at least in his mid-seventies, though still fit. He had a full head of gray hair and dressed in a perfectly ironed blue suit, white shirt, and a red tie. *His attitude. A commanding attitude.*

"I appreciate your help. I am on an assignment from Deputy Director Ranchenkov, acting on orders from the Kremlin."

"May I see the papers so I can be of greater help."

It was not said as a question; more as a military request. A former Soviet military request. Without thinking, Gomenko answered, "Yes, sir."

Kleinkorn read the authorization. He raised an eyebrow upon reading the last paragraph.

"This is ancient history. What is the need for this today?"

"My need is to prepare a report. Beyond that I cannot say." There were multiple truths in the last statement.

"There are those who would not want the information you seek known."

"Mr. Kleinhorn," he stated with authority. "I have a job to do. Will you please lead me to the correct files so I can conduct my research?"

Kleinkorn appeared put out, but waved Gomenko to follow.

Arkady Gomenko rethought how easy spying was.

HELENA, MONTANA

Roarke had all the details Perez could remember. Make and color of the other car, basic age of the driver, and a verbatim of everything that was said on the ride to Montana. That was the easiest part. It consisted of *yes, no*, and *stop at next exit.*

He'd gone as far as he could without a sketch. Like clockwork, there was a knock at the motel door.

"Mr. Roarke?" It was SGT Barnes. "Can you come out please?"

Roarke excused himself again. A few steps down the hall the recruiter stood with a young woman, who looked to be about sixteen or seventeen. Before Roarke even dared ask, SGT Barnes said, "Mr. Roarke, this is Cheryl Gabriel. She's a junior in high school here. The art teacher recommended Cher for your," he paused, "portraits."

Roarke nodded to the teenager and gave Barnes a troubled look. "I'm sorry, but I don't believe SGT Barnes really explained things."

"Oh yes he did." The teenager offered her hand to Roarke. He took it noting her poise and confidence. "I'm pretty good at drawing people. Wanna see?"

"Yes, but it's not a portrait of someone in the room, it's drawing someone, two people, from a description."

"Oh," the girl said.

The Secret Service agent was about to dismiss her when she added, "Well, I'd be happy to give it a try. I love to draw. It's what I'd like to study in college."

Roarke did like her spunk. She was pretty in a natural way, about five-seven with wavy brown hair. Going to college might be a problem, though. He came to that opinion because her coat was ragged and her winter shoes appeared to be seasons old. He surmised that Cheryl's family had very little money.

"Maybe I should talk to your parents first and explain what this is all about."

"I live with my aunt. She's working at the truck stop. I can try to get her, if you really need."

"You're pretty confident."

"The sergeant told me I could earn some money. How much?"

"You are confident, Miss Gabriel."

"It's Cheryl or Cher."

"Well, Cher, what art school do you want to go to?"

She laughed. "Well, I've been looking at Savannah. It's a lot warmer there in the winter. But really far away."

"Yes it is. Tell you what, let's see how you do, then we'll talk. Deal?"

"Deal."

MOSCOW

Gomenko worked under the watchful eye of Kleinkorn. Less than optimum circumstances. It seemed very old school to him. More Soviet than contemporary. But Gomenko chose not to raise eyebrows; not to turn what was reported as a mere government assignment into a suspicious activity worth an archivist's questions. So the more Gomenko appeared bored and annoyed, the more disinterested his watcher became.

An amazing history began to reveal itself box by box. Later material referred back to early files deeper in the vault. It kept Kleinkorn busy. Since the request was based on the specific name, The Andropov Institute, Gomenko stayed with particular items from the era in question. The mid-1960s until whatever the last box would reveal.

This was Russia pre-computer, born from an era full of enemies real and propagandized, foreign and domestic. It was the Cold War, which Gomenko reasoned would have been more accurately described as the Overkill War. Each side had more weapons than humanly necessary. The vast numbers of nuclear weapons researched, developed, tested, built, and stockpiled in Russia and America created unfathomable power, incredible wealth, and a spy network that concocted elaborate plans. Arkady Gomenko quickly learned that The Andropov Institute was one of them. He also discovered that the Institute had another division as well, with an inspiring, patriotic name: Red Banner.

Red Banner was a school, with teachers, classes, assignments, homework, and a rigorous curriculum, but not one found at any other Soviet academic program.

Gomenko read with disbelief. *How could such a thing exist?* Yet it did with great promise and incredible graduates. They were not identified by anything more than a number, but trained over years. They offered an immense expanding level of influence for Soviet politik and perhaps the collapse of America's infrastructure without anyone actually pressing "the button."

Of course, so much of it became obsolete with the end of the Soviet dominion and even more irrelevant when terrorists targeted American buildings with self-guided missiles—commercial aircraft.

Kleinkorn always remained nearby begrudgingly fulfilling requests for more specific boxes. By now, Gomenko dismissed him as a relic of the authoritarian era who still believed he was serving Mother Russia.

HELENA, MONTANA

It took Cheryl Gabriel some time to feel comfortable in the room with Ricardo Perez. She was an innocent country girl. He was an El Salvadorian gang member. A killer. But he was already softening with Roarke's coaxing and discovering that not everyone was as awful as his brother and leaders portrayed. So, he opened up. The more he did, the easier it was for Cheryl to capture the character of the men he described.

A dozen discards were crumpled on the floor and pencil eraser shavings made the bed itchy to the touch. However, in time, as she replaced initial pencil outlines with chalk, real faces emerged with very distinctive features.

This girl is good, Roarke said to himself. Ricardo Perez said it aloud. "That's him! That's the guy I drove."

"Are you sure?" Roarke asked.

"It's like she took a picture of him."

The teenager smiled. "Okay, one down, one to go."

"Either of you need a break?" Roarke asked.

They simultaneously said, "No." They were actually enjoying the creative process and working together.

"Okay then. Go for it."

Roarke then snapped a smartphone picture of her very detailed drawing and immediately forwarded it via e-mail with a short note of explanation.

> Hey, Touch. Run this through the system.
> See what comes up. No hints!
> Oh, and give LT Walker a kiss for me.
> Priority on both. Roarke.

MOSCOW

Every page, every memorandum, every evaluation contained another window to the hell-freezing-over reality of the Cold War. Red Banner offered a variety of courses that couldn't be found anywhere. Red Banner 101 was the introduction. A multi-year introduction. In the most simplistic terms, students enrolled as Russians and graduated as Americans.

Gomenko surmised the program aimed for total immersion. Young men and women were taught to become Americans, to integrate into American life; many fulfilling duties as active spies, others as*sleepers* awaiting wakening.

Drilling down into the details, Gomenko gathered that students never knew or used each other's actual names. Many never saw one another again unless they were sent into the field as couples.

The program was established based on field research. For a long time, the Russians were inept at getting the basics of American life. Prior to Red Banner 101, spies who operated outside of the protection of embassy cover might master an accent or drive an automatic shift car properly, but the little things could blow their cover—things that are so typically American and definitely not Russian. Buying the right sneakers, toothpaste, or jeans. There were too many choices. Frustrating choices. More frustrating than negotiating, bargaining, or, worse yet, arguing over the price. Confused, they'd opt for one product not understanding the other is really what they needed.

Red Banner sought to correct this. It was designed specifically to teach Russians the practical fundamentals of American life. Men and women enlisted. The best became great actors performing on a grand global stage or in small-town America. The student spies lost their Russian accents, learned how to correctly work American idiomatic expressions into their speech, and became respected members of their communities.

Some were even encouraged to marry, have a family, and raise their children to continue their life's work.

Over the years, hundreds of Russians infiltrated American society waiting to be activated.

The plans of such sleepers read like movie scenarios. Graduates were trained to become titans of industry, court justices, and college presidents. By the end of the Cold War, most found capitalism more personally beneficial than totalitarianism and daytime success more rewarding than remaining a sleeper.

Once the Soviet Union fell, it became a moot issue unless the sleeper had other, personal reasons for continuing. Gomenko read the case of one such spy, placed within a family as a result of deadly circumstances. His mission—to become a leading political figure in American life.

Gomenko wondered how close he had gotten. Then he found a notation that made him sit up. In a history full of no names, there finally was one. Colonel Aleksandr Dubroff. The man his CIA contact wanted.

Gomenko decided to research Dubroff further. For that, he'd use his own computer and his own contacts.

HELENA, MONTANA

The three of them were actually laughing. Roarke was convinced that

Perez hadn't done that in a long, long time. He was enjoying the moment when he received two text messages in quick succession.

"Fuck you!" from FBI photo analyst Duane "Touch" Parsons. Then another, with the exact same, "Fuck you!" from army intelligence officer Penny Walker.

They were together because of Roarke. He had played matchmaker between the sexy army intelligence officer and the geeky FBI computer expert. It was working.

The two e-mails made Roarke laugh even more.

"What's that all about?" Cheryl asked.

"Oh, my friends are having a little fun with me. And I guarantee you've given them a great challenge."

Indeed, Roarke was quite certain, though the text didn't say it, that Parsons was already deep into the search at his Quantico office computer station, and Penny would be backing him up.

A minute later Roarke got another text message from Walker.

BTW. He's better than YOU!

Roarke laughed again. "Okay, back to work you two."

"Coffee, coffee, coffee," Perez said playfully.

Barnes made sure they were fully stocked. Roarke grabbed a refill for Perez and paused, cup in hand. *Coffee.* A memory flashed in his mind. Before it was fully shaped it was gone. He hated when that happened.

The next portrait took more back and forth because Perez only briefly saw the second man. After ninety minutes, longer than Roarke had hoped, Perez said, "It's getting close. It's his nose. Still not right. And his chin is too long."

They worked widening the man's nose, shortening his chin, and adding a few days growth of beard, which ultimately could come on or off in Photoshop. A few collaborative finishing touches resulted in another staggeringly realistic sketch of a man, likely early 40s with a distinct Middle Eastern look.

Syrian? Egyptian? Palestinian? Even Israeli? Roarke was unsure. He snapped a photo and sent it on to Parsons. It would be up to the FBI's most creative and dynamic "picto-criminologist," Parsons' own invention, to tell him more.

"I think that's enough for one day," Roarke said, thanking both Ricardo and Cheryl.

Cheryl stood up and Roarke saw the most amazing thing. The gang member did the same and extended his hand. "Hope I didn't scare you too much."

"No, not at all," she said, shaking his hand. "It was really nice working with you."

"Me, too. Good luck."

"You as well, Ricardo. Will you be around for a while?"

Perez looked at Roarke. The agent shook his head.

"Leaving soon."

"Like I said, good luck."

Perez was visibly moved.

Roarke watched and realized he must be feeling like the policeman who had helped him many years ago.

Outside the room, the teenager asked, "Why do you really need these, Mr. Roarke? What did those two men do?"

"I don't really know." Roarke honestly answered. "But, thanks to you, we have a good chance of finding out." Roarke took out two crisp new $100 bills from his wallet. "This is for you, Cher. You have real talent. And I promise, this won't be the last you hear from me."

The girl's eyes lit up. The money would be very helpful, but the compliment meant even more.

"But before you go, I have one very important request."

"Yes?"

"Even though we don't know who they are, or what they're up to, they are dangerous. They, or people associated with them, tried to kill Ricardo."

She gasped.

"And you have to really listen to me now. As far as they know, they succeeded. We have to keep it that way. You have to help us keep it that way."

Cheryl Gabriel nodded, but Roarke felt he needed to go further.

"You can't tell anybody. I need your absolute promise."

She wasn't quite sure how to respond.

"Do you know what national security means?"

It was a tough question for a teenager who lived in rural Montana. "The country?"

"Yes, the country. I work for the government. Pretty high up."

"How high?" she asked with great curiosity.

"Let's just say—very. And I will report to my boss how wonderfully you did today. But you have to keep exactly what you did a secret." Roarke took her hands to make sure he had Cheryl's complete attention. "No one else can know. Not even your aunt."

"But I have to tell her about the money." She clutched the bills.

"You're right. Say your art teacher recommended you do some drawings for the army. That works, doesn't it? It's true."

"Okay."

"But nothing else. It's that important to the country. Can I have your promise?"

With a combination of fear and excitement Cheryl Gabriel proclaimed, "Mr. Roarke, you have it. Now a request from me."

"Oh?" he said surprised.

"Make sure Ricardo does okay."

"Trust me, I will."

• • •

Roarke returned to the motel room. There was more to go over.

"Let's talk about the head of your gang."

"Estavan."

"Yes."

"What do you want to know?"

"Everything. What he's like. Who he sleeps with. What sends him into a rage. Is he ever alone. What he's afraid of. Everything."

They talked for three straight hours. Roarke took it all down.

• • •

Outside again, Roarke phoned the White House. After he downloaded the basics, Roarke added a few personal requests regarding Ricardo Perez and Cheryl Gabriel. Taylor agreed to follow up. After ending that call, Roarke saw that he'd received a text message from Touch Parsons.

Do you have any idea the shit you're into?

Roarke called the photo analyst back in seconds. "Whatcha got?"

"Better in person. When can you be here?"

"Five, six hours. Depends on the winds. But you have to give me something."

Parsons scanned two computer screens. A third was whizzing at light speed through the FBI's Facial Recognition Technology databases, nicknamed FERET.

"You gave me some great stuff to work with."

"And…"

"Solid imagery on eyes, nose, mouth; great work."

"Cut to the chase."

"Matches. Solid ones. Scary ones."

Roarke took a deep breath. "Start with scary."

"Like name, occupation, and best of friends." Parsons enlarged an image on his left computer screen. He enhanced the picture, removing grain and adding sharpness. "I have a positive ID for you from a photo shot in Berlin about eighteen months ago."

"Keep going."

"Mana Al Bushanain. Forty-seven. Saudi Chemist. ID'd right next to the formerly alive Abdul Hassan, who was put to rest by a Homeland Security agent in Houston. His death was kinda front page news, short of some key details."

"I saw it."

"This warrants immediate action Roarke. I can't sit on it. It's got to go upstairs."

"Do it. I'll fill my boss in and see you later today. I'll bring a Starbucks. And don't even think of getting back into that bed with Penny tonight."

"Fuck you again, Roarke. And make it a Venti."

Roarke buckled up and closed his eyes before the Air Force jet took off. The events of the very long day rewound before him. It ended as it began. Christine Slocum shamelessly marching right up to Roarke in the men's locker room, facing him with great delight, and seeing the results. He tried blinking his eyes open to erase the picture. He was sure this was going to lead to something. He just didn't know what.

CHAPTER 35

QUANTICO, VIRGINIA
FBI LABS
JANUARY 13

"Thanks for the Pandora's Box. It's a thing of beauty, Roarke," Touch Parsons explained. "Every picture leads to another, and another, and another. Group photos, surveillance shots at foreign embassy events, soccer matches, awards banquets. You name it. And with so much to work with, it's been a snap cross-referencing locations, names, and dates. The result, a fucking rogue's gallery of characters who will never be nominated for a Nobel. They all interconnect, if not directly, then tangentially through professional associations, university affiliations, and nationality."

"What nationality?"

"Syrian principally. A few Saudis, some Germans, a few Romanians. Even some Indonesians. Here's the kicker: the intelligence computers started ringing like Christmas bells. This is big, Roarke." Parsons laughed. "Hell, I'm on autopilot now, the computer is doing the work for me. I'll need time to sort through it, but Jesus H. Christ, we've got serious trouble here."

Roarke's phone vibrated. He took the call.

"Hey, Penny, I'm with your sweetie." Parsons gave a wave. "He says hi."

"Hi back. Meanwhile, you sure do get around."

"Don't even start with me. I'm wiped. Anyway what's the latest?"

"Here's what I have. Parents dead. Pretty girl's apparently a trust baby. I gather inheritance paid for schooling and everything else. Very little debt according to a credit report. Either she's given freebees everywhere or she has a rich uncle. I'd say she's living beyond her $54 thousand plus per year from the Hill. Oh, and she pays a great deal in cash."

"Suspicious?" Roarke asked.

"Aren't you? That's why you asked, right?"

"That and the feeling that I may have seen her somewhere before."

"There's a good chance you did," Walker stated. "But I need to run this down first."

"Oh?"

"Give me a few hours. I'll get back to you."

"Come on, Penny," Roarke said.

"Later, if this pans out."

"Okay."

"Say *thank you, Penny*."

"Thank you, Penny."

"You're welcome."

Roarke rejoined Touch Parsons. The first thing he heard was "Uh oh." Thoughts that began that way never led to anything good.

"Something new?"

"A familiar face."

"Who?"

"Remember how we met. Your little research job that brought us together?"

Of course Roarke did. Senator Teddy Lodge's campaign for president. And the conspiracy that came out of it. An assassin. Sleeper spies. An assault in Libya. The president's rescue in the Pacific. A talk radio host stirring up hate, and a madman set on bringing down America.

"Look at this."

The sassy FBI photo recognition expert hit a keystroke on his computer. A new image came up; grainy but with enough for Parsons to effectively enhance. Mana Al Bushanain, looking very much like the sketch drawn by Cheryl Gabriel. He was standing with another man. A very familiar man. A most wanted man.

"Holy shit."

THE WHITE HOUSE
1230 HRS

"Boss, we have a problem." Roarke was reporting up the same time Touch Parsons was calling into FBI Director Robert Mulligan.

"Let's have it," the president said.

"I'm not one for conspiracies, but recent history tells me I better become a believer because we have a hell of a one cooking."

Roarke explained what Parsons discovered based on the exceptional sketches from the Montana high school student.

"And it's all pointing to one man. You sitting down?"

"I will if I need to."

"Sit down. It's Haddad. Ibrahim Haddad."

Without missing a beat, Morgan Taylor said, "Get here in one hour. If traffic is a problem, get out and run."

• • •

Roarke was midway to the White House when he reached Katie at her office.

"I'm back and we need to have a serious talk tonight."

"Is everything okay?"

"Yes and no. I'll explain later."

Roarke didn't say it, but it was going to take *delicate* explaining.

CHAPTER 36

LAS VEGAS, NEVADA

Las Vegas, one of the nation's fastest growing metropolitan areas, is thirsty. Its residents and visitors gobble up immense amounts of water every day. In raw numbers, more than 1.2 million residents and more than thirty million tourists each year.

Water flows twenty-five miles from Lake Mead and is pumped up three hundred feet from deep aquifers. The Water District also taps the Las Vegas Springs Preserve, the city's original spring water. The resources fall under the Las Vegas Valley Water District, the LVVWD, which is a member of the Southern Nevada Water Authority (SNWA).

The infrastructure is built on more than three thousand miles of pipeline, a reservoir system which stores seven hundred million gallons of water with high-tech water-quality monitoring controls. However, only a fraction of the water used in the Las Vegas Valley is consumed. Most is used for fountains, lawns, toilets, and cleaning.

Introducing toxins into the metropolitan system is virtually impossible. It would take enormous quantities of chemical or biological substances. But poisoning the water in a few hotel restaurants is another matter entirely. It simply requires a few uniforms and fake IDs, a degree of bravado, and the ability to look like you know what you're doing under the kitchen sink. Such guile is best executed when most of the service staff around are immigrant workers, thankful to have jobs and less likely to point a finger at another hapless worker.

That's how two more of Haddad's men got into four Las Vegas hotel restaurants today. It took only minutes to repipe some lines with their own PVC. In and out in twenty-five minutes. Minutes later, unknowing patrons having Las Vegas' finest with dinner, enjoyed a few hours on the strip, then went back to their rooms and vomited. Based on the amount they had to drink, they might survive the night or another day. But probably not.

It would make the news by the morning; the biggest, most visible scare yet. Far beyond the outbreak of *bacteria legionella* or Legionaire's disease that was reported in Las Vegas in July, 2011. The coverage would lead to other reports. Other reports would lead to regional, then national threats. Then it would turn into a countrywide crisis. All accomplished on Haddad's schedule with precise timing.

This was the story that reporter Paul Twardy was hoping for. This was the report that Bonnie Comley never wanted to see.

ATLANTA, GEORGIA
THE CENTERS FOR DISEASE CONTROL

Dr. Comley continued to compile independent reports from across the country. She looked for commonality: high fever, digestive tract complaints, dehydration—all signs of food poisoning. A few were normal in any demographic survey. But the pile of paper on her desk had moved well beyond *a few*. Now some of the same hospitals updated many of the patients' status to deceased.

Salmonella? There had been so many outbreaks in recent years that it was a first consideration. But the locations were so random, and so widely spread out that it was unlikely they could have been serviced by the same food sources. Still, she called each of the hospitals back and ordered them to immediately send, to CDC specifications, samples of local grocery food, including chicken, eggs, vegetables, and other basics that might contain the bacteria. She also asked that they get samples of the water from each of the victim's homes.

Comley wasn't ready to hit the alarm button yet, but she advised the director of her concern. At the CDC such advice is taken seriously.

NEW YORK
WALL STREET JOURNAL OFFICES

Twardy typed out a story and sent it to his editor, who rejected it immediately.

THE WHITE HOUSE

The meeting began with a cursory, but sincere, "Thank you" from vice president-designee Johnson and an equally quick "You're welcome" from Roarke. Nothing more was needed. There were more pressing things and Roarke had won the argument. J3 and his wife were staying in the White House. No ifs, ands, or buts.

Next, the president asked Roarke to provide a flyover of his Montana trip. The first question that followed was the president's.

"What are we looking at, gentlemen?"

The *gentlemen* sitting around the coffee table were Jack Evans, director of national intelligence; FBI Chief Mulligan; Director of Homeland Security Grigoryan; General Johnson; and Taylor's Chief of Staff, John "Bernsie" Bernstein.

Roarke stood on one side of a white board on an easel, the president on the other.

The floor was open.

"Dirty bombs?" asked Grigoryan.

The president wrote it down without comment.

"Sabotage," added Bernsie.

"Unlikely. Unless it's the electric grid." Still, the president wrote both *sabotage* and *electric grid* on the board.

"Not the electric grid," Roarke argued.

"Why?" Evans asked.

"Touch Parsons is ID'ing these guys as mostly chemists and biologists. A couple of PhDs in geology, but most chem and bio."

Those disciplines resonated and took on even greater meaning as Taylor added them to the grease board.

"WMDs," General Johnson added. The abbreviation hung in the air. "A fucking WMD attack on our own soil."

Morgan Taylor stood with his hands at his sides. Once uttered, the threat of WMDs was so heavy a concept that he could hardly move.

"I don't think so." Roarke said, breaking the long silence.

"You don't think so? And this comes from your expertise in exactly what?" General Johnson said, his voice rising to a shout. In three seconds flat, Scott Roarke felt the full force of General Johnson's Patton-like personality.

Taylor, taking Johnson's side, added WMDs to the list.

Roarke stood his ground. "Does it have to be *mass destruction* to be effective?"

"What are you talking about?" J3 responded.

"From what we know, these guys may be traveling in pairs. Assuming for the moment that they came in via different cities, which we'll know soon, their objectives could be smaller. No doubt deadly, but smaller. Only in aggregate does it become bigger. But think of these as a series of forest fires. Coming from Los Angeles, I've long worried about the destruction five terrorists with a dozen flares could accomplish driving independently through the hills and Santa Monica Mountains. Tossing them out every few miles along the Angeles Crest Highway or Mulholland Drive could paralyze the city, possibly the county, or worse. In league with accomplices hitting other areas, a fifty-buck box of flares could destroy the economy of California overnight. Is it a weapon of *mass destruction*? Yes, in the long run. A box of flares. I'm just suggesting we consider the *micro* as well as *mass.*"

"Point taken," the general said, exhibiting vice presidential timber.

"Okay, taking Roarke's narrower view, what would the enemy, with such special skills, be capable of doing?" the president asked.

The Oval Office went silent. Halfway across the country a teenage boy was going to put the answer up on YouTube.

AURORA, NEBRASKA
THE SAME TIME

At seventeen, Kyle Glasgow was like so many of his peers. Smartphones came easily to him, videogames could fill endless hours, and Facebook, tweeting, texting, sexting to his girlfriend were normal ways to stay current and visible with friends. Kyle was also into posting videos on YouTube. He made silly vignettes out of knives, forks, and spoons and longer productions about the short day in the life of an ice cream cone, the boring existence of a stop sign that could never move, and the utter despair of lint. Thanks to his Twitter account, he actually developed a sizeable following. With today's video he'd positively go viral.

"Hello, I'm Kyle Glasgow. This is my bedroom and I live in Aurora, Nebraska. Did I say live? I'll come back to that because although it sounds so permanent. It isn't." He coughed. "Sorry about that. Anyway, Aurora is a good community to grow up in. It's in the heartland of America, just off Interstate 80. I always thought my biggest choices would be East or West. I'm not going to get to decide that."

Kyle stepped forward to the camera then picked it up, narrating for a while. "I'm going to just give you a tour of my home. We don't have a lot of people in Aurora. Maybe five thousand. It's going to be less soon." Another cough, this time off camera.

He walked out of his room, down the hall, pointing at pictures on the wall. "My parents. My younger sister and brother. You know, soccer pictures, birthdays; they're all on the wall. I'm sure it's the same at your place."

He zoomed outside through a living room picture window past an anyplace-USA kind of quiet street. In the distance, a tall white water tower emblazoned with AURORA painted in red and a graphic image of two trees. The camera microphone picked up some sirens wailing. "That's the outside world. Let me show you inside."

Kyle panned over to his father who is sitting on his favorite easy chair. "That's my father, Doug Glasgow. I love him. He's dead."

Kyle said it so dispassionately as to be completely shocking.

"My mom's in the bedroom. Come look. She was the best. He walked the Canon camera around the corner and stopped in the hall, zooming into his mother. "My mom's name is, or I guess was, Sheila. Mom, I love you, too. She's also dead." He coughs again. "My sis and brother aren't dead yet. But they will be soon. So will I. And you're not going to get to see this if I don't upload it soon."

He put the camera on a bureau and then walked in front of the lens. "I just want you to know, I didn't do this. I've called for help, but 911 is pretty busy right now. Can you hear the sirens?" The sound was audible in the background. "I guess we're not the only ones who got sick really fast. You want to know what I think?"

Kyle grabbed his side. "Hold on a second." He fought back stabbing stomach pain. "I better get this online now and tweet word around. Please forward it." He felt another sharp ache. "What was I saying? Oh, yeah. I think it has something to do with something we ate here. Maybe you can find out. Wanna hear something crazy? I wanted to become a movie director. Does this count? Thanks for watching."

Kyle stumbled off screen holding his stomach. The screen went black as he turned it off.

Friends got his Twitter posting a few minutes later, and the last YouTube video of "Kyle's Korner," as he called it, went online.

NEW YORK

Somebody forwarded the boy's tweet to Twardy. He began screening it.

THE WHITE HOUSE
THE SAME TIME

"What did you get out of Perez about his gang?" FBI Chief Robert Mulligan asked.

"Lots," Roarke replied. He consulted his notes. He had the names of the MS-13 gang leaders in Houston, the location of their principal residences, bio info, and details right down to the make and models of their cars. The main guy is a badass named Manuel Estavan. I'm sure you'll come up with a scary dossier on him," he said to FBI Chief Mulligan.

Taylor wrote MS-13 on the board.

"They're heavily armed and ready to kill. You'll know them by their tattoos. And if you're close enough to read them, then you're already in trouble."

"MS-13? What's it stand for?" Bernsie asked.

"It's an abbreviation for Mara Salvatrucha. Have you heard about them?" Mulligan and Evans knew about the gang, the others didn't, so Roarke explained. "*Mara* meaning gang in *Caliche,* a Salvadoran slang. It actually has an interesting root. It's taken from *marabunta* which is a local ant that's extremely fierce and able to defend the colony. Then *Salvatrucha,* a combination of Salvadoran and *trucha* or trout. In local lingo, it's slang for being alert."

"And the thirteen?" Bernsie wondered.

"Good question. *M* is the thirteenth letter of the alphabet. It's synonymous with La Eme or the Mexican Mafia. MS-13 members like to wear sports shirts, sweats, hats, all with strategic numbers—three, thirteen or twenty-three. The numbers of players like Allen Iverson or Kurt Warner."

"Jesus, how do you know this shit?"

"I came from the streets around the time that MS-13 was getting a stronghold in Los Angeles. Let's just say I got picked up by a cop at the right time and here I am, one of the good guys."

"Anything else on them?" J3 asked.

"Oh it goes on and on. They're guerilla-trained in El Salvador, Guatemala, and Honduras. They control the train routes and the roads, trafficking weapons and people through Mexico. Right to the U.S."

Jack Evans looked at Morgan Taylor. Taylor nodded. He had to make another call to the Mexican president.

"The gang has spread from Los Angeles to more than thirty states. They basically move into the Hispanic community and sink their teeth in. Eventually, they've been able to absorb other gangs, consolidate power, and move on. They have a phenomenal history. Most of it's written in the obit pages. Director Mulligan can probably tell you more."

"A good introduction, Scott. Along with customs enforcement agents, we've made wide-scale raids against known and suspected Maras. Hell, hundreds of arrests and hardly a dent."

Jack Evans jumped in. "We're watching them, too. The next natural step for the Maras, considering they're already multinational, is to tie in with al Qaeda, Hamas, or Hezbollah. Not for the sake of theology or politics. Money. Money through arms and drug sales."

"It's the fastest-growing gang in America in terms of numbers and territory," Mulligan added. "I've had to issue advisories for our agents to take extra care dealing with them. They're vicious. They don't play by any rules and they out-number us two-to-one. We've got about fifteen thousand agents against their thirty thousand. That disparity increases daily."

"And these are the guys who are doing the transporting?" the president asked before turning to Evans.

"Extrapolating from what I've learned, yes," Roarke stated.

"So what do we do?" Bernstein asked, bringing the burning issue to question. "Seems like it's an FBI action."

"Precisely. Roarke," Mulligan continued. "Do you really trust this kid up in Montana?"

"I do. But he needs our protection. With the Maras everywhere, he'll be recognized the moment he surfaces."

"He knocked on my door," General Johnson said, referring to Perez asking for asylum. "How 'bout we bring him into the service."

"He might be willing," Roarke added. "But not until we get his tattoos off. Fortunately, he's not completely covered like other gang members. After that, he could be interested. The army, with some high school education, could turn him around. In the meantime, he's willing to tell us everything. We just can't scare him."

"Then talk to him again. What's his name?" Mulligan asked.

"Ricardo Perez."

"Let Mr. Ricardo Perez know that we trust him. And to make it through this, he has to trust us."

CHAPTER 37

HELENA, MONTANA
JANUARY 14
0615 HRS

Richard C. Montclair, an extreme state's-rights advocate all of his thirty-three years in state government as a legislator and ultimately the governor, did not take kindly to the pressure from Washington. He consistently voted against or outright vetoed federal aid for purely political reasons and was damned sure he wasn't going to put on additional state police because an unwanted highly mortgaged Uncle Sam said so.

That was until he got a call on a direct line only known, he thought, by his mistress.

"Governor," the voice said in the most unpleasant tone, "this is Robert Mulligan."

"And who the hell is Robert Mulligan. You have the wrong number."

"Oh I have the right number, sir. I have a lot of right numbers. I know exactly who I'm talking to and what line I got him on. I'm the director of the FBI."

Montclair swallowed hard and swung his legs out of bed. Not his bed.

"What do you want?"

"You know exactly what, Governor. You can argue any fucking thing you want till the cows come home with the president and the party. But not with me. Not now. Not on this. For the past twelve hours we have been requesting Montana law enforcement officers on an assist. You have ignored the calls and ordered others to do the same. So now you get to hear from me on this very special telephone number of yours. The request remains the same, but with an additional message. If you do not cooperate immediately, I promise that you will become front page news for your utter and complete incompetence and disregard in a matter of national security."

"I don't take threats lightly, Mulligan."

"Neither do I."

The response made the sixty-one-year-old state leader catch his breath. Mulligan had turned the phrase and applied far more sinister meaning.

"How many men?"

"Fifty."

"I'll give you ten," Montclair offered smugly.

"Fifty men and *women* in marked and unmarked cars, on the road in sixty minutes," Mulligan shot back. "And if all you have is forty-nine, then you better get out in your Cadillac, the one parked right outside on Viscaya Drive, and do the job of the fiftieth." Then strictly for effect he added, "If yours isn't gassed up, borrow the Lexus you arranged for your real estate girlfriend to have. It's in her garage just a floor below you."

"You'll get your fifty," Montclair acknowledged.

"I'm sending special agent Shannon Davis to Helena. He will

coordinate. And you, sir, will cooperate and instruct others to do the same with each and every one of his orders. Davis will need everyone's frequencies and phone numbers the moment he touches down.

"You mean you don't have everyone's phone numbers already? Just mine?"

"Fifty cars, Montclair! And watch out. Someone may whisper the wrong thing in your wife's ear when she returns home tonight."

"I got it. But the cost."

"The cost?" Mulligan cut him off. "You have no idea," the FBI chief said. He wasn't talking money.

Montclair sent word to the Montana Highway Patrol Supervisor to get the fifty vehicles on the road, most on overtime. In turn, local police departments were also alerted. They were all e-mailed photographs and descriptions of two foreign nationals believed to be operating within Montana. The information was sent with explicit FBI orders:

> PERSONS OF INTEREST. IF LOCATED: DO NOT DETAIN OR ARREST. REPORT. USE EXTREME CAUTION NOT TO BE OBSERVED. BY ORDER OF THE FEDERAL BUREAU OF INVESTIGATIONS.

GREAT FALLS, MONTANA

"Slow down, that could be it," said SGT Mary Perkins to her rookie partner Carl Boardman.

She was a nine-year veteran with enough savvy to know that no matter who they were after, their suspicion could trigger flight and that was not what the FBI wanted.

"Easy does it." They rolled past the Quality Inn Ponderosa Motel on Central Avenue in Great Falls, Montana. She looked at the car. "Green Toyota Camry, right. License plate…slower. Bravo Sam George 498. We've got a match. Okay, forward and do a u-ey at the corner. Breakfast time. Maybe they're eating.

Boardman was excited. "Got it."

"But don't blow it. Take everything calmly."

Boardman parked the squad car and they calmly went into the Ponderosa, covering the steps with jovial conversation about nothing in particular, saying hi to the staff. It wasn't unusual for them to grab a free coffee or continental breakfast.

Perkins gave the layout an obtuse glance. Three long-haul truckers at the counter. Alone at one table a middle-aged man, likely in sales due to the spreadsheets he was laboring over. A family of five and two men who appeared to be completely out of place in the far corner. The possible subjects.

Perkins pointed to two seats against a far wall. She claimed the one that would give her a constant view of the corner table simply by looking at Boardman. But first, as the senior officer, she said,

"Make me some of those griddle pancakes," Perkins told Boardman. "And a fruit cup and java."

"Yes ma'am," Boardman obliged. Perkins picked up a newspaper left at a nearby table and pretended to read. When her partner came back with the food, she joked with him and then casually sent a text message that was sure to get relayed very quickly.

And that's when things started speeding up.

The pair looked like they didn't belong. Neither Haim nor Calib knew the first thing about espionage; not when they were spotted or if they were being tailed. They tried to blend in with jeans and parkas. It only partially worked. They did know that the less they spoke, the better off they'd be. That was about it.

The one thing they did have down was how to accomplish their mission. Considering what they were handling, one misstep would—not could—cost them their own lives instead of those others.

After ten minutes, the men rose and avoided the two Great Falls police officers on their way out.

Perkins was reading a return text at the time.

stay with them…do not apprehend unless
ordered report all movement. feds on the way.

The thirty-three-year-old police woman had a deep desire to make the arrests, but she also aspired to an FBI appointment. Besides, the younger Boardman was unproven in the field. *Play it safe,* she reasoned. *As ordered.*

After watching the subjects clear the door, she told her partner, "Let's go. When we're outside, stand on my left facing the street. Talk to me about anything. Your dick size. Who you want to fuck. I don't care. I won't be listening. I want to see where they're going."

"Okay."

Perkins nonchalantly watched the men return to a ground motel room adjacent to the lot where their car was parked. Once they were inside, she directed her partner to return with her to their squad car. Still completely normally, they pulled into traffic, and at the next intersection did another 180, drove past the Quality Inn, pulled over, and took up a position fifty yards down the street from the motel in a nonthreatening position and with a clear line of sight.

Perkins texted their status and waited.

• • •

Haim sat at a desk and traced a route on a AAA Montana state map. Next to it was a topographical map from the U.S. Geological Department. He'd circled a destination on both, identifying a location ninety miles to the south.

"Number two today," he said. "Another tomorrow, then Denver airport and home, my friend," he told the young Calib.

"Praise Allah. Allah is good," Calib chanted.

"Allah is good, and Mr. Haddad shall be great for our bank accounts," the more experienced man responded.

They laughed, packed up, and prepared to leave. There'd be no tip for the woman who cleaned the room.

• • •

Shannon Davis's government Gulfstream 450 touched down at Helena Regional Airport after a four-and-a-half-hour flight from Washington. He was completely caught up with Perkins's surveillance texts by the time the plane came to a stop. Now he needed to speak with her.

"This is Agent Davis of the FBI. Is this SGT Perkins?"

"Yes, sir."

"Sergeant, your texts were forwarded to me. What is your status?"

"We're parked down the street, diagonally across from the suspects"

"Exactly where?"

"The suspects are in The Quality Inn Ponderosa on Central Avenue in Great Falls. They've been there for," she checked her watch to be precise, "twenty-two minutes."

Davis and his men transferred to a black Lincoln Navigator that the bureau called in from a local dealership in Helena.

"Looks like we're ninety minutes from you. Straight up I-15. Unless…" Davis considered jumping back on the jet and flying to Malmstrom Air Force Base. It would cut the time by more than half. The bureau could arrange for another vehicle. "Perkins, I've got another idea, instead of driving… ."

"Wait."

"What?" Davis asked.

"They've just exited the room. They've got rolling suitcases. Putting them into the backseat. Now getting into their vehicle."

"Okay, follow them, but do not, unless under my order, take any action. Do you understand?" He felt she did. She'd done everything right so far.

"Affirmative."

"Will do."

"And call in backup with the same instructions. I want to talk to everyone in pursuit. Nothing aggressive. No cowboy stuff. You'll switch off."

"Yes, sir." *By the book,* she thought again.

Which way? Which way? Davis played with the car's GPS display. He calculated distances and driving time. If it was north, Davis and his team would hop back on the jet. If the subjects headed south, then intersecting them on the road would be faster.

"Let the pilot know we may be wheels up again," he told his associate Greg Ketz. "We'll need enough fuel for about ninety miles."

Ketz got out of the SUV, ran over to the G4, and explained the possible change of plans. He flashed a quick thumbs-up to Davis from the open door.

"Any word?" Davis asked Perkins.

"I'll know in a moment, sir. Pulling onto Central now. Going west. Stand by."

The wait, only a minute, still seemed insufferable. Davis wanted to get on the way.

"Okay, we're starting now, too. Their blinker is on. Making a right onto Park Drive North. I expect they'll make a left on the 15 spur, which is Central again. Stand by."

"Don't lose them and don't get spotted."

"Whoa, making a right onto Central. Heading east. Repeat. Heading east, not to the 15."

"East?" Davis zoomed in on the GPS. "Options, Perkins?" Things suddenly got much more urgent and out of control.

"Well, there's the 87 North and 87 East. Don't know."

"Roger. Stay on them."

Ketz returned to the Navigator. "What are we doing?"

"Staying put for another few minutes. Other airports are north and east of Great Falls?"

"I'll find out." Ketz returned to the G4.

"Talk to me, Perkins," Davis said.

"Slow going. Decision point about two minutes."

Davis stayed in the car where it was quieter and he could look at the map. Intercepting would be quicker than catching up, so he was already ruling out Malmstrom.

"Left on Fifteenth Street North," Perkins reported. "That's 87. North it is."

"Roger. Hanging up. Will call you from the plane. Checking airports now."

"Wait! What are you flying?"

"Gulfstream 450." Davis was impressed. "Why?"

"Runway requirements. There's an airport at Fort Benton. I've seen jets go in there. Not sure the runway length, but you'd get there about the same time as we would. It's about forty minutes from here. Maybe even quicker."

"Terrific. Thanks. I'll get back to you in a few." *This gal's sharp.*

The pilot told Davis the Gulfstream generally needed a 4,000-foot landing strip, though he could bring it in shorter. Fort Benton Airport had two runways. One was 1,700 feet. The other: 4,300. "We'll do just fine."

The next call was to arrange for another car. He had the bureau take care of that request. Midway into the flight he had word that a new Ford Expedition would be at the terminal, delivered by Jim Taylor Motors by the time they landed.

• • •

Thirty-three minutes to be precise, the Gulfstream touched down. The Expedition with #2 tinted windows was right in front of the terminal. A salesman held the keys. He was very willing to drive and more interested discovering who the VIPs were.

Davis took the car with a thank you and a signature on an agreement, leaving the young man wondering.

"Perkins, jogging onto State Highway 387 out of the airport. I see a right ahead on 87. Where are you?

"About four miles to the south."

"We'll take it slow. Come up on us. Then we'll get a good look at the subjects."

"Roger that."

"Hey, Perkins. Very good suggestion on the Fort Benton."

"Thank you, sir. Thank you very much." SGT Mary Perkins was very pleased.

Three miles ahead, the Toyota passed Davis's Expedition.

"Okay, I have them. Hang back."

"Then what?" *Mistake.* She wished she'd worded the question differently.

"They'll determine what we'll do. And when."

"What did they do?" she asked.

"Nothing good, SGT Perkins."

The SUV speeded up. "Call you back."

Davis kept driving. Ketz pointed a Canon SLR camera at the Toyota as they passed on the right. The subjects couldn't see them through the tinted windows. The coating made for darker images, but they'd serve the purpose. Seconds later, Ketz e-mailed the photographs to Quantico and photo recognition expert Touch Parsons.

CHAPTER 38

MONTANA RANCH COUNTRY
LATER

"Switch off," Davis said. He eased back and let an unmarked Montana Highway Patrol officer that had joined them to take point on the green Camry. "Give him a good two hundred yards. No closer."

"Yes, sir,"

It was the sixth change in an hour without incident.

"Subjects pulling up to a convenience store," the state trooper reported.

"Drive past. Don't pull over. I'll check it out." They were just south of Havre.

Davis rolled up slowly, but there was no good place to stop without drawing attention.

The Toyota was at the side of the store. He saw the two men park next to another vehicle. The trunks were open on both, and some boxes were transferred from the second vehicle to the Camry.

"Shit. Something's going on. I want an unmarked car to get me the plates on a blue Ford Focus."

A third highway patrol officer responded. "Be there in two."

The passengers returned to the Camry, drove back to 87, but in the opposite direction. South.

"We're on the move again. South. Get those state vehicles out of sight. Fast."

The tail began again retracing the route roughly eighty miles to Great Falls. They got back on Fifteenth Avenue, but instead of returning to the motel, they made a left heading west on 89. Davis widened the GPS screen again to see what might be ahead.

The road took them south of Malmstrom Air Force Base, beyond Belt and Stanford, and farther into Big Sky Country.

• • •

After a total of four hours on the road, including their stop near

Havre, they pulled into Lewistown, a town of 5,900, squarely dead center in Montana. Haim had heard the expression. It amused him.

Dead Center. They'd make certain it would become that tonight.

• • •

"Slowing down," Davis said, now in the lead. "And somebody please tell me where the hell we are?"

"Old Montana town," Perkins reported. "Haven't been here in years. Used to go fishing with my dad. Think we'll catch some big ones tonight?"

"We just may, Perkins," David responded.

He followed his subjects off Route 200, Main Street, onto Seventh Avenue. They parked in front of The Onyx Bar & Grill at the Calvert Hotel. Davis found a spot across the street.

"Why don't you stop a block back. No need for you to raise eyebrows here with your Great Falls markings."

"Good idea."

"Okay folks," Davis said on open radio frequency they were all tuned to now, "looks like we're staying put for a while. Don't know if it's for an early dinner or for the night. If they settle in, we'll take breaks in shifts, always keeping a driver in place."

Two unmarked highway patrol cars went past. Another was a block away.

"Keep warm and be ready to roll," Davis said, feeling a shiver go through his body. It was fifteen degrees outside, and it would get colder as the sun dropped behind the mountain range behind them.

The zoom lens on the Canon gave Ketz a closer view. "They're out. Suitcases staying in the car. I'd say they're in for dinner."

The comment made Davis's stomach growl. The only louder sound was his cell phone ringing.

"Hey, how's my favorite G-man doing in Montana?" Scott Roarke asked.

"Trying to stay warm. How'd you know?"

"Called Mulligan. Wanted to see if you can check out a name for me, but then I heard you picked up the ball from my last trip."

"Hard to catch without gloves, buddy. It's fucking freezing here."

"That cold?"

"That cold."

"Are you on to them."

"Like a moth to light. They're dining at some restaurant in the Calvert Hotel."

"Where's that?"

"Lewistown, Montana. Small town, mid state."

"Hold on, I'll look it up."

"You at the office?" Davis didn't need to say The White House.

"Yep. Hold on."

Davis was getting hungry. He dispatched Ketz to the McDonald's before turning onto Seventh. He heard fingers on a keyboard as Roarke did a Google search.

"Lewiston or town?"

"Lewis – L-e-w-i-s town, sounds like frown."

"K," Roarke said when he opened to a Montana map. What year is it there?"

"Asshole. It's a nice place and it's the same fucking year where you are. Tell me something I don't know."

"Gimmie a second."

"How's Katie?" Davis asked.

"We're working something out."

"Oh? What?"

"Something. Part of which I was calling you about. In person, not for the phone."

"Got it," Davis said, appropriately backing down.

"Okay, Lewis-town," Roarke said, emphasizing the *town*. "Quaint. Nice place to visit."

"Right, but I wouldn't want to…"

"No, it's a nice place to live, too. Historic. Former trading post. For some reason Croatian builders and stonemasons settled there. Lots of well-preserved buildings. Interesting, huh?"

"Oh, continue professor."

"Population 6,000. Well, to be precise, 5,901 in the last census. Median annual income for a family, $36,888. Principally agricultural community with few tourists because it's off the beaten path."

"I'll grant you that."

"Beautiful, for spacious skies. Western town, wide streets, sits within five magnificent mountain ranges, The Snowies, the Judiths, the Moccasins, the Belts, and the Highwoods."

"Thank you National Geographic Channel."

"And you gotta love this. It was the site of a gold rush in 1880, and recently the recipient of a federal grant for an important EPA cleanup and a state grant for conservation reclamation." Roarke read on. "It even has a Mickey-D's."

"I know. I just sent out for a Whopper."

"That's Burger King, idiot."

"Whatever."

"More good stuff. It'll be on the test, so pay attention," Roarke joked. "Lewistown is also known for Big Springs and Big Springs Creek which supplies Lewistown with its entire water supply…a natural resource which…"

Roarke stopped short.

"And?" Davis asked.

"What?"

An italicized subheading on the Lewistown Web site triggered his memory to a few days ago—a conversation in a diner, a warning scribbled on a mirror.

"What?" Davis pleaded.

"I know why they're in Lewistown."

"Why, for God's sake?" Davis's pulse picked up in anticipation.

"Take them down. Take them down now, Shannon."

"Huh?"

"Take them down."

"Roarke, what did you find?"

"Lewistown, Montana—Home of Big Springs and the purest drinking water in the world. They're going to poison the water!"

CHAPTER 39

"Forget the burgers." Davis radioed to Ketz.

"Here, you eat 'em," Ketz told the next person in line. He handed the bag to a grateful teenager and ran back to the Expedition. Davis was already putting on his Kevlar vest he brought from Washington.

Mary Perkins was at the SUV along with her partner, Eric Boardman, and four other highway patrol officers.

"Here's how we'll play it." He looked around and picked one of the two plainclothes officers they'd picked up en route. "What's your name?"

"Erwin."

"First name or last name?"

"Last. But it's close. Ernie."

"Geeze, your parents had no imagination?"

"Not much."

"All right Ernie Erwin. You're elected to get a drink at the bar if there is one. A soft drink. Position yourself so you can see their location and any civilians that could be in the way. I want to avoid a hostage situation at all costs. If anything…I'll say it again just because…if *anything* looks too dicey, we will wait and get them as they exit the hotel. Everyone hear this. We *must* take them alive. Alive and very well. Do you have that?"

Shannon Davis looked at each of the Montana officers. The two uniformed troopers were Iraqi War vets that were used to taking orders."

"Yes, sir," they said in unison.

"Officers Perkins and Boardman?"

"Yes, sir."

"Outstanding job today. You'll stay on the outside with Ketz, me, and…. ." He addressed the two other plainclothesmen and the uniformed highway patrol officers. "Names?"

They sounded off.

"Klugo."

"Melnick"

"Tamburro."

"Gentlemen, thank you for your assistance. "Officers Klugo and Melnick you look like you can run the hundred in ten."

They laughed.

"Each of you flank the sides twenty-five feet out. If anything happens, use that football experience and tackle the suckers."

"Yes, sir."

"Mr. Tamburro will do us all a favor and contact the locals. Let them know we're here and not to interfere. In fact, I don't want to hear a siren, see a cop car, or see the glare of a badge. Then take up position to the left of the door. Four feet."

"Now for you, SGT Perkins. Do you have any authority in this city?"

"None whatsoever."

"Then you have it from me. FBI agent in charge. You've earned your way into the dance. You're on the right side of the door, opposite Officer Tamburro. I'll be front and center. I'm good at bumping into people. When I do that, you take each of them down. If anyone runs, it's up to our tackles, Mr. Klugo and Mr. Melnick. Any questions?"

There were none.

"Good."

"Ernie Erwin. Got a cell?"

"Yes, sir."

"What is it?"

The trooper told Davis. He entered the number and called it. Erwin's number rang. "Now you have mine. Call me when you get settled. Let me know everything.

"Understood."

Davis checked his watch. "Okay, go. They should be ordering now. So this is going to take a while. Don't be impatient. But when they leave, you fall in behind them ever so carefully. Don't think cop. Think spy. Okay?"

"Okay."

Erwin left. The others took position, and Davis texted his status to FBI Chief Robert Mulligan.

Three minutes later Davis's cell phone rang. Erwin.

"Talk to me."

"A family in the booth beside them. Some toughies behind them who might not get what we're all about. Too risky, on site. Sticking to your plan. I'll call when they get the check and keep the line open until they leave. I'll fall in behind them."

"Nice work Erwin." Davis texted Mulligan again.

Twenty-eight minutes later, Davis answered the phone again. "Cash on the table. They're not sticking around. No, wait. Bathroom stop. Back left, wall side."

"Damn," Davis said to himself. He realized he should have had Erwin check exits near the bathroom. Too late now and too obvious. He crossed the street to Melnick and asked, "Any idea if there's a window out of the bathroom or a back entrance?"

"Don't know, sir. I'll find out." The senior of the two officers ran to the corner and around the block to the back of the hotel. There was a back door to the hotel. There was a back door, but not off the bathrooms. The kitchen. The bathroom window was too high to be considered an easy route.

Melnick returned and nodded no. It was all Davis needed.

"On their way," Erwin said on his open phone line.

Davis established eye contact with each of the officers. He tapped his watch and mouthed, "Now." Davis put the phone up to his ear and pretended to talk as he crossed the street, hardly paying attention.

• • •

The door to the restaurant opened. Calib and Haim were armed, but they were definitely not ready. Had they been ready they still wouldn't have had a chance to fire. As soon as they opened the door and stepped outside, the cold make them shiver. They stopped for a moment to bundle up. A man approached them chatting away in fast English. They ignored him but he stumbled and bumped into them, separating them slightly and throwing them off balance.

It was over in three seconds, without even a broken nose or a bullet wasted. Walker and Tamburro nailed them against the window to the restaurant and cuffed them in five seconds flat.

The local ranchers, the toughies that Erwin had described, watched the operation go down from inside. They were on their feet and out the door ready to come to the aid of the two men who were, from their perspective, just mugged.

"Hold it right there," Perkins called out. Her uniform gave her instant authority; her gun even more. "Federal crime scene." She actually liked the sound of that. "Turn around and back inside. Everyone else remains there, too."

"They were too shocked to move. "Is there something you don't understand, gentlemen? Back inside. Now!"

The ranchers complied without another word.

Davis was concentrating on his captives, but still caught Perkins's command of the situation. He made a mental note to talk to her later. Right now, there were other things to deal with.

"I'm an officer from the Federal Bureau of Investigations. You are under arrest for attempted murder. You have the right to remain silent. You have the right to…" Davis continued to recite the Miranda by heart as the other agents disarmed them. "Now, let's check out your car."

"We haven't done anything," Haim stated. Calib was too nervous to speak. "We are visiting."

"Looks like you made a very funny turn to end up in Lewistown." Davis found the car keys in Haim's right front pocket.

"You have no right," Haim, the chemist, said.

Calib began praying in Arabic.

"Shut up!" Haim shouted.

Perkins and Tamburro walked them to their car. Davis unlocked the trunk. "Flashlight?"

Perkins had one on her belt. "Here, sir."

Davis put on plastic gloves and took it. Next he examined the trunk, now narrating into a recorder.

"Inside the trunk of suspects' vehicle, blanket covering…cardboard boxes. Observed boxes put into the car by suspects in Havre, Montana, earlier today." He gave the date and appropriate time. "Opening the top of the boxes now." He did so, then described what he saw. "Appears to be six gallon paint cans. Three in two rows. Both boxes. No label."

"What is this?" he asked the talkative of the two.

"Don't answer!" yelled Haim.

Davis lifted one can. The label had been ripped off. He checked the others. The same.

"This can't be good."

Next Davis opened the front door of the Camry where he found two maps. An AAA road map and a state topographical map with circles around local bodies of water: Lewistown's reservoirs, which as Scott Roarke observed, contained "the purest drinking water in the world."

CHAPTER 40

WASHINGTON, D.C.
FLORIANA
1800 HRS

Many patrons described Floriana, a restaurant in the Dupont Circle section of Washington, as one of the best kept secrets in town. That was doubtful. But Roarke wanted to have a quiet conversation with Katie, and Floriana seemed perfect.

Floriana was located in an historic red brick row house, converted to a comfortable Italian restaurant with a seasonal menu and a welcoming atmosphere. The reviews called it "casual elegant." Roarke chose it tonight because the conversation was likely going to go better in the hushed tones of the romantic setting. It could very well go the other way in their apartment, and Roarke needed time for Katie to listen before she reacted. With their voices down they could blend in with the other customers and she'd be less likely to leave in mid sentence. At least that's what he hoped.

Roarke practiced the conversation on the way over from his office. He prayed he'd be able to stick to his script.

He arrived first, entered the small bar in the basement. That's where they would meet. For chemical support, something he normally didn't do, Roarke ordered a glass of Trefethen 2007, a silky Napa Valley Merlot that unleashed the taste of sweet plums and cherry. Roarke was into his second glass when Katie arrived.

"Hello, honey," she said.

"Hey, darling."

They kissed, but there was something missing from Roarke. She picked up on it. A seat was open and she took it.

"What are you having?"

"A nice Merlot."

"May I try?"

He smiled affirmatively.

Katie held the glass up to the light. The wine had a magnificent deep red color. She took in the bouquet and liked what the wine delivered. After a sip she ordered her own.

"So, how was your day?" The rules were never to say much. "Productive?"

"Busy. The trouble with charters, no frequent flier miles," Roarke joked.

"Bummer," Katie responded. "Everything else okay?

"It'll take some time to sort stuff out." This was their code for *not really.*

As an attorney she listened for clues. Suggestive. Descriptive. Revealing. It's actually what brought the bright, attractive brunette together with a man quite opposite to her in life experience and personality. But opposites surely attracted enough to turn them into a couple. Tonight, however, she felt a distance, a separation, that troubled her.

"Scott, is this about us?"

"Let's get a table."

MOSCOW
THE SAME TIME

Arkady Gomenko was playing chess over breakfast at Pushkin Café. His opponent was a disheveled Russian whose real name he never learned. The man was, in fact, not a Russian. He was CIA agent Vinnie D'Angelo. And at almost any given point he could checkmate Gomenko, who was too nervous to concentrate on the game. Not that it mattered. The match was simply a cover for a few words passed between long, thoughtful pauses. Thankfully, no one paid attention to people playing chess. It was too boring.

Considered over ninety minutes, Gomenko's comments provided D'Angelo with a clear background of Red Banner. Insightful information. History, missions, and goals. The CIA needed more.

"Dubroff? How does he figure in?"

"Still researching." Gomenko told him what he found. He also mentioned his watcher, an old man named Sergie Kleinkorn. "I swear, he must think Khrushchev is still in power the way he hovers. Like a bee over pollen."

"Did you check him out?"

"No. He feels ancient. Pre-Internet."

"Do it anyway," D'Angelo said with a warning tone. "And see if the name Ibrahim Haddad comes up at all." He spelled it.

"Any hints."

"Nope. Not a one."

They played for another thirty minutes before D'Angelo gave in, unnecessarily.

WASHINGTON, D.C.
THE SAME TIME

Roarke led Katie up a short flight of stone stairs into the main dining room at Floriana. Once settled, he ordered a bottle of an Italian Pinot Grigio; a 2009 from Lagaria, Veneto, Italy. This was one of Katie's current favorites. The smooth, fruit-forward flavor worked perfectly in concert with the toasted ciabatta and vine-ripe tomato bruschetta and the steamed mussels they shared. The conversation, however, wasn't to her taste.

"I have to talk to you. It's serious," Roarke finally said. He had a brusk unemotional businesslike tone.

"What, honey?" Katie asked reaching across the table for his hand. It was there for her, but not with the warmth she expected. Not like the other night at the Mansion on O Street.

"It's about a woman."

Katie froze. She pulled her arm back. Their relationship had developed at light speed. Katie and Roarke met under the most trying, yet exciting and sexually explosive of situations. They saved one another, and helped the country. It was dangerous and erotic. Their romance was full-barreled, like the bullets that flew around them.

"Scott." She couldn't bring herself to say another word.

They were already off his script. Roarke reached forward to touch her arm. She wasn't there for him. Katie pushed her chair back and was ready to walk out.

"Katie, wait. I started this wrong. Give me a minute. Please."

She relaxed into her chair but not into the conversation.

"I don't want to hear this."

"I'm not involved with her."

Was there a *yet* missing? Katie wondered.

"She's stalking me. I have to find out why."

Katie gave Roarke the eye contact the comment deserved. She wasn't comforted, but she was willing to listen. "I don't understand."

"Neither do I. But nothing happens in this town without a reason."

Katie didn't give in completely. "Where did you meet her?"

"The Y." Roarke intentionally left out the most provocative elements. "Not my doing, hers. She works on the Hill and has had some dubious relationships. That's what makes it so suspicious."

"And what do you want me to do? Let you go off and fuck this twit for the sake of national security?"

"Almost."

CHAPTER 41

WASHINGTON, D.C.
JANUARY 16

Roarke had complications to handle. Home and office. He texted the president, requesting an early morning meeting, which was quickly confirmed. Then he dialed a new number he committed to memory. On the third ring, Christine Slocum answered her cell.

"Hello." Her voice was soft and sexy.

Roarke was nervous. He was sitting at Filter, a coffee shop not far from his apartment.

"Hi," he said. "This is Scott Roarke, from the gym. The guy you saw a lot of the other day."

"And hoping to see more," she replied.

"There's nothing left you haven't seen."

She laughed. "I mean, we ought to get together. I hope that's why you're calling."

"Yes, but I have to admit I'm a little fragile right now."

"You, fragile? Come now, Mr. Roarke? You must be the least breakable man I've ever encountered."

"I had a fight with my girlfriend," he blurted out.

"Over?"

Roarke took a deep breath. "Over you."

"I'm flattered and sorry. We've only had a few minutes together."

"And in that last minute you left an impression on me."

She paused, and with an enticing smile added, "I guess I did. I was pretty bold. But that's what you get with me."

Roarke considered that the understatement of the conversation.

"So are you single, Scott?"

"Meaning?"

"Your breakup?" she offered with no apology.

He sighed. "Probably."

"You're not sounding so fragile now."

"Maybe not."

She thought about inviting Roarke over, but that would be too quick. Slocum loved the game. It could go on for a while longer. *At least a day.*

"Are you exercising tomorrow morning?" she asked.

"Yup."

"Let's talk then. Okay? I promise I'll stay on the girls' side after we workout."

"I'll hold you to that."

"I'm hoping you'll hold me to a great deal more," she offered seductively.

CIUDAD DEL ESTE

Ibrahim Haddad hadn't shown much happiness in the years since his wife and daughter were killed. But the reports from rural America made him smile. It was an evil smile in an evil city.

Ciudad del Este, Paraguay's second largest city and center of the Tri-border region, would be Haddad's last home. That would be fine, because as his health worsened, so did the health of the United States.

Haddad, of course, was not alone in his conspiring against the West. Ciudad del Este was a haven for Muslim extremists ever since some twenty-five thousand Arabs immigrated to the region from Lebanon after the 1948 Arab-Israeli war and again after the 1985 Lebanese civil war.

A network of thieves, smugglers, and terrorists protected Haddad. Some were members of Hezbollah, others fundamentally capitalists in Muslim garb. They trained young zealots and empowered Hispanic gang members who doled out terror on their own terms in the United States. Ibrahim Haddad had money, followers, and a cause.

Money came from traditional investments, some on the American stock exchange that were beginning to do extremely well. And there would be more. Ciudad del Este was literally sitting on a gold mine.

Just a few more days, he thought. The smile, born out of revenge, returned. Then he smiled for another reason. The assassin named Cooper was alive. The report came from his mole deep in the FBI; a mole with a serious gambling problem that Haddad learned about years ago and had the means to solve. *Cooper lives,* Haddad thought. *Perhaps I shall see him kill again.*

THE CENTERS FOR DISEASE CONTROL BUILDING 21

The first four water samples that Comley ordered up days earlier arrived by courier.

"Howard, I need your help," she said to a favorite technician.

"What's cooking, doc?" The twenty-six-year-old lab tech from Atlanta was thinking about going to med school. After five years with the CDC under Comley, he was ready to follow in her footsteps. Comley was a big fan and had already sent in a glowing recommendation for him to the University of Miami.

"Something potentially hot."

"Then let's get to work.

They donned full positive-pressure white suits, which had replaced the older glove boxes. Once zipped up, they checked each other's oxygen tanks and looked for any leaks in the fabric. All was secure. But this was just the first safeguard. Now they stepped into a BSL-4 modular lab, isolated from the rest of the floor through airlocks, showers, and autoclaves. Though they didn't breathe it, air within the chamber passed through high-efficiency particulate HEPA filters.

WHITE HOUSE
THE OVAL OFFICE

"Are you sure, Scott?" the president asked. He was seriously concerned about what Roarke proposed.

"Yes. I've got to do it this way."

"You're putting a great deal at risk. Maybe for no reason."

"I'll sure as hell find out soon."

"This is way beyond your job category," Taylor added.

"I'm not so sure," Roarke said. He told the president what he had planned. That was enough.

"Your game." Taylor accepted Roarke's request. He signaled Louise Swingle to send in General Johnson, Bob Mulligan, and John Bernstein.

The president offered everyone coffee. It was hardly anybody's first of the day.

"Bob, you start."

"Thank you, Mr. President. Last night the bureau made what we consider a significant arrest in Lewistown, Montana. Based on intelligence gathered by Mr. Roarke, we apprehended two suspects who had been driven to Montana by the MS-13 gang member currently seeking political asylum. Montana Highway Patrol also arrested two others, believed to be associates of the men in custody, outside of Havre, Montana. They're being held on one charge of murder and a charge of attempted murder, and we're waiting to see if we can charge them with conspiracy to commit murder."

"Waiting?" Bernsie asked.

"They had six cans of undetermined substances in their trunk and maps of local reservoirs, and upon further searching, detailed information on access to water district buildings. The substances will be analyzed at FBI facilities."

"When will the analysis be complete?" General Johnson asked.

"First level, within four hours. Confirmation will take longer."

"In your estimation are we looking at a real threat?"

"Very real."

Roarke interrupted. "If I may, sir?"

"Yes, Scott," Taylor answered.

"I have no doubt what they were up to. And what others are up to."

"Others?" Bernsie was the master of one word questions.

"You're all drinking coffee."

Nods.

"A few days ago I was in Mayville, North Dakota, maybe only hours behind Richard Cooper. He, of course, is the man quite intent on killing General Johnson."

"Thank you, Mr. Roarke," the general offered. "You were right. I was wrong."

"Just stay put, please."

"He will," the president stated. "Trust me. He will. But go on."

"While I was in Mayville, the price of coffee went up overnight."

"Oh, Jesus," Bernsie whispered.

Roarke ignored him. "Nobody raises the cost of coffee overnight. But if a restaurant had to, why would they?"

No response.

"The water. They switched to bottled water because there was concern that people might be getting sick from the local water. From potentially poisoned water. Not that they knew it then. But compare the Mayville samples with what's in those six cans confiscated in Montana, and I bet they're going to smell a lot alike."

Everyone was utterly silent. "And if there are six cans, there could be six hundred cans. Maybe six thousand. Yes, *others*, gentlemen."

Roarke was the first to say what was certainly becoming a collective thought.

"I believe the United States is under attack."

CHAPTER 42

JANUARY 17

The story hit the Internet while the president was meeting on the subject.

> Associated Press, Las Vegas, NV, 0555
>
> Hundreds of tourists at numerous Las Vegas hotels have contracted a serious illness. Area hospitals are treating cases of severe abdominal pain. Health officials have no official comment as to the cause, but waterborne disease is suspected.

The booker for *Coast to Coast AM* did some very fast research. Five minutes later Lois Douville was on the telephone to the CDC in Atlanta. After five redirects, she ended up with a public affairs officer.

"May I help you?" Jim Kaplan asked.

"Yes. I don't know if you've seen the news, but Las Vegas is reporting a major health emergency."

As she talked, Kaplan typed Las Vegas into Google news. There was definitely a filing dated only minutes earlier. "I have it up now. What's your question?"

"Questions. What's going on? Are you on it? What is the cause? And what are you doing about it."

"Look, Ms. Douville, I appreciate the call. I'm in public affairs. I'm not a doctor, but I'll be happy to pass the information on. Let me take your number. If we find out anything, I'm sure you'll get a call back," Kaplan lied.

"Then you can confirm that it is a crisis?"

"As I said, I can pass the information along. What's your phone number?"

Douville tried every trick she knew to get something from Kaplan. Nothing succeeded, principally because he couldn't really help her. The radio booker hung up, convinced she had the lead topic for the night's show.

Kaplan fired an e-mail over to a friend in Building 21.

THE OVAL OFFICE
MINUTES LATER

Taylor summoned Homeland Security Department secretary Norman Grigoryan. He joined the others.

"And Louise," the president said, "get the CDC director on the line."

"Yes, Mr. President."

The connection was taking longer than he expected. But there was a reason.

"Mr. President, Dr. Snowden was called down to a lab by one of his staff. His assistant has promised to get him for you as soon as possible."

"Thank you, Louise. We'll stand pat."

Five minutes later Louise had Director Snowden on the line.

"Mr. President, thank you for your patience. To tell you the truth, your timing is uncanny. I was minutes away from trying to reach you. Suffice it to say, it is an honor to talk to you, but I wish the circumstances were different."

"Thank you, Dr. Snowden. I have you on the squawk box with FBI Chief Robert Mulligan, National Security Advisor General Johnson, and Homeland Security Secretary Norman Grigoryan." He didn't mention John Burns or Scott Roarke. "Please speak openly and explain the timing."

"Well we normally operate on quick turnaround to both validate and to disprove. But there is a special urgency now. Accordingly, joining me on this call is Dr. Bonnie Comley, one of my top team members. With your permission, I would like Bonnie to take over."

"Certainly." The president wrote down the doctor's name. He referred to it now. "Dr. Comley, you have the floor."

"Thank you, Mr. President," she began nervously.

One sentence into the briefing, Taylor interrupted. "Please repeat what you've just said, doctor. Slowly. Don't be nervous. It's important we get this."

"Yes sir, sorry. I believe we are facing a problem of epic proportions. We're charting catastrophic illnesses across the country."

Phrases like *epic proportions* and *catastrophic illnesses* were guaranteed to get Oval Office attention.

"Dr. Comley, am I correct to understand that you are point on this research?"

"Well, I suppose so, but not by appointment. More through circumstances."

"Then it is either your good fortune or bad luck. Now you said illnesses. Plural?"

"Yes. Different symptoms, potentially different causes, but all occurring in a short span of time."

"Dr. Comley, this is Homeland Security secretary Grigoryan. Do you have a theory as to the cause?"

"I personally do, but it is unsupported."

"Unsupported or not, what is it?"

"I believe water supplies are being intentionally poisoned."

The president looked at Scott Roarke. His man was right again.

"Dr. Snowden, Dr. Comley, put your top researchers and staff on this immediately and get your butts up here. We're going to do this in person."

"Mr. President," Comley nervously interjected. "I'm running some critical tests that I'd prefer not to turn over. Not just yet. And more samples will be in this afternoon. I'll have much more to report by tomorrow. Will that be okay?"

"Mid-morning Dr. Comley. No later." It was not a request. "If you have any difficulty booking seats, call my secretary, Louise. She lives for solving problems like that."

"Thank you."

"Noon. My office. I'll have coffee on." The president picked up his own cup now and examined the brew. "I have the distinct feeling that time is not on our side."

RUSSIA
CULT BAR

Arkady Gomenko was sitting with his new best friend. Together they replayed the World Cup heroics and disappointments, the years when steroids ruled the Olympics, and other chatty topics that only required liquor and opinions and no action.

Anyone watching would have seen two men getting drunker by the pour. Anyone listening would have gotten bored at least an hour earlier.

The signal finally came when Vinnie D'Angelo folded his napkin twice. Gomenko moved closer and whispered to his companion. He said it in the softest tones possible. D'Angelo heard it as if it had been shouted.

"Dubroff is alive."

Despite the impact of the news, the CIA agent did not react. He looked in the mirror to see if anyone took notice. No one had. *Dubroff alive?* D'Angelo had to get to him. He put his hand on Gomenko's shoulder and pulled him forward the way one drunk might do to another. But D'Angelo was stone cold sober. "Where is he?"

Gomenko fought off the effects of the vodka he had been consuming. "In a secure ward at Burdenko General Military Clinical Hospital."

D'Angelo was familiar with the facility. In the old Soviet days some certain people were admitted healthy, but came out in a body bag. Dubroff was even suspected of *doctoring* the reports. Now he was there himself.

"Get me inside."

THE SAME TIME

It was amazingly easy for Haddad's men to roam the floors of America's hospitals. Doctors and nurses from every corner of the world now treated patients who had trouble pronouncing their names. The service staff was increasingly Hispanic; engineers and plumbers largely Eastern European. So why would two more immigrants in drab grey uniforms and well-worn tool belts raise an eyebrow? Ibrahim Haddad believed they'd be virtually invisible.

A little diversion, one quick jab of a syringe through a plastic water cooler, followed by a fast push of the plunger and it was over. The terrorists came with vials of *Chlamydia psittaci*, *Coxiella burnetii*, and *Shigella*, all fiendish once they dissolved into the previously untainted water. Incredibly simple. A few minutes per floor was all it took, and amidst the typical commotion, no one paid any attention.

The targets were patients in their beds and visiting friends and family. These *plumbers,* and others like them, moved from hospital to hospital, city to city, with a variety of deadly toxins in their arsenal. There was an expression in English that Haddad's men probably never heard, but it described their work today perfectly.

Like shooting fish in a barrel.

DENVER, COLORADO
FBI REGIONAL HEADQUARTERS

"So far one of them is talking," Shannon Davis told Robert Mulligan, from just outside an interrogation room. "If what he says is true, and I have no reason to believe it's not, we're well beyond containment."

CHAPTER 43

FBI LAB
JANUARY 18
0300 HRS

Due to the level of importance, the FBI lab put out a no-frills preliminary report; fast and to the point. Mulligan received an annoying, sleep-interrupting alert on his cell phone and a one word text.

INCOMING

It was his preprogrammed indicator that a sensitive transmission was coming through on his secure desk computer, which he could also access at home. The FBI director shook off the sleep and rose without disturbing his wife. He threw on a bathrobe and lumbered into his home office.

Minutes later, Mulligan went online. He keyed in his password and opened his office e-mail.

Words began standing out, surrounded by qualifiers.

"Substance...cancer causing...death in higher doses...toxic analysis benzine."

"Oh my God!" Mulligan certainly wasn't a chemist, but he knew that, along with anthrax, benzine was bad business.

He dialed the White House switchboard, which never slept, and asked to be connected with the president. It was one of those 3 a.m. calls.

THE WHITE HOUSE
MINUTES LATER

Secretary of the Department of Homeland Security, Norman Grigoryan, could not mistake the president's intent on the phone call that in turn woke him up.

"Norman, I need a full analysis on the nation's water supplies and our vulnerability. In particular, measure and rate the terrorism threat on wells and rural water supplies. If you don't have a study on the computer ready to spit out, make one ready. I need it in four hours."

Grigoryan checked his bedside clock. 4:20 a.m. The overnight desk would get the next call.

"We actually started that yesterday, Mr. President," he said without equivocation. "When do you want it?"

"I can have it for you by nine."

YMCA
0815 HRS

Scott Roarke's drill consisted of a mix of two hundred sit-ups, one hundred marine push-ups, ten minutes on the punching bag, free weights, stretches that would make others scream with pain, and, if he had the energy, five miles on the treadmill, alternating between marathon pace and a fast walk. This menu of hardcore physical fitness kept him fit and focused. It kept him alert and alive. It also allowed him his most private time, which today was spent thinking about where, with all this motion, his life was going.

It looked like that decision was made for him when Katie Kessler stormed into the YMCA gym and dumped a full duffle bag right beside him. "Here. It's everything," she coldly said without concern over his reaction or that of anyone else at the Y. Katie's voice shook. "Have a nice life." She turned to leave.

"Katie!" Roarke looked around. They were drawing everyone's attention. "Let's take this outside."

"No." She breathed in deeply. "No," she added for emphasis. "Your clothes are all there. A couple of pictures. Thank God I didn't invest more time in you." She took two steps toward the door.

Roarke looked stunned. "Please!"

She stopped, but didn't face him. "What?"

"Not like this. Give me a few minutes. We'll talk outside." He grabbed his towel and stood up.

"I heard everything you said. No more."

All of this was with her back facing him. As she spoke, she took in the whole gym and all the people now watching. "Good-bye, Scott. I've got work to do."

Katie Kessler left and didn't look back.

Roarke's powerful body seemed to shrink under Katie's guerilla assault. He was speechless; defeated. That's when Christine Slocum moved in.

Roarke watched Katie's last step out. If he felt Christine's hand on his shoulder he didn't show it.

"I'm sorry," she said.

Roarke nodded slightly.

"Look, if she won't talk, I will. Let's go for some coffee."

He turned to look at her. Roarke was suddenly aware that Christine had incredibly beautiful blue eyes.

"My treat," she added with a smile. "Go in and shower. I'll leave you alone this time. Let's meet in fifteen. I can get to work late today."

Roarke considered her offer then added, "Okay. In thirty."

THE WHITE HOUSE
0830 HRS

Grigoryan, the son of a Russian immigrant physicist, had been chief of police in Boston. He took three things most seriously: law enforcement, threats to America, and the will of the president; especially this president. He was actually at the Oval Office by 8:30 a.m. with a thirty-seven-page report he and his staff prepared. Morgan Taylor was prepared to see him early. Grigoryan gave him the study.

"Thank you, Norman," the president said. "Appreciate the head start before the CDC folks arrive. Louise says their plane landed at 8:17. If they're here earlier, we'll bring them right in. Now, take me through this."

The gray-haired department head started slowly. "Before I get to the heart of the matter, Mr. President, will you allow me to provide some overall perspective?" Grigoryan was aware that Taylor was a cut-to-the-chase leader, but he also encouraged members of his administration to frame their pictures before they hung them.

"Absolutely, go."

"Perspective it is," he said, without working from notes. The proposal remained on his lap not to be reviewed yet. "The Mississippi. One helluva big river. On average, at any moment 2,100 billion liters of water flows across its bottom. That's more than 5.5 billion in gallons. Immense volume, right?"

"Without a doubt," Morgan Taylor replied.

"But at any given moment, that 2,100 billion liters represents only one percent of the water in the Mississippi system."

"Now you have me confused."

"One percent in the river that we see. Ninety-nine percent beneath, within the rock, sand, and sandstone. The aquifer, Mr. President. The water underneath."

"Mary, mother of God, I had no idea."

"You're not alone," Grigoryan noted. "Moreover, ninety-seven percent of the Earth's fresh water is in the aquifers. The supplies we now tap took thousands of years to accumulate, typically less than an inch a year. Now, because of our use of water, the aquifers are being depleted at a rate that surpasses replenishment.

"Add to that, in the last century, as the world's population has nearly quadrupled, we've seen rivers become more and more polluted by cities and toxic runoff. The soup, for lack of a better term, is absorbed in the sediment and ultimately feeds back into the aquifers. The waters are becoming increasingly polluted below ground. So depletion and pollution are up against world need. And selfishly, America's need.

"Before we even consider the issue of terrorism, understand that ninety-five percent of the rural population of the United States relies on groundwater for drinking. Truth be told, water is our most critical resource; our most valuable natural resource in the world. Americans use about a hundred gallons of water at home each day. If our water resources are threatened, we'll have to look elsewhere."

"Look?" Morgan Taylor asked.

"Look and take."

"Like oil."

"Yes sir, like oil."

Grigoryan paused to allow his boss to consider what he just heard.

The meaning of Grigoryan's preamble wasn't obscured by his slight accent. While it may have made President Taylor listen harder, it also made him listen more intently.

Taylor reached for a glass of water on his desk. He held it then examined it as if it were a fine glass of wine.

"It was only when I was shot down and roaming the desert in Iraq that I realized how much I'd taken water for granted," Taylor said. "For a time, I thought there would be nothing more magnificent." He took a sip and contemplated its powers. "I would have died without it."

Grigoryan did not fill in the silence. Protocol. He waited for the president's cue. He didn't have to wait long.

"Well, Norman, I feel you're just revving up."

"Yes, Mr. President. In so many words you asked me to assess our vulnerability to attack. The truth is the United States has been of two minds on the subject of water and terrorism. Social and political. Like so many debates, it comes down to considering regulations to protect environmental health against the need for establishing homeland security measures. We don't have to dig any further for the answer than a well."

"A well?"

"Plain and simple, a well. A single well or thousands of them. EPA calls for transparency in the locations of the nation's wells. At Homeland, we want to keep well locations off the books."

"And who's winning?" Taylor asked.

"It varies from state to state, but if you're asking me can even an unsophisticated terrorist easily find the location of a water well and poison it? The answer is yes."

"What's our greatest vulnerability statewise?"

"Again, it's completely without uniformity. Texas, Illinois, and many others disclose locations of wells. California, for example, does not. I have a list. All a willing terrorist needs to do is go to gov.org and look right on our own government mapping systems."

"Even after 9/11?" Taylor was incredulous. Grigoryan was right. *So simple.*

"Hate to say it, water was not a top focus largely because the regulations were really governed state-by-state. As a result, our water supplies are extremely vulnerable."

"More than vulnerable."

"Yes," Grigoryan agreed. "Contamination of water wells is an absolute risk. More for private wells which have shallower well seals and are more exposed to groundwater contamination. Generally speaking, metropolitan areas are more challenging a target for terrorists because of their volume and communities' reliance on wells with deeper seals. But independent academic and even Pentagon studies have shown it's not the poisoning alone that can lead to catastrophic results.

"What then?"

"Surely, we project tremendous casualties from such attacks. Tens of thousands of deaths. But nonstop press coverage in a zero-turn-around-time news cycle will lead to a breakdown in civil order on a scale too horrible to contemplate."

All of this, Taylor realized, without a sworn-in vice president. Confirmation coming at Washington partisan speed would not be fast enough.

Before the meeting with Grigoryan was over, Taylor hit his intercom to Louise Swingle. "Get me the Senate leadership in here today. Tell them it's urgent."

FILTER CAFÉ
THE SAME TIME

Christine Slocum's objective was Roarke. She hadn't been told why by her benefactor; a man she'd never met. But he had made so many things happen for her. College, arrangements, and introductions that opened doors to executive offices and important bedrooms. Senator Teddy Lodge was one. Speaker of the House, Duke Patrick, another. And now, Scott Roarke. The possibility of sleeping with him pleased her greatly. It might take a few days, given his state of mind, however she'd get there. *Three dates,* she thought. *Maybe two.*

"I'm really sorry about this morning," she said over a latte.

"It's not your fault," Roarke said. He played with his coffee, but decided not to drink it.

"Are you sure. I mean, I came on to you pretty strongly. Did you say anything to your girlfriend?"

Roarke took his time answering. "I talked around it."

"Women have a certain radar. I'd say hers was up."

"I guess."

Christine extended her hand across the table, much as Katie had a few days earlier. "I really am sorry. That's the truth." It wasn't. "But I do want to see you."

Roarke laughed. "I think you already have."

She liked that he lightened up and she went with it. "There's still a good deal left to the imagination," she cooed. "Dinner, Mr. Roarke?"

"If you take it slowly."

"I promise." Christine's legs were crossed.

THE OVAL OFFICE
0915 HRS

"Barbara, Gentlemen," the president said, addressing Senator Majority Leader Barb Rutberg, Democrat from Massachusetts, and Senate Minority Leader, Dick Webb, a staunch South Dakota Republican. Also present, Senate Pro Tem Joel Solomon of Maryland. "What's the hold up on the general's nomination?"

The hold up was plain and simple. Political stalling. General Jonas Jackson Johnson would clearly get confirmed, but the Democratically controlled Senate was doing what any opposition party did. Delay.

Webb pointed a thumb at Rutberg.

"Wait a second," she said angrily. "We've got questions about an active military officer serving as vice president."

"Active until he raises his right hand swearing allegiance all over again, Barbara," Webb stated. "Same flag, some country."

"Don't get smart with me, Dick," Rutberg replied. "You've sat on court nominations for months for no reason while you hoped for regime change here."

"So now an election in this country is viewed as a regime change?" Taylor shot back.

"I'm sorry," Rutberg replied. "A misstatement."

"Why don't you limit that kind of talk to cable news. You're in the Oval Office now."

The senator bowed her head indicting she would take more care.

"Joel," the president continued, "your assessment?"

Solomon was a thoughtful, politically astute deal maker and a veteran with far more experience in Washington's machinations than even Taylor.

"General Johnson will have the necessary votes; a clear majority with support from both sides of the aisle, as soon as Barbara is willing to wrap up the hearings."

"Barbara?" the president asked.

"We still have some witnesses to call. A few weeks. Perhaps a month to clear the decks."

Morgan Taylor rose from his captain's chair and pulled his jacket straight. He walked to his desk, once used by Abraham Lincoln, and sat on the edge. "Barbara, you don't have a few weeks."

"With all due respect, Mr. President," Rutberg interrupted.

Taylor held up his hand.

"You don't have a few weeks because *we* don't have a few weeks. In fact, we don't have a few days."

"What?" the three senators either said or expressed nonverbally.

"I am waiting for verifiable confirmation. It should come into this office at noon today. But it is the administration's belief that the United States is currently under attack."

The reactions took the form of guttural sounds.

"At this moment I cannot disclose the details. Not even confidentially. But terrorists are targeting vital American resources."

"Oil?" Rutberg blurted out. "Where?"

"I cannot get more specific now except to say it is within our borders. I will inform you before addressing the country at large, which may be as early as tonight. For now, I absolutely insist that you do not leak the substance or nature of this conversation. You will not want to stake your political careers getting out in front of this. It is vitally important to our investigation. Is that clear?"

Looking around the room from Webb to Solomon to Rutberg, the president read acceptance.

Barely above a whisper, Solomon asked, "How serious?"

"Very. And Joel, we'll leave it at that. Now, I need a vice president. The nation needs a vice president. If I speak to the nation tonight, I want the vote tomorrow," Morgan Taylor stated without any chance for misinterpretation. "Tomorrow."

Taylor rounded his desk, sat, and busied himself with reviewing a file labeled in bold print with only a number designation.

The members of the Senate leadership got up and left without another word.

THE WHITE HOUSE

"Next," Taylor said.

John Bernstein had the list. "Hernandez."

"Okay, get him."

Five minutes later Mexico's president was on the line.

"President Hernandez..." Taylor's voice was rock steady. "I hope you've seriously considered my proposal."

"Your ultimatum," the president of Mexico replied.

"Your words," Taylor replied.

"Your intent, Mr. President."

"Call it anything you want. What is your answer? There is a situation developing that I *will* take care of with or without your approval."

This was Morgan Taylor at his best: the commander in chief, the president in charge. Most people never saw this side. Those who did grasped clear distinctions between Taylor and other presidents in recent history, Republican or Democrat. He was president of the United States, not the president of any one political party.

"You've seen how this government has been prepared to strike; quickly and strategically," Taylor continued. "In previous administrations and my own. In Indonesia under my watch."

"My intelligence department says you have crossed into my country."

It was true, but Morgan Taylor only confirmed it through silence.

"We have global enemies, Oscar. Global. Yet we view each another as neighbors and friends. Your decision to help the security of the United States should represent the best interests of both our nations."

Taylor hoped that Hernandez would hear the determination in his voice, for there would be no brokering today.

"In the interest of our long-standing relationship," the Mexican president slowly said, "I grant you permission for unimpeded flyovers."

"Mr. President, that is not good enough."

"And permission to identify strategic targets. But," using Taylor's own words now, "*in the best interests of both our nations*, the armed forces of the sovereign Republic of Mexico will prosecute the targets."

This was not the mission Morgan Taylor had set forth. General Johnson, listening on the open line, pursed his lips and mouthed a nonverbal, *No!*

Taylor took a deep breath and organized his thought. He couldn't say too much, but he had to lay the foundation.

"Mr. President, we are investigating a serious infiltration of foreign nationals with terrorist objectives. I can say no more except that these individuals are finding support and comfort by groups who operate with impunity in your country. Should the security and safety of the United States of America be compromised, I assure you that we *will* act to protect our citizenry. I give you fair warning now, Mr. President. I am deadly serious. If you hear the news about a terrorist attack of any nature on our people, consider it too late for another conversation. As of this moment, you are forewarned. I hope I've made myself clear."

Taylor heard some muted arguing on the other end of the phone. *An argument between Hernandez and his chief of staff, Elder Cabrera?* he assumed. Then, after nearly a half minute, "Mr. President, we will discuss this further."

"You may discuss it all you want, Mr. President. But if you hear it on the news, you've discussed it too long. Good-bye."

Morgan Taylor disconnected.

"Next?"

CHAPTER 44

THE OVAL OFFICE
1200 HRS

The president greeted Dr. Comley and her boss, CDC Director Glen Snowden. They did what everyone always does when they entered the Oval Office. They stopped and stared while history overtook their emotions. Here was where the world's most momentous decisions were made; where the country's history was charted; where slavery was debated and erased; where the development of the atomic bomb was approved; where a missile crisis was averted; where incriminating tapes were recorded; where orders to neutralize terrorists were signed. This was the home of every United States president since 1800 when John Adams and his wife Abigail moved in. Within its walls, leaders aged faster than their years and learned more than their memoirs would ever report. Here was more than two centuries of history itself in the fifty-five thousand square feet known to the public.

"Come in, come in," Morgan Taylor urged, recognizing the difficulty Comley and Snowden were both having.

"Yes, thank you, Mr. President," the director said. Protocol required that he speak first. "It is our honor."

"I'm afraid it'll be your job and not so much an honor based on what you'll present to us today, Dr. Snowden."

"We're here to figure that out, Mr. President. Let me introduce Dr. Bonnie Comley."

The CDC investigator stepped forward. She had a briefcase in one hand and large charts in another. She fumbled trying to get her right arm free to shake Morgan Taylor's hand.

"Let me help you," the president said.

"Thank you, sir," she said, obviously nervous.

Taylor took the charts and handed them to John Bernstein, who, along with General Johnson, Directors Evans and Mulligan, Homeland Security Secretary Grigoryan, Attorney General Eve Goldman, and Scott Roarke had been invisible to the awestruck visitors until now.

"Please set up whatever you need and have a seat. We have sandwiches and drinks on the table behind the couch. Don't stand on ceremony; you can get them at any point. In the interest of time, I'll start with introductions." Taylor went around the room and ended on Scott Roarke, who he simply identified as one of his Secret Service handlers.

Comley needed a few minutes to organize her notes and put the charts in order on an easel the White House staff provided. When finished, she stood next to the stand and everyone quieted down. She didn't begin until the president was seated directly opposite her in a famous wooden captain's chair. Like everything else in the Oval Office, it had its history. Taylor set the stage for the meeting by telling the story of its origin.

"This chair belonged to Admiral Isaac Hull, commander of the famed American frigate, the *USS Constitution*, 'Old Ironsides.' It's right off the ship, though the *Constitution* is still officially in service."

"In Boston?" Comley seemed to remember.

"Actually, Charlestown Navy Yard, just north of downtown Boston."

The president liked the fact that she was engaged in his story. He would certainly be engaged in hers.

"It has a celebrated, illustrative history, which came down to a blustery August 19, 1812, when Hull sighted the Royal Navy warship *Guerriere*. The British captain, well-experienced in broadside combat, fired first. He scored hits, but there was little damage. The *Constitution* delivered a quarter hour of intense firing in return. Eventually, the ships became entangled. Both sides readied boarding parties. However, America's marksmen persevered, wounding the *Guerriere* captain. As the ships separated, the British frigate's foremast collapsed, bringing the main mast down with it. It was over by early evening. The *USS Constitution* defeated the *Guerriere,* inspiring the Navy to greatness and heralding the beginning of America's dominance of the world's seas. Which, of course, we have never given up."

"And so, Captain Hull's chair is a reminder to me of *my* responsibility to defend and protect our shores," Morgan Taylor noted.

In her work, Comley also lived on the edge of the deadly war threats. The significance of Hull's achievement and the president's retelling of the account was not lost on her.

"Now to the reason we're all here. Homeland Security Secretary

Grigoryan presented a critical political analysis to us. Now we're ready for the health risk assessment. Let's have it, Dr. Comley. Straight and to the point."

Comley cleared her throat. She looked at everyone before beginning. She studied them individually. These key decision makers had to follow her in a methodical manner, but she couldn't bore them with too much scientific explanation. She chose to wear a simple black two-piece suit, with a navy blue blouse and a red scarf. Comley had practiced in front of her mirror before going to bed. She knew what to emphasize, the correct pace to take, and the points to underscore. She decided on low-tech poster boards rather than a PowerPoint presentation and handouts. Close up and focused because she had to report the worst.

"Mr. President, with your permission, we can live only minutes without air. Of course, under dire circumstances, we can hold out for thirty-six, forty-eight, or more hours without drinking, and in some cases weeks without food. But none of us deliberately goes without water. Not for even a day. It's part of our everyday life. As Americans, we take for granted our access to clean, potable water. Why? Because U.S. water systems deliver some of the safest water in the world. We've long trusted that we're free from deadly waterborne epidemics of the past.

"However, as Dr. Brad Roberts, from the Institute for Defense Analysis once warned, 'What we think we know can be misleading. Dangerously so.'"

Comley had turned the corner on her introduction. So far no interruptions. She had the complete attention of all the president's men and the lone woman, Attorney General Goldman.

"I would leave it to General Johnson's good offices to support the contention that it's unlikely that the United States can be seriously challenged by *conventional* military means in the sense of a traditional wartime attack."

She didn't expect an acknowledgement and didn't get one. The Cold War was over and no matter what breast-beating politicos argued to ramp up patriotic fervor, America was probably more vulnerable to strategic terrorist attacks than Russian missiles.

Now her inflection changed. She added more timber. "Why?

Because this sense of U.S. superiority can actually leave us blind to potential asymmetric attacks against weaknesses in our infrastructure."

"Make that *has* left us blind, doctor," the president noted.

"Has," she said. "The vulnerabilities were pointed out in a 1999 air force analysis titled *A Chemical and Biological Warfare Threat.* They include telecommunications, energy, banking and finance, transportation systems, emergency services, and," she paused again for impact, "water."

This was her second dramatic characterization of the importance of water. She was a long way from finishing.

"But we can go back to 1941 when FBI Director J. Edgar Hoover issued a warning." She read from a file card. "'It has long been recognized that among public utilities, water supply facilities offer a particular vulnerable point of attack to the foreign agent, due to the strategic position they occupy in keeping the wheels of industry turning and in preserving the health and morale of the American populace.'"

She looked at Morgan Taylor squarely in the eyes.

"Nineteen forty-one, Mr. President. "We've been living on borrowed time."

But Comley didn't stop there.

"Getting back to more recent history, President Clinton called for an assessment in *A National Security Strategy for a New Century.* How vulnerable were we in 1999 and now? Depending upon the actual objectives, an enemy could attack water in two ways. Physical or cyber attack on controls, including the destruction of dams, pumping stations, or distribution lines, could deny us water and degrade emergency services. On the other hand, to kill Americans, terrorists could deliberately contaminate our water with CW/BW."

She intentionally employed the stark abbreviation knowing the power it would have on everyone in the room. "CW/BW, Mr. President, Chemical Warfare and Biological Warfare."

Comley now turned the first board over on the easel. It read Vulnerability.

"Now I'm going to go through some history. Quickly, but it's highly relevant considering where we are today. First a quote that bears telling. '*…and he that will not apply new remedies must expect new evils; for time is the greatest innovator.*' The author, Sir Francis

Bacon, in 1601. And Mr. President, I can honestly say, we are facing new evils.

"The record shows that for thousands of years, city states, nations, and both advancing and retreating armies have deliberately contaminated water supplies as a means of achieving victory or revenge. Attacks have been crude and as simple as dumping human and animal cadavers into wells and watering holes to well-planned contamination by cholera and anthrax.

"In ancient Rome, Emperor Nero dispatched his enemies with cherry laurel water. If it sounds inviting, you're wrong. Cyanide is the chief toxic ingredient. In the Civil War, Confederate soldiers shot farm animals and left them rotting in ponds, compromising the water for General Sherman's soldiers on the march. During World War II, the Japanese laced water in China with anthrax, cholera, and other bacteria. The Nazis released sewage into a Bohemia reservoir to sicken residents. It goes on and on. Through Kosovo in 1998, Afghanistan more recently.

"Under President Clinton's authority, The President's Critical Infrastructure Assurance Office, the CIAO stated, 'The water supplied to U.S. communities is potentially vulnerable to terrorist attacks by insertion of biological agents, chemical agents, or toxins. The possibility of attack is of considerable concern…these agents could be a threat if they were inserted at critical points in the system.'"

Comley changed the poster board. Threat Analysis. She still had everyone's attention and no interruptions.

"Foreign nations have developed programs and arsenals with substantial chemical and biological weapons. Our evaluation of our own vulnerability has revealed that local, state, and federal infrastructure is already strained as a result of dealing with other important health problems, so little effort was placed on detecting and managing threats to public health through what was the *probable*, now the *actual*, use of these agents as weapons.

"In an unpublished, 2000 CDC Strategic Planning Workgroup titled *Preparedness and Response to Biological and Chemical Terrorism: A Strategic Plan*, steps were outlined for strengthening public health and health care capacity to protect the country against such dangers. It called for the CDC to join with law enforcement, defense, and intelligence agencies to address a national security threat. Participating with the CDC in this effort was ATSDR, The Agency for Toxic Substances and Disease Registry. It was determined that a) recipes for preparing homemade agents are absolutely available; and b) use of these agents will require rapid mobilization of public health workers, emergency responders, and private health care providers.

"The United States Air Force, in its own studies, focused on potential threats. The term they used —*Centers of Gravity*. Drinking water being one such COG. Injecting deadly chemicals or insidious infective agents into air base water supplies could functionally disrupt or destroy operations. In fact, in late September, 1990, during Operation Desert Shield, a mission was scrubbed, and base combat effectiveness was reduced to fifty percent for a week because aircrews were sick in bed, the result of*unintentional* water poisoning."

She flipped the poster board again. Weaponized Water.

"How can it be accomplished here? How is it being accomplished? In our estimation, not by poisoning lakes, rivers, and aquifers. The amount of toxins required would be too risky for terrorists to transport. Eighteen-wheelers, train cars—too visible, too likely to be inspected. Moreover, biological agents dumped into a city's water source would become highly diluted by the time they reached a treatment plant. But contaminants in smaller doses are easy to transport, and at specific critical points in the supply system, easy to insert.

"Here's what compounds the problem. We don't have a system to rapidly access whether an attack has occurred. We're quite reactive rather than proactive."

"Why?' Attorney General Goldman asked quite sincerely.

"Simply put," Comley explained, "water supplies are really only monitored for a limited number of contaminants, and even those results can take hours or days. Also, local monitoring is fairly concentrated on screening for microbial contamination from human waste. Not the presence of bio and chem weapons. Mostly sewage."

"Shit," Bernsie whispered. It was not meant as a joke.

"To put it another way," Comely continued, "we are not prepared to defend or test our water resources from an attack. And that brings me to a report from *The Journal of the American Medical Association.* The AMA reviewed the likely ways lethal or near-lethal agents could be used in a biological attack. Some can survive better in water than others. It depends upon how much water and whether the toxins have to pass through sophisticated filtration systems."

The CDC doctor scanned her notes. She hadn't missed a thing.

"So, where would a terrorist lace water with positive results? In rural wells, in critical *downstream*points of the delivery system, in unpressurized, typically passively defended water bladders, in water towers, through valves at control points where maintenance and supervision is lax, in building holding tanks, and in common public, office, and home water coolers.

"Through these delivery routes, CW/BW toxins can have deadly impact. A saboteur with four- and-a-quarter hundred-pound bags of sodium cyanide, with access to clear wells or water storage bladders, could create a deadly blend that could kill or incapacitate a small town right through their faucets. Just .21 kilograms, or less than a half a pound of botulism toxin in a two hundred thousand-gallon supply would do just as well. For less than ten thousand dollars, anyone with something as simple as a home brewing kit, protein cultures, and personal protection gear can cultivate trillions of bacteria, effective threats to drinking water. It's incredibly easy. If a treatment plant isn't manned twenty-four hours, and not remotely monitored, then a terrorist could shut off the online chlorinator and dump in any number of nasty toxins. Within hours of consumption, well, let's just say this doesn't end well."

Dr. Comley flipped the board again. Response Time.

"The covert dissemination of toxins may not be noticed on a wide scale for a variety of reasons. Local doctors may not be experienced in sophisticated diagnoses. They may not have been trained to report CW/BW cases. As a result, regional or national CDC investigators could remain unaware of the threats for days or longer. This is what has just occurred. Patients have been infected in rural areas and small towns with little notice. But over the last week, news began to spread through late night talk radio, blogs, and social media. It is surely to be followed when reports from Las Vegas hit the wire services, television, and the Internet. Inevitably, we face the possibility of widespread panic.

"Before I take questions, I'd like to refer to America's Safe Drinking

Water Act which identifies contaminants that have posed risks to public water systems. It categorizes levels of toxins and deployment by their danger to humans. In its *Susceptibility Analysis,* critical factors include potential poisons, proximity of the contaminants to water sources, geological considerations, and the likelihood of actual release and dissemination.

"Contaminants that *could* be released are given a factor of x1, or as I like to say, *Times 1.* Those*close to release*, with still indeterminable impact are rated x2; *Times 2.* And contaminants that pose a real and present, quantifiable health hazard on a grand scale are given the factor of x3. As a physician, a research scientist, and a mother, I never wanted to see America at *Times 3.* But I'm here to tell you, without any equivocation, we are."

CHAPTER 45

Morgan Taylor held Scott Roarke back as the session ended. "Scott, one quick thing."

"Sure, boss."

Taylor thanked everyone and asked them to wait in the cabinet room, get caught up with phone calls, and be ready for further briefings. When the Oval Office was clear, the president put his hand on Roarke's arm; a sign of endearment and trust.

"We're going to move at light speed. I need three of you. Unfortunately, there's only one."

Roarke laughed.

"So expect calls 24/7, meetings at any time, and be ready to move on a dime."

"Always packed." He didn't need to add *armed.*

"Starting in fifty in the Situation Room. You earned a seat at the briefing. But no sitting. Stand in the back. Wear your damned lapel pin for a change and read the faces. They're going to be shocked and I want to know who can really handle this crisis with me."

Roarke didn't do it often, but this time the request called for a formal, command reaction. "Yes sir."

"Thank you, now take a hike. I've got to give Patrick and a few other members of Congress a preview so they don't shit a brick."

Congressman Duke Patrick's name reminded Roarke about his dinner with Christine. It was getting complicated already.

CONGRESSMAN DUKE PATRICK'S OFFICE

The congressman's secretary buzzed Patrick. "Mr. Speaker, the president is on the line."

Patrick and Slocum were reviewing talking points for an MSNBC interview. He stumbled the last time on the air. Now with Slocum's coaching, he would be better.

"What the hell does he want? Kelly, find out if it can wait."

The secretary was back on the phone within ten seconds. "No, it has to be now."

You should take it, Congressman," Christine recommended.

He reluctantly agreed. "Put him through." Patrick pressed the speaker button.

"Mr. President, nice to hear from you."

"Are we on a squawk box, Duke?"

"Yes, but I'm alone. What can I do for you?"

"Pick up please."

Patrick mouthed *asshole* to Slocum, but obliged the president. He held the phone out so his speechwriter could also hear. "Okay. Better?"

"Yes. I'm calling you and other party leaders with advance word that I will be addressing the nation at 8 p.m. eastern on a most serious subject. I'm afraid that under the circumstances I can't say anything more at this time…"

Patrick shot Christine a quizzical look. With her pen and paper already handy, she scribbled "specifics" and underlined it twice.

"…because of the severity of the crisis and the danger it poses to the nation…"

"Excuse me, Mr. President, if I may, can you provide specifics if this is so serious? I don't understand what…"

"You will before the evening is through, Duke. This call is purely to alert you on the time of the speech, not the subject. However, because of the importance, I have asked the Senate leadership for the ratification of General Johnson as vice president."

"What?" Patrick exclaimed.

Punctuating the question was the ring of Christine Slocum's phone. She pulled it out of her pocket. Scott Roarke's number came up. She let the call go to voicemail.

"Ultimately this may involve the declaration of a national emergency."

"Mr. President!" Patrick yelled.

"I'm sorry, Congressman, I am not prepared to say anything further on the open line. I recommend you have your TV turned on at five. We'll talk after that. Believe me, I'll have a lot more to share with you then."

"Take your pick of the channels, Duke. I'm asking for the widest coverage possible."

The Speaker hung up frustrated and angry. He said a few choice words to Christine Slocum whose mind was elsewhere. The president was probably blowing dinner plans with the Secret Service agent she was cozying up to.

THE WHITE HOUSE
SITUATION ROOM
1345 HRS

"Here's how I see it. Correct me if I'm wrong."

The president addressed his principal advisors and cabinet members. If there were corrections, these people would make them without hesitating.

Roarke stood, as ordered, against the left side wall.

"One," the president continued, "the United States is under attack. The story is out in bits and pieces. It will be our story to own and I will be in control rather than reacting. So at 2000 hours I'll speak to the nation from the East Room. At a podium presenting a national security issue of the highest order. No questions. Five minutes on and off.

"Two. I state the country is now on alert. We will need to be prepared for panic, looting, and violence.

"Three. Because of one and two, I may—that is *may* not necessarily *will*—sign an Executive Order establishing a State of Emergency. The attorney general, White House Counsel, and the Supreme Court will put it under review. If I do so, FBI Chief Mulligan will coordinate with state and local law enforcement and the National Guard on proper, coordinated, and measured response.

"Four. I postpone my State of the Union Address. Reagan did it after the Challenger Space Shuttle disaster. And this is not the time to assemble all the members of Congress, the Supreme Court, and the Executive Branch in one building.

"Five. General Johnson moves into the vice president's residence at Number One Observatory Circle, under full Secret Service protection, once confirmed. I have called for immediate Senate ratification of his nomination, which will provide for the normal line of succession should it be necessary.

"Six. We proceed with arrests around the country based on the information the bureau is assembling. I want live leads not body bags. You make that clear up and down the system. Find the bastards in our backyards who are poisoning our water and we can nail the power behind them."

"I trust I have your support." It wasn't a question and there was no disagreement. Morgan Taylor was right on every point.

"Then, if you'll excuse me. I have a speech to write."

• • •

The major broadcast networks, along with the principal cable news channels, were alerted by the White House press secretary. Only a few calls needed to be made. Texts, e-mails, and tweets worked fine. Considering most of the networks were owned by just a few media conglomerates, it was just as easy to reach forty channels as it was three in the old days.

The major network news departments called back. John Bernstein took the calls, which surprised the executives. They said that management at local stations were reluctant give up the airtime. They'd be happy to pick up highlights from CNN, Fox News, and MSNBC for later airing.

The president's chief of staff used Taylor's words. "National security." The speech would take five minutes and cover a most serious development.

That got news directors' attention; local and national. The phrase had not been dropped in more than a decade. Still, one mid-level executive over a group of network stations told Bernsie in no uncertain terms that since *American Idol* winners often got more votes than a president in an election, Morgan Taylor could go to cable. That message was communicated verbatim to the chairman of the FCC, a presidential appointee, who called an even higher-level executive at the network; one with a brain and a memory of when broadcast networks used to show more responsibility. Minutes later, Bernstein had what the president demanded: network and independent stations, CNN, MSNBC, CNBC, Fox News, Fox Business, HLN, Telemundo, and Current TV, along with the hundreds, if not thousands of Internet channels, what was left of radio news, and international news outlets.

And then the pregame speculation began.

An MSNBC host: "For a president to invoke *National Security* it is either a powerfully political move or the nation is facing a crisis on the order of the Cuban Missile Crisis; the defining moment in President John Kennedy's term."

A Fox News analyst: "Morgan Taylor is a war hero, a president cut from the mold of Teddy Roosevelt and Ronald Reagan, and a leader who's willing to give 'em more hell than Harry. We better pay attention this afternoon. I know I will."

A CNN talking head admitted, "He's more of a Rockefeller Republican than a neocon and a party loyalist. And as much as it pains me to say it, he's the kind of president we need."

A Current TV anchor: "Let's hope this is not the Oval Office's version of a *trumped up* crisis. We don't need Morgan Taylor to be the star of his own reality show. But giving the man his due, let's see what he has to say."

KATIE'S OFFICE

Katie found it hard to concentrate. This was all so new to her. A true, deep relationship, a job advising and counseling the world's most important leader, and things going very wrong.

As she reviewed her recent past, she'd given up stability in Boston. *No, that's not true. Stability was snatched from me the moment I met Scott.* But with it came powerful love and excitement on a global stage.

Now she faced issues of trust, national security, and her own insecurity.

"Damnit, Kessler! Get to work," she said aloud in her office. She blew out a long breath and hit the computer. The first key words she typed:

> precedent, U.S. president, declaring federal state of emergency

CHAPTER 46

THE WHITE HOUSE
EAST ROOM
2000 HRS

The president of the United States walked to the podium. This is where presidents tended to give serious addresses. Here and from behind the desk in the Oval Office. Morgan Taylor preferred to stand today. He wanted to show strength and resolve. Sitting would not deliver the required body language.

Morgan Taylor turned and squared the camera. The broadcast,

cable, and radio commentators back-timed their introductions, basically to the effect of, "And now, we'll find out from President Morgan Taylor."

The president wrote the speech himself. The only argument he had with this chief of staff over the content was the opening line. Bernsie argued that the president remove *Good evening*. Taylor agreed. Instead he started by raising his eyes to the teleprompter and slowly starting with the tried and true, "My Fellow Americans."

He struck the right tone. People quieted across the country.

"Tonight I come before you with the most serious news. Through coordinated efforts of our intelligence services and the Centers for Disease Control, we have determined that foreign nationals have targeted vital water supplies within the United States, systematically poisoning sources we have always taken for granted.

"Poisoning water has long been the tool of scoundrels, mad dictators, and advancing and retreating armies. Today it is also the weapon of terrorists bent on our destruction. I view this as an uncivilized act of war, and having now occurred in this country, at this time, under my watch, I will treat it as such.

"We are monitoring reports of tainted water in twenty-two states, from rural communities to major cities, from schools to hospitals, wells and water towers to office coolers. Within days our medical facilities will be strained and we will need to rely on one another to deal with the hometown as the home front.

"Without a doubt, this is an attack on the United States. Cruel; inhumane and deadly. At this hour, law enforcement agencies are working with the FBI, the CIA, and health care officials to analyze toxins as a means to locate these enemies of the state and the people behind them.

"We will find you and we will survive this unprecedented attack."

The president brought his delivery down. "Now I ask every American to help. You can start by only consuming water that we can confirm as safe. That should include bottled water already in your refrigerator, purchased more than ten days ago."

Should was the operative word. Reporters circled it in their notes and the president saw the scribbling. He clarified his own point.

"...Bottled water with a seal that has not been broken or has no leaks. Rain water you collect yourself. Old ice in your refrigerators. Regional and national offices of the Centers for Disease Control are on their way to critical areas across the country. They are charged with the supervising and distribution of safe bottled water. But until we catch and stop each of the terrorists, we must be vigilant. That does not mean taking to the streets, fighting neighbor to neighbor. It does not mean looting. It does not mean taking aim at strangers. These acts, unprincipled in every measure of the rules of war, have been perpetrated by people who blend in rather than stand out. That means you probably will not recognize them. It does not mean, however, they will escape our net.

"The United States of America is the greatest nation in the world. Our intelligence resources are immense; beyond comprehension. We will survive. We will endure. We will bring these war criminals to justice or to death.

"While we pursue this enemy, the Centers for Disease Control, under Presidential Decision Directive PDD 39, will coordinate their efforts with the Federal Bureau of Investigation. The CDC is already on site at hot locations around the country to ensure the availability, procurement, and delivery of adequate medical management and disease control. Further, the CDC, in conjunction with the U.S. Environmental Protection Agency, has activated its laboratory response network for bioterrorism. This links clinical labs to public health agencies in all the states, districts, territories, and selected cities. In other words, help is on the way.

"I have asked the leaders of Congress to join me in a joint resolution of support; not a declaration of war, but support that allows this administration to employ every available tool in intelligence and information gathering. Attorney General Eve Goldman will address those issues tomorrow at a nine a.m. Eastern Time press conference. I have also asked Congress to swiftly ratify my nomination of General Jonas Jackson Johnson as vice president of the United States to insure proper succession, as provided for in the Twenty-fifth Amendment.

"I have also spoken with President Tyler of Canada and President Hernandez of Mexico regarding our ability to pursue any leads in their countries." Canada was a courtesy call. Jack Evans was already focusing on MS-13 conclaves in Mexico that the government or police had never dealt with. A follow-up conversation with Hernandez was on Taylor's list.

Now the president focused sharply on the camera lens, bringing his speech to a close.

"We will not wake up tomorrow with a cure or a solution or the sense that everything is all right. It's not. We will wake up to a new normal. Accordingly, I ask every one of you tonight to demonstrate your resolve not to panic. Show your community your unity. Show the world your courage. Show these heartless fiends who seek to hurt us that they cannot bring us down; that we are stronger than they are. And give me your support to do what I have to do; what I must do to track our enemies to the ends of the earth and punish them for the harm they have brought upon our sovereign shores.

"Thank you and God bless America."

Just as Morgan Taylor did not begin with *Good evening,* he did not end with *Good night.* It surely wasn't.

CHAPTER 47

TEN MINUTES LATER

The president's secretary buzzed the intercom.

"Yes, Louise."

"Mr. President, President Hernandez is on and he said he must talk to you immediately."

"Put him through, Louise."

"Well, J3, let's see what our friend to the south has to say."

Louise Swingle sent the call in. On the third ring Taylor pressed the flashing button.

"Yes, Oscar," the president intentionally employed Hernandez's first name. "I'm here with General Johnson. I'm sure you have a witness to the conversation as well."

"Ah, yes. Elder is with me."

There was a long pause as if the Mexican president was expecting chit chat from the associates. Without any, he proceeded.

"Morgan, I want to assure you that this office, my administration, and the Republic of Mexico will stand by you. We watched your speech and the peoples of Mexico extend their sympathy to the families stricken by this horrifying attack."

Taylor looked up at Johnson. The president of Mexico had just given him the authority to deploy America's forces against targets in his country.

"I want this in writing, Oscar. For the record."

"You will have it within the hour, Morgan. But I cannot allow or condone attacks on civilians. You must understand that."

"I do. We will be strategic and judicious."

Hernandez read that more as boots on the ground rather than drones from above.

Taylor continued, "I will alert you before any action is taken. Your public compliance and acceptance, noting it as a joint effort, will be required.

"Understood and agreed."

"Thank, you Oscar. These are difficult times. I wish the nature of this call and the possible defensive actions to follow were not necessary. However, America is under attack, and our intelligence shows that operatives have been working and training in Mexico, using a supply line and money from the Mara Salvatruchas. It is in our mutual interests that they be dealt with immediately."

Taylor was certain that the Mexican leader would have to tighten his own security. MS-13 and its offshoots were liable to come after him.

"Again, I understand."

"We will be better for this, Oscar."

"What is the old saying, '*What doesn't kill us makes us stronger.*'"

"Friedrich Nietzsche," Morgan Taylor replied. "And mark my words, we will become stronger."

THE WHITE HOUSE
2300 HRS

The Senate sped up the vote. Instead of making it the next day, they affirmed General Johnson an hour after the president's speech.

The White House hastily called for a small, but necessary, formal gathering. The president and his wife stood with General Johnson and his wife. Present in the West Wing were the Speaker of the House, Senate Pro Tem, Majority and Minority Leaders of the House and Senate, the Secretary of State, Supreme Court Chief Justice Leopold Browning, and members of the press. Six Secret Service agents were at the doors.

The first order of business, difficult and emotional for General Johnson, was for him to resign his commission. He did so by handing a letter to the president.

"Thank you, General," the president said.

Johnson, one of the toughest individuals Taylor had ever met, fought back his tears.

"It has been my honor to serve you as a member of the United States Army," he proclaimed.

"Thirty-seven proud years in the military. One of the country's most esteemed and decorated African American officers," Taylor remarked. "A brilliant military strategist. A true leader. I have no doubt about how your experience will transfer into your new job. Thank you for accepting, Jonas."

"You're welcome, Mr. President." Johnson's wife squeezed his hand.

"So let's keep you off the unemployment line. Mr. Chief Justice, you have the honor."

It was Leopold Browning's duty to administer the oath of office. The Supreme Court justice began without flourish. "Place your hand on the Bible and repeat after me."

The actual text for the vice presidential oath of office is not in the Constitution like the presidential oath. The wording, approved by Congress in 1884, is the same that's used to swear in all members of Congress and other government officers required to take an oath. It is, with every word, declarative and precise.

"I, state your name, do solemnly swear that I will support and defend the Constitution of the United States…"

"I, Jonas Jackson Johnson, do solemnly swear that I will support and defend the Constitution of the United States… "

Two hours north of Washington, a doctor at the St. Francis Medical Center in Trenton, New Jersey, pronounced a fifty-four-year-old farmer dead. He followed his wife to the grave after their well was poisoned.

"…against all enemies, foreign and domestic," Chief Leopold continued.

Johnson responded, "…against all enemies, foreign and domestic…"

In Pahrump, Nevada, a local policeman keeled over on the job. His partner immediately called for paramedics to take him to Desert View Hospital.

"…that I will bear true faith and allegiance to the same… "

"…that I will bear true faith and allegiance to the same… "

Ten-year-old twins from Ghent, New York, were being cared for at Columbia Memorial Hospital, up the river in Hudson, NY. The attending physician felt they might have a chance.

"…that I take this obligation freely…"

"…that I take this obligation freely," Jackson recited.

A long-haul truck driver along I-70 in Kansas had no chance. He grabbed his stomach, leaned over the steering wheel with sudden and severe cramps. The action caused his 18-wheeler to swerve.

"…without any mental reservation or purpose of evasion…"

"…without any mental reservation or purpose of evasion…"

At eighty miles an hour the big rig jackknifed, flipped to the side, and slid four hundred feet down the interstate. When it hit a van in the right lane, the truck exploded into a fireball. The truck driver died instantly. The family in the van really never knew what hit them. They never would.

"…and that I will well and faithfully discharge the duties of the office on which I am about to enter: So help me God."

Johnson concluded, "…and that I will well and faithfully discharge the duties of the office on which I am about to enter: So help me God."

The Chief Justice shook his hand. "Congratulations, Mr. Vice President.

As the death toll mounted outside, Jonas Jackson Johnson became the third man named Johnson to become vice president of the United States.

Morgan Taylor certainly hoped that his vice president would not succeed him the same way Andrew Johnson and Lyndon Johnson succeeded Abraham Lincoln and John F. Kennedy.

PART III

CHAPTER 48

THE WHITE HOUSE
JANUARY 19

The news was the same. All bad. How could it be any different. Americans were sick and dying. Random as it might be, it created a wave of national fear.

Political perspective notwithstanding, the headlines were interchangeable from the *New York Times*to the *Manchester Union Leader*. And Hannity, Limbaugh, and Rachel Maddow were demanding answers to the same question. "What is the president doing about this?"

The debate echoed in America's homes; from dinner tables to bedrooms and bathrooms. From elderly couples to teens and mothers nursing. To fathers arming for the worst.

What water can I trust? Who's going to tell us what's safe to drink? What if we run out? And predictably, *When is Taylor going to attack?*

Of course, attacking required a target. As for what was safe to drink, no one could safely answer.

"It's a shit storm," Bernsie said in the morning briefing. The other familiar faces were J3, Mulligan, and Evans.

"I know," Taylor said. He was looking particularly gaunt today. The daily pressure that came with the job was one thing. This was something else entirely. John Bernstein saw how it was affecting the president.

Taylor leaned on his director of national intelligence, the man responsible under the Intelligence Reform and Terrorism Prevention Act of 2004, to oversee the country's complete National Intelligence Program. Of course, national also meant international.

"We're working Russia now. I'll need more time."

"Operationally where are we?"

"Texas. Houston to be precise."

"When, Jack?"

"As long as we're speaking of a domestic operation, I should chime in," Bob Mulligan said. "Just for the record."

"Okay."

"Days, Mr. President. A coordinated air force and FBI op."

"Days?" the president did not like the timeline. "You can't be readied earlier?"

Mulligan looked at Johnson. Johnson gave him a positive sign.

"We'll revise the schedule. Tomorrow. We have the target and I like J3's, excuse me, the vice president's plan. It's damned original. If we pull it off, they'll make a movie about it."

"That good?" Taylor asked.

"That good," was Mulligan's reply. "General, care to share it?"

The newly confirmed vice president reviewed his strategy for capturing the MS-13 gang leader in Houston. The president had to agree, he'd never heard anything like it.

CHAPTER 49

MOSCOW

"Dubroff is in a secure wing at Burdenko Central Military Hospital," Arkady Gomenko whispered over their third shot of vodka. "Top floor."

"Burdenko," D'Angelo repeated. Not good news. He knew the facility, though he'd never been in it. Burdenko Central Military Hospital was a five-building medical center, 275 years old, and rebuilt with state-of-the-art medical equipment and high-tech security systems. Very high-tech.

"I can map where he is. Top floor. But I doubt you'll be able to get to him," Arkady warned. "I hear he's under lock and key.

"Don't have a clue why or what he's there for. But he's certainly the man who can recite the history of Red Banner chapter and verse. Maybe this new Russia is interested in what he has in his head that goes beyond even the files I've been able to read."

That's exactly why D'Angelo had to reach him. According to a coded message from Evans, which he figured was somehow playing into the stateside news, his assignment had turned more urgent.

WASHINGTON, D.C.
THE SAME TIME

"Well, Mr. Roarke, for a while there, I thought we'd never get our dinner in."

Christine Slocum sat opposite Roarke at a corner table in one of Washington's most popular eateries. The Occidental Grill and Seafood Restaurant was favored by White House personnel because it was around the corner from work; almost sprinting distance. The walls were adorned with historic photographs of presidents and twentieth-century personalities. The savory dishes were known for their fresh local ingredients and complicated blends of spices.

They had the choice of tables, because in Washington, like the rest of the country, most people were not eating out.

Slocum picked the quietest corner and calculated that her foot could provocatively reach his thigh. But the evening was too young to make that move. She dressed only slightly conservatively. Her neckline was definitely below *see-level* and she was hoping Roarke would rise with the tide.

They each had bottled water and took care not to order soup or steamed vegetables. Christine ordered the five peppercorn crusted salmon with caramelized cipollini onions, toasted black and white sesame seeds, and carrot-ginger butter. Roarke went for roasted loin of venison, crusted with fennel pollen and juniper seeds, served with chestnut flan tasting all the better because of the wild Maine blueberry grappa sauce.

"I'm sorry," he said responding to her comment. "It's been a little hectic."

"For me, too. I work with the Speaker. Did I mention that?"

Roarke indicated she hadn't.

"And he's running like crazy. The president is throwing a lot at the Hill all at once." She paused to make her next line really count. "Scott, I'm scared."

"With good reason."

Both of them had been following the news. Despite the president's stated hope for calm, panic had gripped the nation. And with panic came looting. And with looting, arrests and clubbings which led to further strain on local hospitals. It was getting worse by the hour.

"I wouldn't recommend walking around alone," he said. "You don't want to be caught in the wrong place at the wrong time."

"The whole country is the wrong place right now."

Christine looked deeply into Roarke's eyes and stretched her arm across the table. Their fingers met and she gently inched her fingers up his arm. "I really am scared, Scott. Tell me the truth, are we going to be okay?"

Roarke took care with what he said. "From what I gather, the FBI is looking everywhere."

"But aren't you close to the president?"

"Oh, some days I see him. But he has his full-time agents. That's not my duty."

He wished he had not said that. It invited a question.

"What do you do?" she asked in an almost flirtatious way. "I mean besides working out in the morning and showering."

He laughed at the reference to her bold encounter at the gym. "Mostly advance work. Sometimes for the president, other times for cabinet members. I've got a bank full of frequent flier miles I haven't used."

"Maybe we'll get to cash them in." Now it was time for her foot to reach his thigh.

Roarke responded by closing his eyes for a moment, which pleased her.

"I've never been to the White House. It must be exciting."

"It's just an office. You get used to it."

"Oh, I don't think I ever would. Especially now."

"Wanna check it out?"

"Really? Even though I work for the enemy?"

"What?"

"You know, the opposition," she explained.

"Hey, it's everyone's White House, Republican or Democrat," Roarke said. "Just like Congress."

"Still, aren't I the enemy?"

"I don't know, are you?"

"No," she said softly.

"Then I can probably get you in."

She worked her foot higher. "That was going to be *my* line."

• • •

After dinner, Roarke helped Christine with her $1,000 black Burberry Brit Double-Breasted Coat from Nordstrom. As she turned into him for help with the buttons, she created the natural opportunity to regard his brown eyes and contemplate his lips. Just as she moved closer to what would be an invitation for the rest of the evening, Roarke's phone rang.

Christine backed away, frustrated as he dutifully answered. She watched him as he said "Yup" a few times and "It has to be now, Shannon?" It ended with a quick "Okay. Bye."

"Duty calls?" she asked when he finished.

"Yes, I'm sorry."

"Me, too."

"I'll get you a cab."

"You don't have to. I'll be fine."

"Are you sure?" he asked.

"Absolutely, but I want a rain check."

"Oh?"

"The White House?"

Then she kissed him and felt him.

"Yes, that, too."

CENTERS FOR DISEASE CONTROL
BUILDING 23

The bad news just got worse. Some eighty-five hundred deaths and counting. More than nineteen hundred in the last twenty-four hours. The causes began hitting the press as news organizations did their own analyses. Some right, some wrong. Sarin, Soman, Sulfar Mustard, and Lewisite—all available on the open market—and shaken, stirred, or mixed with water they created lethal concoctions across the country. Bonnie Comley expected the number of deaths to almost double by the day until Americans got the message. *Turn off the tap.*

The news channels didn't help. They competed for the most disturbing footage: A deadly fight over the last quart of bottled water at a Cincinnati 7-Eleven. A truck smashing into a Birmingham Target after hours and loading up with soft drinks, cartons of juice and milk, and a big-screen TV just because.

Comely recognized that as people got more desperate panic would increase. It was a model she'd mapped on her computer two years earlier as an academic exercise.

It was becoming all too real now.

"We allowed this to happen," she told CDC director Snowden. "The country has one hundred and sixty-eight thousand mostly unsupervised public water systems. Yet, how many people want to get rid of regulations and government infrastructure that we desperately need? And with antiterrorist efforts run basically without teeth, we've thrown open the door to anyone with a little knowledge and a vial of spores."

Comley referred to The Association of Metropolitan Water Agencies which created the Water Information Sharing and Analysis Center (WISAC) as a volunteer program.

"Hell, I went to the last WEFTEC session," she said, recalling the Water Environment Federation Technical Exposition and Conference.

We had a night of speeches about how locks were being changed and monitoring systems had been upgraded. The bottom line is that while our water systems are viewed as predominately safe for human consumption, our infrastructure is choked. And the cost for upgrading?"

Snowden had the numbers off the top of his head. "EPA says $123 billion. The American Water Works Association estimates $360 billion. The Water Infrastructure Network puts it at $1 trillion and twenty years to make things safe."

"Twenty years? Try right now," Comley added.

Snowden was supposed to give the president an update; hopefully something positive. There was no positive news coming out of the CDC today.

THE WHITE HOUSE

"This isn't like most terrorist acts," Taylor said to his wife while he got into bed. Eleanor rested a Kindle on her lap to listen to her husband. The history of women's suffrage would always be there. "Water is sacred. More than electricity, even more than cable TV. They haven't even had to poison supplies everywhere, not that they could have. Enough to make people believe *all* the water is contaminated; enough so people would lose confidence in the safety of *their* water supplies."

"Which they've done," she offered.

"Brilliantly, sweetheart. Absolutely brilliantly." He reflected on his next thought. "And as a result the country has lost faith in me."

"Come here. Give me some good news."

He moved into his wife's arms, but he had nothing to share.

"Everyone's working hard," Eleanor said consoling him.

"Yes they are. The National Infrastructure Protection Agency..."

"The what?"

"Part of Homeland Security. They cover critical review of the nation's electric power, food, and drinking water, our national monuments, telecommunications and transportation systems, chemical facilities, and a whole lot more.

"Oh."

"Well, they're talking with Information Sharing and Analysis Center."

"They're talking with a sharing center. How nice."

The comment actually made Morgan Taylor laugh. Then he explained. "They're dealing more with cyber threats than physical attacks, but maybe this experience will make us smarter for the next inevitable attack."

"So much for less government," Eleanor said. "Thank God the EPA didn't get completely slashed."

"Not completely, but only a little more than a couple of million went into counter bioterrorism efforts."

"What will it take, hon?"

"A blank check and Congress looking the other way while I do a few things they won't want to know about." He pulled the covers up to his chin. "Now, let's go to sleep."

CHAPTER 50

THE OVAL OFFICE
JANUARY 20

The biggest debate over the strategic plan had been between Vice President Johnson and FBI Chief Robert Mulligan. Both argued that they had the better handle on the mission. One required Constitutional review; the other needed a communications link and a Thesaurus.

Morgan Taylor made the final decision.

"Bob, the bureau has the know-how, but you're not hooked up into the Pentagon lingo. If your men read a flash order wrong from the birds, you'd put them and the operation at risk. Special Forces go in."

"You understand the issues deploying American armed forces under these circumstances. It's not legal."

"I do," Taylor stated. "Neither is mass murder."

The president pressed the intercom button at his desk. "Louise, please send in Attorney General Goldman and Ms. Kessler."

Bob Mulligan and the vice president stood as the nation's attorney general and the president's new deputy counsel joined the discussion. After the perfunctory greetings, the president launched into his lead question.

"We're discussing the issue you've been researching. Where do we stand, Eve?"

The attorney general, long a friend of the president and a hard-as-nails lawyer, sat forward on the couch.

"You asked whether there are any constitutional limits to the president engaging in a domestic military action and what constitutional standards apply to its use. I had Ms. Kessler review case law, executive acts, and legal precedence. She has done that quickly and efficiently. Considering time is of the essence..."

"Utmost essence," the president interrupted.

"Granted, utmost essence," Goldman corrected herself. "Ms. Kessler?" She turned to Katie Kessler.

Katie arranged some papers on the coffee table.

"Yes, let's have it, counselor," the president said with real respect. Morgan Taylor had seen the young attorney under fire, real fire—political and physical. She exhibited immense character, courage, and the ability to stand up to the most powerful personalities in government. Morgan Taylor for one; Supreme Court Chief Justice Leopold Browning for another. And then there were the challenges she faced maintaining a relationship with Scott Roarke; a man the president constantly put in harm's way.

Katie Kessler wore an olive green pants suit for the meeting; a little more stylish than business *de rigueur*, yet still courtroom acceptable with a white blouse and freshwater pearls. Her body language mirrored the attorney general's. Proper and formal.

"Mr. President, I began with the Posse Comitatus Act, 18 U.S.C. § 1385, United States Federal Law of 18 June 1878. As originally applied, it intended to remove the army from domestic law enforcement, and it was the result of President Grant sending a *posse comitatus*—meaning 'the power of the county'—to the polls during the election of 1878. Following the Civil War, the army was routinely called to maintain order and to enforce the policies of Reconstruction on the South. The U.S. troops were highly visible at political events and polling places until Southern Democrats, arguing that the army was becoming politicized, passed The Posse Comitatus Act, which removed the army from civilian law enforcement and returned it to the military and the job of defending America's borders.

"Accordingly, many experts maintained that the act precludes the use of U.S. military forces in domestic security operations. But that thinking changed a great deal on September 11, 2001."

Morgan Taylor lowered his eyes out of respect.

"Based on my understanding of the crisis at hand," Kessler continued, " I conclude that the president of the United States has ample statutory and constitutional authority to deploy the military against foreign terrorists operating within the United States."

"What about *against* American citizens," Mulligan asked.

"I'll come to that Mr. Director. But first, in consideration of the president's constitutional powers..." She reached into her open briefcase to the side of her chair and withdrew a file. "This is a 2001 Congressional joint resolution following the attack on the World Trade Centers."

Kessler handed copies of the resolution and allowed time for a cursory reading.

"Enactment of S.J. Res 23 recognizes that the president may deploy military forces domestically to prevent and deter similar acts of terrorism."

"Done deal," the vice president announced.

"There's more, Mr. President. Much in the same vein, but necessary to present." In a brave and almost scolding tone to the new vice president she added, "I take it this exercise is more than academic or rhetorical, so it should not be given short shrift."

"Point taken, Ms. Kessler. Please continue," the president responded at the same time he shot a *don't go there* expression to J3.

"Back to the Posse Comitatus Act and its consideration in favor of military use. It can be argued that Posse Comitatus only applies to domestic use of the armed forces for law enforcement purposes. Taking law enforcement out of the sentence opens up other considerations. But for that application, we need to look at the Fourth Amendment which guards against unreasonable searches and seizures.

"It is my opinion, and the position of White House legal staff before me, that rather than debate whether the Fourth Amendment would apply, we should ask whether it *would not* apply in the 'situation' as I understand it. Given the problem posed to me, I do not think that a military mission against a terrorist cell within the United States would be required to demonstrate probable cause or obtain a warrant, and therefore not be obligated under the Fourth Amendment. The government's responsibility to protect the nation from attack outweighs the inherent privacy interests and trumps the search or seizure protections."

Everyone was utterly impressed with Kessler's command of the law. She was breaking it down into completely understandable bites that seemed to support the vice president's plan.

"Now I want to consider the difference between warring belligerent nations and terrorists. Traditionally, America has prosecuted wars with countries where the theater of military operations was on the battlefield, with men in uniform and absolute distinctions between sides."

She cleared her throat, suddenly a little less confident talking war in front of one of the nation's greatest military minds.

"Today, many of our enemies wear no uniforms. They have little or no formal military training. They can be children or seniors, bicycling or walking to a town square rather than marching to war in a platoon. They may not even represent a nation. In fact, it is their aim to blend into everyday civilian life in a way that disguises their identity, their cause, and their mission. As a result, the rules of engagement change. And protection of an American citizenry, suddenly part of the battlefield that has moved into their hometowns, becomes a challenge beyond the capability of local law enforcement.

"In my opinion, the Fourth Amendment would not restrict or prevent military operations under your authority to prevent or repeal attack or invasion against the United States.

"So tying together history with new world enemies, the established law in the absence of rules of war suggests, in my opinion, that Article II of the Constitution, which vests the president with the power to answer threats to national security, provides for the use of the armed forces in domestic operations against terrorists."

"Amen!" J3 proclaimed.

Katie ignored it. She wasn't finished. Her voice suddenly shook when she realized that what she had said was somehow going to involve Scott. Was she ultimately giving the president and the general the legal ammunition to act?

"Mr. President," she slowly stated, "the Constitution, supported by past administrations, Congress, and the courts indicates to me that you, sir, have the authority to take military actions, both domestic and foreign if you determine that such actions will be necessary to respond to terrorist threats against the United States. However, this is only my opinion. A briefing with the chief justice would be in order."

"Your buddy," the president said.

"In a manner of speaking. I don't believe he's anyone's 'buddy.'"

Katie Kessler had, on her first trip to Washington, stood eye-to-eye with the nation's highest court justice arguing law and precedent and did not blink. She admired Chief Justice Leopold Browning, but the thought of facing him on this issue concerned her.

"I don't know if I can," she admitted.

"I don't know anyone better to do so. But perhaps the attorney general can accompany you this time to reinforce the president's position and the importance. After all, if it comes to a ruling at the Supreme Court, we will need five justices on our side; Browning among them," Taylor explained.

"Yes, sir. We'll set the meeting immediately," Eve Goldman offered.

Katie Kessler melted into her seat, a sure signal that the formal side of her presentation was over.

"Questions?" Attorney General Goldman asked.

"One. Back to search and seizure. *If...*," FBI Chief Mulligan said, not having a better word, "there is such a need, are warrants required?"

Eve Goldman jumped in. "Acting in the nation's best interests and under the command of the president, our forces—and I'll use *forces* as an umbrella term—must be free to search and secure enemy quarters, whether they are within military command posts, cars, or homes. And once those forces are in place they must be able to seize papers, computers, documents, devices, smartphones; anything that could be considered relevant. All of this without having to show probable cause before the court. And, I should add, without having to demonstrate that such actions were constitutionally reasonable."

"What if the potential targets were American citizens and not foreign nationals acting under a flag?" Mulligan asked.

"But still suspected terrorists?"

"Yes, and a threat to national security."

Eve Goldman didn't get a chance to sound like a general or a law enforcement officer much. But she took the opportunity now.

"Then you go get 'em."

• • •

Eve Goldman and Katie Kessler were thanked and excused. J3 and Mulligan remained with the president.

"So here's how it works," Taylor stated. "The general's running the pregame and the game. The bureau takes over *after* the general's through with the postgame. The hand off will be right there on the spot. You have twenty-four hours to set up your safe house.

"We have no margin of error, Bob," Taylor emphasized. "It's J3's show and I like what he's come up with. But then I'm counting on you for actionable intel. You'll be dealing with a thug, not a trained terrorist. Make him talk fast, but don't turn this into a Guantanamo-type investigation."

"Oh believe me; he'll talk just so he won't have to listen to my man Bessolo for too long."

It was intended as a joke, but no one was laughing these days.

CHAPTER 51

THE SUPREME COURT
JANUARY 21
1100 HRS

Katie and Attorney General Goldman were at the chief justice's door precisely two minutes early. Promptness was something Browning required from everyone—employees, visitors, even emissaries from the White House.

"Come right in. May I offer you anything other than water?"

The point was well taken.

"No thank you."

"It's bottled," he said picking up an eight-ounce plastic container.

Browning favored a traditional American décor for his office. Dark wood paneling, free-standing lamp lighting, brown leather furniture, and an antique Colonial rug. Nothing contemporary. It was austere, if not officious, and just the image he wanted to project.

Katie observed the portraits on his walls. Seven in all in equally distinguished frames. Three on one side; four on another. There was something unnerving about the grouping of three.

"Ah, the men who look over me. Start with the opposite side, though."

Katie Kessler turned and examined the four paintings that hung to the right side of his desk. There was a spark to them; life in the eyes; brilliance that shined through. She looked back at the others, then again to the four she found more inspiring.

"You see a difference?"

"Yes, sir."

"So do I. These men, Ms. Kessler, are my conscience. Always sitting in judgment of me. All former justices who remind me to consider the Constitution as the conscience of the founding fathers, interpreted in the best interest of the times. Do you recognize them?" Browning asked

"Earl Warren is on the right." Katie replied. She paused. "Next to him Justice Brandeis?" She stopped.

"Madame Attorney General?"

"John Marshall is on the left. I don't know the fourth."

"Ms. Kessler?"

"No, your honor, I'm afraid I don't either."

"Seventy-five percent between the two of you. A passing grade, but not Magna Cum Laude for the White House. The fourth is Charles Evan Hughes. Former New York governor. Ran for president. Obviously defeated. He opposed many of Roosevelt's initiatives, upheld minimum wage, and helped avoid a terrible showdown between the court and President Roosevelt through diplomacy. Yes, diplomacy, even on the court. His work to keep the court from being expanded to fifteen under FDR was applauded as *The Switch in Time That Saved Nine.* Hughes worked closely with my model you correctly identified, Ms. Kessler, Louis Brandeis."

Browning took a few steps to the opposite wall, drawing his audience's attention. "But it's these men who I argue with as I prepare my rulings."

The three portraits cast a cold, unctuous stare.

"I'll spare you the quiz this time," Browning asserted. "Samuel Chase, James Clark McReynolds, and Charles Evans Whittaker. In my opinion, three of the most notorious Supreme Court justices ever to live. And what do they remind me of?" Browning, ever the judge, asked the visiting.

"Integrity and honesty," Eve Goldman said.

Browning was amused. "Perhaps."

"Your decisions become history and you with them," Katie added. "Rule as Justice McReynolds did, and you risk residing in infamy. Perhaps you would be placed on some future chief justice's wall of shame."

Leopold Browning smiled broadly. "Are you sure I can't lure you over?"

"Your honor, it would be inappropriate to discuss that while I'm representing the White House. I'm sure Justice Brandeis would agree. Didn't he say, 'The world presents enough problems if you believe it to be a world of law and order; do not add to them by believing it to be a world of miracles.'"

"Well, counselor. You have me. Consider the comment stricken. Now to the point of your trip across town."

Katie looked to the attorney general to begin as they had rehearsed. Eve Goldman began.

"We are here to discuss the president of the United States' decision to take military action within our domestic borders. We also can discuss the possibility of invoking martial law and the potential of declaring a national State of Emergency. But let's just start with the first argument."

The attorney general was that direct. "The president, on precedent of prior chief executives, will release 'The National Defense Resources Preparedness' executive order. It will state that under the present emergency, the federal government has the authority to assume control of aspects of American society from farming and livestock to transportation, industry, health care facilities, defense and construction, and…water resources. All will fall under the authority of the president of the United States."

All of this came at lightning speed while everyone remained standing. Leopold Browning directed Goldman and Kessler to sit. He walked to his desk, commanding their complete attention.

"President Taylor is not the first to make such a proclamation. However, that does not make it the proper course of action."

"Mr. Chief Justice, there are extenuating circumstances. In years' past, presidents issued their orders primarily in anticipation of the need, and sometimes in response; never fully implementing martial law, but establishing their right. Actually their authority," Goldman answered.

"An important delineation," Browning scowled. "Government has the power and can establish the authority. But government does not have the right. We, the people, have rights, conveyed by the Constitution. So just to be sure—we agree on the distinction?"

"Yes, sir. We absolutely agree."

"Then please continue. But limit your points to what is intended by the Executive Branch."

"If I may," Katie began, "The president's intent is for the executive order to be in force if and when it is necessary to restore order and to manage the water resources of the nation. This is in keeping with President Obama's order of March, 2012." She read from notes in her Coach leather portfolio. "The domestic industrial and technological base is the foundation for national defense preparedness. The authorities provided in the act shall be used to strengthen this base and to ensure it is capable of responding to the national defense needs of the United States.

"Mr. Chief Justice," she continued, lifting her head above the paper, "the order then, as now, is designed to deliver supplies, resources, and security to the people of the United States in a time of national emergency. We live in such a time right now. At this very moment."

"Ms. Kessler, you are persuasive, but local and state police can provide the first line of authority."

"Can they, your honor? Do you know that as a fact? The national security briefings I have seen, as well as news reports, strongly paint a picture of a breakdown of civil authority escalating on a geometric scale."

"And the president is willing to eviscerate due process and judicial oversight for any action deemed by the Executive Branch as necessary in the interest of national security?"

"In the interest of saving lives, Justice Browning. Saving American lives."

"Ms. Kessler, I may be chief justice of the Supreme Court of the United States, but I am also a father and a grandfather. Do not lecture me on families. I value the lives of all Americans—all Americans including *my* family."

Katie used a technique she learned in law school. She took her time responding and she apologized to the bench.

"Your honor, I sincerely apologize. Perhaps if I take an historical approach." Katie intentionally looked at the wall of the favored justices. "President Roosevelt signed the first national defense resources preparedness mandate, which has been amended over the years by other presidents including Clinton and George W. Bush. Furthermore, the new order is rooted in the Defense Production Act of 1950, which gave the government powers to mobilize national resources in the event of national emergencies."

Goldman rested her arm on Katie's. She'd drive the point home.

"Mr. Chief Justice," the attorney general argued, "The Supreme Court did not rule then, and it is the opinion of White House counsel that the court in whatever accelerated process may be at hand, need not rule now."

Justice Browning straightened his tie. He was an impeccable dresser, though his own wardrobe was rarely seen under the court robes. He adjusted his American flag cufflinks forward and cleared his throat.

"Martial law, counselor, and it could come to martial law… is the suspension of civil authority and the imposition of military authority. That has not happened except on a state level and even then in relation to national disasters. Giving the president the military authority to act as police would be unprecedented. And then there is the issue of Habeas Corpus."

Katie was expecting this argument to come up. When it did, she had the defining response.

"Sir, Article 1, Section 9. The United States Constitution addresses exactly that. Only Congress can declare martial law unless 'when in the Cases of Rebellion or Invasion the public Safety might require it.' Sadly, the times require it. Public safety absolutely requires it."

"Ms. Kessler. Are you sure you don't want a job over here?" Leopold asked, awarding her a clear win.

"Mr. Chief Justice," she said scolding him, "you are out of order."

Browning laughed. She'd gotten to him once again.

CHAPTER 52

GULFTON, TEXAS
JANUARY 23

As a community, Gulfton, in Southwest Houston, had seen better days.

In the 1960s and '70s, booming oil money threw cash in the pockets of thousands of upwardly mobile young men and women from all over the country who were willing to come and work in Gulfton. Money also talked to immigrants from the Middle East, the Pacific Rim, and South America in need of service jobs. Land was abundant, dollars flowed like oil. Builders prospered.

Apartment complexes with *nouveau riche* names like "Chateau Carmel" and "Napoleon Square" were rushed to completion. But developers put little thought into the foundation of Gulfton and planning for the future. The principal goal—perhaps the only goal—was to build quickly and inexpensively to meet the overnight demand and capitalize on deregulation benefits in the financial markets.

However, the boom began to bust in the 1980s. With jobs evaporating and higher-paid oil employees moving out, rents plummeted. The value of many of the buildings, not yet fully amortized, dropped rapidly and went into foreclosure. Foreclosure was followed by bankruptcy. Bankruptcy led to abandonment. And yet, there was still the working class and the underclass ready to occupy Gulfton.

Gulfton became the most densely populated section of Houston with a core demographic of more than 70 percent Hispanic, including families from Mexico and Central America.

Crime rates soared. Much of Gulfton degraded into a lockdown and gun-loaded municipality. Houstonians who skirted the area on their commutes dubbed the densely populated 3.2-square-mile area as Gulfton Ghetto.

It became the perfect breeding ground for a gang known as Mara Salvatrucha—MS-13.

Manuel Estavan lived in one of the dilapidated apartment buildings. Most of the letters had fallen off the marquee, but faded paint managed to bring out the once dignified name, "The Standish Arms."

This was Estavan's home, his compound, his bordello, his bunker, and his bank. He lived here with his army of bullies and killers and their rotating supply of whores. Today there were fourteen. There could be as many as thirty-six. But it was a Saturday morning, and even MS-13 members had to see the kids they had fathered from the women they abandoned.

Estavan had transformed the eight-apartment structure into a fortress with no regard for the owner, who was actually too fearful to collect rent. He was the boss of the building, the dictator of the block, and the emperor of the neighborhood. He controlled an ever-expanding fiefdom where no one dared to cross him.

The gang leader profited from drugs, prostitution, gun trafficking, and, most recently, a unique taxi service to various points North, East, and West. He was a killer without remorse and so far directly untouchable by the FBI and the ATF. But he did have an Achilles' heel known throughout his ranks, right down to Ricardo Perez. The man was deathly afraid of earthquakes.

That's what Scott Roarke learned from his conversations with Perez in Montana. It's what Jonas Jackson Johnson counted on this morning as he walked the floor into the White House Situation Room.

MOSCOW
THE SAME TIME

The snow had been falling for ten hours, blanketing the city streets, making life move at a slower pace. Few people were outside. Those who dared, tried to get inside as quickly as possible.

But doctors had their responsibilities. Among them, Max Yurovich. He trudged through the snow outside the Burdenko Central Military Hospital. He braced himself against the cold and covered his face with a black and white hand-knitted scarf.

Yurovich passed a maintenance crew that was furiously trying to keep the 18-square-inch slabs of cement clear. They took no interest in him at all. But their efforts neatly removed his footprints.

The doctor clutched an old hard leather briefcase. He made sure not to swing it too much. His job was to fit in, not provide anyone with a reason to look twice or remember anything distinctive about him.

Yurovich paused outside the impressive yellow structure, embellished with white columns that began on the exterior of the second floor and extended three stories. He removed his wet glasses, brushed the snow off his topcoat, and blew his nose. All normal acts; all reasonable in one of the coldest days so far of the already brutal Moscow winter.

Inside, when asked for identification, Dr. Max Yurovich provided credentials from Sechenov Medical Academy.

The guard was on his last twenty-five minutes of work. He gave the ID a tired, superficial glance. It looked perfectly authentic and certainly not new. He waved the visiting doctor through without ever looking at his face.

Dr. Yurovich unbuttoned his coat, revealing a navy blue blazer and a boring, nondescript tie. He stood against a wall of the main hall and removed a folder from his briefcase, which he read as he continued his walk. This simple distraction made him fit in even more. He proceeded down the hall, across the complex, beyond a bank of operating rooms, and into an adjoining building. Dr. Yurovich walked slowly, occasionally getting his bearings as anyone so preoccupied would.

In the second building, a guard returning from the bathroom routinely asked if he needed help. Dr. Yurovich responded in perfect

Russian that he was fine, but late. Very few words. Not too little to seem impolite. Not too much to create a real memory. Precisely the way he intended.

The good doctor was, in fact, Vinnie D'Angelo, who served the CIA, not the Russian medical community.

OUTSIDE SAN ANTONIO, TEXAS
THE SAME TIME

Major A.J. Giese beat his wake-up alarm on his iPhone by precisely sixty seconds. He stretched his toes in bed and took in the morning air waiting for this phone alert. He didn't need to check the time. His body was his real clock, just as his experience navigated him successfully over enemy territory.

There'd be no enemy fire on today's mission, but according to specific orders from the Pentagon, it was no less important to the United States of America.

Forty-nine minutes later Giese was in his flight suit and the first in the briefing room at Randolph AFB, 14.8 miles east outside of San Antonio, Texas. Giese would be first on the flightline, too.

The major was solid beyond solid. At exactly 185 pounds, never wavering more than 10 ounces due to diet and discipline, he fit like a glove in the cockpit of his F-15C.

He'd flown single and two-seater versions of this versatile aircraft for years. Over Libya. Over Afghanistan, Iraq, Somalia, and a dozen completely classified global hotspots. For today's flight he would have to avoid obstacles he never encountered over deserts, mountains, and jungles: high rise buildings, apartments, and other aircraft.

Giese had a real target, but his plane, and his squadron of three other F-15s, all tasked out of the 53rd Wing at Eglin Air Force Base, Florida, would fly in tight formation without their normal armaments. Nonetheless, they would pack a wallop.

For this mission, Major A.J. Giese reported to one man. That one man reported to the commander in chief. It was that direct and that important.

That's what Giese told his men in their predawn briefing. "Short and sweet," he said. "We each take one pass. Just like we rehearsed."

The rehearsals occurred only one day earlier, with ten practice runs over the New Mexico desert.

"We've all done this before. A real crowd pleaser. But today, turn it up to eleven," he added. The reference to the classic movie *Spinal Tap* got a laugh from a few of the other men in the room. It was lost on the youngest.

"One more thing. For God's sake, leave everything standing."

Vice President Jonas Jackson Johnson personally selected Giese from a very short list. He'd been one of the military's go-to lead pilots on other vital "exercises." As far as J3 was concerned, there was no one better. That was good enough for the president of the United States.

GULFTON, TEXAS
ESTAVAN'S BUILDING

Manuel Estavan took care of the accounting on Saturday mornings. He maintained that with practice, he'd be able to figure it out himself. Not quite yet. He paid a cousin, Jorge Rojas, well for the privilege of doing the books and keeping quiet.

They worked on the dining room table, which showed evidence of Estavan's machete blade coming down on fingers and other body parts.

"That's it. Eighty-three thousand and change," Jorge Rojas said after counting. "Not a bad week. Not the best week. But not bad. Why won't you let me put it in stocks. I'm seeing some real movement in Coke."

"I move my own coke," Estavan laughed. "And I like my neighborhood market better."

MOSCOW

Vinnie D'Angelo wasn't certain what he would learn, if anything. First he had to talk his way into the hospital without launching an international incident. Then he needed to convince the old Russian to talk, hoping that if he said anything, it would be the truth. Once finished he had to get out alive.

Actual infiltration was less of a problem than dealing with what he might find. Arkady Gomenko had no intelligence on Dubroff's health. He could be on a steady recovery from his gunshot wound at the Gum Department Store in Red Square or in a coma. Since Gomenko's information on the old Cold War Red Banner operation was limited, talking with Dubroff became essential. Yet, D'Angelo recognized that what Dubroff knew was probably important enough for the FSB to stop him from traveling to the West.

Who else is out there? D'Angelo asked Dubroff subconsciously as he walked down the light green halls of Burdenko Central Military Hospital. *They stopped you because it's all still too hot. Right?*

The Andropov Institute, the cloak-and-dagger Russian academy which trained spies to pass as Americans and work their way up into positions of influence in the United States, had nearly succeeded at the highest level. That alone made D'Angelo's operation critical. Somewhere, part of Red Banner was still alive.

OVER TEXAS

Giese's F-15C was the perfect plane for the mission.

The F-15 is an all-weather, extremely maneuverable fighter. It is 63.8 feet long, with a 42.8-foot wing span. The plane stands 18.5 feet tall. It can fly at 1,875 mph—Mach 2.5 plus.

The jet is powered by two Pratt & Whitney F100 axial flow turbofan engines with side-by-side afterburners mounted on the fuselage.

Giese and his F-15 squadron, now in their cockpits, went through the final preflight checks. They sat elevated in their forward fuselages, looking through one-piece windscreens and large canopies that offered exceptional visibility.

Visibility was important today.

The planes' extremely agile handling came from low wing loading or weight-to-wing ratio, with a high thrust-to-weight ratio. What that means to pilots in combat or people watching an F-15 at an airshow is that it can turn tightly without losing airspeed, and it can climb virtually straight up thirty thousand feet in sixty seconds with afterburners blazing.

Maneuverability and afterburners were also essential to today's undertaking. And while many of Giese's accomplishments couldn't be talked about, this one would certainly be heard.

ESTAVAN'S BUILDING

"No taxes, all profit," Estavan said. "For me and you, dear cousin." He peeled off five thousand dollars, handed it to Rojas and put the rest in an open safe that was bolted to the floor.

Rojas stuffed the cash in his briefcase without counting. All would be there or it wouldn't. Either case, he knew not to question Estavan's math. Not today. Not ever. Even though he was the MS-13 gang leader's second cousin, there had been a first, also an accountant, who was no longer in the family, or elsewhere for that matter.

RUSSIA

Vinnie D'Angelo rounded another corner with the self-assurance of a man familiar with the building. He was. He'd memorized the layout of the complex from plans he downloaded. A brief but strategic surreptitious visit the previous night gave him added confidence. D'Angelo could speak rather well-rehearsed generic medical terms and phrases in Russian. He was that prepared. But most of what he needed to do would be in whispers with Aleksandr Dubroff, with a gun to the old man's head if necessary.

A decision point lay ahead. Take the elevator or the stairs from the main floor to the third. He opted for the tired doctor way, not what a fit CIA agent would do. He pressed the lift button and waited.

The door opened. D'Angelo smiled at a young orderly who didn't worry him. He moved on to a grizzled Russian army major who did.

Neither took much notice of him, and in keeping with elevator etiquette it stayed that way.

Both Russians were coming up from the basement. D'Angelo turned to see what buttons had been pushed. Both floors 2 and 3. He hoped the officer was getting out at 2. If so, he would go to 3, his ultimate destination. If the major didn't move on 2, and that was the orderly's floor, he would get out as well and bide his time before returning to the elevator. He needed to be that cautious.

The elevator was slow, clunky, and in need of repair. When it stopped, D'Angelo fumbled with his papers and stood out of the way. It bought him the moment he needed to see who would depart. Without any grace or civility, the colonel brushed past him. D'Angelo didn't call any attention to the move but the orderly did.

"*Byeaz oom yets,*" he proclaimed. D'Angelo knew the phrase and laughed a little. The orderly had just called the colonel an idiot. He responded with a perfect accent, "*Da,*" for yes.

The door closed and elevator rules resumed. There was no further conversation. The door opened, protocol allowed for the doctor to exit first. D'Angelo did so, turned right, and headed to his destination at the end of the hall.

OVER TEXAS

Once aloft, Giese led the squadron almost due east for their 190-mile, thirty-minute flight. They climbed over Bastrop, Texas, crossed between Giddings and La Grange, and reached a peak altitude of 14,480. Roughly five minutes to the target, Giese led the planes in a sharp descent, burning off height and airspeed at an amazing rate.

Major Giese literally aimed the pack lower and lower. Over Katy, Texas, they leveled at two thousand feet and changed formation. Giese held back, allowing the three other F-15s to fall into position ahead of him. Three minutes later, they approached the target at merely 312 feet above the ground and at an astonishingly slow speed of barely 75 knots, or 86.3 mph. They were spaced precisely twenty seconds apart.

RUSSIA

Ten more steps. One sleepy corporal guarding the door.

D'Angelo considered two options as he approached the private room in the northeast corner of the hospital. Stroll in like he belonged there or help the guard sleep a little more soundly.

"*Spa koy ne nawch ee*," D'Angelo said in Russian. "Good night."

The guard lazily opened his eyes and nodded showing no interest. D'Angelo assumed he was used to doctors coming and going and was bored with his duty. He couldn't care less who came at this late hour.

D'Angelo opened the door.

OVER TEXAS

"Alpha, sixty seconds to target," Giese reported on a discreet channel. No acknowledgement was necessary from the ground forces. Colonel Steven Slangman's special ops were ready. They were poised to stage in four tightly orchestrated moves, each in concert with Major Giese's air show. The advance team would act first, then team two, team three, and four would move up to their "execute" positions.

ESTAVAN'S BUILDING

"Next week will be even better, cuz," Estavan said. Rojas reached for his coffee mug and prepared to propose a toast. He noticed ripples, unusual ripples, creating mini waves in the black liquid. Then the mug itself began to vibrate on the table. He automatically steadied it, curious as to what was happening. At first it was quite mesmerizing. But seconds later the room started shaking violently.

Tequila bottles crashed to the floor. Plates on the table slid off and broke. Dust escaped from unpatched bullet holes in the dry wall. A screen dislodged from the window. The heavy safe door, still unlocked, swung back and forth as the rumble grew. Windows shattered as the poorly constructed frame of the old Standish Arms quaked right to the foundation.

"Earthquake!" Estavan shouted.

RUSSIA

The far corner of the room glowed in green light from Dubroff's monitors that were turned toward the bed. The low volume from the wall-mounted television set filled in the silence. Other than that, it was dark and quiet.

D'Angelo immediately recognized the movie on the old tube screen—a dubbed edition of Hitchcock's *The 39 Steps*. He smiled at the irony of the 1935 classic running at this moment. In the movie, actor Robert Donat was attempting to learn the meaning of a code known only by the vaudeville comedian on stage.

The CIA operative approached Dubroff's hospital bed. The old man appeared to be lying in deep sleep. D'Angelo's eyes shifted to the heart monitor. The line across the screen was flat. The deep sleep would be long and eternal.

D'Angelo's senses sharpened to the sound of someone else breathing. His body tensed.

"Nobody lives forever," a voice said in English from the shadows in the bathroom.

ESTAVAN'S BUILDING

Rojas was already moving faster than he had in years with no regard for anything but getting to safety. He crashed into the three hookers watching QVC who were too stoned to walk a straight line before or after the collision.

The rattling increased, but it was the deafening sound, now accompanying the rocking, that unsettled them even more.

The first F-15C had made its run.

Inside, Estavan caught the safe door from swinging shut. He grabbed the cash and ran for the door, too frightened to take another second to grab his pistol and machete.

Flanked by four equally scared MS-13 lieutenants, Estavan scrambled to the front lawn just in time to see *something* bear directly toward his building. At the last possible second it made an unbelievable ninety-degree turn skyward and ignite; virtually turning into a rocket with fire shooting out the engines. Estavan could feel the heat, but it was the ear-piercing roar that sent him to the ground.

Even if he wanted to run, he couldn't. Primal fear gripped the gang leader, just as Roarke had learned it would.

The F-15 was demonstrating why it deserved its nickname. With the afterburners kicking in, it truly became "The Screaming Eagle."

At the exact moment, Slangman's advance Special Forces team hit. Sergeants Recht and Willerth each fired their M26 Series tasers. The darts connected with two of Estavan's near guards, sending fifty thousand volts across fifteen feet of wire into their central nervous systems. The men flopped to the ground and were hooded and dragged out of sight before anyone knew what hit them.

• • •

Estavan lifted his head. "It's a fucking airplane!" he shouted, though no one could hear him. Not even his cousin who was a foot away. "A goddamned fucking airplane!"

Estavan rose to one knee. But then he saw another jet approach, coming in slower, lower, and louder, with its nose aimed straight at them.

The sound of the two thunderous engines mixed with the noise of the other F-15s, now accelerating and ascending.

"What the fuck?" he yelled. But again no one could hear anything other than the roar that engulfed them. Estavan couldn't even hear himself.

• • •

Slangman's second squad tasered four more men who had scrambled onto the street. They were hooded and out of commission before the fourth and final F-15, Giese's plane, came in even lower.

• • •

All of this occurred in sixty seconds. There was no place to escape from the shock. And at the precise instant that Giese hit his afterburners seemingly straight above Estavan, there was one more surprise that kept the gang leader and his cronies on the deck. The biggest thing they'd ever seen came lumbering right at them.

The last plane in formation was a C-17 Globemaster, piloted by CPT Susan Mitnick, a beautiful career officer and one of the most respected aviators in the service. The massive airplane under her command was 174 feet long, with nearly an equal length wingspan. It was big enough to ferry tanks, a squadron of paratroopers, and even the president's limo and security detail with their black SUVs loaded with unique aftermarket extras. She'd done it all. In fact, she was the White House's first choice when it came to any mission involving a C-17. Like Giese, her work had taken her around the world. But today, Mitnick flew over Gulfton for dramatic impact and to create more racket. Angling low, loud, and threateningly, she piloted her Globemaster into what looked like a sure collision course, though she had complete control.

• • •

Estavan was the real target as the Globemaster rumbled overhead, seemingly close enough to touch.

Slangman rushed him at chest height. Recht came from a forty-five-degree angle off the right, aiming for his ankles. The simultaneous impact from two Special Forces officers resulted in a rib-crashing tackle right out of an NFL game minus referees. Estavan went down hard and fast. His money scattered, and yet no one was watching what was going on at ground level. Mitnick's scary overflight took care of that.

The orders were not to taser the gang leader. The FBI needed a completely, or nearly completely, intact man to interrogate. It was another matter for the accountant. Rojas went down with a hard faceplant courtesy of two other members of the army's elite squad, never to come up with the same looking nose or all his original teeth.

The arrival of the Globemaster also gave the Special Forces coverage to swarm and secure the apartment building as they would a bunker behind enemy lines.

In all of ninety seconds it was over. The hookers looked around totally surprised that they were surrounded by five uniformed men aiming M-4 carbines at them. They were too traumatized to notice that Manuel Estavan and his minions had vanished.

CHAPTER 53

RUSSIA

"My name is Kleinkorn, Colonel Sergei Kleinkorn. I suspect you go by many names," he proclaimed.

D'Angelo turned slowly. He was certain Kleinkorn had a gun aimed at him. He was right. D'Angelo even recognized the model: a Serdyukov SPS Gyurza Vector SR-1. The short recoil weapon had been adopted by the FSB in 1996. It was a very visible calling card.

"Ah, you've taken notice that you are in a vulnerable position."

D'Angelo said nothing.

"Pity you're a day late, but we were expecting you," the colonel continued. "Oh, and just to keep your ledger sheet up to date, too, you won't need to make any more payments to your friend Gomenko. What do they say in the movies? He cashed out?"

D'Angelo remained silent.

"The front desk tells me you're posing as Dr. Max Yurovich. Well, I can assume your Russian is more than passable; very good. But I'm grateful for the chance to practice my English.

Vinnie D'Angelo weighed his immediate options. He ruled out the window for two reasons: bars and height. And undoubtedly the guard at the door had been wide awake and was now joined by others. Time, however, didn't appear to be an issue. Kleinkorn was in a talking mood.

"I'm sure you're filled with questions. Perhaps we can have a discussion before you depart."

The CIA operative did not like the word *depart*. Too precise.

"May I sit?" D'Angelo asked in Russian. He gestured to one of two seats under the television.

"Your command of the language is excellent," Kleinkorn replied in Russian. "Of course you may."

D'Angelo angled away from Kleinkorn and slowly took the three steps to the chair.

"But do take care not to act hastily." He switched to English. "Despite my age, I maintain the highest marks on the shooting range. And I am quite proficient at this distance."

The American sat and faced the colonel, giving up any advantage he may have had to move quickly when he was standing.

"I don't suppose you want to tell me exactly who you are?"

"No thank you." D'Angelo finally used English.

Kleinkorn laughed. "I didn't think so. No matter, we can find out."

Another comment D'Angelo did not like. But he maintained his poker face.

"You expended a great deal of time and effort trying to find out where our revered Colonel Dubroff was, with the hopes of having a serious chat. I commend you for your own dedication. It harkens back to another era when both our nations stood at the brink of war communicating through a red telephone. At least we won the war on the color of the phone."

D'Angelo smiled. "Do you know the origin of the hot line?"

"Well, yes. It was utilized during the Cuban Missile Crisis between Premier Khrushchev and your President Kennedy."

"Actually earlier, sir. It was the recommendation of atomic physicist Leo Szilard in 1957. His discussions led to Khrushchev accepting installation of the hook up between the Kremlin and the White House."

"Well, I stand corrected. Thank you. I love historical anecdotes, as I see you do, as well."

"Then let's pick up the conversation I was going to have with Dubroff," D'Angelo brazenly stated.

"The Andropov Institute."

"Yes. Your Red Banner program to be specific."

D'Angelo had no reason to withhold the question. Kleinkorn had likely gotten it all from Gomenko.

"Well, that may be a bit too sensitive to share even after all these years. Put yourself in my place. Better yet, your government's position. The United States has many secrets that it keeps under wraps. If the situation were reversed and you held the Serdyukov, which I've noticed you desire, on me at your Walter Reed National Military Medical Center, would you provide me details of the Kennedy Assassination or the Iranian hostage release?"

"Point well taken. But I wasn't here to talk with you."

"Timing was not on your side, Mr. …."

"We'll keep it at mister, Colonel. Speaking of timing," D'Angelo looked at his watch and made a mental note.

"Let me rephrase. Timing is *not* on your side," Kleinkorn said, cavalierly waving his pistol outside the kill zone. "But it is on Russia's. The past and present have merged. The new Russia is beginning to look much like the old. Putin put the building blocks in place. Now we are rebuilding. Oh, we won't call it Communism this time. We are far too democratized for that. Business flourishes and multinational corporations make men wealthy beyond the dacha era when a simple vacation house on the Baltic was a sign of great power. Now wealth allows the new International Russian to travel the world, to buy homes in Maui and gamble in Macau's casinos. And yet, we are becoming a global player again with a checkbook and a real economy."

"And a nuclear arsenal."

"Always."

"But do your young leaders have the experience or judgment?"

Kleinkorn laughed loudly. "Of course not. That's why those of us from the old days are still needed. We tolerate them because they get the votes. No more old men in the Kremlin. At least not visibly. But those of us with experience still watch, gather information, manipulate, blackmail, and control.

"People don't disappear like in the old days. They get fired. They're ruined. But little else unless we find a tweet, a text, or an e-mail not to our liking."

"Or a conversation," D'Angelo offered, referring to Gomenko.

"Quite right, or a conversation. And to that point, it's too bad about your friend. So close to enjoying the next chapter of his life. I hated to surprise him so."

D'Angelo made a quick promise to himself. "Ah, but without experience," he continued good naturedly, "those in power can destroy Russia like your comrades did years ago."

"We have learned from the mistakes of the past."

"Maybe you have, Colonel, but how much longer will you be around? And your protégés? Twenty-eight-year-olds have minds all their own."

"I shall make a point to update you on their *education* for as long as you languish in Krasnokamensk. Sadly, I won't get to see you often. It's a prison camp in Siberia, oh, roughly five thousand kilometers away."

In the immediate this meant that Kleinkorn was not inclined to the pull the trigger.

The Russian frowned. "Perhaps years from now someone will want to swap you. Not now. Not like the 10-for-4 in 2010. That was laughable, wouldn't you agree?"

"I would."

Kleinkorn referred to the ten Russian sleeper spies in New York, Virginia, and Boston. They had lived under the guise of Americans for years, delivering messages about American policy. Ten agents tasked with collecting political gossip that might actually mean something. The Russians termed it the "Illegals Program," but it was fashioned after the old Red Banner curriculum.

Time, however, changed the way things were done. Decades earlier, great effort was made to eliminate all traces of Russian accents through rigorous phonetics classes. Russian habits were drummed out of the agents' default responses. Spies were taught to pass as Americans.

Now, with America more of a melting pot than ever, Russians dialects were heard everywhere, from Fairfax Blvd. in Los Angeles to Fairfax, Virginia.

"Not quite old school," D'Angelo said with a chuckle. "Did you see the *Playboy* photos of Anna Chapman?"

"I did," Kleinkorn remarked. "Definitely not old school."

"And leaked by an ex-boyfriend. You probably learned more about her from the photographs than anything she sent back to Russia."

The Russian enjoyed the comment about the former bank employee who gained the most notoriety of all the spies. They were returned during a very un-Cold War transfer held on the tarmac of

Vienna's international airport rather than the notorious Checkpoint Charlie or the Glienicke Bridge in Berlin.

"Ah, and the pictures in Russia's *Maxim*? Even more suggestive," Kleinkorn added. "Like a silly Bond girl with a Beretta in a lace glove. Believe me, she's a far greater threat at the poker table, though you'll never have the opportunity to take her on."

Kleinkorn showed his complete disgust for the new generation of spies. "And what a waste of resources. All she did was post useless pictures on Facebook and send worthless communiqués from Starbucks. We learned more from Google than her communiqués or from anything the others sent. Except for the public relations value, it was an unmitigated disaster. An embarrassment. But, after her return, Anna became Putin's pal, singing patriotic songs and taking submarine rides with photo ops. Hell, she'll open a mini-mall if they pay enough." He laughed, but not because he was making a joke. He was referring to a joke. "The face of the new Russian spy. Mata Hari for Gen Text."

D'Angelo was encouraged that Kleinkorn was in a talking mood. *A little more, Colonel,* he thought.

"The illegals did demonstrate we can still compete with America," the Russian continued, "even if they were failures from an intelligence point of view. Shame though that we had to give up four double agents for them." His tone changed. "You won't be so lucky."

"I bet you've run far better operations."

"Quite so. Fewer rules in the KGB, more autonomy."

"Better talent?"

"Oh, yes. But how do you know so much?"

"I've read the reports of Major General Oleg Kalugin."

Kleinkorn narrowed his eyes.

"Surely you know Kalugin, Colonel. He ran several agents in Washington in the '60s. Back in the day."

D'Angelo read the silence as important. *Of course Kleinkorn knew him.*

"Remember some of his assignments. Classic Cold War. Didn't he control an agent whose job was to blow the power grid in Washington if we were close to a military conflict?"

"The thing that fiction is made of," Kleinkorn said.

"Like Congressman Lodge?" D'Angelo bravely asked.

Kleinkorn's body stiffened. He was not hiding his feelings well; not playing chess like a Russian master.

"If I'm not mistaken, Kalugin ran another spy who, under the same circumstances, would poison the water supplies in the Washington area. Am I right?"

Kleinkorn's hand tightened on the handle of his gun.

His comment hit a real nerve. *Something more in the present than historic?*

"This is not the time for my confessions. You are in my country and you are not a guest."

"I'm sorry, I've probably worn out my welcome," D'Angelo said as he casually checked his Vostok-Europe 8215 Diver Watch.

"You're not in any rush, are you?" the Russian said sharply.

"No, no, but back to old school for another moment," D'Angelo continued, "since I missed my opportunity to speak with Colonel Dubroff about Mr. Lodge, perhaps you can shed some light on the community you're still running in the United States."

Kleinkorn laughed hard. "Now that you've found your voice, I see you're not shy."

"Never been accused of that, Colonel."

"Ah, but what if there are other ears listening to your voice. How do I know you're not wired directly to Langley?"

"Langley?" D'Angelo asked, hoping to push the FSB agent a little further.

"Langley! Your CIA bosses. The ones who are sending you to prison because of this ridiculous assignment! The ones who don't care about you. Maybe we won't wait until a swap. I can just shoot the mystery spy here and now. Wouldn't you if you discovered that a judge or yet another member of Congress, perhaps one of your popular Tea Party members, was actually a long-time sleeper? I think you would. Bury the news. Destroy the evidence so it doesn't contribute to your country falling apart to an even greater degree. It is, you know. You're on the brink of martial law. Martial law in the United States of America." He laughed again. It was a proud laugh. "Now what could possibly lead to such chaos on your streets? Does it happen by accident? By short-term planning? By religious fanatics and ideologues? By twenty-eight-year-olds, as you so rightly noted? No, my friend. It takes exhaustive preparation, an immense amount of money, and a man with the patience—and the hatred of America—to see it through."

Kleinkorn suddenly stopped. "Oh, you are good." He suddenly realized he'd been baited by an expert. He quickly returned to the friendly, but supercilious, tone he'd been using. "But I merely raise questions…nothing more. And we shall have a great deal of time for more of these intellectual exercises."

"Indulge me for a final question, Colonel."

"Final question?"

D'Angelo ignored the retort. "Your goal can't possibly be to bring down the United States like in a melodramatic Cold War movie. I suspect we have more mutual enemies, and in a global economy you need us."

"True. We do need you for business and growth. Your survival is important to us. But your dominance is another thing. Europe with its failed Euros. America with its politicized Congress and every position fought out on your so-called news channels. You have lost your bearings. Your laws are subject to TV ratings more than the ballot box. And you, like Russia, lie about your votes.

"In the next decade, we will rise to greatness as the United States' stature diminishes. And we can, in the end, thank our dearly departed friend who so expertly ran a training program years ago. His dream will continue. It will provide us with dividends into the future. Sadly, Dubroff shall never get the credit. Perhaps that's why he sought to come to America. The historical recognition, quite deserved, will go to a Syrian businessman on his own mad quest. But enough talk. Your time as a free man and your nation's time as a superpower is over."

D'Angelo smiled. "I don't think so." He glanced at his Lithuanian watch again.

"Why not?" Kleinkorn said waving his gun again.

"Because it is fifteen minutes past the hour."

At that moment the building shook with an explosion three floors below them, and the hospital plunged into darkness.

CHAPTER 54

MOSCOW

D'Angelo's quick study of Kleinkorn told him the old Russian colonel was right-handed and therefore likely to focus and fire center and right. But then again, if Kleinkorn correctly read D'Angelo's body language, he would fire straight and left.

The CIA agent judged Kleinkorn's training to be dominant. Therefore, he dodged to the Russian's right, the direction that an untrained shooter would shoot, but not an experienced spy who thought he'd out-psyched his quarry.

Three shots rang out in the dark. Kleinkorn heard D'Angelo's chair fall to the ground, a fraction of a second before he felt a powerful head ram into his heart.

D'Angelo drove the Russian spymaster right off his seat and onto the floor where he wouldn't immediately, if ever, recover. D'Angelo wasn't going to wait around to find out.

Out in the hall, all hell broke out as expected. This wasn't D'Angelo's first visit to Burdenko Military Hospital. He'd come the previous day, disguised as a maintenance worker, and rigged a timed explosive to the facility's principal lighting grid. The backup generator would kick in, but not for at least thirty seconds. Enough time to make his way off the floor.

D'Angelo's sight was as useless as the guard's outside the room. They squarely collided, with the advantage going to the Russian. D'Angelo felt the guard's gun against his ribs. But shock value also counted for something. In a fraction of a second, the CIA agent twisted the gun up and away, breaking the young man's hand. He followed it up with a sharp upper cut to the jaw, sending the man down. Then he yelled in Russian for others to hear, "*He went upstairs!*"

D'Angelo heard the sound of boots on the tile floor—heading away from him to the left toward the closest stairwell. He went in the opposite direction, to the far stairs.

Ten more seconds, he calculated. He reached the stairway in nine and raced down two flights as the lights began to flicker on. His destination was the main floor and to the right. Considering he was still dressed as a doctor, he could move fairly freely. But escape was not an option. Not yet. D'Angelo casually walked into a semiprivate room that he had scouted the day before. Nothing had changed in twenty-four hours. There was only the comatose patient in bed one closest to the door. D'Angelo crossed to the far bed, pulled the covers aside, got under the covers, and feigned sleep while people ran down the halls. Soon, the commotion lessened and he thought about his next move, which wouldn't be until mid-afternoon the next day. Feeling secure, he fell asleep, not to be disturbed by his roommate or any of the Russian guards who would tire of the search, especially since there was no one alive to give them orders.

He would calmly check himself out the next morning.

CHAPTER 55

WASHINGTON
JANUARY 24

Christine Slocum couldn't hide her excitement.

She was about to enter The White House for the first time. The experience reduced almost everyone to a childlike state of wonder. She tried to keep her composure, but Roarke could tell. So could the uniformed Secret Service agent that checked them through.

"Good morning, Mr. Roarke," Agent Wheeler said.

"Morning. I have a visitor from the Hill. Christine Slocum."

"Picture ID, Ms. Slocum." There was no *please*.

Christine handed her wallet to the thirty-four-year-old agent, who looked like he was carved out of marble.

"Just your identification, miss."

She considered correcting *miss* to *Ms.*, but decided not to. Christine slid her Maryland license out of the window compartment and handed it to Wheeler. He examined it, compared her to the photograph, and checked his log. Roarke had called ahead.

"Thank you, Ms. Slocum," he said, returning the ID. Now your purse and jacket through the X-ray."

Slocum removed her jacket, revealing as perfect a figure as the agent had ever seen. She was positive he tried to stifle a smile.

Roarke sent his overcoat, sports jacket, keys, change, pens, and Sig Sauer P229 pistol through the scan. Once cleared, he reholstered his weapon and then handed Christine her items.

"Now you're on the inside. How does it feel?" Roarke asked.

"Pretty remarkable," the blonde said with genuine enthusiasm.

"Trust me. You're going to experience things that aren't on the tour."

She leaned over and whispered, "If your office door locks, so will you,"

"Whoa," Roarke said into Christine's very sexy eyes. She had disarmed him again.

"Okay," she said slowly, "you lead then."

"Do you always think this way?" he had to ask.

"Let's just say you bring it out in me, Mr. Roarke."

She reached up, nibbled his ear and whispered, "Maybe I'll bring it out of you."

"Down girl."

"Yes, sir," she chuckled. As they continued down the hall Slocum asked, "Is this where the president spoke from the other day?"

"No, that was on the other side. We're coming through the Northwest. But do you want to see it?"

"Sure."

Roarke used his access to cut across. He was waved through by people who were already informed of his presence. Slocum was impressed.

"Here you go. The president's podium was," he walked to the spot, "right here."

"Wow," was all she could manage.

"Now do you know any of the history of this section of the White House?"

"Not a darned thing," she replied.

"Well, early on, President Jefferson turned the entrance hall into an exhibition space for artifacts from Lewis and Clark expeditions.

Later, President Grant began the tradition of hanging presidential portraits here and in Cross Hall up ahead."

"There's probably not a square inch of this place where history hasn't been made."

"And still is," Roarke said. "Undoubtedly even today."

"Oh?" Slocum asked, her interest piqued.

"Just speaking generally. They don't tell me much."

Roarke continued the tour through the East Room, which President Madison had used as his Cabinet Room and where presidents Lincoln and Kennedy laid in state.

They passed through downstairs corridors to the Diplomatic Reception Room, which had been the furnace room until the 1902 White House renovation; then on to the Green Room, an intimate state parlor; and the Red Room, originally used by First Lady Dolly Madison for regular Wednesday social gatherings with members of opposing political parties. Slocum also learned that the Red Room was where Eleanor Roosevelt hosted numerous press conferences for women reporters who were excluded at the time from the president's own press conferences.

Roarke's tour took them through the State Dining Room, then into the famed West Wing and Louise Swingle's office. Between Swingle and the president, visitors had to pass through another office. This one was occupied by the Secret Service.

"Hello, Louise."

She was busy proofing a page and lifted her head to Roarke's familiar voice.

"Mr. Roarke. So nice to see you."

Roarke did not react to her formality, nor she to his. She gave a cursory nod to the woman who stood more than business-close to Roarke.

"May I introduce Christine Slocum? She works with the Speaker. This is her first time to the White House."

"Hello, nice to meet you," she said. Slocum offered her hand. Swingle slowly stood and took it in a noncommittal manner. As easily as Slocum read the Marine's interest in her, she felt a stinging coldness from Swingle.

"Welcome, Ms. Slocum. I trust Mr. Roarke is giving you a proper tour."

"I feel I'm in *very* good hands," she said in an only partially veiled retort. She looked at Roarke and said much more with her eyes.

Roarke interrupted her train of thought.

"Is the president in?" He didn't say *boss* as usual.

"In, but knee deep in chicanery. Directors Mulligan and Evans are with him waiting for word."

Suddenly the conversation seemed very inside to Slocum. She frowned, conveying her confusion.

"I guess there's a lot going on right now," he offered in both an explanation and a question. "So no chance we can say hi?"

"Not now," Swingle answered.

"Okay, let him know I stopped by. I'd love for Ms. Slocum to meet him, and I have a few things to go over."

"Yes," Christine added. "That would be great."

"Perhaps later. We'll see how things go. I'll buzz you. Where will you be?"

"Downstairs, in my office."

Swingle's good-bye was as cool as her hello. Roarke and Slocum left, and the president's secretary typed a note on her computer and then went back to her proofreading.

"She's a tough one," Christine said when they were out of earshot.

"Just protective. That's her job."

"I guess." Slocum slid her arm into Roarke's as they walked. "Speaking of protection."

"Excuse me," he said.

"I meant *your* job, silly."

Roarke laughed at the comment. For once she wasn't being sexual, but it came out that way.

"What's it like being a Secret Service agent, and how come you don't dress like the other guys. What's that all about?"

"Well, first of all it's not all guys. Second of all, we have different duties. Rookies, for example, aren't on the presidential detail. They have to work their way up. Third, a lot of us do research."

"Like you? Funny, I see you as more than simply a researcher."

"Don't get me wrong. Research isn't what you think. It's computer work, but we're also in the field. Typically, the president receives more than three thousand threats a year. The number has grown by leaps and bounds since the rise of terrorism. And with the Internet, it's bound to get worse. We have to know who's out there, and in some cases, we even fraternize with the threats."

"You do what?"

"We call them class 3s. They're subjects who must be supervised if the president is visiting where they are. They're people who, given the chance, might attack the president. Crazies, but not yet arrest-worthy or convictable criminals. Maybe they're medicated. Maybe not. We know about them and we watch them. Sometimes we even take them out bowling or for lunch when the president is coming to their area. Agents will even go to the movies with them to keep them busy."

"I had no idea."

"You're not supposed to."

"And other kinds of bad guys?"

"What about them?" Roarke asked.

"Are you tracking them, too?"

"Am I personally?"

"I don't know, yes," she asked.

"I do a little of this and a little of that."

She stopped him in the stairwell leading downstairs. "Come now, Mr. Roarke. You can reveal yourself to me. After all, I've seen all of you."

"Allow me some mystery," he said.

She leaned close and kissed his lips lightly. "Mmmm. I like figuring out mysteries." She inched away. "I guess that's why they call it the *Secret* Service."

"I never actually thought about that," Roarke said. "Come on, I'll tell you more while we walk."

"You work out all the time?"

"As often as possible."

"And when you can't?"

"Push-ups and sit-ups in hotel rooms," Roarke explained.

"What a waste of a good hotel room," Christine said, reverting back to her normal self.

"Who said they put me in good hotel rooms," he joked.

"So what's it really like?" She was really interested, more interested in Roarke than the tour.

"Like I'm on alert 24/7 for years. From training after I got out of the army. And if I thought the service was tough, I had a real awakening at Rowley."

"Rowley?" she asked.

"Sorry. The Rowley Training Center. RTC. It's where we train and retrain. Outside of the city. Four hundred ninety-three acres of a pure, excruciating playground of extreme driving courses, firing ranges, and tactical shoot houses, including a mock-up of the White House and grounds." He didn't mention that RTC also had a small section of the secret underground White House tunnel system. "We get it all, along with a lot of pain."

"Sounds like it makes the Y look like a cake walk," the blonde beauty added.

"Yup. And every year I have to go back for a refresher."

She stopped again and felt his abs. "Even in your shape, Scott?" Scott came out softly with inviting notions.

He took her hand and kissed it. "It's not always about the physical training. There's the mental side, too. Computer work, classes on nasty chem and biological agents. You name it."

"Today's news."

Roarke punctuated her sentence. "And tomorrow's. We have to be ready for anything including an assassin squirting toxins onto chopped lettuce at a state dinner. And we screen for substances that could kill the president in his hotel suite while he's showering or rolling over on his pillow."

"Wild."

"Daily and serious Secret Service work," he politely corrected.

They rounded a hallway on the lower level and stopped in front of a metal door. "I live inside. It's pretty boring."

"That's okay. Take me in." Again, another suggestive comment. Christine Slocum was never more than one breath away from a sexual comment.

There was no standard key to the door, just a key pad. Roarke quickly entered a series of twelve numbers. The lock clicked and they entered. Lights automatically turned on and the door closed behind them.

Roarke was right. Slocum observed that it was stark and boring. A desk and a computer. Files on the desk. A bank of locked cabinets. Three 35-inch Sony TV monitors. A white board with some notations. And definitely no couch.

"They stick me down here," he explained. "But at least I get an office."

Slocum nodded and went to his desk. She moved some paperwork to the side and sat on the top. She extended her hand, which he took, then pulled him closer.

"I want to hear more," she said. "But closer."

"It excites you?"

"You excite me," Slocum whispered in his ear. It was followed by a sexy nibble.

"We have to be ready for anything and everything: from immediate threats to the president, to threats to the country. We practice everything. Assaults on motorcades. Mortar blasts to *The Beast*."

"The beast?" Her legs tightened around him.

"The president's limousine. If it's disabled, we push it out of a kill zone. And if the president is outside and in jeopardy, we have to be his *meat shield*."

Slocum understood the meaning of that reference. She'd seen the footage of the Secret Service agent covering President Reagan when he was shot in April, 1981.

"Tactically, it's like trying to scare off a bear," Roarke explained. "You rise up as big as possible, getting the president, first lady, children, or vice president's head down and covering the vital parts. If they fall, you pick them up. You have to get them to move. Hoping that your Kevlar—if you're wearing it—stops the bullet from first killing you, let alone the president. Literally, you're the shield. And when you can, you move. Fast. Hell, the word was that on 9/11, two agents grabbed Cheney out of his desk. His feet never touched the ground until he was out of there.

"Oh, and there's one more part of the training that they want you to keep current."

He paused for a moment for impact. "An up-to-date signed will."

Christine Slocum had always been taken care of. Her school had been paid for. Jobs just came. She slept with powerful men—all arranged. It had been easy, fun, and profitable. She'd never been in danger and never knew what her contributions meant except to further a political agenda. But today, now, she had a sense of the other side that trumped her master's degree in political science and her unbelievable skills in the bedroom. She was with a man who would die for his country or kill for it.

Christine pulled him closer. She looked into his eyes and at his lips. This was a moment that would be real for her.

But the phone rang.

"Oh come on," she said dejectedly. "Is this going to be the story of our lives."

"It's already mine."

Her whole body deflated. Her legs slid down and away as Roarke turned to the telephone.

He held up a finger indicating one minute, then answered on the fourth ring.

"Roarke." He listened to one short sentence. "Got it. I'll be right up." He hung down and shook his head. "Duty calls. The president needs ten minutes. Sorry."

"Not as sorry as I am. Can I stay here?"

"There's not much to do."

"No cold shower?"

"Not here," he laughed.

"Go. I'll be fine."

Roarke went for the door. "At least ten minutes. He checked his watch and left.

Ten minutes, she thought, totally frustrated by the interruption. Slocum sighed and looked around the room. *Nothing. Not even a painting.* She continued her survey, which ultimately brought her back to the desk that she sat on. Four folders were to her right. The top was marked *CHICANERY: TOP SECRET.*

Chicanery? She had heard that only minutes earlier. Swingle said the president was reviewing something called *Chicanery.*

Slocum was drawn to the secret file like a moth to a flame. She was in the White House, about to seduce Scott Roarke, as prompted, and now here she was with a secret file. She closed her eyes and visualized the coded e-mail, *Get close to him. Learn everything you can.* A file marked top secret certainly qualified. She touched the folder, wishing the information would intuitively come to her and she wouldn't have to actually open it. Opening the file and reading it took her commitment to helping the loyal opposition, which is what she thought she was doing, to another level. *Would she? Could she? It's right here.*

She slowly picked up the file, placed it in her lap and started rocking back and forth. Her eyes narrowed and her nose crinkled. Tears formed. She rocked more, weighing the options and the consequences. She looked down, then up at nothing in particular.

In another room, the Oval Office, Morgan Taylor, Scott Roarke, FBI Chief Mulligan, and DNI Evans watched the troubled woman over a closed-circuit television camera, simultaneously being recorded on a computer hard drive. Roarke was uncomfortable.

"Crisis of conscience, Mr. Roarke?" Mulligan asked noting his reaction.

"Yes, as a matter of fact. I don't like this."

"Give it five more minutes, Scott." The president understood how he felt. "It's an awfully big step to go from Capitol Hill mistress to International Mata Hari."

"Especially if she doesn't know who she's working for," Roarke offered.

"What do you mean?" Evans asked the question without taking his eyes off the screen.

"We know what she's done. But none of it is illegal. Ill advised. Reprehensible. Yes. But I think she's naïve and maybe innocent."

"Like a hawk innocently eyes a mouse," Mulligan snickered.

Roarke ignored him. "Let me go back in and talk with her before she fucks up her life. She could help us."

"No wait," Mulligan said. "A few more minutes. She's tasted too much of the forbidden fruit to not take a bite of this apple."

CHAPTER 56

CIUDAD DEL ESTE, PARAGUAY
THE SAME TIME

Ibrahim Haddad watched life in America get worse. Thanks to CNN International, the NBC and Fox news channels, and Telemundo, he monitored the unraveling of the infrastructure. Fear spread, perhaps not as quickly as he hoped, but it was surely reaching the heartland. So was distrust in the government. What he hadn't accomplished before was close at hand now. There were things that concerned him, however.

Haddad's plant within the FBI was being more cautious. Communications had slowed when he wanted more information. He'd have to find out why. It made him nervous.

And then there was the woman—Slocum. If there was trouble with his FBI man, there could also be trouble with her. He believed that, if questioned, she couldn't possibly provide any trail that would lead directly to him or Ciudad del Este. But electronic fingerprints were another thing. Haddad had been her benefactor for half her life, but through sheltered foundations. Maybe it had been a mistake to connect her so directly with the Secret Service agent. *Maybe*… He thought about the possibilities. Then his mind fixed on his ultimate target: *the so-called nation of Israel.* With the United States focused on its own troubles it was time to set his last move in motion. Haddad dialed a cell phone number reaching a man conducting some unrecorded business on Av San Blas, one of the city's main shopping districts.

"Midhat, it's H," he said in Spanish. "Tomorrow night at my home. Bring Ahmad and Mustafa. Seven o'clock."

The man confirmed the information and hung up.

The meeting was set. *A month, maybe less, we strike.*

With the call completed, Ibrahim returned to his concern about the American woman.

THE WHITE HOUSE
MINUTES LATER

It had been more than ten minutes. Fifteen now. After coming to her decision Christine Slocum pulled herself together and awaited Roarke's return.

The door opened but it wasn't Roarke who came in first. It was President Morgan Taylor. Roarke followed a few steps behind. Though she didn't recognize the other two men, she'd soon find out.

"Ms. Slocum, it's time we have a chat."

The sight of the president drained her. After all, this was *the* president of the United States.

"Mr. President," was all she could manage.

"Mr. Roarke doesn't have a lot of places to sit. So why don't you just return to his desk where you were a few minutes ago."

She looked at Roarke and the others, confused. Roarke pointed to one overhead light fixture that contained a camera, then another in the clock facing her.

"I…" She choked as she tried to get more out. "I didn't…"

"We know," Roarke said in a comforting tone. "We know. If you had, you would have only seen or photographed a fabricated plan. But you didn't, and it's time you come over to the other side."

"I'm…"

"You, my dear, have been knowingly or unknowingly manipulated almost your whole adult life. We want to find out who and why."

She looked at Roarke again, now frightened.

"Who is he? What…"

"Christine, this is FBI Chief Mulligan and the Director of National Intelligence, Evans."

"Oh my God, am I under arrest? I haven't done anything."

"Oh, you've done a great deal, Ms. Slocum," the president said, "with puppet strings attached to you. Your contact with Mr. Roarke after your associations with the Speaker and Congressman Lodge were much too coincidental. Were you told to seduce him?"

The direct question from the president explained it all. She had been instructed to connect with Scott just as she had with Lodge and Duke Patrick. Lodge had been exciting. He was a powerful man on the rise and was destined to be president. Patrick, on the other hand, was a political buffoon yet fun to tease. She hadn't slept with him... yet. And Scott? Scott Roarke could have been real...*if he was real*, she thought. *But he isn't.*

Tears flowed for more reasons than she could count. "I didn't read anything. I didn't know... "

CHAPTER 57

THE CAPITOL ROTUNDA
THE SAME TIME

The Speaker of the House approached the pool microphone. The video cameras, smaller by the year, were locked on him. Still cameras, looking just like many of the video cams, snapped away. A hint of what Duke Patrick was going to propose had been leaked strategically by Christine Slocum to*Huffington Post*. One blogger. One sentence. From there it went viral in thirty minutes. This was going to be the most important address of the Speaker's life. *And now, where the hell is Christine?* he asked himself. The forty-nine-year-old congressman relied on her for focus, rehearsals, quotable sound bites, even the right tie. Everything. Including this speech, word for word. *Christ!* He couldn't wait a second longer. He was live across the nation, on Fox News, CNN, MSNBC, and progressive and conservative syndicated radio shows.

"Thank you for giving me your time today," Patrick said without a hint of his characteristic smile. "I will get right to the point." He gave the reporters a long, somber stare and took a beat before continuing.

That was a trick Slocum taught him their first day. "Wait and think before you speak," she instructed. Another trick: "I always want you to have a paperclip or a dime in your fingertips. Casually transfer it from one hand to another as you talk. We won't see the object, but it'll keep your gestures from feeling awkward."

"Today, with profound sadness, but for the good of the country, I call for an investigation into what did the president know and when did he know it." He borrowed the phrase from Tennessee Senator Howard Baker's cross examinations during the Watergate Hearings.

Career defining and explosive. That's what Slocum had told him. Patrick felt it as he spoke the words.

"We have lost confidence in Morgan Taylor as a leader. He has not demonstrated the ability to end this horrible crisis, to save American lives, and set things right. By setting things right, I mean find the perpetrators and kill them. But we must also discover how long the administration delayed going to the public, which, in turn, continues to result in the deaths of thousands upon thousands of Americans. Where this will go from here, I cannot say. But it is Congress' responsibility to find out.

"I am compelled to demand, on behalf of the American people, that the House of Representatives examine the facts leading up to this horrible attack. That we do it now. That we do it with or without the president's help. Thank you."

There must have been close to forty reporters who called out "Mr. Speaker!" simultaneously. He chose one, a reporter from MSNBC.

"Congressman, according to my sources, the president only recently learned of the attack and then moved on it. What is there to investigate?"

Patrick counted to three and transferred the paperclip he was manipulating with two fingers in his left hand to his right. *Time to ignore the question and reframe the argument;* another Slocum tip.

"President Taylor failed the nation," Patrick said dead seriously. "According to my sources at the Centers for Disease Control, the White House was briefed on this in time to do something. How many people would be alive today if he had brought this act of terrorism to the American public when it started? I can't answer that, but I certainly can demand an answer to the question."

"Congressman, you are certain the White House knew? How early?" asked AP.

"A week or more." He invented the time frame. "And now Americans are afraid to turn on their taps; afraid to have their morning coffee;

afraid that their faucet and even bottled water will mean death. Next will come martial law and a complete usurpation of our rights."

A question from Fox News. "Will you call for Morgan Taylor's resignation?"

"The president did not prevent or contain this crisis. He has not brought it to an end. He has lost the confidence of the American people. That's all I'll say until we convene our investigation."

More questions. More dodging and pontificating. The Capitol Hill two-step.

"In short, America is at war and we have no evidence that President Taylor has done anything to protect us."

"Mr. Speaker!" shouted the young woman CNN reporter. "Based on the present situation, the impact on the public's confidence in the available water supplies, and the subsequent surge in beverage-related stocks at the expense of the rest of the market, won't your investigation lead to more uncertainty and unrest?"

Patrick filled his lungs, transferred the paperclip again, and peered directly into the camera.

"No. The answer is no. I am seeking to restore stability and show the world how we re-establish confidence that has been lost. Confidence that Morgan Taylor cannot personally regain."

It was the sharpest attack the reporter ever heard on camera. The thirty-five-year-old Columbia School of Journalism graduate was about to have her defining moment on TV, too.

"Mr. Speaker, is this more about you than President Taylor? If he had not requested quick approval of General Johnson as vice president, then you would be next in the line of succession."

"This is not about me!" The reaction had the effect of calling out the reporter for her insolent comment. "Not one bit." Patrick took another deep breath, transferred the paperclip and calmly approached the question. "This is about the health and well-being of the United States of America. And for that reason, Morgan Taylor must do the right thing. Submit to an investigation."

His actual speech was hardly more than 150 well-rehearsed words. There would be much more spoken and written about it in the next ten minutes, let alone in the nation's history.

Career defining and explosive. Absolutely. But Duke Patrick's timing couldn't have been worse.

THE WHITE HOUSE
SCOTT ROARKE'S BASEMENT OFFICE

Morgan Taylor wasn't watching Duke Patrick's tirade. He had no time and certainly no regard for the bombastic House Speaker. But Christine Slocum was another matter; a political chess piece on the other side of the chessboard. *Are you a pawn or a knight?* he wondered.

"Ms. Slocum, now that you're here, you can be of great help to us."

"Help?" she said regaining her exposure.

Taylor cued Robert Mulligan to join in. Roarke and Evans watched.

"You've been at the apex of some high-level activities. And as best we can determine, though you are a very bright and accomplished young woman, things have come your way very easily. Without you having to do much. Am I correct?"

She acknowledged that fact.

"Your Congressional appointments. Your scholarship, internships, and jobs just happened, along with a monthly stipend."

"Trusts and foundations," Slocum replied. "Merit awards in school."

Mulligan stepped closer. He'd been holding a file under his arm, which he now presented.

"You didn't look at Mr. Roarke's folder. You're going to want to read this one."

"What is it?"

Mulligan opened it up and put it in her hands. "Did you ever wonder how your parents died?"

CHAPTER 58

THE WHITE HOUSE

Christine Slocum now answered direct questions posed by Roy Bessolo, one of the most unpleasant men she'd ever met. She knew one other in the room, by sight. The attorney general. The only comfort she had was seeing Scott Roarke, who stood against a wall and listened intently.

"You never questioned where your support came from?" Bessolo barked. They were well into the so-called "informational session."

"No. It all looked legitimate. I'll show you the letters. They always came from foundations I thought my parents set up."

"And the foundations told you you'd be fucking a presidential candidate?"

Eve Goldman cleared her throat; a signal for him to calm down.

Bessolo barely corrected himself. "Excuse me, I meant who you needed to cozy up to."

"No, that was all me."

"Bullshit."

"I've always…"

"Fucked anyone you wanted to? No need to respond, Ms. Slocum. We're getting a pretty clear picture of how you operated and who your conquests were."

"But no one told me to," she started to explain.

"They didn't have to. They knew your serial behavior and counted on it."

Slocum turned to the AG. "I think I need a lawyer. I'd like to call a lawyer." She reached for a tissue as an additional layer of her resolve slipped away.

"Ms. Slocum, you are not under arrest," Eve Goldman explained again. "As far as we can tell, you have not committed any crime. But that does not mean you were not involved, even unsuspectingly, of assisting others who evidently duped you. We need your help. We need it now."

"Okay, I'll try."

Bessolo returned to his last point.

"You were apparently very creative in all areas. You wrote campaign speeches, position papers." He put undo emphasis on *position.* "And you filled in for Mrs. Lodge rather well."

"Agent Bessolo!" Goldman commented in a scolding town. "Please."

It was definitely a game of good cop/bad cop.

SAN ANTONIO, TEXAS
RANDOLPH AFB
THE SAME TIME

Much has been written and debated about "enhanced interrogation techniques," a euphemism in some circles for torture; "applied encouragement" to others.

This would be neither. Though his name might have hinted he'd be attaching electrodes to testicles, Raymond Watts entered the isolation cell within the airplane hangar without any such equipment. He was prepared to offer Manuel Estavan a straight-forward take-it-or-leave-it deal, with a few key caveats.

"Mr. Estavan, we don't have a great deal of time," the career FBI agent stated, even before the door behind him slammed shut. And it did slam with a huge bang.

Estavan sat at a metal chair bolted to the floor, adjacent to a stainless steel table. On the surface, a half-filled paper cup of water and a pack of the gangster's unlit Chesterfields. They would remain unlit.

The MS-13 gang leader followed Watts as he walked around the room. He saw that age was not a factor in the man's strength. He calculated that the agent was around fifty and at least twice as powerful as he was.

Watts circled the perimeter, staying clear of Estavan. He took off his sports jacket, revealing upper arms twice as large as most men's thighs. He swept Estavan's water off the table, and laid his carefully folded jacket on the surface. He picked up the cigarettes, crumpled them, and said, "This is a federal building. No smoking's allowed."

Then Watts circled the room again.

"There are cameras up there." He pointed to a half-moon metal bowl in the center of the ceiling. "Four in fact. Microphones are planted in the table. They'll pick up everything." He approached Estavan and spoke softly into his ear. "Even a whisper. Right?" Watts looked at a mirror facing them.

They heard a knock through the glass.

"One-way mirror. We're being watched, listened to, and recorded. Live to the FBI officers on the other side. Live to Washington. And, if the conversation doesn't go too well from my perspective, it'll go viral to your family and friends back in Guatemala. Your mother and sister still live there, Mr. Estavan."

The gang leader tried to ignore the veiled threat, but couldn't. He flinched.

"Yes, we know all about them." Watts came closer and squatted across the desk. He looked at Estavan squarely in the eyes. "How long do you think they'll survive if the video goes out on the Internet? You know we can dub, subtitle, zoom in. It's really amazing."

This was not how Estavan thought it was going to go down. Beating, yes. Threats to his family, no.

Watts stood up and resumed his pacing. "That's the nice part of technology. Smart phones everywhere. We can even go live from this room. Right here. Right now. One call to your family. We have their number. I'm sure they'd be surprised to hear what kind of man you've become. What you've done with your life. For that matter, we can make sure your rivals get dialed in. Of course, at some point, the conversation would inevitably lead to how you've sold everyone out. You might deny it, but you think they'd buy it? I don't. They'd probably want to make an example of you…through your mother and your sister." He paused for a beat. "Natalia's pregnant, you know. Her first child."

This was news to Estavan. Staggering news. His eyes swelled with tears; the first time in years.

"You wouldn't," he finally said.

"Oh, we would, Mr. Estavan." He looked back at the one-way mirror. Two taps came back at them in confirmation.

"Live. Here and now," the six-foot-two retired Marine made his point. "But that won't end it. We'll let you back out on the streets. What will your life expectancy be? Days? I'd say minutes.

"You know how painful and difficult beheadings are. Nothing simple about it. Maybe you'll man up to the moment. But your mother and Natalia? Would they make your mother watch your sister die or the other way around? How would you stage it? Or maybe they'd record your death, show it to them, then cut their throats. So many options."

THE WHITE HOUSE

"Ms. Slocum, the attorney general said we're not charging you with anything." He paused. "But should we?"

"No. I just did what I was told."

The comment hung in the air.

Roarke stepped forward. He showed real compassion when he quietly asked, "Who told you, Christine? Who?"

She took his hand. "I never knew. I just got some instructions over the Internet. Nothing that seemed really wrong. In fact it was exciting. I thought that's how Washington works."

She was right, but Roarke didn't say it.

"And sometimes I had to send some messages out..."

• • •

There are many ways to get information from an asset to a handler. The traditional method is through a dead drop, so named because it involves a person dropping off a message. It's usually coded information inserted into a container of some sort and left at a prearranged location. Another person then picks it up and moves it along or decodes the communiqué. It's the thing of John LeCarré novels and Cold War intrigue.

Dead drops, like live drops—a face-to-face meeting, are still used. But with the development and proliferation of the Internet, a whole new world of anonymous data transfer has emerged.

That's how Christine Slocum delivered her information.

"In pictures," she offered. Slocum reached for another tissue but didn't let go of Roarke's hand. "A kind of nerdy guy came over a year ago and showed me how to do it."

"How to do what?" Bessolo barked none too politely.

"To send and receive through pictures. But it was always gossip. You'd find better stuff on *TMZ,*" she complained.

• • •

For years, there had been rumors that Al Qaeda embedded coded messages in Internet photographs. It wasn't until 2010, however, that the FBI was able to confirm the actual use of high-tech data concealment.

The technique requires a degree of technological training, but not a lot. Basically, it involves changing the numeric code that computers assign to a picture's colors. To produce a computer picture on-screen, the computer gives every pixel three numeric values. They refer to the amount of primary colors—red, green, and blue that are generated in each pixel. Changing these values even to a small degree, allows spies to hide computer language of 1s and 0s in the picture's pixel numbers.

This doesn't change a picture's appearance. However, it does create an electronic dead drop. With billions of pictures on the Internet, analysis by the CIA or NSA is virtually impossible.

While the technology is new, the act of concealing messages within images is not. *Steganography,*as it is called, is as old as governments and regimes themselves. It goes back at least as far as the ancient Greek messages tattooed into the shaved scalps of couriers, which became invisible as a head of hair regrew. Truly simple in its day; technologically elegant in modern times.

Christine Slocum was as adept at the computer as she was in the bedroom.

• • •

"Look lady," Bessolo said, leaning right into her face, "this isn't a god-damned reality television show. You are in serious trouble…"

"I thought I was okay as long as I…"

Bessolo didn't let her finish. "Quite honestly, the attorney general has told you some things that I'm not happy with. And when I'm not happy, I am committed to make you unhappy and very, very miserable. So confine your answers to specifics and save the commentary for your best-selling autobiography five years from now."

Roarke patted her shoulder. "Just answer, Christine. We'll be through soon."

"I'm trying."

"Did you ever know who you were sending reports to?" Bessolo asked.

"A think tank in Maryland."

"What think tank?"

"I don't know."

"And you didn't want to find out?"

"I should have."

"Damned straight!"

"Mr. Bessolo," Attorney General Goldman chided. "Let's stick to the questions."

"Yes, ma'am," he said only somewhat apologetically. He returned to Slocum barely changing his tone. "What kind of information did you pass, Ms. Slocum?"

"Like I said. Gossip. Sex stuff mostly. Short on details." She looked at Roarke and pleaded, "I wouldn't have said anything, Scott."

"People you were ordered to sleep with?" Bessolo demanded.

"Yes. No. Not ordered to."

"Doors opened up for you pretty automatically," the attorney general offered from a few feet away. "You never thought that was odd? That these partners came so easily to you." Goldman hesitated to measure her next words, and then proclaimed what should have been abundantly obvious to Slocum. "You never realized you were spying?"

"No. No! Why do you say that? Scott, what are they trying to do?"

RANDOLPH AFB

"We have a problem that you helped create. Now you're going to help us solve it. You're going to do it without me having to lay a hand on you—which I'm quite capable of doing. Or worse, my colleagues will step in. They cut their teeth in Iraq, and what they didn't learn there, they sure made up for in Afghanistan.

"They're all muscle. I'm what they call the negotiator. They don't believe in what I do a lot. And I don't like what they do all that much. But at the end of the day, we need information. So one way or another we'll get it."

Watts moved closer and said, barely above whisper, "So here's the deal. You answer all my questions without any hesitation; without any lying."

"If I do?" Estavan asked tentatively.

"If you don't!" he shouted as he turned to the mirror. They heard a loud knock back. "If I were you, I'd just open up right now."

The killer looked like a little boy who had done something terribly wrong.

"And *when* I do?"

"*When* is *now.* And we will come to an arrangement."

The word confused Estavan. "An arrangement?"

"A business arrangement, Mr. Estavan. Because you will be out of the business you were in and we couldn't possibly allow you to continue."

"And then?"

"We'll talk about a new job. You'll be working for us."

"And if I don't like this *arrangement?*"

"We will always have the recordings. We'll always know where your family is. Where your*friends,*" he stressed in a sarcastic way, "are. You *will* work for us. The details, of course, are a bit sketchy at this moment. But as the responsible adult in this equation; responsible to your mother and sister, I think you get it."

Estavan's will, all but drained, barely held him in his chair. He had no fight left.

"Shall we begin," Watts said.

THE WHITE HOUSE

"Christine, you were being used and you used other people," Goldman added softly. "By definition, you were a spy. And knowingly or not, you were reporting to someone. Perhaps a foreign national. Think. Do you have any idea at all?"

"No. Honestly no."

"Okay," Bessolo said completely changing his tone. "I believe you don't."

Christine cried grateful tears.

"But your computer will."

Over the next twenty minutes Slocum described everything in detail; how she chose noncopyrighted photographs to manipulate; those unlikely to be pulled from Internet use. She provided the names of URLs she found instructions on and how she signaled through innocent-looking, but coded Facebook postings.

The session concluded with Roy Bessolo telling her exactly what would happen next. "Now you will, with full knowledge, help us. You'll tell lies and you'll help us find who and where your handlers are. You'll feed them information that will trigger responses…that will chip away at their armor…that will lead us to them. More of the game, as you said. This time, we make the rules. Do you understand, Ms. Slocum? Do you fully understand?"

"Yes sir, I do."

"Mr. Roarke is going to get you something to eat. Take your time. We've got a team over at your apartment now checking for listening devices and cameras. They'll clone your computer, laptop, and iPad. Figure a few more hours and you can go home. Tomorrow, you slip back into your normal routine and continue to see Mr. Roarke as if nothing has happened. It will require some good acting, but apparently you already have that talent."

RANDOLPH AFB

In the end, no real interrogation was required. The MS-13 gang leader gave Watts phone numbers, bank routing numbers, dates and locations, pseudonyms, call signs, his transporters still on the road, and other Maras likely to be involved in different cities. Estavan explained how money was wired to his accounts in Cyprus and St. Vincent, how cash was withdrawn and brought into the United States by couriers, and how he first got involved with a well-dressed foreign businessman two years earlier.

Watts called his boss, FBI Director Mulligan, after the "discussion" concluded.

"Did he ever directly meet his contact?" the FBI chief asked.

"No," Watts said. "But it wasn't simply a *contact*. Estavan indicated that he wasn't speaking to a go-between. This was the guy. He knew everything and berated and threatened the gang leader like someone who was in charge of facts, money, and the plan."

"No name?" Mulligan asked.

"Only a pseudonym. *Solon.*"

"Solons? What the hell kind of word is that?"

"Don't know. We're running it now. Feels Middle Eastern. And even though Estavan doesn't really have an ear for accents, we ran some tape for him and he seemed to feel that Solons fit a Middle Eastern voice pattern."

Given the threat, Mulligan wasn't surprised. Given the scope of the attack, he had one man in mind.

"Can Estavan dial Solons again?"

"Not according to the last conversation."

"But can he?"

"Well, why don't I bring him a cell phone and find out," Watts said.

"Do it. Now. And keep him on long enough for an international trace. In the meantime, stay on those numbers and bank accounts and let me know the soonest you have something on this *Solons.*"

CHAPTER 59

WASHINGTON, D.C.
LATER

Roarke and Christine returned to the apartment at 9:45. The "exterminators" left a note on her door indicating that they found no evidence of cockroaches, but they would be back in two weeks to check again. They also tagged three other doors on the floor requesting a time and date for an inspection. Of course, it was for show.

"You definitely had bug problems," Roarke said as planned. He'd gotten a text confirmation from Bessolo's FBI team that indeed she did, hidden in the walls and the phone. Now they ran the conversation they rehearsed at the White House.

"I saw some run through the kitchen and under the stove," she added. This building has had problems." Bessolo backed that up with some false paperwork with the exterminator company, an agency cover that actually performed two jobs. Removing insects and rodents and installing listening devices and cameras.

"Same with my building, especially in the winter. Guess they're trying to stay warm, too."

All of this was outside her door.

"How about you, want to get warmer?"

"Warmer?" he asked.

"Actually, I was thinking more about *hot.*"

This was off the script.

When first told about the hidden microphones, Christine was embarrassed. Then she felt violated and angry. Now she didn't seem to care. She stood on her toes, dropped her purse and keys on the floor and found his lips giving him a very real, though short kiss. Then she worked up to his ear and whispered, "Got to make it sound real."

Christine Slocum was right.

• • •

And so it went. A bottle of Pinot Noir, light classical music, candlelight, a move from two chairs at the table to the living room couch to Christine's bedroom.

That's where they rested making fitting noises for twenty minutes. Just noise. When the playing was over, Christine rested her head on Roarke's chest. He held her and ran his fingers through her hair, feeling her body shake as she wept, resigning herself to reality. Christine longed to make love with him, to feel him inside, to feel protected by his strength. There would be none of that, and Slocum cried more.

Roarke touched her tears with his finger. She nestled in closer. He held her affectionately, but not lovingly. And there, they feel asleep.

At 2 a.m. Roarke whispered loud enough for the microphone to pick up, "I have to go."

"Why?" she asked quite honestly.

"Got an early meeting with the boss on what's going down." It should have been enough to interest anyone who might be listening live or playing recordings later.

"Oh?" she said, again rehearsed.

"Can't talk about it now."

"Please stay. I really want you to stay." She meant it.

"I'm sorry." Roarke was.

There was the sound of dressing staged for the microphones. "Can I see you after work?"

"I hope so," he answered. "I'll call you."

"Will you really?" It was a typical question after a first night in bed.

"Really." He returned to the bed and kissed her on the forehead.

"Wait, I'll walk you to the door. She slipped out of bed with the sound of her bare feet adding to the authenticity.

"I wish you could stay." She meant it.

"Me too." He didn't.

At the door, Slocum took the chance again, raised up on her toes to reach his lips and kissed him. He separated from her and smiled. And she knew there would be no more.

• • •

Two transcripts of the conversation would be made in the morning. One going to the FBI from their microphones; another eventually to

Ibrahim Haddad from his mics with what would confirm very credible contact. However, it really wasn't necessary.

CHAPTER 60

RANDOLPH AFB

"Hello Solon, it's Estavan. I have to talk to you."

"What? No! Do you have any idea of the hour?" Haddad was furious with the gang member. Another loose end he would absolutely have to deal with.

"Wait it's important. There's a problem."

That got Haddad's attention.

"What kind of *problem*?"

Estavan spoke slowly as he had been rehearsed. He was also told to use longer sentences to give the CIA computer tracers more time.

"One of my drivers got away. He called and said someone tried to kill him. I listened to him. Of course, I didn't say anything. But he's alive."

"That's your problem not mine. Take care of it."

"He's in jail in Montana. The police found him on the side of the road after his car blew up. They started doing some checking and…"

Watts watched on his iPad as the trace worked its way from Houston to Bonn, Germany, to Istanbul, Turkey…

He gave Estavan a stretch, as if pulling an invisible string apart with two hands.

"If he starts talking, it's going to come back to me."

"Look. You take care of this now."

The trace continued to Jakarta, Indonesia…

"You do it or I'll have someone who will. If that happens, then your usefulness to me will have ended."

Jakarta to Mexico City…

"I can do it," Estavan said. "I've got people nearby. Someone can slip in the jail where he is."

"Then we don't have a problem." Haddad stated.

"No, Solon." Estavan was running out of ways to stretch.

...Mexico City to Ciudad del Este, Paraguay. That's where the signal terminated.

"No more calls. Ever."

"Yes, Solon. But..."

The line went dead. Watts was satisfied.

CHAPTER 61

WASHINGTON, D.C.
JANUARY 25
0125 HRS

The January cold slapped Roarke in the face. He'd done what he'd been ordered and he wasn't happy. He couldn't say *nothing* happened. Not now. But *nothing else* would happen.

The frigid wind made it all the more clear to him. Katie Kessler was the one and only.

Roarke's personal thoughts did not prevent him from noticing a man who suddenly slinked down into a black Thunderbird parked down the street.

Roarke avoided eye contact. But there was no conceivable reason for a man to sit in a parked car in the middle of a twenty-degree night pretending to be asleep. No one in his right mind.

He passed the car and continued down the street away from Slocum's apartment. Roarke kept his ear cocked for the sound of a car door opening, which it did not. He peered back before turning the corner of Dumbarton onto Twenty-ninth Street NW.

Intuitively, Roarke recognized that he was dealing with someone equally cautious.

He crossed the street and waited for some coverage to allow him to double back. A minute later he had it. A *Washington Post* delivery truck approached. The driver already had his blinker on to turn left back onto Dumbarton where Slocum lived.

He ran alongside the truck and ducked behind a van diagonally opposite the Thunderbird. The limited street light made it hard to see. He looked for movement again, a beep of a lock unlocking, the door opening.

Still nothing. Worse. Less than nothing.

Roarke crouched down, retraced his steps, and crossed the street with the cover of a passing car. He slowly crept up. Only feet away now, with his Sig Sauer in his right hand, he raised up.

"Shit!" he exclaimed.

The driver was gone.

Roarke raced back to Slocum's. The downstairs door had been jimmied open with a screwdriver.

Roarke had three flights to cover. He calculated the time lost. Two minutes at the most that *Bird,* the name he dubbed the man, had on him.

Do the math, he told himself as he took the stairs two at a time. *Fifteen seconds to get to the door. He took another fifteen to get through the lock. Forty-five seconds to climb the stairs. Another fifteen at the upstairs door. What's that?"* Roarke added it up. *Thirty seconds to play with!*

Roarke ran faster. A lot could happen in thirty seconds.

When he reached the landing on the second floor he heard a door close one more flight up. *In or out?*

Out. He saw Bird approach the steps.

Bird saw Roarke as well and fired first. The only thing missing as the bullet sped through the silenced barrel was his aim. Roarke dove down and leveled his weapon, more prepared than his quarry, but now without a target. Bird ran up to the fourth floor.

Roarke followed, passing Christine's door with single-mindedness.

A floor above him, the door to the roof flew open. Roarke felt the cold air as he rounded the landing. Bird fired a second shot. It was wide but only by inches. Roarke pressed his body flat against the wall, creating an awkward obtuse angle for the gunman. Neither man had a good shot or an advantage…but the power of a bullet fired from a Sig Sauer at a distance of less than twelve feet, and the resulting impact it can have against a one-inch dry wooden door, can be significant.

Roarke saw the end of Bird's Walther barrel four feet above floor level. He traced back to where the arm and torso would be. He stepped out into the hall and fired three quick shots into the door.

It wasn't just the bullets that killed Bird. Wood shards had drilled through the man's heart.

Roarke ran back down the stairs to Christine's apartment. He used his full body weight to crash through her door. Once inside he saw the most beautiful blonde he'd ever met dead on her lonely bed.

• • •

Two hours later, Roarke stood outside Katie's apartment totally drained. He looked up to her second floor bay window. The bedroom light was still on. He had a key, but he rang the doorbell instead. Moments later, she called through the intercom.

"Yes, who is it?"

"Me."

There was a long pause, then soft-spoken "Okay," and the buzzer that unlocked the front door.

Upstairs, Katie stood in her doorway. She recognized that something was terribly wrong. All other thoughts disappeared with his distress.

"What's the matter? What happened?"

Roarke looked lost for the first time. "I couldn't save her, Katie. I tried, but I couldn't save her."

"Here, come in." She took his hand and led him inside.

"What? How," she asked, drawing him to her couch.

"I set her up and they killed her."

The words hadn't fully sunk in yet. Katie looked perplexed. Then it all came to her. She whispered, "Oh no."

"Christine Slocum, Katie. Christine. Shot in her bed."

"Oh my God."

"It was my fault, Katie."

"No! It wasn't."

"It was. I left. I shouldn't have left."

She let go of his hand. He sensed why.

"Nothing happened, Katie. Nothing was going to happen. But if I hadn't left, or if I had gotten back there in time? I tried."

She took his hand again and squeezed it gently.

"I set her up."

"Wrong," Katie said defiantly. "She set you up. I've talked to Eve Goldman. Christine pursued you, on orders, like she pursued others."

"And I tricked her. Entrapped her."

"Don't go legal on me. You did not entrap her, mister."

"The scene at the gym where you walked out. *We* set her up, Katie."

"And how do you know that had anything to do with her death? She'd likely outlived her usefulness to..." Katie suddenly stopped, shocked at what she'd said and the *we* he used. "Jesus, Scott, what did we get into?" she said.

CHAPTER 62

OMAHA, NEBRASKA
JANUARY 28

It started with a brick. One brick against a Department of Water and Power truck windshield window.

Sharon Fitzgerald had never done anything remotely illegal before in her life. But she'd never held a dead child in her arms either.

The brick smashed through the front driver's side. It happened too quickly for Sam Masters, himself a father of two, to swerve out of the way of the woman who threw it; the woman holding some sort of package. He'd never find out what it was.

Sharon Fitzgerald died on the spot. Sam Masters would join her shortly. He slammed into a utility pole at forty mph. It collapsed on his cab. The impact didn't kill him. That honor went to three men who witnessed the impact.

"Hey, he killed the mom and her kid." A fact that was only half true and not his fault; a fact that was lost on the scared men. They saw the DWP as the embodiment of the means by which poisoned water was reaching their homes. Sam Masters worked for the DWP. He was an instrument of death. They made the connections that fast. And they beat him to death and then torched the truck.

A crowd gathered and cheered at the spectacle. These were the same people who would have helped Masters to safety barely a week earlier. But not today. Not in Omaha or many other cities and towns across the country. Frightfully similar scenarios were playing out in Fort Meyers, Florida; Portsmouth, New Hampshire; and Albany, New York. Eight hot spots yesterday. Twenty-five today. Probably one hundred tomorrow.

The anger was lit by fear, fueled by bloggers, fanned by talk radio, and impossible for local police to contain.

THE WHITE HOUSE

John Bernstein tossed the morning's *Washington Post* on the president's coffee table. The front page was uncharacteristically all pictures, all bad. Rioting across the country. People running through the streets looking for targets and finding them with nothing but dread in their hearts and nothing in their minds. Inside, more pictures and articles to go with them that depicted and described looting in supermarket aisles; police barricades and fires. Inevitably, thefts expanded their bounty from soda bottles and prepacked juices at Safeways, Publixs, Ralphs, and Shaws to items that had nothing to do with water. They hit the big box stores like Best Buy, Walmart, and Fry's Electronics. Self-preservation gave way to chaos. Poisoning was the trip wire for turning a country of laws into a lawless third-world nation.

"It's going to get worse," Bernstein predicted. "By the hour. You've got to get the National Guard in. Bush put four thousand troops and one thousand federal officers on standby in Los Angeles in '92. At this rate we could have five hundred LAs, maybe a thousand, by the end of the week."

Morgan Taylor focused on a notion shared by millions and celebrated by one. "How can this happen in America?" He knew the answer. In the age of hate speech and demagoguery, too many people were only a flashpoint away from reverting to primal behavior. The worst, and often most popular, talk show hosts encouraged it. The best couldn't stop it.

The president answered his own question. "This happened because it can. A total breakdown of civil authority. No missiles or bombers, but in a matter of days, civil authority as we know it will be at risk of disappearing."

Taylor stood and looked out the West Wing window where John Kennedy had contemplated where and how the Cuban Missile Crisis would end. This is where Lyndon Johnson realized he had lost the America people and the Vietnam War. Where Ronald Reagan fashioned an end to the Cold War. Where George W. Bush strategized over lost causes; the world's and his own. Now it was Morgan Taylor's time to wonder. *How many would die?*

He turned to the TV sets in his office. The sound was down, but the images were virtually all the same. CNN, MSNBC, FOX News, NBC, CBS, ABC, HLN. All the same.

CNN cut to a camera outside the White House. District police were moving forward, driving protesters away from the iron fence along Pennsylvania Avenue. A young man tried to climb over. An officer grabbed him and slammed him to the ground. This only encouraged others to go for the fence. A stupid and deadly move. It wasn't a problem with one or two, but when it became twenty…

Snipers on the White House roof had them in their sights.

Taylor heard the shots through the walls that couldn't be heard over the muted TV. A horrible situation had, as Bernstein said, just gotten really worse.

• • •

The rioters never expected to see the president. But as he rushed to the gate, running faster than his Secret Service detail, the crowd hushed. Men, women, and children traded the rocks in their hands for their cell phone cameras. Their coverage would go viral.

Morgan Taylor knelt down beside the victim. He took off his suit jacket and covered the young man's head. The president was exposed to the freezing cold in only shirtsleeves. Taylor shook his head revealing his utter sorrow; an emotion that few presidents would dare show the world. Then he rose and looked around. More than three hundred people at the foot of 1600 Pennsylvania Avenue were stone silent. The fight was out of them.

Taylor seized the moment.

"This is America," he said in a sweeping hand motion across the landscape. "And this is America." He gestured to the young man. "Everything that we believe in will be gone as quickly as this man's life unless we regain our senses and get control of our actions.

"We are under attack, but we cannot turn on ourselves. We're all frightened. Yes, all of us. But I am charged with dealing with this, and deal with it I will. I will not rest until the hideousness of the act perpetrated against our nation has come to an end, until the perpetrator is punished, until order and reason are restored. I will not rest. And I, we, will end this insidious plot with a vengeance armed with a cold, cold heart and the firepower of the greatest nation in the world.

"That's what I will do. Now I ask you to go home. I plead with everyone to go home. Here and across America. Watch over your families, but don't destroy what we have. That's what our enemy seeks—an enemy that is empowered and emboldened by your actions; by events like this.

"Go home. For God's sake go home. For your own safety go home. For the sake of America, please go home."

The president knelt one more time and patted the head of the dead man. A quiet minute later, Morgan Taylor rose and walked back inside as the crowd loaded their smart phone videos and pictures on YouTube and Facebook, launching them around the world.

Ibrahim Haddad saw it five minutes later. The image of the president beside the victim reminded him of how he held his dead child in his arms. He was hurting his enemy deeply.

WEST VIRGINIA BACK ROADS

Richard Cooper could slip into dozens of characters on the outside.

But on the inside, he would always be a man on the run, alive only to himself; dead to his family.

Money was not a problem. It never would be. The assignments he'd accepted from the Middle East would cover him for life—however long that might last. Unless he changed his own strategy, it might not be too long. He had put himself in a far too exposed position.

Richard Cooper was a brilliant operative and a resourceful combatant. And right now, he considered himself lucky to be alive. The same could be said for General Johnson and the Secret Service agent who was always barely a step behind him.

It was time to disappear again. Away from Washington. Out of the cold. On the beach.

The word that best described the fiasco he barely escaped was *reckless*. Maybe *brainless,* Cooper thought as he drove through a light drizzle into the West Virginia mountains. *No, never again.*

He steered well clear of the Interstate and kept at the speed limit in a used 2008 Ford Fiesta he bought two years earlier under one of his aliases. This was one of four cars he strategically garaged around the country and drove only when necessary.

With every swipe of the windshield wiper blades, Richard Cooper, for now Rengal, ran his next moves in order like a calculating chess player.

Forget the general, he realized. *Let politics kill him. Death by a thousand political swords. Far more cruel.*

And what of his own future? The buyers of his services thought he was dead. Resurfacing would unduly expose him. And then there were the good guys. The FBI, the Secret Service, *that damned Roarke*, and every satellite dish linked to the NRO. They'd all be searching for him.

No matter how hard he had tried to avoid photographers at the party, he was undoubtedly in some pictures. They'd be in every police cruiser by now.

His disguise as Rengal was good, but not great. Rushed. He'd dyed his hair blond. And a black William and Mary sweatshirt covering a blue checkered shirt, jeans, and boots was hardly a full disguise. The only real accent came from thin-framed designer glasses. He knew he needed to do better.

The rain came down heavier now. He had five more miles to Fairmont, West Virginia, and the Super 8 motel he'd found on the Internet where he planned to hide. Richard Rengal would check in for three days. His plan was to abandon his car, not such an unusual sight in the backwoods, catch a cab to Morgantown, then buy a ticket on the Mountain Line Transit bus. After four switches, he would end up in Knoxville, Tennessee. Beyond that he wasn't sure yet.

Where? he wondered again as he drove. Richard Cooper didn't know and Rengal sure as hell wasn't telling him. Maybe it would come to one of them.

He rolled into the motel lot and paid cash for his stay. Dinner consisted of a boneless steak, peas, and mashed potatoes at the Poky Dot, a rock-themed restaurant. He ate undisturbed at a corner table, biding his time reading a day-old *USA Today.* There were more reports about poisonings from coast to coast; random cities, but enough to create nationwide panic.

Insidious, he thought, even by his standards. But Cooper knew the cause and the perpetrator. He'd been offered the opportunity to participate by the man who funded his exploits. However, mass murder was not Cooper's calling.

He read on. Reports of riots in major cities and deaths in communities stretching from Maine to Florida on the east coast, Oregon to California in the west, and ten states in between up the Mississippi into the Ohio Valley and…

Cooper froze. One sentence in the article, one cold sentence, written without shading or emotion, spoke to him. His eyes never left that one sentence until the full paper was reduced to the size of a baseball in his grip.

A young couple opposite him saw what he had done, but they kept to their own dinner, avoiding eye contact with the visibly obsessed outsider.

Not that Cooper would have noticed them. He was in his own deep thoughts.

That one sentence he read over and over now dictated where he would go and what he would do. One sentence in *USA Today.*

WASHINGTON, D.C.

"Scott, it's Penny," CPT Walker said without a hint of her typical flirtation. She caught Roarke walking from Katie's apartment to the White House.

"Yup," he answered, not even pausing to recognize how serious she sounded.

"I've got something new for you. But there's a lot of wind noise. Can you find someplace to duck in?"

"Sure."

Roarke shifted the cell to his left hand and shoved his cold right hand that had been holding the phone into the pocket of his parka. But he wasn't feeling anything other than rage, and something even colder—revenge.

"Okay, better?" he asked from inside the lobby of an office building down from Dupont Circle on Connecticut Avenue.

"Better. First of all, I'm sorry. I heard what happened."

"Right."

"I also know that there was nothing you could have done, Mr. Roarke."

"Wrong."

"No, you're wrong," Walker replied. "It was a hit. No one could have seen it coming. Not you or anyone. So stop beating yourself up. Anyway, what I have should get you thinking about something else."

Roarke shifted his weight and straightened up, prepared to pay attention. "What do you have?"

"I'm still checking any usual deaths across the country that might correlate to Cooper. Apparently no one else in the service. But..."

The "but" centered him.

"General, ah the vice president, was Cooper's final target, right?"

"We think so."

"Considering the security around him now, I'm betting that Cooper will be more cautious."

"Or more determined. Penny, a minute ago you said that Christine Slocum was the target of a hit and I couldn't do anything. Now you think Cooper doesn't care about J3 anymore. No way."

"What if Cooper has something else on his mind."

"Like what?"

"Someone who died. Poisoned."

"Where?"

"Ohio."

"So?" It was a cold, dispassionate response.

"So, look if you're not interested...."

"I am, I'm sorry. Who?"

"The name only came up because of my random search."

"I don't understand."

"You will."

CHAPTER 63

PITTSFIELD, MASSACHUSETTS
JANUARY 29
2150 HRS

Two DPW workers in their early forties parked their Ford Taurus outside the West Street pump station, one of six that maintained pressure for the Pittsfield, Massachusetts water system. They wore standard uniforms and flashed what looked like proper identification badges when they entered.

"Gotta check some valves on the line," said the first man to the security officer.

Given the number of Russian plumbers working in New England in recent years, even their accents didn't raise any suspicion, though the fact that they drove up in a non-departmental vehicle should have. But nobody checked cars, particularly on a raw, rainy January night well into the night shift.

"All yours," replied the guard who quickly returned to his CSI rerun on cable.

The two men wore web belts with the requisite tools. They pulled a luggage cart stacked with three sealed boxes.

The guard didn't even ask what they were taking in.

The Pittsfield Department of Public Works and Utilities provides services to the city's forty-two thousand citizens. Drinking water is supplied by six water reservoirs, running through 241 miles of distribution pipes, two flow control stations, and five pumping stations. At this moment, the pair, presumably from DPW, concentrated on one of two pumping stations that filled the Lebanon Avenue storage tank. An hour earlier they had visited the North Street station, quickly and efficiently completing their assignment. They expected the same ease at their second and final stop.

Inside and unobserved, they made some adjustments to the piping, adding an extra few feet of PVC they brought with them. Next, they introduced the substance they had transported two thousand miles cross-country.

Finished, they left, waving to the security guard who was much more interested in what the team of investigators on TV would accomplish in New York than the terrorists in his midst in Pittsfield.

That might have been the last anyone would have known about them had the weather not turned colder in the last thirty minutes. The drizzle that started before the men went in turned to black ice on the city streets.

The driver, Yuri Pavel, the one who spoke to the guard, was indeed a Russian immigrant. He was used to driving in brutal weather, but not used to the automatic transmissions that dominated American driving. This became a problem when he drove down North Street heading for the intersection of East Street. He was unfamiliar with antilock brakes, which actually offered far safer handling in a skid than pumping the brakes. Details were important to him in his field of chemistry, but not driving American cars. So the manual had remained unread in the Taurus glove compartment.

The traffic light was just beginning to turn from green to yellow. He had a choice: speed up and get through the light, or brake. He tested the brake. It felt wrong to him; like the car was locking up. So he hit the gas.

At first, the intersection looked clear; no one was at the light on the cross street. That was until a Chevy Silverado judged the driving conditions and timing of the light from his perspective. Thirty yards from the corner, the driver accelerated, which was precisely what Pavel was doing.

"Shit!" he yelled. He slammed on the brakes fast; once, twice, three times. This put him into an uncontrollable spin. The Silverado outweighed the Taurus. Taking the physics, the speed, and the weather into account, upon impact on the driver's side, Pavel's rotation increased. He hit a telephone pole at forty mph.

Russians didn't like safety belts, and the air bag only helped Pavel's coconspirator, another Russian chemist, Igor Romanovich. Pavel died either on the first hit by the Chevy or when his head went through the windshield. It actually didn't matter much.

Romanovich survived the crash and was rushed to nearby Berkshire Medical Center.

It took four hours before the Pittsfield police put the pieces together. The chief of police made the call himself to the FBI.

CHAPTER 64

WASHINGTON, D.C.
JANUARY 30

"We caught another break, Mr. President."

"Explain," Taylor replied over the phone to Robert Mulligan.

"We have one in Pittsfield, Massachusetts."

Morgan Taylor had campaigned in Pittsfield during his first run for office. He remembered citing that in 2005, Farmers Insurance had ranked Pittsfield twentieth in the nation as "Most Secure Places to Live."

He considered, *Maybe they should move up in the ranking.*

"A pair infiltrated two pumping stations. The whole department's been shut down until they can flush out whatever bad stuff they piped into the system."

"Thank God," Taylor said. Then he added, "You said you had one, but there was a pair?"

"Was. One's dead. The driver." The FBI Chief explained. "Car crash. According to the local police, the passenger started talking pretty quickly. We've sent our team in and we're running his prints and pictures against everything we have. We're doing the same with the dead man."

"I don't have to tell you how urgent it is that we get more," Taylor stated.

"Understood. I'm sending the same team up to Pittsfield that delivered on the MS-13 thug. They'll be there in under ninety minutes."

"Thank you, Bob."

"It's the third leg of the stool. We should be able to zero in on more now."

Scott Roarke, Vinnie D'Angelo, Raymond Watts, CPT Penny Walker, and Touch Parsons were having a very busy day dealing with pieces of the same puzzle.

Parsons, the FBI super geek, sat in front of a bank of computer screens. Sometimes his eyes and his mind seemed to work faster than the technology at his command. In the past year, Parsons had helped unravel the plot to bring down the president by utilizing and laboring over FERET. Now he was cross-referencing 140 million photographs worldwide, searching for that unmistakable *something* that would tie two captures in Montana and another in Massachusetts to the *someone* who was responsible.

But as the computer moved at light speed through databases, Parsons already had an image front of mind that he expected the computer program to confirm.

While the computer dove in and out of FBI files; local, national, and global news services; Getty photographs, Google images, and more, Parsons called across town to his girlfriend, CPT Penny Walker.

"Hey, anything more?" he asked.

"Into every database I can find and I just gave Roarke some startling news." She told him.

"Holy shit!" Parson exclaimed.

"Anything on your end?"

"My pet is sniffing around." His pet was FERET. "He's feeding right now. Bits and bits. Really hungry. Something tells me all of us are triangulating on the same man."

LANGLEY, VIRGINIA
CIA HEADQUARTERS

D'Angelo lived for open spaces and ways out. The CIA, his home, felt too confining. However, Jack Evans called him in after his escape from Burdenko and subsequent flight out of Russia.

"A pity," Evans said. "Dubroff would have been a great get. He could have unlocked the entire Russian sleeper network for us. We've done okay with the dumbass freshman class they've put in play over the last few years. But those deep plants. They're still out there, Vinnie. Dubroff knew them all."

"Sorry. He was dead when I got there. Not so sure Kleinkorn didn't pull the plug on him once he was on to me. It was a perfect trap. I'm lucky I got out."

"No luck there. You had it all planned out," Evans said.

"As a matter of fact…"

"Glad you're on our side."

"It sure isn't for the retirement benefits," D'Angelo joked. The government plan, even at the CIA, hardly stood up to what D'Angelo could get in the private sector. *Maybe one day,* he thought. *Could go into business with Roarke.*

"So, no names?"

"Nothing exact," D'Angelo responded. "But close enough. Kleinkorn said that internally Dubroff gets the credit for running the spy program that will—in his words now—*provide benefit into the future.* I didn't like the ring of that. Then he added, *the historical credit will go to a Syrian businessman on his own mad quest.*"

"Yes, a Syrian on a mad quest."

Evans removed a folder from his upper desk drawer; a folder that never made it to the filing cabinet or the shredder. An active folder. He laid it down, opened it to a picture of the one Syrian most on his mind for the past year. "Do you believe in coincidences, Vincent?"

D'Angelo nodded no.

"Neither do I."

THE SAME TIME

The FBI computers at the Quantico labs in Virginia delivered for Touch Parsons. One photograph cross-referenced with another, then ten more and a hundred beyond them. Ultimately the computer landed on a picture shot at an academic conference in Rome, Italy, three years earlier. Parsons examined the photo. It depicted a group of chemists flashing happy grins for the camera and one man trying to step out of range. It was this very man—the one who was avoiding the snapshot—that Parsons hoped to find…the man who would support his theory. He smiled and thought to himself, *I am good.*

Roarke wrote a single name on his grease board. Richard Cooper. Then he added Gloria Cooper's name and stuck a line through it. *Dead.* Then he added a question mark. Intuition told him something that others were discovering through their own means. He erased the question mark and printed a name in red. He felt this was the man who would lead him to Cooper, or Cooper to…

Richard Cooper had intended to disappear in Aruba. Not anymore. He booked a ticket with multiple layovers and stops, circuitously traveling from Atlanta to Los Angeles, connecting to Panama City and Asuncion, with the final destination Guarani International Airport in Paraguay. For most of the thirty-seven-hours-plus trip, Richard Cooper thought of what he might say to the man responsible for his mother's death. Then he recognized that there'd be no need for conversation. No words mattered any more when it came to Ibrahim Haddad.

CHAPTER 65

THE WHITE HOUSE

"It's probably the last place in the Western Hemisphere you'd want to go." Jack Evans explained.

Morgan Taylor read the briefing that the Director of National Intelligence brought. He was relatively unfamiliar with the TBI, the Tri-Border Region of Brazil, Argentina, and Paraguay, and Ciudad del Este in particular.

"The city was close to the top of the CIA's list of the most dangerous locales in the world. We tell people to go at their own risk."

"What do we have in Paraguay, Jack?"

"Well Bush 2 strong-armed the Paraguayan Senate to allow us to—quote/unquote—'train' their troops. He threatened to cut off millions in aid if Paraguay didn't grant the United States entry. We wanted in for counterterrorism efforts. This was after U.S. troops discovered a poster of the nearby Iguacu Falls on the wall of an Al Qaeda operative's home in Kabul. The bureau then sent in some forty agents to investigate terrorism networks, and Rumsfeld took charge of the program on orders from Cheney.

"To a great extent we were trying to establish a game-changer in the region. We'd been subject to a degree of bullying given Venezuela and uncertain relations with Colombia. So we talked Paraguay into giving us some ground to establish a presence. We still have a few assets watching what's going on. But the visibility back then actually created more paranoia than useful intelligence."

"How?" Taylor asked.

"Well, it was rumored that the Bush family was buying up property. State Department denied the reports. But that didn't stop them from flying across the Internet; food for conspiracy theorists and foreign governments."

"About what?"

"Now that's a great question, especially under the present circumstances. It's something we *should*have been paying attention to over the years."

The president was intrigued.

"Water, Mr. President. Water. Below Ciudad del Este is one of the largest aquifers in the entire world. Fresh water, Mr. President. Maybe today, more valuable to most Americans than oil. Fresh water that fed those rumors about Bush's land grab. And, since this crisis began, fresh water that *is* being sold and exported to major distributors in the United States. You tell me that's a coincidence. I suspect that rise in share price and the profit taking is going to flow right back into Hamas, Hezbollah, and Al Qaeda coffers right there in Ciudad del Este.

"Mr. President, I have never seen such a well-orchestrated terrorist plan resulting in moral and civil breakdown in the United States, simultaneously funding the global terrorism network with billions of legal dollars quite legally through U.S. corporations. It required a mastermind."

CIUDAD DEL ESTE

"My friends," Ibrahim Haddad began, "you are aware of my great accomplishments."

"Yes, Ibrahim," said Midhat Al Faras, leader of Ciudad del Este's drug smuggling network run by Hezbollah. He was the most outspoken of the group assembled by Haddad. The others were no less dangerous, simply quieter.

Sitting around the dining room table were Ahmad Almana, economic envoy in the Iranian embassy; Mustafa Ladas, who handled the early recruiting of MS-13 for Haddad; and Jalal bin Jassin, the senior Al Qaeda operative in South America.

They all had different agendas but answered to the same master. Money. Religious beliefs barely played into their quest for power. These were very powerful, dangerous men, all in their mid-fifties, looking to build enough wealth to retire in luxury while zealots under their thumbs did their bidding and their dying.

Ibrahim Haddad had the financial resources. He also provided them with a goal that brought legions of terrorists and ideologues flocking to their camps.

"What I did to America is only the prelude," Haddad said very quietly. "Next, I will bring Israel to its knees. They've lived off the Jordan River for too long, leaving little drinkable water downstream for our people. They have fresh water running from their faucets. We have a toxic mix of salt water and liquid waste. They irrigated their lands while ours have gone dry. No more. Death will flow from their faucets and chaos will spill over to the streets. Then we shall bomb the squares, the schools, the hospitals, police stations, airport terminals, and synagogues. I will create fear and panic on a scale never known. Civil authority will break down, highways will be clogged as Israelis try to escape. Then we will bomb those highways. Beirut of twenty years ago will look like Disneyland compared to what I create."

Haddad caught himself. "Ah, but I sound so egotistic. My friends, this shall be *our* accomplishment. Our homelands are different, but our cause is one. The end of Israel. What is left and how it is to be divided will be up to you. I will have done my part."

Haddad held his audience by offering them a stake in the new world. It was an irresistible lure.

"When will we strike?" asked Ahmad.

"May fourteenth. The anniversary of the founding of the Zionist State."

"Five months? Why not sooner," asked the Al Qaeda terrorist.

"It took great planning to achieve such success in America. But the task ahead requires more thought and more help."

"But five months?" he repeated.

"There is the time-honored saying: '*He who acts without knowledge causes more corruption than good, and he who does not consider his speech to be part of his actions sins repeatedly. Satisfaction is scarce, and the true believer should rely on patience.*'"

Haddad's tone now suddenly changed. In a cold and cruel voice he added, "I recommend you rely on patience, my friend.

"As we read in the *Qur'an*, '*Surely the patient will be paid their wages in full without reckoning.*'" He paused and peered directly into the eyes of the man who dared challenge him.

"If you are in such a rush to reap your spoils, I can see that you attain true heavenly pleasures much quicker.

Jalal bin Jassin got the meaning completely. "May fourteenth."

"Good," Haddad said. "Next week I will give you your assignments. It will take great coordination, much strategizing and travel, and..." he looked at the Al Qaeda representative again, "patience."

WASHINGTON, D.C.

"I need to speak to the boss right now," Roarke explained over the phone to Louise Swingle.

Twenty seconds later the president's trusted secretary put him through. Connected, Roarke didn't even say hello.

"I know who we're after."

"And we know where he is," the president replied.

CHAPTER 66

THE WHITE HOUSE SITUATION ROOM FEBRUARY 1

"Gentlemen, Vice Admiral Seymour Gunning has the floor."

That was all Morgan Taylor said in introduction. Everyone knew and respected the ranking Navy officer in the room. He commanded Navy ST-6, Navy SEALs Team 6, on missions rarely or never reported; the deep black ops that earned Team 6 the highest regard and virtually no credit.

Gunning had been a SEAL. That was in George H.W. Bush's day. Now, decades later, he was the same weight, with nearly the same level of body fat. The only hint to his real age was his graying temples that he wore with pride like one of his medals.

The sixty-one-year-old vice admiral rose out of his plush leather chair, setting his six-foot frame into a perfectly vertical stance. He was in full uniform, not always required in the White House. He conveyed unmistakable authority and experience.

"Thank you, Mr. President. Lights."

An aide, not needing a second more, switched off the overhead lights in the Situation Room, located in the basement of the West Wing just below the Oval office. The space was arguably one of the most buttoned-down conference rooms in the world. This is where the president discusses, debates, and rules on global strategies, from national security to secret missions. It was from here that President Obama watched the raid on Osama bin Laden and where they would likely watch a takedown of Ibrahim Haddad.

A 60-inch digital screen drew everyone's attention at the front of the room. *Everyone* meant President Taylor, Vice President Johnson, FBI Chief Mulligan, DNI Jack Evans, Homeland Security Advisor Grigoryan, Secretary of Defense Bradley Marks, Chief of Staff John Bernstein, Chairman of the Joint Chiefs Paul Coss, and ranking Pentagon officers from the army, navy, marines and air force. They all sat around a huge, long wooden conference table with binders that read NOFORN or "Not for Release to Foreign Nationals." It also was labeled CLASSIFIED, NOT FOR REMOVAL. All of the binders would be later collected and disposed of in a burn bag.

The documents couldn't leave the room. Neither would the HP laptop computers with their SCI or "Sensitive Compartmented Information." On the other hand, smart phones, iPads, and other devices weren't allowed in. Attendees deposited them in hallway cubbyholes outside the Situation Room.

"Please follow me as I go through my presentation," the vice admiral instructed. They all focused on the first of Gunning's PowerPoint slides. There was only one word in fire engine red over a black background: MERCURY.

Gunning's staff had considered calling the operation "Antidote," but J3 quashed that notion. "Too many people don't know how to spell the damned word today. They confuse it with *anecdote.* And this isn't a fucking anecdote."

The president had another reason for vetoing it. Nobody wants an antidote that doesn't work.

So it became MERCURY, recalling the Greek God and the planned swiftness of the mission.

"Our objective..." Vice Admiral Gunning switched to the second slide, a revolving space-view of Earth. Next he triggered the embedded animation to zoom into South America, then tighter to the Tri-Border region of Paraguay, Argentina, and Brazil. "Here. The country is Paraguay. The city is named Ciudad del Este, Paraguay."

Gunning gave a quick summary of Ciudad del Este and the dangers it presented.

Having gone as far as Google satellite would take the eye, the video dissolved to a classified NSA view which continued to zoom tighter and tighter to the Paraná Country Club along the Rio Paraná and into what was obviously a heavily fortified compound with armed guards patrolling every twenty feet.

"This is a real-time sat view of our hard target. Some one hundred miles up. We get about a ten-minute window every ninety minutes, so timing is critical. Also mission worthy—predators which can loiter for hours. They'll fly high enough that they won't be seen from the ground. They shouldn't be picked up by Paraguayan radar. But *shouldn't* isn't *won't.* We'll test their area air defenses before we launch."

He clicked through to another web source. "Now, real-time video. You're looking at a mansion with twenty-foot walls, guerillas with AK47s patrolling the grounds, cameras, and perhaps mines on the property. The sentries seem to know exactly where to walk.

"What you see is what we'll be taking. A three-story mansion patrolled by armed guards. Once inside, we will locate, identify, capture, or kill this man."

He changed the slide.

"Ibrahim Haddad."

The screen showed a single photograph. Seconds later, with another command, it separated into a quad split with three other pictures, then multiplied to sixteen pictures, all from different places and events over the years.

"Location. Target. Now for the timing."

A digital timer came on screen. It counted down days, hours, minutes, and seconds.

"We are on the clock now, people. Our first asset, courtesy of

Director Evans, is arriving in the country," he checked his watch, "in two hours and forty-five minutes. We'll have reliable, on-ground intel coming in by the evening."

Gunning switched to the next slide. It showed a photograph of a Navy SEAL in full tactical gear ready for battle. "Now here's how we're going to do it."

CIUDAD DEL ESTE

Vinnie D'Angelo spoke Spanish with an impeccable accent. Anyone with a trained ear would swear he came from Madrid.

The CIA operative arrived at Aeropuerto Guarani in Minga Guazá on TAM Airlines from São Paulo, Brazil. He cleared a very lax customs without incident and grabbed a taxi through Ciudad del Este to the Paraná Country Club, which is in Hernandarias.

The lack of security at the airport was more than made up for by what he faced here. Armed guards were posted at the entrance. Cameras mounted on posts, at the corner of the guard gate, and in trees provided overlapping 360-degree views to unseen eyes.

"*Pasaporte, señor.*" The order came in Spanish from a very serious and well-trained paramilitary figure. *Likely a former mercenary*, he reasoned. D'Angelo vowed to not underestimate them.

"*Si,*" D'Angelo responded warmly. He opened his briefcase, retrieved the passport identifying him as a Spanish national, and handed it over to the guard.

The sentry examined the picture closely against the man. "Do you have additional identification?"

D'Angelo was surprised, but not flustered.

"Other identification? Certainly. Just a moment."

The CIA agent reached for his wallet in a zippered front pants pocket. He had backup IDs from a driver's license to credit cards. "Here," he said handing over the license.

Again the guard studied the picture against D'Angelo. *Overly thorough or on alert?* he wondered.

Holding the license and the passport, the guard stood erect and keyed his radio. D'Angelo read and memorized his nametag. SGT Julio Octavio. "I have a Señor Rafael Gonzales. Check."

Thirty seconds went by. The meter on the cab continued to run and D'Angelo, Sr. Gonzales for this expedition, settled into his seat beginning to look mildly impatient and inconvenienced as *normal* would suggest.

Octavio got clearance in his earphone and bent over into the passenger side window again. He held onto the identification.

"Your business, Sr. Gonzales?"

Now D'Angelo launched into his legend, which could be easily confirmed thanks to friends in the Spanish business community under CIA payroll.

"I'm a travel industry executive, and quite honestly…"

"Your business, Sr. Gonzales?" Octavio said with more authority.

D'Angelo relaxed for effect. "I work with Exotica International. We are looking to establish ecotravel adventures to the Tri-border region with a luxury stay at the Casa Blanca." He decided to tickle the tiger and gauge whether he was subjected to a degree of heightened security. "But I'm not sure I would recommend the property if this is the way tourists are treated when they arrive."

It worked. Ocatvio's concern lessened. "We are simply being cautious, Señor. We live in a beautiful place, but one must take extra precautions."

It was the *extra* that alerted D'Angelo. He'd convey that to Washington later.

"And how long will you be staying?"

"Likely four days. I will be touring, setting up meetings, and writing a blog." All of it was true. Then there was the part he didn't explain.

"If you need a guide, don't hesitate to ask."

That was the last thing D'Angelo would do.

"Gracias. Perhaps."

Now D'Angelo made an obvious attempt to examine the man's badge, which of course, he had already done. "I will certainly let you know, SGT Octavio." He also assessed all of the immediate threats on the man. His Glock, a taser, and nightstick.

Ciudad del Este was living up to its reputation as a smugglers' paradise, a haven for outlaws, gangsters, and terrorists. A place … be taken lightly.

"In the meantime, is everything all right?" D'Angelo held his ha… out for his identification.

The guard smiled. He was not quite ready. He peered at D'Angelo's wallet. Now the CIA agent recognized that Octavio worked for three masters. The country club, the terrorist, and cash.

D'Angelo casually removed five hundred thousand Guarani, the equivalent $100, and offered it in trade for his IDs. Octavio casually took it and released the IDs, but not without saying in plain English, "Thank you."

It didn't throw the CIA agent. The ploy was as old as a George Sanders depiction of a cold Nazi commander from a 1940s Hollywood B-movie. "*Perdóneme?*" D'Angelo asked.

"Nada," Octavio said waving the cab through. "Nada." Five hundred thousand richer, the guard reasoned there was no need to place a call to the man in Casa del Zuma, and no reason for the cab driver, also on salary, to report anything suspicious.

Vinnie D'Angelo was in.

THE WHITE HOUSE SITUATION ROOM

"Scott, got a second?" the president said following the briefing.

"Sure," Roarke said without his usual lightness.

"This Slocum thing has weighed heavily on you."

"Yes, it has."

"And all indications point to our man Haddad."

Roarke nodded in agreement.

"You were not responsible, Scott. Not in any way."

Roarke still didn't accept that fact, even though it's what everyone was saying.

"Focus on Katie. You're lucky to have her. She's so good for you. Try to think about that future together, will you?"

Taylor saw that his words of consolation were not hitting home.

…derstood what made Roarke tick better than probably anyone. …believed he had a solution that could help.

"Look, if you want in on MERCURY, I'll speak to the vice admiral."

Roarke raised his head and stared into the president's eyes.

"I want in. I want to be there for the kill," Roarke said with the unmistakable desire to pull the trigger.

"It'll be tough. The SEALs are animals. Only a few days for you to train with them."

"Get me in. I'll be ready. I'll be so ready."

The thank you was implied.

CHAPTER 67

THE OVAL OFFICE
FEBRUARY 3

"Duke, thank you for coming in."

The president dispensed with the formality of *Mr. Speaker* or *Congressman*. He purposely didn't rise from his desk.

"You know the Director of the FBI," he continued, indicating Robert Mulligan's presence.

"Yes, of course. Good to see you again Mr. Director."

But Patrick, feeling an icy stare from Mulligan recognized it was not *good.*

Morgan Taylor added further evidence. "Take a seat, please." He motioned to the couch facing Mulligan who sat in one of two captain's chairs.

Patrick cut to the center of the Oval Office and did as he was instructed. Only after he was seated did Taylor stand, cross the room, and take the seat next to the FBI chief. Mulligan opened a file, which Patrick showed obvious interest in. Mulligan closed the file shut when he saw what Patrick, reputed to be able to read upside down, was doing.

"Duke, you had a young woman working with you by the name of Christine Slocum," Taylor stated.

Patrick smiled. "That's right. A crackerjack writer and legislative aide. She'll make a great chief of staff some day." He had other designs on her as well.

"That's not going to happen," Mulligan said.

"What? She's a real pro," Patrick said, taking obvious exception. "Why?"

"She's dead," the president said solemnly.

The declaration caught Patrick completely off guard. His mouth gaped open, but no words came out.

"She was murdered last night."

"Taken out would be more like it," Mulligan interrupted. "Shot in her bed. Assassinated."

"Assassinated? What are you talking about?"

The president looked to the FBI director to continue.

Mulligan opened the file again and turned to a tabbed page. "Christine Slocum was a plant in your office, just as she had been for Teddy Lodge. Groomed, trained, and put there by the terrorist behind the nation's poisoning, the same mastermind behind last year's coup attempt and the election fraud before it."

"I can't believe this. This is ludicrous."

"Mr. Speaker," Mulligan continued without raising his voice, "She was in the process of expanding her sphere of influence directly into the White House. Infiltrating, if you will, through a relationship with one of our Secret Service agents. Infiltrating here, just as she had in your office. She had hoped to co-opt this agent, learn vital information, and relay it to her handler."

"You're making this up to get to me," Patrick blustered. It was an automatic response. "And, Taylor, I promise you this will get nasty all the way up the Hill."

Mulligan was about to react when the president tapped his arm and bore down on Patrick himself.

"You *will* rethink what you just said, Congressman."

Taylor was more serious than Patrick had ever seen him.

"In basic terms, you had a spy in your office. How do you think that will play on the networks news, let alone back home. You. On your payroll. Someone who, through intermediaries you are also dealing with, reported to a foreign national, now the enemy of the people of the United States."

Patrick started to form a rebuttal, but Morgan Taylor cut him off.

"I am not finished. There is more. We've scrubbed her computer and researched her phone records. Slocum's Svengali may have been a foreign national. But there were intermediaries. Others in the Beltway. It's all in the director's report."

"Which I presume I can see?"

"No. As long as you cooperate," Mulligan declared. "Yes, if you don't. In the *Post*."

"This is unbelievable," Patrick stuttered. "You're trying to blackmail me not to criticize you. Not to run for this bloody office."

"The only thing you have right, Duke, is that this is a bloody office and it's about to become much bloodier."

The impact of the revelation was that Patrick would never be able to run for president. Never, in his mind, become the most powerful man on the face of the earth. All of this in one short conversation. And considering this was Washington, it also meant that the president had something in mind to ensure Patrick's acquiescence.

"What do you want?"

• • •

Duke Patrick stood before the cameras and microphones in the Capitol Rotunda, ready to deliver a short statement.

"I'll make this as simple as possible. I come before you today in support of President Taylor's call for calm. We live in a perilous time that tests us beyond our means and imagination. Rather than showing our differences to the world, we must stand united; brave and determined to right the wrongs that have been perpetrated against the United States of America…against the good people of our nation…against the freedoms we hold so dear. Go to your homes, as the president said, and trust in your government that we will see this through to a brighter day. Thank you."

Patrick left without taking any questions. It was a signal to many in the press corps that he was not happy.

CHAPTER 68

THE WHITE HOUSE
LATER

"It won't work going through Paraguay," Secretary of State Bob Huret explained to Morgan Taylor. Huret was still in the air over the Atlantic on his way back from briefing NATO partners in Europe. The president sent him to speak with America's allies; to reassure them that the United States was not paralyzed by the attacks and that they should increase their security, but not feel alone and vulnerable.

Huret, a former international businessman, fluent in French, German, Spanish, and Mandarin, did his best to relieve anxiety abroad. Now he appraised the president on our relations with the Paraguayan government.

"The new regime is, what shall I say, cash rich. The cash comes from, let's just say, dubious sources."

"Dubious?" Taylor asked. "Dubious as in Ciudad del Este's businesses?"

"Evans can probably answer with more authority, but yes. Twenty percent of Paraguay's $9 billion gross domestic product comes from illegal trafficking. President Ruben deJuan is in the hip pocket of any number of the crime families."

"Hold for a minute. I'll get Jack on the line."

Taylor made the request to Louise Swingle to patch the Director of National Intelligence in. It took less than the minute he told Huret.

"Jack?"

"Yes, Mr. President."

"Thanks for joining. I've got Bob Huret on from the air. We're talking about our travel destination and el presidente."

"Hi, Bob."

"Hi, Jack."

"Your thoughts?" the president asked.

"Well, he's sure not my favorite," Jack Evans quickly stated.

"Go on."

"Liberal party on the face of it, but his ties with Hamas and Hezbollah were what got him up the food chain to the top."

"Can he be trusted with any inside baseball?"

"Not if you want to keep it a secret."

"Bob, are you in agreement?"

"One hundred percent, Mr. President. I'm sure you'll tell me what this is all about in a few hours, but give him anything sensitive that might relate to his keepers, and rest assured, they'll hear about it. We've had a cordial relationship, but since he took over two years ago, he's not anyone I would ever expect to engage in any *normal* dialogue. Very guarded."

"Jack?"

"There's more that I can get into. As for a flyover, Bob's nailed it."

"Okay, gentlemen. Give me the next best neighbor. For the sake of this conversation, Bob, we need a friendly nation we can rely on or one where a little subtle arm-twisting will work. Your specialty."

"On the Tri-Border there is, of course, Argentina and Brazil," Huret explained. "I'm not the person to give you strategic information, just political ramifications. I'd have to defer to Jack."

"No on Argentina. We'll have easier access with stopovers in Brazil and a straight shot across the Paraná River," Evans offered.

"How are we doing with Brazil, Bob?"

"That's a touchy subject. We haven't delivered on some promises, and Lydia Santiago is as shrewd a politico as they come."

"Can she be trusted?" Taylor asked. It was probably the most important question so far.

No one jumped in.

"I need to know, gentlemen."

"Let me put it this way, you can negotiate with her," Huret stated.

"That may be enough. Okay, I have a thought about that and maybe the leverage that will work. When are you due to touch down, Bob?"

"In about three hours."

"Get a good night's sleep. You'll need it. Not sure when your next one will come. Tomorrow I'll run through my idea. Take the first crack at the call to Lydia. If she agrees, then I can follow up through the diplomatic route.

"We have to choreograph this with the Joint Chiefs. I'll order up their plan based on this conversation right now."

• • •

Roarke packed lightly. Toothbrush, underwear, socks, sweater, jeans, and three shirts. It was all laid out on the bed next to a black backpack.

"You can't tell me where you're going, can you?" Katie asked.

"No, I'm sorry, honey."

"That's the part that's really hard for me." She folded the last of his shirts. "Nothing for the cold?"

"Not this trip." It was more information than he wished to share, but Katie was Katie. A smart attorney and an astute packer.

"Why do I feel this time will be more dangerous? That when I say good-bye, it will be for good?"

Roarke stopped. He turned to the love of his life. Tears came to his eyes, then to hers. The past few weeks had been very difficult for them. The pressure of their jobs, the upheaval in the country, and the complications with the Christine Slocum assignment amplified the level of stress. They needed to reconnect.

She stood up on her toes and kissed his tears. He did the same.

"This can wait 'til the morning. We can't." He slid everything onto the floor. Roarke pivoted quickly, grabbed Katie's hand, and pulled her to his bed.

He started what they both needed—a long, passionate kiss that, for now, erased her fear and his thoughts of the days to come. The kiss melted into a clinging hug. Then their fingers moved in concert on each other's buttons and fasteners.

Soon they were both naked and needing the closeness that they foolishly let slip away.

Katie's hands found him and she smiled inches from his face. "Oooo, you're ready."

"So ready," he responded in a voice and twitch she immediately felt.

His fingers discovered that she was as well.

Katie kissed him deeply as he explored her wetness and she continued to feel him swell to her touch. Her heart was beating faster. His body was tingling, and she proposed a question that excited him even more.

"Top or bottom, Scott?"

"Oh," he sighed rolling onto the side of her exquisite body.

"I love you come-pletely," she said with completely intentional emphasis.

At that instant, in one swift motion, he reached under her, rolled her over and on top of him.

"Top and right now."

"Now," she gasped, looking down at the two of them as he disappeared inside of her, filling her with passion and desire. She wanted *now* to last forever.

Scott Roarke had the exact same thought.

And together their word for the night was "Now!"

CHAPTER 69

VIRGINIA BEACH, VIRGINIA
NAVAL AIR STATION OCEAN
FEBRUARY 4

"Roarke, how would you describe your physical state?"

Scott Roarke wasn't an equal to the Navy SEALs. But he was as fit as a Secret Service agent gets, maybe more.

"Good shape, sir. Healthy. I work out." For a moment Christine came to mind. As quickly as she did, she was gone.

"You won't have to be looking over your shoulder for me."

"Then good to have you here lieutenant," Commander B.D. Coons replied, noting Roarke's old rank.

Here was ST6's home base in Virginia Beach. Never formally acknowledged, of course.

"By the way, we're a little less formal. No need for all the sir stuff. We try to blend in. Short, tall, not so super-sized. We're not auditioning for the WWF. We've got our job, and the fewer people who know it, the better."

To the average person, Coons would look fit, but not a member of the nation's most elite and lethal fighting force. His hair wasn't stereotypically military. He wore a brown T-shirt and loose matching khakis and boots. Roarke figured him to be five-eleven and about two hundred pounds, but he hid his muscle and zero body fat.

Though he had an open personality, Roarke knew that all of Coons's niceties would be switched off well before stepping into the kill zone. His job was to distinguish friend from foe, dispatch the enemy without a second thought, and bring everyone back alive.

"Come on, I'll show you around," Coons offered. "You can preview the objective right on the base."

Roarke reached for his backpack.

"Forget your gear. It'll catch up with you tonight. After you've run the course."

Roarke was tagging along to report to the president, but he would take his orders from B.D. He figured the B and D were Coons's first and middle names, but the letters also seemed to say he was someone who could Beat Death.

• • •

SEAL Team 6, or DEVGRU, the Naval Special Warfare Development Group, operated outside military protocol. They were all "black" operatives, working at the highest level of classification and well outside the boundaries of international law. Their unit is shrouded in such secrecy that even the Pentagon won't confirm that it's housed at Navy Air Station Oceana.

Even the girlfriends and spouses of DEVGRU rarely heard much about their men's work, assignments, or deployment. And when the team returned, as they did after taking out Osama bin Laden, there were no welcome-home parades.

They blended into the more than 14,600 military personnel and

2,000 civilians at Oceana, and on any given day they could be training anywhere at the 5,916-acre station.

Today, it was at a remote section of the facility where walls of a building had been quickly erected and scaffolding provided multilevel floor access.

"Let your imagine fill in the brick and mortar, Roarke." Coons brought his jeep to a stop. "There's the target. Welcome to Casa del Zuma, an armed mansion on the footprint of the Paraná Country Club in Ciudad del Este, Paraguay. Memorize every square inch of it. You'll be taking it with your eyes closed before we leave this base."

Roarke was impressed. The team had constructed a replica of Ibrahim Haddad's stronghold from satellite photographs. The grounds included a fifteen-foot high wall covering what appeared to be about a seven-thousand-square foot property. In the center, protected by another inner wall of equal height, was a four-story tiered structure, with either a master bedroom or command center at the top. There were also sentry posts throughout the layout, both within the first walled area and the inner wall.

"Looks like it would make perfect pickings for a drone, but we've been ordered to seize the computers like Pakistan." Roarke got the reference. "I gather that POTUS wants to know what's on them. That's mission critical."

Leaving with Haddad was not.

"What do we know about the inside layout?" Roarke asked.

"We're working on that. Radar imagery and some intel on the ground will tell us a great deal. But we'll have to feel our way as we go."

Intel on the ground meant D'Angelo. Roarke didn't offer up the name any more than Coons did.

"We'll be getting remote eyes in a few hours through some pretty cool gear from our asset. Then we'll assess the location of threats minute-by-minute."

Coons's face was already changing; Roarke's attitude as well.

CIUDAD DEL ESTE

D'Angelo walked the grounds with a modified Canon 5D Mark III that wasn't sold in any retail or online store. It was modified to toggle between two drives with three fast taps on a locking apparatus. This allowed him to sight and take typical tourist pictures, which were stored on a regular Sun Disk USB 16GB flash drive, and other critical shots snapped from his hip which went to an embedded 84GB drive that could be erased onboard or remotely. He was careful not to venture too close to Casa del Zuma, but he didn't avoid it either. He appeared to be just another visiting photographer in sandals, shorts, and a loose button-down shirt.

The country club was filled with luxury minicastles, expensive shops, and a beautiful golf course. The property houses a number of hotels, Casa Blanca the most beautiful. That's where he booked a suite.

The CIA operative heard motors of tree-mounted cameras as they panned and tilted to follow his walk. He made a mental note of where they were to mark them on a map he would later e-mail to command with his surveillance photographs.

Security tightened as he approached Casa del Zuma. But he continued his self-guided tour, politely nodding to others who strolled the grounds. All the while, D'Angelo gauged where the blind spots would be and where he would soon place some unique monitoring devices of his own. He'd accomplish that on another walk in a few hours with the sun at its highest and Haddad's men at their hottest, desperate to stay out of the sun.

He took it all at a leisurely pace. Following his walk, D'Angelo went through the Mediterranean-designed lobby of the Casa Blanca, out to the pool where he had a Tequila Sunrise, and did what most tourism executives would do. He reviewed the pictures on his camera—only the ones on the standard smart stick. Forty minutes later, D'Angelo returned to his villa and e-mailed the other images to Langley.

THE WHITE HOUSE

The president's impromptu speech outside the White House gate had done the impossible. The streets were quiet. But Morgan Taylor knew this couldn't last. The network *noise* channels reported the calm by the hour with the hopeful expectation that they'd have more interesting video soon.

"Like walking on egg shells, Mr. President," Chief of Staff Bernstein proposed during a meeting break in the Oval Office. "It won't take long to break them. And then you're going to get slammed for not initiating martial law. Both parties. Both barrels."

"Bernsie, they would have come after me if I had already. What did Harry Truman say, '*If you want a friend in Washington, get a dog.*'"

"Actually, with all due respect, Mr. President, it's credited to Truman, but etymologists would take you to task on that."

"Come on. It's pure Truman."

"Truman reinvented on stage. For a play. Not for real."

"Then who gets the damned credit?"

"Quite a few people, in fact," Bernsie explained. "It's been attributed to Carl Icahn when he was chairman of U.S. Steel. Also, Selig Robinson, a Truman cohort; Donald Devine in the Reagan administration. But even Devine couldn't recall where he heard it—maybe a line in *Give 'em Hell, Harry.* There was even a variation uttered by Gordon Gekko."

"Who?"

"Gordon Gekko. Michael Douglas's character in *Wall Street.* The movie."

"How in hell do you know so much about one fucking made-up quote?"

"I'm your chief of staff. You pay me to know. After all, I wouldn't want you to go public with something so obviously wrong and then get nibbled to death by twenty-five million tweeters."

John Bernstein was right about that. Twitter had the power in 140 characters or less to boost an unknown to national prominence or contribute to regime change in Third World countries.

The wrong message could mean a national viral shift in public opinion as it became zeitgeist. Taylor acknowledged that such messaging, no matter how insignificant, would one day unseat a president. Not over a misquote of Truman, but it could happen over something equally insignificant.

"Suppose I'll have to come up with some original homilies for *my* autobiography. What about you?" Taylor asked. "How will you judge me, old friend? What will you recall when you decide to leave and walk into a million dollar advance? The juicier the better."

Of course John Bernstein had considered the question himself. But this was the first time the president personally posed it. He'd probably leave a year before Taylor's second term was over so he could market himself as a talking head on Fox News or MSNBC prior to any book publication.

"You'll have to work harder to give me some real dirt. As a president you're pretty boring. I'd have to make up smack. Nothing titillating. Hell, you're going to make for a boring read."

"There's still time."

"I'm counting on it," Bernsie said with a chuckle that made his belly bounce. Then his mood changed. "Morgan," he said very personally, "you're a man of convictions. A decision maker who bucks political wisdom. It's probably how you flew your F-18s. You followed a prescribed flight plan when you had to, and hit your targets with conviction, relying on your experience and judgment. Not sure how that sells books, but it sure makes me proud to be working with you."

"Thank you, Bernsie. Ultimately, I feel some moral authority in this bizarre second term. I can be president of the United States rather than the president of one political party. It's what diminished everyone from Clinton on. Four years, eight years, you're beaten down by the opposition most days. The leadership scrambles to deliver counter punches. I suppose I have the luxury of saying fuck you to partisan politics. And you can quote me on that!"

"Finally something to work with," Bernsie joked. And there's always the Lodge campaign and election. The last-minute huddling on succession. Lamden's departure, bless his heart. Elliott Strong's radio broadcast and coup. And how you jumped into the cockpit of Air Force One. Christ, the more I think about it, this would make a helluva movie!" Bernsie exclaimed.

"See, you have something good to work with after all. Now let's see if I can help spice up your middle chapters. Call the press room and schedule me for an hour from now. Then get me Gregory at NBC. I have an idea," Morgan Taylor said with a crooked smile.

THE WHITE HOUSE
EAST ROOM
THE SAME DAY

"I'll be short and sweet. Then I'll take your questions," the president began. He wore his classic blue suit, white shirt, and red tie. The requisite American flag was on his left lapel. His tone before the pool cameras and microphones was even. His voice was clear, authoritative, and measured.

"Americans have demonstrated a unity of spirit unknown in recent years. The United States has shown the world that we are a nation of people who stand up to adversity at home. When, under attack, we come together. We become stronger rather than weaker. We help our neighbors, and we survive.

"No enemy of the people will bring us down. Not now. Not ever. I am proud of the way our citizens have shown extraordinary courage despite the threats of death and the loss of friends and family. I am proud of you.

"And so, I continue to urge you to stay home. Be safe. Do not take to the streets. Trust in the might of the United States armed forces. We will find the terrorist behind the evil act. We will bring him to justice."

The emphasis made it clear the speech was over. Now Morgan Taylor would create a masterful diversion. The members of the Fourth Estate shouted to get recognized.

Taylor pointed to the NBC anchor. "Mr. Gregory?"

"Mr. President, you maintain that you will find the terrorist behind the poisonings that have brought much of American life to a standstill. Have you actually identified who he is and where he is hiding?"

It was a total set up, played perfectly, although the talent didn't know it.

"I'm sorry, as you can well understand, for the sake of national security, I can't get into specifics," the president stated. "However…"

Everyone held on that one word.

"We have narrowed our search to the islands of Indonesia; home to other terrorist groups. That's all I can say."

At this point, the other reporters shot their hands up and shouted questions that would send everyone with a camera, a microphone, or an opinion running in the wrong direction.

Most of all, Morgan Taylor hoped his deceit would lead Ibrahim Haddad to lower his guard, even just a little.

It wasn't the first time a sitting president used television to lie.

CIUDAD DEL ESTE

While the president was tricking the world, Vinnie D'Angelo was on his second stroll through the Paraná Country Club property.

Less than a hundred yards from Casa del Zuma, he cut across an undeveloped, wooded area, photographing scenes for a brochure and Web site that would never exist.

He heard laughter from the nearby villa. Boisterous, victorious laughter; a mocking tone with the air of superiority. D'Angelo felt that if it continued for another hour the revelry might even drown out the evening's symphonic cacophony of the frogs and cicadas.

Indeed, it was getting late, but the sun was in the perfect place for D'Angelo to approach Casa del Zuma. The cameras and guards would be looking in his direction, but directly into the setting sun.

Barely fifty yards from the mansion, the CIA agent tripped over a log and fell hard on the ground. It was quite a performance; completely believable. With his back to the cameras, D'Angelo simultaneously rubbed his ankle with one hand, and flipped his backpack he carried forward with the other.

Using his body as a shield to block any observing eyes, D'Angelo reached into his pack and removed the items he brought along.

Minutes later, he struggled to his feet, wobbled a little, reached down for the pack, now pounds lighter, and flung it over his shoulder. He faced the cameras, without offering any visible eye contact, and limped back toward the road and eventually his hotel room.

• • •

"Idiots. They're idiots," Haddad shouted while watching the

American president on CNN International. "They look where they've been before." He was speaking to his chief aide, a functionary who believed he would eventually be rewarded in heaven with his virgins for serving his earthly master. Haddad, however, believed his reward was only in the here and now with the planning and execution of his personal *jihad*.

"They're on a fool's errand," Haddad bellowed. "Much to my surprise, we will live to see another day."

Haddad wasn't certain, but he thought he saw true disappointment in the religious zealot at his side who thought it better to die.

CHAPTER 70

CIUDAD DEL ESTE
FEBRUARY 5

During his days, D'Angelo kept to a regular schedule touring Ciudad del Este, eating at the city's restaurants, and taking cabs to the nearby tourist sites. He also made certain to grab a siesta in the late afternoon and hold off on dinner until 2100 hrs because of his nighttime assignments.

Occasionally he'd interact with other guests at Casa Blanca, chatting casually, turning down offers to play golf or tour together. But he always excused himself, complaining about the schedule his Spanish travel agency had him on.

That didn't prevent him from creating dossiers on anyone who spoke to him or seemed to take interest in his routine.

There was a group of four forty-something golfers from Buenos Aires who were in Ciudad del Este before he arrived. They seemed more interested in the hookers than hooking their drives. The day he checked in, he bumped into a British college professor on sabbatical, writing about Ciudad del Este politics. The fact that he admitted it showed how ill-informed he was about the danger. Then there was a pair of Mexican "businessmen." D'Angelo surmised their business was drugs. Also staying at Casa Blanca, a Saudi prince; likely a prince among thieves.

Two days into his stay, he met a husband and wife vacationing from Madrid. D'Angelo definitely wanted to steer clear of them for fear his cover story might not hold. Finally, he met a very private Chinese "investment banker" who was constantly scanning every room he entered. The CIA agent pegged him for a member of Tai Chen, the Cantonese mafia. D'Angelo learned that the man regularly commuted between Taiwan and Ciudad del Este. No doubt they managed the ever-expanding smuggling business. D'Angelo noted that he carried a gun in a shoulder holster. Given the areas of town where he traveled, he probably needed it. D'Angelo hoped that the British professor wouldn't follow him.

For safety's sake, D'Angelo sent profiles back to D.C. for analysis and confirmation. So far there were no red flags on the Saudi prince, the Mexicans, or the Argentine golfers looking for a hole in one or another. Nor was there any report on the Brit or the Tai visitors. Experience told him to steer clear of both.

THE WHITE HOUSE

"I have President Santiago on the line for you now, sir."

"Thank you, Louise. Put her through."

This call was going to require deliberate political gamesmanship. Morgan Taylor worked out the staging with Secretary of State Huret. They talked about the president playing her like they were in a high-stakes poker tournament.

"Hide most of what you hold," Huret reminded Morgan Taylor again. "Reveal your face cards when necessary. Bluff, raise the ante. Let her win the first hand."

"Got it."

On the third ring, Morgan Taylor picked up. "Madame President, good afternoon. Thank you for calling me right back."

"Well, urgent from Morgan Taylor's secretary is a sure way to move up my list," replied Lydia Santiago, the fifty-three-year-old former CEO now president of Brazil. "What do you need?"

Need, not *want? She's already interested in what the dealer has,* thought Taylor. He decided to answer head on.

"I applaud your directness," Taylor replied. "Need is exactly the topic of our conversation. And in the interest of transparency, I have Secretary of State Bob Huret with me." He failed to mention that his vice president and Homeland Security secretary were also listening in. "Am I correct to assume you are not alone as well."

"Yes."

"Good. This may require some consulting."

"You have my undivided attention, Mr. President," Santiago replied.

"You know our problem," he said declaratively rather than as a question. Time to throw out some low cards.

"I do. I only hope that you are able to restore order and make the proper arrests."

"We have a tentative calm now. The best way to ensure it will last is by finding the perpetrators." Taylor didn't use her word—*arrest.*

"As for your need, Mr. President?"

"Our nations," Taylor continued, "have had a long and friendly history. We have been economic and political partners. We have served in Pan American associations together, looked out for each another's mutual interests and the interests of our hemispheric neighbors."

"Perhaps, but recent promises..." She left the thought hanging.

Santiago was raising the stakes. Taylor knew exactly where she was going, but first he had to keep her on track. His track.

"You asked about our need. I will tell you."

Now to show a higher card.

"I *need* clear airspace; unobstructed; unfettered. I *need*..." he continued with more emphasis, "two airports in support of an exercise."

"An exercise?" she interrupted. "An exercise in exactly what?"

"An exercise, Lydia," he replied directly. "The United States, as we discussed, is under attack. Accordingly, we are deploying forces to strategic areas around the world as we gather credible intelligence. Just as we are talking today, I have calls out to the heads of state in seven," a made-up number, "nations."

"Unobstructed and unfettered? That's much more than I could grant under normal circumstances."

Moran Taylor smiled at Vice President Johnson and Secretary Grigoryan. She was totally engaged.

"We are not living under normal circumstances, Lydia. As a member of numerous western hemisphere defense coalitions, I appeal to you in the same manner that I will be privately appealing to our NATO and ANZUS partners." NATO referring to the North Atlantic Treaty Organization and ANZUS, the Australia, New Zealand, U.S. Security Treaty. Again a bluff, for now beyond her confirmation.

"Such approval is not mine to grant. Our alliance notwithstanding, we have laws regarding our sovereignty and regulations governing our airspace, Morgan."

"I am not asking you to violate Brazil's law. I am, however, asking for your permission. With your approval there is no violation."

"But there is political risk," she said, doubling down on where she was taking the conversation.

"And political gain," Taylor countered, laying down a stack of chips.

The two-term Brazilian president, a cunning player herself as former head of Citibank South America, wanted to see what else Morgan Taylor held.

"Oh?"

Now J3 gave President Taylor a thumbs-up.

"Madame President, you've been waiting for quite some time for the receipt of the F-35As." Taylor thought she would actually come through the telephone with the mention of this long dormant promise.

"Twenty-four," she quickly replied. "For six years!"

"You'll have them in thirty days, with technicians, trainers, and spare parts."

She remained silent, as if to ask for more.

"And the Ford plant, delayed in our trade rigmarole. Congress will approve it."

"Your Speaker of the House has not been in favor of it."

"He will approve it now," Taylor said without any equivocation. Then he stopped.

"Unobstructed and unfettered?" Santiago asked again.

Taylor remained silent, wondering if she would bargain for more. For fifteen seconds no one spoke. He reasoned she was getting advice or cues from her chiefs of staff. There was a great deal on the table. Brazil had waited years for the F-35As, and the automotive plant had been so tied up in committee, no one believed it would ever see the light of day. Now both were within reach. Taylor's face cards. He had put down the equivalent of ten, jack, queen, and king, all of the same suit.

"When do you require such access, Morgan?" she finally said.

Taylor made a triumphant fist and thrust it in the air.

"Beginning at 0400 your time tomorrow, Lydia."

He heard an audible gasp. "Mr. President…"

"Tens of thousands of America's men, women, and children are victims of a vicious attack. And, in case you weren't aware, nineteen were Brazilian citizens." That was his ace. A Royal Flush.

"I didn't know," President Santiago humbly responded.

"Lydia, we are doing what we have to."

"Two questions, Mr. President."

"Yes."

"Are there really other countries you're talking with? And will you take action with or without my approval?"

"Lydia, I am asking for your permission to flyover, land, and stage an exercise unobstructed; unfettered *with* your cooperation. There will be no offensive action within your borders or airspace."

Taylor would not go any further, and she knew it.

"So where do you want to do this, Mr. President? I'll make the arrangements."

The president had the SOCOM mission plan on his desk. Santiago remained stone cold when he identified the second airport. Surely she recognized the proximity of Florianópolis, Brazil, to the crime capital of the western hemisphere.

CHAPTER 71

CIUDAD DEL ESTE, PARAGUAY

They were called *snakebots* and they were nothing short of phenomenal in the field. They blended in, moved stealthily, and put focused eyes on the target that were seen thousands of miles away.

The *snakebots* were robots designed to look like snakes, camouflaged in a green and white dotted pattern. Fully extended, they were six feet long. But working their way up a tree and across a branch, their smart bodies wrapped around into whatever form would be necessary to corkscrew upward.

D'Angelo controlled them as they slithered across the tropical floor. He then wiggled the robots high up into the canopy created by Lauraceae, Myrtaceae, and Leguminosae trees.

The fantastic inventions, created by a team at the Biorobotics and Biomechanics Lab at the Technion-Israeli Institute of Technology, were born of polymer, electric motors, and artificial intelligence. They were developed by studying actual snake locomotion, which employs many internal degrees of independent freedom that drives a wave of motion. Reimagining and engineering the movement into practical models, scientists transferred the intelligence into the robots which looked and acted like snakes.

Their onboard 360-degree field-of-view cameras scanned the surroundings, determining distance and maneuverability and generating a "print cloud" of readings which mapped the terrain in a 3-D model. Four directional microphones enabled the *snakebots* to detect the movement of approaching humans. By comparing the time that incoming sounds took to reach the microphone, the robots could process and access a threat's proximity, direction, and speed. That data triggers defense programs that constantly allowed the *snakebots* time to blend in and hide. All real; all instantaneous.

At the same time, the *snakebots* transmitted streaming video to Vinnie D'Angelo in his room, the ST-6 command team in Virginia Beach, Virginia, CIA headquarters in Langley, and the White House.

"Describe the scene for me," Vice President Johnson said over the squawk box from the Situation Room.

Vice Admiral Seymour Gunning, who actually preferred being called "Sy," watched the three incoming video feeds along with Commander B.D. Coons and Scott Roarke. Jack Evans participated online from the CIA, while National Security Advisor Grigoryan joined J3 in the White House.

"Remote cameras on the objective, Mr. Vice President," Gunning replied.

"They seem to have some focus issues and a lot of movement."

"It's because they're moving into position, sir. Climbing trees, inching across branches."

"Climbing trees, I thought they were remotely operated."

The vice admiral described how D'Angelo was zooming in on Casa del Zuma from his closet in the Casa Blanca Hotel.

"Zooming. Zuma. I like it. I want to see full specs on this *snakebot* thing after our call," J3 barked.

"Yes, sir." Gunning made a note that he quickly passed along to his aide.

Soon a second camera, positioned some thirty feet to the right, focused on Haddad's villa. Finally, the third camera steadied. Its shot was fifteen yards closer and off to the left. The three positions gave an amazingly clear view of the fortified mansion.

As the head of each *snakebot* panned, a computer at the CIA mapped the layout, determining range, size of the windows, live bodies that passed by inside, location of power lines, sentries, and obstacles. A complete schematic would be in Gunning's hands within the hour.

"What about down-looking?"

"We'll have them online shortly, J3," Evans offered. The KH-11, launched from our Delta 352 will give us high-rez electro-optical reconnaissance. Hell, we can drill all the way down to two centimeters if we need to. With optical and digital enhancement, close enough to read the brand off a cigarette pack. We'll see what kind of weapons we'll be up against on the deck and who's asleep on the job."

"Amazing," Grigoryan commented. "Absolutely amazing stuff. It never fails to astound me."

"We're plotting shift changes with the video," B.D. Coons added. "Looking for weaknesses in the line, pee schedule, cell phone users and the smokers. I want to know who's lighting up and how often. When they're not paying attention. We need it all. In fact, Director Evans, can your brainiacs calculate the density of the walls?"

"Yes," Evans replied.

"Roof construction?"

"Yes."

"Evidence of any missiles?"

"Harder until they're fired up, but we know what size containment to look for. If they're there, we'll find them, and you'll have the locations."

"Mines in the courtyards?"

"We have to expect that. We're plotting where the Tangos walk. And our birds will not set down on the deck."

"Good, because I want my men to know exactly what's off limits."

All of the detail would be incorporated into the mock-up of Haddad's complex at Naval Air Station Ocean. It would be everyone's job to memorize the layout.

Roarke realized he had extra studying to do. It's a good thing Katie didn't know what kind of danger he was about to jump into.

"Here come the sat images," Evans said. "Log into our secure site."

CHAPTER 72

FEBRUARY 6

The relative quiet on the streets didn't help the hungry news cycle. Nor did the silencing of the president's avowed political enemy, Speaker of the House Duke Patrick. Talk radio began to fill the void, first with questions, then with rhetoric, and hours later with rumors of terrorists switching from poison to sniper attacks and the White House close to ordering a suppression of citizen rights. All unconfirmed. All wrong.

The reports migrated to television where talking heads quoted research they'd heard or made up.

"More than a third of Americans agree that in times like this, we must deprive other people their basic liberties," claimed a first-term North Carolina Congressman who was quickly getting the airtime Patrick turned down.

"No, it's more like fifty percent," added a political spokes-liar from Ohio. "And from the polls I've seen, two-thirds of the American people agree that law enforcement should be able to indefinitely detain anyone suspected of terrorism. If Gitmo is out, then ship them off to Puerto Rico or Guam."

"I predict full-scale rioting in America's cities because the president failed to establish martial law," added a self-proclaimed expert on such things. The former Arizona sheriff was more than pleased to be back in the limelight. "And if Morgan Taylor doesn't take control, which he obviously won't, then it is up to us, as citizens."

"Are you suggesting, as a former law enforcement officer, that Americans walk their neighborhoods armed?" the anchor asked over the satellite uplink. He tried to make a fair-sounding question, but it was as soft a pitch as imaginable.

"We're under attack. Thousands have died. But all Taylor does is tell people to stay inside. What kind of America is that? Stay inside. Give me a break. If the president isn't doing anything, then we must."

THE OVAL OFFICE

"The strike force will land at MacDill in four hours, then turn around, fully loaded for the mission," Sy Gunning stated. "The quiet birds are already at the staging point. If the weather holds, it looks like we'll drop in on schedule."

"I'll take hourly updates, Admiral. J3 will be awake when I'm asleep. Any change in plans, the White House gets them first," the president stated during the latest briefing.

"Yes sir."

"And thank you, Sy. We'll all be in communication throughout. Good luck to you and your men."

"Thank you, Mr. President. Thank you for your confidence in us."

• • •

The president hung up and segued into a briefing that including Johnson, Secretary Grigoryan, Bob Mulligan, and Jack Evans and SOCOM General Jim Drivas, the officer in charge of the operation.

SOCOM, an acronym for the country's Special Operations Command is a key component in the U.S. unified central command or USSOUTHCOM. It's headquartered at MacDill Air Force Base in Tampa, Florida, and is comprised of the best, most carefully selected combatants in the United States military. SOCOM was created in 1987 to execute overt and covert operations, which can be authorized under CIA command and the White House. Each branch of America's armed forces is represented in SOCOM units. They are also the most elite units which are deployed when the most special of talents are required.

The agenda for the briefing: the timeline for "neutralizing and eliminating" the MS-13 supply lines through Mexico and the domestic assault on the Mara Salvatrucha strongholds. This was to follow on the heels of MERCURY.

"Mr. Hernandez will be informed three minutes before the strikes," Gunning noted. "What isn't taken out by the drones will be cleaned by the five SEAL teams already spread out across the supply routes."

Taylor was satisfied with the oral report. He'd already read and approved the written. Next up, Mulligan's report on MS-13.

"Based on what we've learned from the Houston MS-13 leader about the Maras and the splinter MS-13-30 gangs, we've pinpointed targets from Providence to Miami, Chicago down to Dallas, San Francisco to San Diego and dozens of cities in between. This will be the biggest roundup of thugs in American history; enough to keep the gangs' lawyers busy for years. The FBI is lead dog, with support from ATF, some of whom have been working undercover for years."

"All in, what can I expect to see?" Taylor asked.

"Forty-three simultaneous strikes. All in the middle of the night. No time for any one cell to prepare. We anticipate some will not go down easily. Others will. We have warrants in hand. We consider computer records as important as human intel."

"What will be the standard charges?" the vice president asked.

"Conspiracy, sedition, money laundering, murder. Pick a letter in the alphabet and we'll have a charge that starts with it."

"And the law of unintended consequences, Bob? There always are," Taylor noted.

"The night will change the face of organized crime in America. Some other group is likely to move in. But it sure is going to make a lot of junkies shaky and seriously hurt the tattoo business in America," Mulligan added.

Morgan Taylor also knew it was going to give the news channels and talk show hosts something new to talk about. So much for the president doing nothing.

CIUDAD DEL ESTE

The *snakebots* crawled closer under D'Angelo's skillful maneuvering and trained eye. They slithered their way from to tree to tree, mapping the exterior of the mansion, capturing the guards' routines, and providing actionable information.

High overhead, the CIA's satellites peered down with amazing clarity and detail. Closer to earth USAF drones sent more real-time images back to MacDill in Florida and the CIA in Langley.

As good as the eyes in the sky, Jack Evans relied heavily on HUMINT, an abbreviation for Human Intelligence. Boots on the ground. In this case, Vinnie D'Angelo. It was his experience that delivered beyond what the high-tech lenses reported. The career CIA officer communicated mission options, personal analysis, and opinion. Because he was there, he could interpret manner, attitude, intent, and the degree of professionalism.

He saw camaraderie rather than authority. Cavalier Latin machismo instead of military discipline. And he saw no leadership. That worried D'Angelo. They'd fire at anything, releasing everything in their magazine, indiscriminately killing instead of looking for hard targets. That kind of enemy had to be dealt with *before* they aimed their weapons and squeezed their triggers. One by one. Stealthily. Efficiently.

Vinnie D'Angelo's recommendations evolved the more he observed the target. He sent e-mails in short blasts and beyond anyone's decoding ability.

Guards most lax final 30 min before shift change.

He found their weakness and he would exploit it. The relief team was reliably late, casually strolling in independently, replacing tired and upset sentries.

Target 0233.

As for the country club security gate, he recommended a way to keep the rent-a-cop detail busy.

Create diversion.

He presented the rest of his plan, which the agency bought, SOCOM affirmed, and, after study, ST-6 approved.

D'Angelo also put in a personal request.

Want in.

That appeal went all the way to the POTUS. With the approval came another message that made him smile.

Observer with birds. Top Gun VIP. Known.

D'Angelo smiled. This could mean only one man. A friend with benefits. *Scott Roarke.*

TAMPA, FLORIDA
MACDILL AFB

Roarke and the ST-6 team touched down at MacDill for refueling and an updating briefing. The base was manned by approximately twelve thousand military personnel and thirteen hundred civilians. Nobody except those few who were cleared saw the Navy SEALs. Of the twenty-six assigned to MERCURY, more than half had previously worked together in Indonesia, Afghanistan, and Pakistan. For the newbies there was no hazing, only the strictest insistence on team work and efficiency.

"Gentlemen," General Drivas began, "we are *go* for a four-phased operation, as planned. Upon insertion, the clock ticks for twenty minutes. That's the time we calculate you'll have before first responders arrive. No time to buy postcard. Not that any of you Tweeters would even know how to put a stamp on one."

The team laughed. But it was entirely true.

"Of course, we'll be watching those nice live hi-def videos from your helmet cams back here at MacDill and monitoring your vest iPhones and your other doodads. You break 'em you pay for them," he joked. "Oh, and the POTUS will be watching, too. And you know he's Navy. So do him right. Got that?"

In unison, all the military team members shouted, "Yes, sir."

"Mr. Roarke, where are you?" Drivas asked.

Roarke waved his hand from the third row.

"Stand up, please."

He complied.

"Take a good look at this man. You've been training with him, and for a civilian, he's not done half bad keeping up. If you're wondering why the fuck he's here, Roarke works for the big boss. He's tagging along to observe and report on a separate channel. You make sure he comes back in one piece."

Roarke sat down.

"Ah, and Mr. Roarke, even though you'll be armed, please return the favor. Be damned careful where you aim."

Roarke tipped two fingers forward just off his forehead in partial salute. "Understood, sir."

"Okay then, let's go through the operation. You're on the C-40s in two hours and we have a lot to review."

CHAPTER 73

Two Boeing 737-BBJC transports, business and military versions of the commercial 737, were slowly towed out of adjacent hangars at

MacDill. One plane would have sufficed, but SOCOM flew two with the SEALs contingent split. No one talked about the *what ifs*, but they were obvious. Command accordingly took the necessary precautions.

The planes, repainted forty-eight hours earlier, rolled out with the corporate identity of Colgreen Jet Charters and a gold CJC company logo on the fuselage. But the crew and the passengers were all red, white, and blue. Colgreen was a faux cover just as the paint jobs were over the U.S. Navy Reserve modified 737s or C-40s.

The SEALs had a long flight ahead. These specially adapted 737s carried twelve fuel tanks, which extended the normal range from 3,500 miles to at least 7,000. Their trip would be 4,137 miles, taking eight hours and thirty-eight minutes from MacDill AFB in Tampa, Florida, to Florianópolis Air Force Base on the coast of Brazil.

The teams rested for the first four hours. About halfway they awoke, hit the head, and got to work, which consisted of studying real-time satellite, air, and ground imagery, running through slight changes in the mission, and reviewing their personal hard targets. It all had to be automatic with the ability to call audibles.

No joking now. The SEALs were in the zone, and Roarke was right there with them. Katie was a world away. She had to be. And Christine Slocum never existed.

CAPITOL HILL

Duke Patrick showed no remorse at the death of his young speechwriter. This had his staff perplexed. Even more troubling was that he was not getting out in front of the story; using his political capital to get airtime and hammer Taylor.

"Senator Aderly is calling again," his secretary said.

"Take a message."

"I've done that every time he's phoned. This is the umpteenth time. And the same for Shultz and Maddow. They're looking for soundbites, sir."

"No calls!" the emasculated Speaker of the House shouted. With his career in shambles and the threat of exposure and ruin, the former party stalwart wondered what kind of life, political or otherwise, lay ahead.

His secretary interrupted his depression again. "Mr. Speaker, he absolutely insists on talking to you."

• • •

The overnight assignment editors watched the wires for action. Any action. They got it. The networks and newspapers were conducting their own tests and coming up with a litany of deadly toxins.

"*Yersini Pestis*—stable for weeks or more," reported Fox News out of Lexington, Kentucky.

"Worse Case Scenario," was the headline in the *Baltimore Sun* after their analysis in College Park, Maryland, turned up *Bacillus anthracis* spores—active in water for up to two years.

ABC doubled down on the story, interviewing a medical expert who warned that boiling contaminated water with spore-forming *Bacillus subtillis*, a substitute for anthrax, could result in the release of bacteria particles into the air.

In Milwaukee, an article in the *Journal Sentinel* recalled the massive 1993 outbreak of cryptosporidiosis, the result of *Cryptosporidium* organisms passing undetected through two water treatment plants. It caused an estimated four hundred three thousand illnesses and forty four hundred hospitalizations. Now Wisconsin families were rushing to buy or steal bottled water, treating it as if it were gold. "In a few days," the paper reported, "the escalating prices might well set a new gold standard."

But the news got even worse when CNN announced that *Botulinum* toxin had been found in milk processed at a local Poughkeepsie, New York, dairy farm.

The *New York Times* front page asked, "What will be next?"

CIUDAD DEL ESTE

George Brewer and Nick Segaloff were part of the team that was going to provide it. The Delta Force lieutenants were on the ground, in advance of MERCURY. They each had specific missions, which they performed during the moonless night. Their jobs involved the use of plastic explosives they had smuggled into Paraguay from Brazil across the Friendship Bridge.

Brewer's two targets required 35 grams of C-4, or about 1.5 ounces. Segaloff carried 2 ounces for his objectives.

They worked separately and undetected. In the morning they would check into local hotels and be ready for any further orders.

BRAZIL
FLORIANÓPOLIS AIRPORT

The C-40s touched down and taxied without particular notice into two Brazilian Air Force hangars that had been turned over to U.S. operations.

Once inside, the crews deplaned for ninety minutes, enough time for a shower and refueling and weapons check.

Depending on the man and the specific duty, they carried both heavy and light weaponry: standard issue Heckler & Koch MP5 submachine guns; lightweight, air-cooled with 30-round capacity magazines; MK23 Mod 0 handguns with .45 ACP cartridges; and Benelli M4 Super 90 Shotguns with night-visions sights.

Also on their tactical vests—extra magazines, grenades, and multipurpose knives that really had one principal purpose.

They all wore camouflage, boots, watches, personal GPSs and multichannel communications equipment.

Take away all the equipment, the ST-6 remained a lethal force because each of the SEALs stood by the basic special ops truths. *Humans are more important than hardware. Quality is better than quantity. Special Operations Forces cannot be mass produced and Competent Special Ops Forces cannot be created after emergencies occurred.*

They were trained and ready. Scott Roarke among them.

Fifty-five minutes later they reboarded for the next leg, a 354-mile hop to Cascavel Airport, northwest of Florianópolis.

WASHINGTON, D.C.

"What the hell's going on, Patrick?" Senator Aderly Shaw complained. "Williamson's pissed beyond all measure. He says if you don't get out in front of those cameras, he'll find someone who will."

Duke Patrick didn't respond.

"Are you deaf as well as brain dead? Do you understand English? We will shut down the pipeline. Everything. The PACs, the support. It all goes away. We have a chance to score big here and you're the go-to face. It's now or never."

"We have a problem, Shaw," Patrick finally admitted to the Missouri senator, his likely running mate for the presidency.

"What? What kind of problem?"

He explained what Taylor had told him, concluding with a volley of direct questions. "Tell me. No lies. Tell me you didn't know about Slocum's history? About her connections with God knows whoever? About why you recommended her to me? You, Shaw. You. Sure looks like a set up to me. The truth, Senator. You were using me to get to the White House. What were you going to do when we got there? Shoot me? Or was that Williamson's job?"

"Oh come on. We recommended the girl to you. That's all. No conspiracy about it. She'd come off of Lodge's campaign bus and she looked like she'd be a good loyal addition to your staff. Hell, you wanted to fuck her."

Aderly paused long enough to switch on some feigned charm.

"Look, Duke, Slocum was a bright enough woman. I'm sorry she's dead."

"A dead spy is what she was!"

"You don't really know that. Taylor's just trying to throw you off. Remove you from the equation."

"The way I see it, my future has turned to shit because of you and your buddies."

"Because of us you had a future. And I suggest if you want to keep it, you do exactly as I say. I'll get back to you on how to manage this crisis. That's all it is. A crisis. And we'll get through it one way or another."

It was the *or another* that scared Duke Patrick even more than the president's threats.

• • •

Given the hold that terrorists and crime lords had on Ciudad del Este, threats were part of every day life. Tonight, D'Angelo figured it was going to get worse by an almost incalculable violent and political scale. He'd only worry about the violent part. The suits would deal with the politics.

Two hours earlier he had assigned control of the *snakebots* to MacDill. From now until exfiltration he was going to remain on alert in the battle zone. GPS signals, relayed to the airborne team, constantly pinpointed his location. It was imperative that he be viewed as a friendly at all times.

"Quiet and normal," he reported at 2245.

He updated SOCOM every fifteen from a hollowed-out tree he'd found on his first day of surveillance into the woods between the Paraná River and Haddad's mansion.

"Quiet and normal," he continued to broadcast.

• • •

Here is where Morgan Taylor's conversation with Lydia Santiago paid off.

Ten minutes into the forty-two minute flight to Cascavel, the airport plunged into darkness. The official write up? Power surge. But it was a Brazilian officer who cut the circuit.

Operating only on auxiliary power, with General Jim Drivas calling the shots, the tower diverted all incoming traffic back to Florianópolis where the U.S. transports had departed.

While in the air, the SEALs tested their cameras, GPSs, and devices and double-checked the other tools of their trade.

Thirty-minutes later, the big jets landed two minutes apart without the benefit of runway or landing lights. They quickly taxied to the end of the runway, barely fifty yards from three UH-60s, specially equipped Black Hawk helicopters which had made the trip to Cascavel under the cover of darkness the night before.

• • •

The teams split up according to plan, quickly boarding the Black Hawks. Five minutes later they were aloft again.

The next eighty-one miles would take two hours and one minute on a southwest course over rural Brazil, to the Brazil/Paraguay border that cut through the Paraná River, and the final two hundred yards to Ibrahim Haddad's compound. The schedule was all back-timed to precisely 0235.

FEBRUARY 7

Morgan Taylor looked at his watch. 12:35 a.m. He buzzed Louise Swingle who insisted on staying late.

"Yes, Mr. President."

"Is everyone comfortable and coffee'd-up?"

"Still waiting for a few. The vice president is already in the Situation Room along with the Joint Chiefs, Secretary Huret, and Mr. Grigoryan. Director Evans will be at Langley with his evaluators, and Director Mulligan, Mr. Bernstein, and Attorney General Goldman are due at 1 a.m."

"Thank you, Louise. I do have one other person to add to the list, but I don't want you to place the call quite yet." He gave her the name and when to call.

CHAPTER 74

WASHINGTON, D.C.

A telephone ring in the middle of the night is truly one of the most disturbing sounds on the face of the earth. It usually means something terrible has happened. When two phones ring, it must be worse. By zip code and city, there are probably more of those calls in metro D.C. than anywhere else in the country, if not the globe.

First, it was Katie Kessler's cell phone. She left her BlackBerry in her pocketbook in the kitchen. So even though the sound woke her, she didn't reach it in time. Four seconds after it stopped, her landline rang. She ran back to the bedroom but just as she reached for the handset on the fourth ring, her voice mail picked up. She heard her announcement, but when she said hello, no one was there.

Katie was wide awake now and worried. The noise and the alarm it raises had fully shaken the sleep out of her. She turned on her bedside nightlight, grabbed Scott's T-shirt that she liked to wear when he wasn't there off the floor, and slipped it on.

Just as Katie was trying to convince herself that everything was okay, both phones began ringing again. She quickly answered the landline. With great urgency she said, "Hello, who is this?"

"Kate?" replied a woman, speaking precisely and authoritatively.

"Yes. My other phone is ringing, too. Can I…?"

"That's me too. I'll drop that," the woman said.

Katie's cell stopped ringing.

"It's Louise Swingle. Will you hold for the president?"

"Yes. Yes, but why."

Katie's fears, the ones she lived with and shared with Scott overwhelmed her. Her heart rate increased. Her body tensed and her chest tightened. She gasped for a breath as she waited. Katie never had had asthma, but she believed this was what it must feel like.

Five seconds. Ten. Fifteen. All agonizing as she waited for the president of the United States to get on the phone at, *God, what hour?* She looked at her clock radio. It only made her feel more anxious.

"Katie," Morgan Taylor began.

She immediately tried to gauge the quality of his voice. Comforting? Serious? *It was serious*, she thought.

"Yes, Mr. President." Without waiting for what she now considered the inevitable, she said, "It's about Scott. Isn't it?"

Tears welled up.

"Yes. He is on a mission right now. But he's all right."

She let out a long, relieved, and cleansing breath that the president heard.

"I'm sorry my call alarmed you. But I decided you had earned the right to join us in the Situation Room for the operation. That's if you want to come."

"What operation?"

Taylor interrupted. "Can't explain now. There's a driver waiting outside your apartment. I recommend that you get here in twenty minutes. We'll have someone ready to bring you on in."

Katie was already standing, figuring out what to throw on. A sixty-second shower would bring her to her senses. After that jeans, a warm shirt and… *No,* she thought. It's still the White House. *Business. But the UGGs would have to do*. There was a new snowfall. *Not a good time to trip and break a leg.* Oh, and *makeup in the car.* She ran the entire exercise in her mind between Morgan Taylor's sentences.

"Is that okay, Katie?"

"Yes, sir." She wanted more reassurance that Scott was really safe. But that wouldn't happen on the phone. Not now. Whatever he was about to get into was going to be dangerous. Monitoring from the White House Situation Room was a true indication. *Better to be there.* "I'll be downstairs in ten minutes at the latest."

She made it in nine.

• • •

It was a combination of the medication he was taking, his insatiable appetite for the news from the United States, and his personal desire for revenge. The three combined to keep Ibrahim Haddad awake most nights. He spent hours logging on to local American newspaper Web sites, searching for updates about the great price he was exacting from America for something it had never done. His sworn enemy and its president were not responsible for the death of his wife and daughter, but his hatred of Israel fully transferred to the United States.

He felt untouchable now. Beyond the reach of any civilized law in one of the world's most lawless places. Maybe the only thing missing was the attention and notoriety. He was, after all, America's Number One Most Wanted. The aging terrorist didn't doubt they had some vague suspicion of his involvement by now. However he took no credit; made no pronouncements. After his narrow escapes from

Miami and Chicago, he concentrated on remaining committed to achieving his goal and remaining as off the grid as humanly possible.

"Get me a sandwich," he told the guard outside his room.

"Are you certain, sir? It's well after two."

"A sandwich," he barked again.

The guard, a member of Hamas hired a month earlier, radioed downstairs to the control center on the ground floor.

"He wants a sandwich."

"Did he say what kind?"

Idiot, the guard thought. *He only eats turkey.*

"The usual. And make it quick."

• • •

Katie was driven to the White House Southwest Gate. Her identification cleared her past the Marine Guard. A Secret Service agent on night duty accompanied her up what was called West Executive Avenue to the West Basement entrance. Here, she was checked again and allowed to pass.

They went down a flight of stairs and came to the White House Mess on the left and the Situation Room on the right. Another Secret Service agent examined her ID outside the closed door to the Sit Room.

"Katie Kessler?"

"Yes, sir." The agent checked her picture. Once satisfied he said, "I'll need your cell phone and tablets."

"Only a cell." Katie handed her BlackBerry to the agent.

"Thank you, Ms. Kessler. The president is inside. You may go in."

Katie said thank you in return, not knowing if she'd be really grateful for what she was about to experience.

This was her first time in the Situation Room. She took it all in. The multiple workstations, computers, and communication equipment. The bank of programmable TV screens, the austere long oak desk.

The president was talking quietly to J3. Everyone else seemed completely engaged in their own space, monitoring video feeds, typing quickly on laptops, and speaking to various people on headsets. She'd just walked into a hot command center and it scared the living hell out of her.

On the multiple TV screens in the front of the rectangular room were what seemed to be three different angles on one building. One was a shot that constantly panned from windows to doors. The camera operator, whoever it was, zoomed to a man with a cigarette dangling out of his mouth and a rifle slung over his shoulder. Next to that monitor was another video image. This one appeared to be pointing straight down at a man. Under the images, running time on a twenty-four-hour clock and a reference: SAT 535. When Katie grasped that she was viewing a live shot from a satellite that showed, with amazing clarity, the same man, she was astounded. On another monitor to the side, a clock that was running backwards; a countdown. She watched the seconds tick down to fourteen minutes.

"Oh my God," was all she could muster. That brought the attention of the president.

"Katie, thank you for coming."

"Coming to what?" she asked.

"Operation MERCURY. Quick in and out of a building and a country."

"A country?"

Less than a year ago, Katie Kessler was a young junior attorney in a Boston law firm. Today she stood in the White House Situation Room before what appeared to be *a target.*

"Paraguay, Katie. A city on the Tri-border with Brazil and Argentina. Not a particularly ideal spot for a week away, which is why we're planning on doing this in under twenty minutes."

"I'm sorry Mr. President, doing what and why?"

"Scott figured out who we were after. We discovered where he was."

Suddenly it became all too apparent why Louise Swingle called.

"Scott's there."

"On his way. I thought you'd want to be here."

"Oh no," she said, covering her mouth with her right hand.

The president extended his arms for a hug which she gratefully took. "It'll be okay. He's with SEAL Team 6. They're the best in the world. He's there only as an observer. My observer. He'll be yours, too."

Katie stepped away and worked to compose herself.

"There's a seat across the table there next to Eve. It's yours. Just toss your coat on one of the chairs behind you. Water?"

"I'll start with that," she said, trying to see if a joke would calm her.

The president reached for one in the center of the table and handed it to her. "Maybe we'll crack something stronger in an hour."

The *maybe* did not set her mind at ease. Not one bit.

• • •

"Nervous, Roarke?" asked B.D. Coons.

Roarke nodded. "On alert. I've been here before."

"You'll have to tell me about it sometime. I tried to read up on you and there's not much. You're listed as Secret Service and you served in the army with distinction. But even that's not public record. I can figure out your pay grade, but beyond that little else. A Facebook page would have helped me, that's for damned sure."

Roarke laughed. "I like to keep a low profile."

"Low doesn't begin to describe it. More like spook level."

"Well, I'm not that," Roarke laughed. "Not even close."

"Whatever, you're one of us now. Stay alert. Drop in *only* after we have secured the target. On my order. Got that, Mr. Roarke."

"Affirmative."

Roarke did understand how dangerous it would be and how he could compromise the SEALs operation. But he was there to certify Haddad's capture or death.

CHAPTER 75

CIUDAD DEL ESTE

D'Angelo continued to report all normal as it had been night after night…until 0225.

At ten minutes prior to execution he stared into his binoculars and did not like what he saw. He adjusted the focus on his tricked-out Night Optics USA/TG-7 Digital Thermal Imaging Binocular Goggles, switched to 2x and whispered, "Shit" into his open mic.

Vice Admiral Gunning beat everyone to the response. "Say again, Enterprise?"

D'Angelo adjusted his focus and steadied his body.

"You watching this back home?"

They were—at MacDill AFB, the CIA, on the incoming C-40s, and in the White House.

Shit, shit, shit, he mouthed.

• • •

Haddad's guard knocked at the door of his master bedroom suite.

"Yes?"

"Your food, sir."

"Fine. Bring it in."

The guard opened the door for the cook who brought in a silver tray.

Haddad glanced over. "Good, over there on the table," Haddad said.

"May I move the papers, sir?" The table was covered with printouts from Internet coverage across America.

"Yes…no! Leave them." He pointed frantically. "The table in front of the TV. And turn CNN back on."

That assignment went to the guard, not the cook.

As soon as the guard found the right channel, Haddad left the computer and moved to the TV.

"Sit down. Watch," he implored. It was part of the evening ritual. Someone had to listen to Haddad reminisce. They caught the news just as American deaths were being updated.

"Eighteen more cities have reported incidences," the anchored intoned. He stood in front of a graphic of the United States swollen with red hot spots.

"Another good day, Ali."

"Yes, sir."

"Though I would have preferred to see more dead by now," Haddad offered.

A on-screen list ticked upward nearing twenty-eight thousand deaths.

He completely ignored the Prophet Muhammad's actual teachings on revenge and Quaranic passages that spoke against it. Haddad's fight began as personal and remained there, with a degree of radical religious and political fervor thrown in whenever necessary. He never questioned what he was doing on an ideological or theological basis. Ibrahim Haddad, driven by hate, had become a mass murderer who liked turkey sandwiches, chips, warm coconut cake, and a glass of fresh water from Ciudad del Este's abundant source, the Gurani Aquifer.

"Perhaps tomorrow we will break thirty thousand," Ali added.

"I shall pray for that," Haddad said as he took his first bite.

At that moment, the doorbell rang two floors below.

• • •

D'Angelo zoomed in tighter.

"Civilian." It was repeated by another, "Shit."

"Describe."

D'Angelo followed a man walking to the door. He carried three flat boxes.

"Pizza delivery?" It was clearly more of a question than an observation. He hadn't seen any such activity before and wondered, *Why just before a shift change?* It would put the guards on the move, in the wrong place and off schedule.

He looked at his watch. Nine minutes to infil. *Come on pizza man, take your fucking money and get the hell out of there.*

• • •

The American commandos were coming in low and fast in helicopters that the government had basically kept under wraps until the killing of Osama bin Laden. These UH-60s had modifications which boggled the mind. They no longer sounded like helicopters.

Generally speaking, helicopters produce a distinctive percussive chop-chop rotor sound caused by the positioning of the blades. Adjust the blade angle, increase the number of blades in the main and tail rotors from four to five or six, and the noise diminishes, blending into the background sounds. Moreover, these Sikorsky Black Hawks had been re-engineered and reimagined with swept stabilizers and a noise suppressing "dishpan" cover over the tail rotor. Further refinements included reducing the rpm, especially in forward flight below maximum speed. To the untrained ear, it appeared that the helicopters were much farther away, not heading in, but away from a target.

There were also changes that reduced the chances of returning radar signals. Retractable landing gears and fairings over the rotor hubs cut down the radar cross-section (RCS). And sharp edges, standard on the UH-60s, were replaced with curved surfaces coated in a special silver-loaded infrared skin. These important conversions served to scatter incoming radar hits, sending them in multiple directions and confusing an enemy's air-defense systems.

Multimillion dollar changes that transformed noisy machines into stealthy aircraft.

• • •

Take your money and leave! D'Angelo thought.

But his best efforts to will the delivery man away didn't work. He tilted up to the bedroom. Target Alpha, the man they were coming for, walked past a window. He tilted down again to watch the front door. *Shit.* Pizza man was still there.

"Uncle." He used Command's sign. "Definite civilian in the zone."

"We're watching, Enterprise."

"Schedule?"

"As planned."

"Options?"

Command had none to offer. "No."

"Roger," D'Angelo said more quietly.

With that, he decided to follow the SEALs into the compound and try to avoid any *collateral damage.*

• • •

Roarke heard the interchange between D'Angelo and Command. He watched the feed from the CIA agent's Night Optics USA/TG-7 on a make-shift bank of 5-inch monitors facing the passenger compartment.

Judging by the door frame, the man was about six feet. Maybe a little more. He wore a hoodie and slacks and sneakers. It struck Roarke that a hoodie might be too warm for the surroundings. But it certainly was *derigueur* for so many young men today, and at night it could be in the low '70s. Still he had a nagging thought as he flew closer and closer to Ibrahim Haddad's lair.

• • •

At exactly 0229 cell phone service throughout the country club and the neighboring area went dead.

This was George Brewer's work. Two electrical detonators wired to a timer fired a brief charge, which in turn set off a small amount of explosive material. This applied an instantaneous shock wave that triggered the C-4 to explode. The 1.5 ounces didn't have to bring the cell phone towers down. Brewer just needed to take out the power supplies.

• • •

Get the fuck out of there! D'Angelo wanted to shout!

• • •

"I need an open line to Enterprise," Roarke keyed into his mic. He could hear D'Angelo, but he couldn't speak directly to him without SOCOM's help.

"Too late. We're under two minutes."

"Do it!" Roarke shouted. The Navy SEAL beside him read the urgency.

"What's up?" Commander Bob Shayne asked loudly over the sound of the rotors.

Roarke pointed to the monitor displaying the video from

D'Angelo's binoculars. The front door opened and a guard looked at the pizza boxes.

"I need Enterprise. Fast."

Shayne tapped his watch and shook his head. They were very close to the drop.

"Tell them!"

Shayne, who had hopes of working in the movies post military, barked into the mic in his helmet.

"Link up Sidekick."

A few long beats later Roarke heard a scratchy, "Putting him through. You have fifteen seconds. Go."

"Enterprise, this is Sidekick." Roarke's handle. "Can you ID the civvie?"

D'Angelo whispered. "Negative, Sidekick."

They both watched as the guard took the three boxes of pizza and walked to his right. The delivery man followed him in and closed the door behind him.

"He's inside."

"Do you let your pizza man in?" Roarke asked. But the comm line was already closed. They were slowing down over the Paraná River. Another thirty seconds.

CHAPTER 76

The three Black Hawks bore down on the target.

Directly above the Brazil-Paraguay border; about the midpoint in the Paraná, the lead helo cut to port side, flew another six hundred yards, then banked starboard, cutting over the Paraná Country Club. Twenty seconds later, another starboard turn brought it dead on to the southwest wall of Ibrahim Haddad's compound.

Black Hawk Two made a coordinated mirror move up the river, with a sweep that put it on course for the northeast courtyard wall.

Black Hawk Three had a straight-in flight path to the largest and lowest point, the southeast wall.

The moonless night, the noise suppression, and the perfectly coordinated maneuvering allowed the SEALs to sneak up on the target, manned with guards who were ready to leave their posts and unprepared for the surprise assault.

• • •

"It's going to unfold fast from here on," J3 explained. At this moment, he was more general again than vice president.

"They'll hit exactly at the same time. The first copter will hover a few feet above the courtyard, drawing attention. Two and three will sit higher, and the SEALs will rappel down. Based on the intelligence and live pictures, they each have a specific target. The objective is to eliminate the external threats first and swiftly proceed inside."

Katie now wished she weren't there. This was too real; too scary for her. The president sensed her fear. He rose and walked around the table. "Scott's only job is to report back to me," Taylor whispered. "His audio is being fed to the computer in front of you. When this is over, you'll be able to IM him. He'll see it on a heads-up display."

Katie reached back and took the president's hand.

• • •

Haddad's three-story compound provided natural objectives and some real problems. Surprise was the most important element, but surprise never dictated how real people would react. That was the X factor computers couldn't plot. An added unknown—the civilian on the property. B.D. Coons radioed down the line to identify the non-com and remove him from the kill zone. If necessary by force. It added a variable that he did not like.

• • •

A red light flashed at the cargo doors of the Black Hawk. Time.

Roarke wanted to be part of the first wave, but that was not to be. He was in Black Hawk Two under orders to hold back.

It happened quickly. "They're dropping now," Roarke narrated for the White House. He described how Shayne rappelled down from Black Hawk Three, followed by SEALs Steve Smoller, Joe Hilton, and Anthony Formichelli. All coordinated; all focused on their specific target.

Meanwhile, the same was happening diagonally across from Roarke's helicopter with Commander B.D. Coons's team from Black Hawk One. The third-story master suite blocked much of his view, but he described what he could. "Team One hitting the deck and firing. Obstructed view, but seeing flashes. One fully in play. Three same. Hard targets being neutralized."

The *snakebot* videos and the satellite images told the White House even more. In fifteen seconds, three teams took out all the men in the courtyard; kills that would never need their reliefs.

Roarke's Black Hawk Two moved clear of the perimeter, taking up a position one hundred yards away and four hundred feet up. He had a clear view of the compound and continued his reports.

On ground, the objective was to get inside. Team One's Walter Canby fired a M203 Grenade Launcher, underslung to his rifle. The single 40mm shot blew out the sidewall to the first floor, creating a much more dramatic way to enter than the door.

Two other SEALs followed the blast through the wall. Guns ready. But Canby had done the work for them. Three of Haddad's men were dead on the floor and another on the stairway leading to the second floor.

The exact same move came from under Black Hawk Two's squad when Formichelli fired his grenade launcher and opened up the northeast living room. Not that anyone in there was still living.

"Through second wall," Roarke radioed. "SEALs taking up position in the courtyard. Others converging inside. More shots from first floor."

It was apparent from his coverage that Roarke was itching to be in the middle of the action.

Commentary from Coons added to the coverage. "Ground floor

secure. Eleven confirmed kills. Two floors to go. Sidekick cleared to proceed."

Katie watched breathlessly 5,300 miles away as Roarke's helmet cam went live.

"Roger," Roarke replied.

Roarke's UH-60 moved back into position. Through his point of view Katie saw a line check and then a fast rappel to the courtyard. The sight of the ground rushing up made her gasp. She felt like she was there with him.

"On ground," Roarke called in.

This was too intense for Katie. She was virtually watching through Roarke's eyes. Hearing the gunshots. Seeing the carnage. Too much.

"I can't," she cried.

Attorney General Eve Goldman grabbed her arm.

"It's okay, go outside."

Katie nodded and exhaled a cleansing breath. "I'll be okay."

Goldman glanced over to the president and gave him an indication that Katie needed attention. The president returned to her side and pulled up a chair next to her. He put his arm on her shoulder and softly said, "He's going to be okay. He's the last man in and we'll see to it that he's the first out. How about that?"

Katie turned and said, "Please."

• • •

The team converged on the first floor. They stepped over bodies and body parts, around shattered glass and utterly destroyed furniture. Three SEALs tagged items that they'd take home. That meant anything that might have intelligence value—computers, memory sticks, papers, cell phones, answering machines. Anything. The small items went into a duffle bag. The larger prizes would be hauled out by the other team members. On his own discreet channel Formichelli verbally logged what he saw, including three pizza boxes strewn across the floor with tomato sauce indistinguishable from the enemies' blood.

Moving to the second floor, Shayne was surprised to meet less resistance. Two guards rushed out of adjoining rooms. They'd been shocked awake barely twenty-two seconds earlier. The moment they hit the hallway the SEALs gave them a way to make up for the sleep they missed.

Four seconds later, Black Hawk Two's Rob Perlman and Jim Kaplan met on the first landing taking the lead up the next flight.

One by one, the shocked enemy combatants, no match for SEALs, fell. A drunk guard urgently and unsuccessfully trying to dial his cell. The cook with a knife. Another sentry on a toilet break. Another reaching for his gun.

There were all eliminated from humankind with extreme prejudice. None with the honor of a national hero. All destined to die because of the man who hired them. Some shot so cleanly it would be hard to find the bullet entry point. Others who lost their heads with a blast of the Benelli M4 Super 90 shotgun in the hands of SEALs from each copter.

Roarke cautiously followed the SEALs. As they made their way up to the second landing he realized he was not providing the commentary promised.

"Cleared the ground floor. Two minutes in. Sirens beginning outside."

• • •

D'Angelo was very aware of the sirens. But thanks to the preparation by the advance team, the main road would be relatively impassable, buying extra minutes.

The SEALs scoped the second floor. Without speaking, Coons pointed, *There, there, there, there.* Four fingers. Four nods from his men. And with his command, four more of Haddad's men would not go home tonight. It seemed like the only lucky ones would be those late for the guard shift change.

Next, the third floor. Here, resistance was stronger. Higher ground.

"We're pinned down. I count six guards protecting the bedroom. Need cover. Hang on."

Suddenly they were off the game plan. The SEALs were pinned down and cut off.

"Count?" Coons shouted to his men. "Whoever has a target."

"One to the left top," Shayne called out.

"Got another to right. Behind a post," yelled Kaplan.

"Two more. One at the door to the right of the stairs, another firing from a room down the hall," added Perlman.

"Saw a shadow duck into room at the end of the hall," Formichelli said.

Two more SEALs reported what they saw.

"Enterprise, what do you see inside the bedroom?"

D'Angelo brought his binoculars into focus on the room. "Can't say."

Coons signaled to Shayne to take care of the easiest problems. The men directly above who had them immediately pinned down.

"Formichelli, Canby, left-right. He pointed to the cross shots for the men carrying the grenade launchers.

Affirmative nods. They backed down the steps. The guards above continued to fire across the hall, hitting the plaster on the walls and the stairs, but not the SEALs.

On the second floor landing, Formichelli and Canby took aim. It wasn't going to be pretty. But it was going to be effective. A fraction of a second later, two dead guards fell through the holes in the floor created by the firepower of the M203s.

With momentary quiet Shayne heard a transmission from MacDill.

"Any sign of Target Alpha?" asked Command.

"Negative," answered Shayne. "Stand by."

• • •

Those in the Situation Room watched it all via live, hi-def, streaming video. Only one other administration had witnessed such similar startling video. It was a world apart from the way war used to be fought. And it was episodic, hypnotic, and compelling.

• • •

"I'll take a new count," yelled Coons.

The report came immediately. Four visible; others unseen.

The captain checked his watch. It had seemed like an hour. But so far, only four minutes.

"Let's light up the tower, Dog One. Southwest," Shayne keyed into his mic.

"Roger that," Milt Frome, the pilot of the Black Hawk One responded.

Captain Frome eased his helo back 250 yards, targeted the roof of the third floor, and let loose with his two machine guns.

In ten seconds, twenty-five hundred rounds plowed into and across the roof. Portions of it caved in over the hall. The remaining guards on the third floor scrambled for safety. But there was none within the crosshairs of the Navy SEALs.

For the first time since the men rappelled, there was quiet.

"Up to the third floor," Roarke radioed. "Visible assets taken out. Alpha ahead."

The SEALs stepped over bodies on the stairs that would remain there until the local police got through. They took a particularly large step over two dead, one on top of another, their blood flowing down to the second floor landing below.

Coons silently signaled for Shayne and Smoller to flank the door to the master bedroom suite ahead, ten feet on either side. This was the scenario they'd run dozens of times in the Virginia Beach mockup.

Now Shayne held up five fingers for his men to see; then squeezed them into a solid fist. He held that in the air, getting nods from his forward team. Roarke remained behind him.

Ascertaining that everyone was ready, he returned to a five finger count, each second dropping one finger starting with his thumb.

On four, Shayne and Smoller took aim on their cross shots. On three, Shayne aimed his HK MP5 at the left side of the door frame and the hinges. Smoller had the lock and the right side. On two, they took a deep breath. On one, they released and fired.

• • •

It was an unbelievable experience for Katie Kessler. She witnessed the SEALs' precision kills. She watched as they meticulously pushed forward, eliminating the enemy, blowing down walls and floors, taking strides over dead bodies. She stopped counting at fifteen. Katie jumped at the thundering noise as part of the roof collapsed under the heavy fire from the Black Hawk. And now she grabbed Eve Goldman's hand hard, preparing herself for the worst. This was beyond anything she had ever been subjected to; a horrific reality playing out on video monitors, Bose speakers, and computer screens. Death everywhere.

• • •

The 9mm rounds spit out of the submachine guns at a rate of 800 rounds per minute. But coming from two SEALs simultaneously, it only required ten seconds and roughly 528 rounds. What had been a solid oak door splintered away, looking like it had been devoured by a Japanese movie monster. On plus eleven seconds, facing no immediate resistance, Shayne and Smoller moved in and cross-scanned their quadrants. The four other SEALs on the stairs proceeded forward.

"No resistance," Roarke whispered. He followed the assault team up the stairs. Out of sight—six other SEALs downstairs. There were pulling computers and files into the courtyard and transferring the cache into metal litters which were lifted up to Black Hawk Two.

As the smoke cleared in what had been a bedroom and office, it was apparent that the second phase of the operation was complete. Maybe not exactly to script, but complete.

Ibrahim Haddad was dead. He was sprawled across his desk; shards of wood and shrapnel from the door were lodged in his body. His head was dangling off the end of his workspace.

"We're clear," reported Shayne.

"Clear," added Smoller.

Coons entered the room. "Alpha down. Repeat, Alpha is down."

Roarke added the grace note. "Haddad is dead."

The rest of the squad carefully surveyed the room. "Three on the floor," Shayne said. He checked for signs of life. There were none. Coons okayed the techies in the squad to secure the computers. A Sony desktop computer had crashed on the floor. An Apple laptop was open and still running on a coffee table. Both would be transported to the helicopters along with a room safe that was beside the bed and four file cabinets.

Roarke walked around the desk to examine Haddad. He gasped at the sight.

"Oh, God! Coons! Come over here."

Roarke's helmet cam broadcast the picture to the White House before the SEAL leader saw it.

Coons crossed the room never expecting a discovery like this.

• • •

Roarke radioed D'Angelo. "Enterprise, are you still with me?"

"Enterprise here."

"Subject is dead."

"Roger that, Sidekick. Caught the traffic."

"But not by us."

CHAPTER 77

The president's first thought watching the live streaming video was *Poetic Justice.* Then came *who* and*when*, which were the same questions the SEALs had.

Roarke knew. It was crystal clear. As crystal clear as the half-empty three-litre water bottle stuffed into Haddad's mouth and sealed tightly around his head and nose with duct tape.

"He drowned to death," Roarke reported. "Likely only minutes ago."

D'Angelo cut in. "The pizza man. Damnit. I should have realized."

"Realized what?" Roarke asked.

"The British guy at the hotel. The teacher. Wasn't British and wasn't a teacher!"

"Cooper," Roarke declared.

"Cooper," D'Angelo confirmed.

He moved closer. Haddad's eyes bulged out in fear; fear and desperation. He was a man not prepared to die tonight, at least not this way. He was a murderer himself who was incapable of fighting off a killer so personally intent on revenge.

"Shit!" Roarke bolted upright. "He's still gotta be here."

Roarke ran out of the room.

"Careful, soldier," Coons yelled. The commander told his SEALs to continue their mop up and joined the Secret Service agent on the hunt.

• • •

Katie stood up; her fingernails digging into the palms of her hands.

• • •

Roarke and Coons ran down the stairs nearly tripping over a body between the third and second floors. When they reached the first floor, Roarke scanned the premises. The ST-6 team members assigned to removal were shuttling take-away to Black Hawk One.

Suddenly a distinct picture came to Roarke.

"Quick, back up!" he shouted.

Roarke took two steps at a time, making the first flight in three seconds. Four more leaps and he was there. At *the* body he had stepped over moments earlier. At the single body where there had been two dead men; one on top of another only minutes before.

"Enterprise, Cooper is alive! Scan the second floor."

"On it!"

D'Angelo trained his Night Optics USA/TG-7 Digital Thermal Imaging Binoculars on the windows and porches. Nothing.

Meanwhile, MacDill, listening on the comm line, remotely redirected the *snakebots* to the second floor.

"No movement, Sidekick," D'Angelo reported.

"Stadium reports negative as well." The second view came from MacDill, code named *Stadium* for the mission.

"Back me up," Roarke said to Coons.

• • •

Katie tightened her grip on Eve Goldman's arm. She shot an anguished glare at the president who had assured her Roarke would be fine.

Now, Roarke was fully in the mix of it and no one could put her mind to rest. Not until he got out safely.

• • •

Coons radioed for additional support. Formichelli and Smoller rushed down from Haddad's suite. They took signals from Coons and lined up on two sides of a second floor door, one of three.

Weapons at the ready, night vision goggles on, they moved forward. Formichelli, on the right, turned the knob and pushed the unlocked door open. Smoller knelt down and angled into the room at a lower perspective. Coons, standing, scanned the opposite side high. Roarke moved forward in the center, following Shayne's hand signs.

No heat signatures on the infrared. The team edged forward in complete synchronization. Nobody in the public space. Nobody in the single closet. No one under the bed. And the window was locked.

They backed out the same way they entered, then proceeded to the neighboring bedroom in the same manner.

"Clear," Coons whispered. He motioned for his men to check the bathroom.

"Clear," they responded thirty seconds later.

One more room. Shayne gave the signal silently. Palm down. Go slow. They moved even more cautiously. High, low, cross covering the room. Roarke was prepared to fire, to end his chase once and for all.

"There!" Roarke spotted the open window. He broke rank and ran forward. No ledge. Two floors up. He calculated the jump. *Twenty, maybe twenty-two feet.* Then he heard some rustling below and to the left.

"I need eyes over there!" He pointed. Formichelli came up to the northwest window and peered out where Roarke was pointing. He caught a man on the run. He was on his way into the woods, some thirty yards away.

"Enterprise, moving north on the ground, your three o'clock!" Roarke shouted.

D'Angelo blew a confirmation into his microphone saving the time to speak.

It didn't matter. Roarke jumped the two stories concentrating on not breaking his legs.

• • •

The ground looked as if it were rushing up again. It was. Katie gasped; then screamed as the view jostled and went out of focus.

• • •

Roarke cushioned his jump rolling on the ground. Safe, he sprung to his feet and radioed, "Dog Two what do you see?" Dog Two was the second Black Hawk.

"On point, sir. Recovering the packages," the pilot said. The same response came from the other helicopters when Roarke asked if they could pick up the target.

"Enterprise?"

"Catching up."

Roarke ran at breakneck speed toward the Paraná River, Cooper's obvious destination.

He cut through the woods. Branches slapped at his face. Night vision would have helped him on the moonless night. Now he relied on the crunching sound of leaves ahead of him and his own personal radar—skill.

Roarke checked his constantly updating position against D'Angelo's. They both showed up as blips on his handheld PDA dubbed DAGR for Defense Advanced GPS Receiver He saw that D'Angelo was not going to be able to close the distance. Cooper kept up maximum distance between them. But the sound was getting louder to Roarke. He was gaining on his prey.

• • •

Richard Cooper always had an exit strategy. Sometimes it was a quick-change disguise. Other times, a diversion; a shot in the air, an explosion; a scream. He lived longer because he planned his escapes to the same detail that he planned his assassinations.

This time he had a Zodiac 150 horsepower inflatable launch ready. He jumped in his hidden craft, powered up, and set a straight course for Ciudad del Este where he could disappear among the other thieves and murderers.

"Damnit. I need help here!" Roarke exclaimed. "Calling an audible. Someone get me authorization."

Command could see exactly where he was. The trouble was authorization. Black Hawk One, nearly packed, could rise, swing east, and pick him up in the basket at river's edge. But it would cost time and it was not on the playlist.

• • •

"Mr. President, Stadium is asking how you want to respond?"

Morgan Taylor quickly got thumbs down and negative nods from Jack Evans and Secretary Grigoryan. Secretary of State Huret felt he didn't have a vote.

"The mission was the kill and exfil with the computers and files. That has been accomplished. Mr. President, let's get everyone out as planned," Evans stated.

"J3? Your vote? The man tried to kill you. If we abandon the pursuit your life will still be at risk," Morgan Taylor asked.

"Yes, Mr. President, but I agree with Jack. Get the boys out. Get them out now."

Katie, however, realized that the decision made in the Situation Room would not deter Scott Roarke. Not now. Not ever.

"Mr. President, I want Scott out, too. But if you don't help him, he'll do it on his own. So you better back him up."

• • •

As right as she might be about Scott, the president made a decision for the sake of the mission. "Everyone gets out now. That's an order." Roarke was alive and Morgan Taylor wanted to keep it that way.

"Stadium," the vice president stated over the line, "Tell Sidekick to return for extraction."

"Yes, sir," came the relieved response from Vice Admiral Gunning at MacDill AFB. He also wanted his SEALs safely out. "Affirmative."

The order was relayed to Roarke.

"Negative, Stadium. Need to pursue."

"Repeat, return to Field Goal."

"Negative, Stadium," Roarke repeated. "New objective in view."

"Overruled Sidekick."

Roarke understood what *overruled* meant. His request went to the top. "Damn," he said aloud.

Just then, Roarke heard another boat coming up river and a flashlilght signaling in Morse Code:

...I..I-..I.I-.-I..I-.-.I-.-

Sidekick.

D'Angelo had commandeered a docked Pride Cheetah Ski Boat powered by a 115 Mercury outboard motor. Just another thing stolen in the crime capital of South America. He honed in on Roarke on his DAGR. A half minute later, Roarke was his passenger in pursuit of Richard Cooper.

CHAPTER 78

"Mr. President," Vice Admiral Gunning asked from MacDill, "We're reassessing."

"Say again?" Morgan Taylor demanded over the scrambled line.

"Reassessing, sir."

"What in hell does that mean?"

"Enterprise acquired Sidekick." The rest remained unstated.

"Oh no." Taylor shook his head sensing Katie's eyes burning into him. He turned away from her, but she figured out the situation.

"Jesus. He's still after him," she said.

Katie wanted to leave, but was too angry to do so. Angry at the president for putting Roarke in the field. Angry at Roarke for taking on the hunt.

"For God's sake, help him," she pleaded.

• • •

The best the Cheetah could do was keep Cooper's Zodiac in view, not catch up. With less than a few kilometers to Ciudad del Este and no support, it seemed likely Cooper would get away—again.

Two minutes in, Roarke and D'Angelo saw the lights ahead on the Friendship Bridge which linked Brazil and Paraguay. D'Angelo sharpened the focus on his binoculars. Cooper's craft was angling closer to the shore.

"Got any suggestions?" the CIA agent asked.

"Yes. Kill him."

D'Angelo laughed. "Don't count on it. He's a nuclear cockroach."

Roarke kept his attention forward, fully aware that D'Angelo was right. They couldn't possibly catch up.

Suddenly a whirring sound came up on and over them. Water churned almost violently, which was nothing compared to the ear shattering volley that spit out Black Hawk Two's side-mounted M60D machine gun.

At first the aim was short, but Captain Frome brought the UH-60 nose up, and the next rounds hit the Zodiac's motor dead on, which ignited the fuel and created an explosion that lit up the dock that Cooper was only yards away from reaching.

Satisfied, Frome banked the Black Hawk toward the Brazil side of the Paraná and waved good-bye.

"Enterprise, proceed to Farmer's Daughter for reunion." The order came from B.D. Coons who was observing from one thousand feet in Black Hawk One. The order was to tie up with two other SEALs who attacked the country club entrance before the national military tightened exfiltration routes.

"Roger, One," D'Angelo responded.

Roarke disagreed. "You said he's a nuclear cockroach. Get us closer."

"One pass. But let's lighten up."

They tossed their tactical vests, helmets, and heavy weapons in the middle of the Paraná and washed the grease off their faces.

• • •

D'Angelo steered around the debris and burning rubber. Pieces floated where there had been a whole craft. Nothing else.

"We've gotta go, Roarke. Sorry."

Roarke continued to look for signs of a swimmer; or any remains.

"He's gone, buddy."

Gone, Roarke thought. He reached for D'Angelo's binoculars. "Give me those."

D'Angelo handed them over. Roarke brought them up to his eyes and scanned the water ahead, then swept farther up river.

"We've got to…"

"Damnit! Give me one more minute!"

• • •

The binocular images were transmitted back to MacDill where an extra pair of eyes jockeyed between the video monitor and a computerized waveform monitor that distinguished objects Roarke might not.

"General, check out the incoming vid from Enterprise," Seaman Garrett Dettling requested.

Gunning looked up at the video feed in the op center. There was nothing significant to his mind.

"What?" he asked.

"I'll give you playback in slo-mo, sir."

Dettling typed in time-code from thirty seconds previous. The hard drive instantly cued to the image the $10,752-a-year enlisted man had viewed before.

Dettling crept the video forward. "Coming up." He froze an image. "See?"

• • •

"Enterprise, subject on the move. Forty-five degrees off your nose. Two hundred twenty feet." The transmission immediately got D'Angelo's attention.

"Get your eyes up there and hold on!" D'Angelo yelled. He revved the engine and speeded to the riverbank. Roarke nearly lost his footing. "You just might have another shot, buddy."

Roarke trained the binoculars on the embankment. "There!" he shouted loud enough for Richard Cooper to hear.

D'Angelo could see him now, too, Cooper was slightly illuminated by the reflection of the city lights in the water.

Roarke yelled, "Faster," though he didn't need to. D'Angelo was already at top speed, closing the distance to the swimmer.

• • •

Nothing the president could say would have mattered to Katie Kessler. Roarke and D'Angelo were determined to get Cooper.

Moments earlier they had all been relieved that the assault was over. Now they were compelled to listen to the drama. No more pictures from Roarke's POV camera. That went into the river along with his tac vest.

"The two Bobs." The president got the attention of his FBI Director and Secretary of State.

Taylor motioned with his index finger for them to come around. Bob Huret, a member of his cabinet from the beginning, kneeled next to Taylor. The FBI Director stood.

"Yes, Mr. President," Secretary of State Huret said for both of them.

"Alarms have got to be going off down there. It's time to get Gutierez on phone."

"Absolutely. When?"

"Five minutes. I'll bet you dollars to donuts you're not the one to wake him up."

Huret agreed. By now, the president of Paraguay was certain to be very busy and very confused.

• • •

Cooper scrambled up the slope that rose from the Paraná. At the crest, more woods, then the bustling streets, market venders, and shopping malls of Ciudad del Este. A perfect place to escape even at this hour.

First, get lost in the crowd. Cooper thought as he ran. *Then lose whoever was following him.* But he had a strong feeling he knew who it was.

• • •

Roarke leaped off the bow of the craft milliseconds before D'Angelo beached it. Inertia gave him a boost up the hill but no direct shot.

• • •

Cooper made the street thirty feet ahead of his hunter. He bumped into hawkers still selling perfumes, cell phones, cigarettes, tents, and suitcases. He careened off one merchant, knocking him into stacked boxes of hot flat screen TVs. They came crashing down and bought him a few extra seconds of space.

Roarke had to jump over the boxes.

• • •

Cooper smashed into a makeshift gate holding fifty or more multicolored soccer balls. The structure collapsed and the balls bounced into the street and sidewalk giving him more broken field running room.

Roarke dodged and slipped. When he rose, Cooper was gone.

• • •

"Mr. President, I'm sorry to call you at this hour," Morgan Taylor began.

"I'm a little busy. Would this have anything to do with it?" the Paraguayan chief executive replied in a completely unfriendly tone.

"I will be direct, President Gutierez. Tonight the United States acted unilaterally in defense of its national interests. In the most specific of terms, Special Forces, under orders of the president of the United States, located the terrorist known to be behind the attacks on this country. This action occurred within Paraguay outside of Ciudad del Este. The terrorist's guards were *dealt with* and our enemy was removed."

Taylor kept to the truth, but avoided detail.

"We are currently extracting our men and we will cover the actual cost of physical damage to public and private property. Any interference, Mr. President, *any* will be considered collusion in the unmitigated attack on the peoples of the United States of America. Conversely, your cooperation will be noted in our ongoing discussions." He intentionally left out promises.

"I will turn further dialogue over to Bob Huret, in anticipation of the questions surely to follow from the press."

Morgan Taylor stopped, not to invite dialogue but to end the conversation.

"Mr. President, I must ask," Gutierez began.

"I'm sorry, my first duty is to my men. Secretary of State Huret will be calling back within the hour. Thank you, President Gutierez."

Taylor hung up.

He was becoming someone else—fast. Cooper quickly grabbed a short-sleeve shirt off a rack, a baseball cap, and a blue backpack and paid the indignant shopkeeper a hard right in his gut for the goods.

• • •

Roarke searched left and right. He removed slower people from those moving faster and people who weren't trying to be invisible from one who was.

• • •

Around a corner Cooper ripped off his wet shirt, put on the new one, then slung the backpack over it. The hat rounded out the quick change. Ahead, in front of the Americana Mall, were rows of parked yellow motorcycles and a few arriving and departing.

He made a wide sweep around them, blending in with the pedestrians, and identified a biker who was going to lose his bike.

• • •

Damn! Roarke narrowed his focus. *Where are you?* The sounds were impossible to filter. A cacophony of music emanating from ramshackle apartments interspersed with the malls and shouts of "coke!," which is easily available and definitely not in a can. His training told him to stick with the motion and look for someone trying to blend in.

Roarke stepped out into the street. Little chance of being hit by a car. Traffic was backed up. The only things moving were the motorcycles. He searched again left, right, and straight ahead. Cooper was a tad taller than most, so he looked above the heads. That's when he caught a figure in a garish shirt and a baseball cap moving quickly amongst the late-night shoppers and hookers. *Not him.* But just as Roarke was about to shift his attention elsewhere, he saw a man ever so slightly casting about as if he were checking for something. Checking for an escape route.

Cooper!

The assassin rammed his elbow into the solar plexus of the twenty-four-year-old tourist from Denmark who had just bought some of the street coke and was now ready to drive back to his hotel. It was such a natural movement that no one noticed it came with near lethal intent. The man doubled over; the wind knocked out of him. Cooper saved the motorcycle and let the young man fall face first onto the pavement and into his own vomit. Cooper skipped the yellow helmet and gunned the throttle.

That caught Roarke's attention even more. Everyone else had a helmet. He cut across a line of cars, back into a street vender, and knocked down a display of Black Market Bobbi Brown cosmetics under a red, blue, green, and yellow umbrella. The merchandise broke, releasing the powerful perfumed scents into the marketplace. When Roarke found his footing again, he drew a forty-five-degree bead on Cooper. A clear shot. But a boy, likely no older than twelve, stepped out in front of him. He held a Smith and Wesson .380 semiautomatic on him.

"Detener!" the boy yelled. "Stop." From barely ten feet, he aimed his pistol at Roarke's stomach, a bigger, easier target than his head. He wasn't the only one armed on the street. Other vendors—men,

women, and children—had shotguns. The small semiautomatic was just easier for the kid to handle.

Roarke froze. A child with a gun; a child who spoke no English and who thought he could earn some street cred for stopping this thief, was not someone to tempt.

"*Por favor. Que el hombre*," Roarke said in his best Los Angeleno Spanish. "Please, that man." He motioned to the motorcyclist barreling down on them.

The kid would have nothing of it. He had his own man, the one who had just destroyed hundreds of dollars of merchandise.

Roarke was pushed forward by the pedestrians who made way for the motorcyclist.

"Detener! Detener."

Roarke found his footing. It didn't seem like the boy would.

To him, Roarke was big, strong, and very threatening. The child steadied his grip with the standard two-hand stance. He obviously had trained for this moment. The safety was off. Adrenaline coursed through his veins.

"No!" Roarke shouted.

The child had seen others do it. Aim and fire. A rite of passage for many others who had also grown up in the most dangerous environment imaginable. A lawless city, a throwback to the old West where guns spoke the loudest and young people proved their worth by using them.

Roarke cautiously angled his body to give the boy a narrower target. "No, mi amigo," he said.

It wasn't enough to deter the child from his defining moment.

He fired, but his aim went high as a form that seemed to come out of nowhere tackled him. A much bigger force. Vinnie D'Angelo.

"Get going!"

Roarke turned to see if he could catch Cooper on foot, but he'd already put too much room between them. Then he remembered the other motorcyclists. He changed direction, ran to the parking rack, and with even greater urgency than Cooper, also commandeered a motorcycle.

"*Por favor*. Sorry," he said to the young woman he left stranded. Roarke gunned the engine, circled, and tore off after Cooper. He caught a glimpse of D'Angelo helping the kid up and screaming at the others to calm down. His Spanish was far better and more authoritative than Roarke's. He was also one hundred times more lethal than anyone congregating near him now.

• • •

Roarke saw Cooper ahead about fifty yards. He maneuvered straight for the Friendship Bridge which linked Ciudad del Este, Paraguay, with Foz do Iguaçu, Brazil. Even while steering through the traffic, Roarke wondered why Cooper would abandon a crime capital where he could easily disappear for a border crossing and military guards. But the thought vanished when a car sideswiped him. Roarke went down. He was okay, but the motorcycle was not. Fortunately, there was no shortage of others on Avenida da San Blás. He yanked another driver off one, this time without an apology.

• • •

Cooper crossed over to the main bridge road, Route 7. He looked back and didn't see Roarke.*Breathing room.*

• • •

Roarke's new bike was just a little bit faster, and he began to close the distance. Once again, he searched for Cooper. The streetlights helped. He spotted him. Cooper raced along a parallel road that would soon put him on the bridge.

Not waiting for a proper turn, Roarke darted across a greenway, leaning sharply to his right, then to his left. He straightened his bike, swerved around a Jetta, and merged onto the bridge access road.

He was getting better with the traffic and had speed on his side.

Ahead, Cooper veered to the left onto a dedicated motorcycle lane. Another break for the assassin.

Ten seconds later Roarke drove into the bike lane. It would be impossible for Roarke to pass others in the narrower space. He honked and screamed for people to get out of the way. Mostly, he had to slow down.

Cooper passed a blue sign which read *MOTOS Controle Migratõrio e Aduaneri*, indicating an immigration control station. A guard in a blue shirt, khaki slacks, boots, a tactical jacket, and a blue cap stood holding a clipboard, but did nothing. Why would he? People had spent money in Paraguay. Their problem would be on the Brazil side.

• • •

Cooper knocked down other slower-moving motorcycles, further affecting Roarke's chase. Now he was actually on the Friendship Bridge, 1,812 feet long, more than 130 feet above the swirling river. The motorcycle lane fed back into the main traffic; more room, but more deadly dodging.

• • •

Roarke darted around the downed motorcycles, doing his best not to break his own neck. Cooper still had the advantage. What's more, Roarke was without a plan of action, and crashing through armed guards at the opposite end of the bridge wouldn't make his job any easier. His best option was to get off a killing shot and then disappear into the swarm of tourists and smugglers returning to Brazil with their cheap cigarettes, electronics, and drugs.

• • •

A little past the midpoint over the river was a hand-painted sign on the cement railing. It had two words that delineated the precise geographic border point on the bridge. *PARAGUAY* was painted in capital letters on the near side. Next to it, *BRAZIL*. The words completely stood out.

Cooper quickly cut to the far lane and stopped. He dismounted and pushed his motorcycle into the traffic, snarling the flow. Horns blared. Angry drivers cursed. The backlog caught up to Roarke seconds later. He strained to see what was going on. A van in front of him blocked his view. Roarke managed to find an opening between the traffic and the six-foot fence between the road and a pedestrian sidewalk. And there was Cooper, leaping over the fence.

Scott Roarke realized he'd do better on foot now, too. He dumped his motorcycle, which added to the tie-up. Three vehicles up, he climbed atop a sedan and used the height to jump over the fence. Cooper was only feet ahead of him just stepping over the short cement barrier, the only thing between him and the drop to the Paraná below.

"Cooper!" Roarke shouted as he dove forward. The force brought them both to the ground but left them six feet apart.

Cooper was the first on his feet. He shot his right foot forward at Roarke's head. Roarke deflected the move with a sweep of his right hand. But he didn't expect Cooper to come in with a left hook which landed on his chin.

The blow stunned Roarke.

Richard Cooper smiled. "Roarke. You're one persistent son of a bitch." And with that, the assassin bent down and grabbed the shoulder straps on his backpack. He wedged the pack into an opening of the cement wall precisely under the border demarcation. The straps dangled over the bridge. "No more."

Cooper's cold eyes lock onto Roarke's.

"You're right, no more!" Roarke said sitting up spread eagle. He had his Sig Sauer in hand and fired just as Cooper used the straps to swing under the arch bridge. Roarke ran to where Cooper had leaped. The backpack was there but Cooper was not.

The lights of the bridge illuminated the roadway and spilled over to the side. At 3:32 a.m., the rising moon added more light. Roarke leaned over the side. He saw one hand clinging onto a single strap.

"Cooper. Hang on," Roarke said, not even understanding why he was offering help. Instinct? Training? Evidence that he was different than the assassin only feet below him?

Roarke dislodged the backpack. He lowered it, giving Cooper the chance to grab the second strap; a lifeline. "Take it." He dangled it. "Grab it for God's sake!"

What happened next seemed to play out in slow motion. Roarke saw Cooper's other hand reach for the strap. He felt the balanced weight on the other end. Roarke began to lift Cooper. He anchored his feet against the cement wall and began to lift Cooper using his stomach muscles. "Hang on."

Then Roarke swore Cooper laughed. After that, he fell flat on his back as the weight disappeared. From where he lay, he couldn't see, but Roarke heard the sound of a hard thud against the curved cement arch under the bridge, followed by a splash in the water.

Scott Roarke scrambled to his feet and peered over the edge. Below, concentric circles spreading out in the water. The impact point. He strained to see Cooper's body, but Rio Paraná had swallowed it up.

CHAPTER 79

"Scott, are you all right?" Katie's voice shook. She was patched through to Roarke from the Situation Room.

The line crackled.

"Scott! Can you hear me?"

More attempts, still nothing.

J3 checked with Command at MacDill. "Are you tracking Sidekick?"

"Yes sir. He's on the move. We have him almost at the other side of Foz do Iguaçu. About twenty miles per hour along main streets. But no communications. His transceiver went dead on the run."

"Is he on a motorcycle?" the vice president asked.

"Don't know, but he is proceeding to exfil point Charlie."

"Patch him in when he re-establishes contact."

"Roger."

"A few more minutes," Johnson relayed to the president. Taylor told Katie.

Those few minutes turned into thirty. Then Roarke's distinctive voice came over the Situation Room speakers.

"Sidekick airborne. Understand you've been calling."

"You gave us more than one scare there," Morgan Taylor said.

"Sorry, sir. I did go a little off the reservation."

"A little," the president countered. "Anyway, there is someone here who wants to talk with you."

Taylor whispered to Katie. "No real information. Just hello and how are you?"

She nodded and then started on Roarke with, "Are you crazy?"

• • •

Katie left, but the night was not finished for the president. In coordinated air force drone attacks, strategic MS-13 targets were attacked in Mexico, killing drug lords and destroying supply lines. Names and places provided by Manuel Estavan.

Simultaneously, the FBI and ATF raided Mara Salvatrucha strongholds in the United States, in Boston, Providence, Baltimore, Washington, Philadelphia, Atlanta, Miami, Houston, Phoenix, Los Angeles, and Chicago. Three hundred fifty gang members were rounded up before dawn. Hundreds more wished they had darkness to crawl into because their fellow gang members would soon be giving up their names, too.

• • •

At noon the next day, President Morgan Taylor addressed the nation from the White House.

"Last night and through the morning, the United States carried out deliberate attacks on those people responsible for the mass murder of Americans. The terrorist mastermind is dead. His name was Ibrahim Haddad. He was killed during a Special Forces assault on his compound in Paraguay. No American servicemen were injured in the action. Upon confirmation of the death of Haddad, and under my orders and with full cooperation of Mexico's President Oscar Hernandez, unmanned drones destroyed twenty-four staging points in Mexico that were involved in the operation. In the course of the aerial bombings, we made a serious dent in one of the hemisphere's most lawless gangs, the Mara Salvatrucha or MS-13, which has also participated in the reign of terror against the United States and the deadly drug wars in Mexico. For that reason, and based on the strongest intelligence culled from America's law enforcement agencies, the Federal Bureau of Investigations, working with agents for Alcohol, Tobacco, Firearms, and Explosives and the Drug Enforcement Administration, moved in on twenty-two related operations in cities coast to coast. The immediate result: hundreds of arrests. More will follow.

"While it is clear that our crisis is not over, and that the Centers for Disease Control has a great deal of work ahead, this government took decisive action. Our plans have been developing since the first report that toxic substances had been introduced into our water.

"Secrecy was key to the successful implementation. Now I hope that public disclosure will bring renewed confidence to all Americans.

"I promise, you'll have no shortage of details in the coming days and weeks. For now, however, I continue to urge that you stay home, be safe, and remain calm.

"Thank you."

The president left the podium in the East Room. The press secretary took over, introducing Secretary of Homeland Security Grigoryan and the CDC's Bonnie Comley to answer questions. The press conference continued for ninety-five more minutes.

• • •

Taylor had more calls to make. The president of Paraguay. A brief apology. The president of Brazil. A heartfelt thank you. Then he took a brisk walk outside into the freezing February air. It had been an unusually harsh winter for much of the country. He bent down, picked up a handful of new-fallen snow, and let it melt in his mouth. This was the way a lot of people were getting their water.

CHAPTER 80

FEBRUARY 11

In his debriefing at MacDill with Vice Admiral Gunning and his friend, FBI agent Shannon Davis, Roarke relived the last minutes on the bridge. He described in detail how he took the motorcycles, darted through traffic, caught up to the assassin, fired, and ultimately tried to save him. One thing troubled Roarke. "Why did Cooper stop precisely at the border between Paraguay and Brazil, right at the painted sign? Why there?"

"Dunno," Gunning said. "Too much traffic ahead?"

"No, it wasn't any worse or any better."

"He realized he wouldn't get through Brazilian immigration easily," Davis added.

"He could have shot his way through. No, he just stopped right at that sign, as if he had planned to. And the way he used his backpack," Roarke continued. "It was a tool."

"Roarke, let it go. You got your man. Go home and remind that beautiful girlfriend of yours what she's been missing."

Roarke smiled. Davis was absolutely right about that. He couldn't wait to be in bed with Katie. But was he right about everything else? He wondered for only an instant until his libido took over.

"I'm outahere."

• • •

In Helena, Montana, a high school student opened two unsolicited letters that had arrived. One from Rhode Island School for Design, another from Savannah College of the Arts. Each institution offered Cheryl Gabriel full four-year rides—scholarships and living stipends, all thanks to a personal phone call from the president.

• • •

In the same city, a young man raised his right hand and swore to support and defend the Constitution of the United States against all enemies, foreign and domestic. Ricardo Perez joined the U.S. Army, though under a new name he personally chose. Eduardo Roarke.

• • •

At her CDC lab, Dr. Bonnie Comley was developing new standards to test for contaminants in local water supplies. Morgan Taylor assured her he would make it a presidential directive as soon as it was off her computer and on his desk for signature.

• • •

Water shipments were airlifted from Paraguay to U.S. cities, drawn from the Guarani Aquifer beneath Ciudad del Este. It was part of a new trade alliance, quickly forged with the Paraguayan president. Something that benefited both countries and a few terrorist organizations along the money train.

• • •

The FBI tracked down and arrested more of Haddad's accomplices. The trial backlog was going to be enormous.

• • •

Christine Slocum was buried in Philadelphia next to her parents who had died in a car crash twenty years earlier when they failed to make a dangerous hairpin turn along The Stelvio Pass in Italy's eastern Alps. Bad brakes were cited at the time. Working on information from Haddad's computers, the CIA learned that the two right tires had been shot out.

• • •

Ibrahim Haddad's computers provided more valuable information. One of the first names to come up: FBI Agent Curtis Lawson. Director Robert Mulligan made the arrest himself. Further investigation revealed that Lawson had marital problems, a huge debt, childhood self-esteem problems, and unresolved father issues; all signs that made him a prime candidate for betrayal.

• • •

Katie Kessler turned in her resignation as Deputy White House Counsel. Morgan Taylor hadn't lied to her when he said Scott Roarke wasn't going to be involved in any action. That had been the plan. But it had the impact of a lie and created far too much worry.

She left her White House job on Friday to begin another job in a week. Her new boss was an even stronger personality. Supreme Court Chief Justice Leopold Browning.

• • •

Roarke wanted to take a needed vacation in the U.S. Virgin Islands. However, Katie was eager to start her new job. Instead, he moved into her apartment for a week and did two things he had never done before. Scott Roarke really kissed up to the love of his life and he followed recipes in a Wolfgang Puck cookbook, creating what he thought were five near-perfect meals in a row. Saturday night Katie insisted on taking him out to dinner—in St. Croix.

EPILOGUE

THE CAPITOL

Duke Patrick just couldn't resist going on camera and tickling the tiger. Taylor was getting standing ovations wherever he went and non-stop praise. What wasn't shining on him spilled over to the new vice president and SEAL Team 6.

Haddad was dead. His operatives, inexperienced and untrained, were being rounded up across the country.

MS-13, though not destroyed, was crippled by federal raids which netted cash, names, and plans. The Justice Department was certainly going to be busy for a long, long time.

But Patrick couldn't stand it. He hungered for airtime. And so he called a press conference at the House of Representatives.

Dressed in his favorite blue suit, with a white shirt and a red tie, he aimed for the fences.

"While I applaud the president's ability to bring our crisis to an end and his resolve to restore calm amidst the possibility of utter collapse, he did so violating international law, not once, not twice, but by my count dozens of times…in Paraguay, in Mexico, and, if the reports are true, with executions around the world.

"Moreover, our enemy had lived here. In the United States. Under the nose of Taylor's FBI."

Senator Shaw Aderly insisted that Duke Patrick stress that point. He believed it was his winning argument.

"For years, Ibrahim Haddad plotted within our borders, long before he hid in South America. Had Morgan Taylor gotten to this terrorist, rather than allowing him to escape…not once, but twice as we've come to learn, then we would not have faced this horrible crisis and suffered such losses.

"And now, to placate a nation, whose sovereignty we violated, Taylor seeks to rush through a long-dormant and controversial arms deal."

Duke Patrick's energy and vitality visibly grew the more he pontificated for the cameras.

THE WHITE HOUSE

"He said what?" Morgan Taylor exclaimed after Bernsie briefed him.

"The F-18s deal to Brazil. The Ford factory. He laid it all out and invented a few other things that we'll have to answer for."

"That son of a bitch," the president shouted. "How?"

"All right on the air. He'll use the House Appropriations Committee as a platform to kill it."

"That was revealed in a closed-door session."

"Apparently with a wide open window," John Bernstein replied. "And a wide open mouth. Is the man that crazy?"

"No," Taylor stated. He's crazed. A megalomaniac who's very short on memory. For God's sake, we successfully prosecuted a dangerous mission without inflicting any U.S. military casualties, and we've begun to restore a semblance of order right here. Christ sake, does anyone have a bullet left I can use?"

"Mr. President!"

"A turn of a phrase, Bernsie. Some dirt for your autobiography." Still, Morgan Taylor slammed his fist on his desk and stood abruptly.

"He just couldn't keep his goddamned trap shut. He couldn't stay out of the limelight. Not even for two weeks. Unbelievable. He couldn't let things rest."

"He still wants to be president," Bernsie offered. "That urge is unstop…" the chief of staff caught himself.

"Say it, Bernsie. Say it."

"Unstoppable."

"Oh, you're wrong. I'm going to stop him starting today."

"You can't be thinking…?"

"Christ, Bernsie, I'm not going to kill the man. Just destroy him." Morgan Taylor seemed to glow with excitement now. "And when I'm through, if he has one ounce of dignity left, he'll wish I made it quicker and less painful."

"I'm not sure I should be party to this, Mr. President."

"Of course you can. We're going to go public about his association with Slocum and her connections to Haddad and let the press go wild filling in the blanks. Even his closest aides won't deny how she manipulated him. And while we're at it, let's see how many degrees of separation there are between Shaw Aderly and our dead terrorist. I have a suspicion you won't have to go further than three."

"But Patrick was being used. He's not a terrorist," Bernsie suggested.

"Maybe so. But he's going down."

ACKNOWLEDGMENTS

There are so many people I'd like to thank for their love, encouragement, and willingness to share their knowledge and resources.

Michael Messinger, for his insight into the "inside." His work with every U.S. president of the modern era has to be a record all on its own. Peter Loge from Milo Public Affairs for his Beltway savvy and key help for the third time. Then there's Bruce Coons, U.S. Army retired and my oldest friend in the world. Let's just say Bruce has been around. He knows "things" and makes sure I get them right.

Marc Kusinitz and Gordon Rubenfeld get my thanks for their incredible assistance with health and medical information; key to the plot.

In the realm of publishing, Roger Cooper for launching my career as a novelist, and putting the right words in the right ears. Those ears belong to Scott Waxman at Diversion Books. Thank you, Scott, for taking me into the phenomenal world of eBooks with *Executive Actions*, *Executive Treason* and now*Executive Command*. Also, true and sincere special thanks to Mary Cummings, Diversion Books Editorial Director, who has been wonderful every step of the way.

Additional thanks to Barbara Schwartz and Deborah Collins for their attention to detail, and readers and fans who have taken the time and effort to write me. I hope Executive Command delivers for you!

I also want to thank authors and friends W.G. Griffiths, Dwight Jon Zimmerman, Larry Bond, Michael Palmer, Dale Brown and

Allan Topol. Add to that list, screenwriters Bruce Feirstein and Gary Goldman. You've all helped inspire me and move me forward.

Of course there are my colleagues, mentors and friends Dick Taylor, Vin Di Bona, Stan Deutsch, Robb Weller, Barry Kibrick, Sandi Goldfarb, Kathy Scheets, Jeffrey Greenhawt, Jeffrey Davis, Nancy Cushing-Jones, Shelley Frieman, Michael Blowen, Mike Brown, Tom Cooper, Jim Nolt, and so many more friends and colleagues I'll just have to write more books to acknowledge everyone.

Special thanks again to Bob Bowker and Bianca Pino at iNet// Web Solutions, Inc. for their wonderful and creative development of my website, www.garygrossman.com. Friends and colleagues forever.

Thanks to my wonderful family, Helene, Sasha, Zach and Jake. I also have to point skyward to Stanley and Evelyn and Maish and Jean for all your love, too.

GARY GROSSMAN's first novel, *Executive Actions*, propelled him into the world of political thrillers. *Executive Treason*, the sequel, further tapped Grossman's experience as a journalist, newspaper columnist, documentary television producer, reporter and playwright. The third book in the series, *Executive Command*, nearly brought his trilogy to a conclusion. But there was more—and *Executive Force* covers new ground. Grossman has written for the *New York Times, Boston Globe,* and *Boston Herald American*. He covered presidential campaigns for WBZ-TV in Boston, and has produced television series for NBC News, CNN, NBC, ABC, CBS, FOX and 40 cable networks. He is a multiple Emmy Award winning producer, served as chair of the Government Affairs Committee for the Caucus for Television, Producers, Writers and Directors, and is a member of the International Thriller Writers Association. Grossman has taught at Emerson College (where he is a member of the Board of Trustees), Boston University, USC, and Loyola Marymount University, and is a contributing editor to *Media Ethics Magazine*.

For more information visit
www.garygrossman.com

Follow Gary Grossman on Twitter
@garygrossman1

Printed in the USA
CPSIA information can be obtained
at www.ICGtesting.com
JSHW031706140824
68134JS00038B/3535